Todd leaned forward and turned up the radio. The country & western DJ spent more time jabbering than playing music. He wished the guy would just shut up and get on with the tunes.

"—unusually high number of breakdowns, making traffic on all Bay Area freeways a real mess. Two cars stalled or out of gas on the Golden Gate Bridge, one on the Bayshore Freeway, three on the San Mateo Bridge. Dumbarton's clear—so far. You cowhands must have had one rough weekend to forget to fill up your cars! The rest of you all, be prepared for a long ride into the city."

Finally, the DJ played a new Ray Stevens single, "The Wreck of the *Oilstar Zoroaster*" to the tune of an old Gordon Lightfoot song. Todd slapped the steering wheel and guffawed.

He glanced at his watch; in Wyoming it would have taken him less than twenty minutes to cover twice the distance. He tried not to let it get to him. Short of ramming the car up front, there was little he could do about it.

Another ten minutes passed before he moved far enough ahead to see the amber, blue, and red lights of a CHP cruiser. Three new vehicles cluttered the right-hand lane: a wine-colored Lexus, a Honda Accord, and a Mitsubishi Something-or-other. What the heck was going on here—nails in the road? A pileup? New cars didn't just break down by themselves, all at the same time. Smiling to himself, he muttered, "Next time, buy American!"

ALSO BY KEVIN J. ANDERSON AND DOUG BEASON

Lifeline
The Trinity Paradox
Assemblers of Infinity
Virtual Destruction
*Ignition**

*forthcoming

ILL WIND

Kevin J. Anderson
& Doug Beason

TOR®

A TOM DOHERTY ASSOCIATES BOOK
NEW YORK

ILL WIND

Cover art by Tim Jacobus

A Tor Book
Published by Tom Doherty Associates, Inc.
175 Fifth Avenue
New York, NY 10010

Tor Books on the World Wide Web:
http://www.tor.com

Tor® is a registered trademark of Tom Doherty Associates, Inc.

ISBN: 0-812-55018-8
Library of Congress Card Catalog Number: 95-6314

First edition: June 1995
First mass market edition: May 1996

Printed in the United States of America

0 9 8 7 6 5 4 3 2 1

Dedication

To my parents, who tolerated my crazy insistence on wanting to be a writer, on majoring in astronomy and Russian history, and doing just about anything else that made it impossible for me to find a "normal" job. I'm proud of them for reading my stories and grateful to them for offering their encouragement even back when my fiction wasn't as . . . er, polished as I hope it is now.

—KJA

To my parents, for allowing me to experience the world.

—DB

Acknowledgments

Kristine Kathryn Rusch for her major text and plot surgery and sharp editorial eye; Marina Fitch for her prompt and thorough overhaul of (what we thought was) the final version; Laura Anderson for the inside scoop on working for an insurance company; Roberta Leong and Doug Rountree for a tour of the floor of the Pacific Stock Exchange and making it (somewhat) comprehensible; Mike McGuire and Ken Williams for their help with economic speculation; Rita Anderson for transcribing some of the chapters written with a microcassette recorder; members of the Wordshop—danl danehy-oakes, Michael C. Berch, Michael Paul Meltzer, Claire Bell, M. Coleman Easton, Avis Minger, Lori Ann White, Gary Shockley, and Dan Marcus—who provided the usual test read of the first draft and offered numerous helpful suggestions; Patrick Nielsen Hayden for his insightful editorial suggestions; and my wife Rebecca and stepson Jonathan for their love, patience, and shameless pride in my accomplishments (KJA).

Special thanks to Dr. Clifford E. Rhoades for the citrus connection, and Dr. Don Petit for working it out; Dr. Stu Nozette and his graduate students for the orbits; Dr. Charles Sheffield for being a mentor; Lt. Col. (Dr.) Don Erbschloe for the flying; Dr. D. Allan Bromley, former Presidential Science Advisor, for allowing DB to work with him on the White House Staff; Rat Zeringue for the "coon-ass" dialect; Tamara, Amanda, and my wife Cindy for being there (DB).

Dramatis Personae

San Francisco, CA

Connor Brooks—Seaman
Miles Uma—Captain, *Oilstar Zoroaster*
Ed Dailey—Second mate
Dr. Alex Kramer—Oilstar microbiologist
Maureen Kramer—His wife
Jay Kramer—His son
Erin Kramer—His daughter
Dr. Mitchell Stone—Alex's assistant
Jackson Harris—Environmental activist
Daphne Harris—Environmental activist, Jackson's
  wife
Todd Severyn—Petroleum engineer
Dr. Iris Shikozu—Stanford University
Francis Plerry—Environmental Policy Office
Emma Branson—CEO, Oilstar
Henry Cochran—Oilstar executive
Moira Tibbett—Sandia, Livermore researcher
Dave Hensch—Stanford student
Officer Orenio—Security guard
Jake Torgens—Environmentalist, radical activist
Reverend Timothy Rudge—Pastor, Holy Grace
  Baptist Church

White Sands, NM

Dr. Spencer Lockwood—Physicist, solar-satellite
  project head
Rita Fellenstein—Chief technician

Dr. Lance Nedermyer—Department of Energy
  program manager
Dr. Gilbert Hertoya—Director, Electromagnetic
  Launch Facility
Juan Romero—Technician
Dr. Arnold Norton—Sandia scientist

Albuquerque, NM

Brigadier General Ed Bayclock—Commander,
  Kirtland Air Force Base
David Reinski—Mayor of Albuquerque
Sgt. Caitlyn Morris—Helicopter mechanic
Colonel David—Commander, Phillips Laboratory
Colonel Nichimya—Commander, Base Personnel
  Group

Washington, DC

Henry Holback—President of the U.S.
Harald Wolani—Vice President of the U.S.
The Honorable Jeffrey Mayeaux—Speaker of the
  House
Franklin Weathersee—Mayeaux's chief of staff
General Wacon—Chairman, JCS

Other locations

Heather Dixon—Insurance adjuster (Flagstaff, AZ)
Al Sysco—Manager, Surety Insurance (Flagstaff, AZ)
Dick Morgret—Gas station owner (Death Valley, CA)
Carlos Bettario—Rancher (Death Valley, CA)
Lt. Bobby Carron—F/A-18 pilot, USN (China Lake,
  CA)
Lt. Ralph "Barfman" Petronfi—Bobby's wingman
  (China Lake, CA)

PART ONE
BLACK TIDE

ONE

DEAD MAN'S CURVE

Crashing through twenty-foot waves, the supertanker *Zoroaster* drove through the Pacific night like a great steel behemoth.

Longer than three football fields and 170 feet wide, the Oilstar supertanker was one of the largest objects ever constructed. Weather and salt water had left a patina of blisters and rust on a deck that had once been painted silver. Behind the ship, the wake looked like a bubbling cauldron of green foam, lit by a wash of moonlight.

Four days earlier, the supertanker had left the Alaskan port of Valdez after filling its twelve massive tanks with crude oil piped from Prudhoe Bay. Fully loaded, the *Zoroaster* had churned out of the Gulf of Alaska, bound for the Oilstar refineries in the San Francisco Bay.

Oilstar representatives claimed the massive ship could function with a minimal crew of twenty-eight, because of highly efficient computer warning and navigation systems. Internal corporate memos included terms like "increased profit margin" and "downsizing." Only the long, exhausting shifts broke the tedium for the crew.

No one wanted to think about what could go wrong with so large a ship . . . and how few people there were to respond to an emergency.

The lower corridor of the *Zoroaster*'s deckhouse was empty. Good. The only sounds were the continuous groans of the tanker, the whisper of the Pacific, and the distant throb of the engines. Everyone asleep. Along the corridor, the gunmetal-gray cabin doors had been sealed against the deep night. This ship always stank of fumes.

Connor Brooks did not hesitate. Sweating with excitement, he yanked down the fire alarm. It would create one hell of a diversion, and he would be glad to destroy the papers and get his sorry ass out of sight. Let the Oilstar pricks do all the explaining.

Electronic whoops clamored through the intercom, making the whole ship echo. Fuck, it was loud enough! Connor grabbed his metal food tray and raced up the narrow corrugated stairs to the bridge. Keep everything moving. His entire plan depended on timing. Come on, come on!

Connor's heart hammered as he bounded up the stairs, the screwdriver in his pocket flopping against his leg. His shaggy blond hair flew backward; his scalp prickled with sweat. That butthead, Captain Miles Uma, would take a few seconds to respond to the emergency, and Connor would get his chance. About time, too.

He had to get everyone off the bridge so he could break into his personnel file, trash the evidence that was going to get him in trouble with the authorities. As the *Zoroaster* approached the end of her four-day journey to San Francisco, Connor's time was running out. The supertanker would pass through the Golden Gate in less than an hour.

He wanted to kick someone in the kneecaps with his heavy work boot. So he had been caught with a few credit cards he had lifted from the wallets of other crew members—big fucking deal! Nobody was liable for more than fifty bucks or so from purchases made on a stolen card anyway. Besides, Connor had never imagined anybody would notice until long after he jumped ship in San Francisco. What would someone use a credit card for on an *oil tanker,* for crying out loud?

Connor deserved a decent break in his life. Just one. He had run to Alaska in the first place to hide from a lot of things he did not want to remember, things that other people refused to forget. The port of Valdez in Prince William Sound was full of dirty jobs, working the slime line in fisheries or scrubbing out tankers before they refilled from the trans-Alaskan pipeline. He had hired onto the *Zoroaster* as a bottom-rank seaman, which meant serving meals and cleaning toilets. Connor hadn't counted on Captain Uma being such a stuffed-shirt butthead! Why was the world so full of pricks?

Uma wasn't going to give him a break, so Connor had to take matters in his own hands.

Still running from the deafening fire alarms below, Connor reached the top deck with the tray of food. A stained cook's apron covered his muscular frame.

He paused a second to catch his breath before stepping onto the bridge. He was tempted to whistle a bit, just to show how casual he felt, but that would be too obvious. Old Butthead had the night watch—didn't the man ever leave his station? Damned Eskimo/Negro mix-up. Short and bearlike, Butthead's swarthy skin, frizzy black hair, huge beard, and heavy eyebrows made him look like a gorilla trying to pass himself off as human. He kept his Oilstar uniform neat, and he didn't drink booze. At all.

Butthead Uma whirled upon hearing Connor enter. "Brooks! What the hell are you doing here?"

Amid the confusion of panicked sounds, Connor put on a big "Yes, sir!" smile. "Brought your late-night snack, Captain."

Butthead ignored him and turned instead to the second mate. "Where is that damned alarm coming from, Dailey?"

The second mate looked up from a display panel, shoving his glasses back up on the bridge of his nose. "Two decks down, sir!"

"Right here in the deckhouse?" Butthead said. "At least it's not out by the cargo holds."

Connor spoke up. "Yeah, I just came from down there. It looked pretty bad, and the others were calling for you. The intercom is busted or something." He shrugged. The alarm kept yammering.

"Fire control activated, Captain," said the second mate.

Uma seemed suspicious. "Dailey, take the conn. Brooks, put that food down and come with me. Why didn't you let me know?"

Connor cursed under his breath. Now he had to go with Butthead! How the hell was he going to get at the records?

The second mate looked out the wide, salt-spattered windows of the bridge, squinting through thick glasses toward the glimmering lights that stood out on the coast. "Captain, we're approaching the Point Bonitas light-house. Only two miles out of the Golden Gate. The Bay pilot is on his way to come aboard and take us through."

"I can't sit around if there's a fire on my ship." Uma dashed to the bridge doorway. "Brooks, get a move on!"

Connor refrained from "assisting" Butthead down the stairwell with a hard kick in the ass. He had to delay, get the second mate out of the picture. The captain's heavy boots clomped down the corrugated stairs like bricks falling on a brass gong.

Connor set the food down on the chart table, keeping the heavy metal tray. The moment the captain disappeared from view, Connor whirled, smashing the metal tray against the second mate's head. The second mate held up an arm to fend off Connor, then fell to one knee; his glasses broke as they clattered to the floor. Two more to the head knocked the man unconscious.

, shipmate," Connor said as he ground the

broken eyeglasses under the heel of his stained boot. "You should have gone with Butthead."

He tossed the tray to the side, and its clang vanished in the throbbing wail of the alarm. He rushed over to the personnel records bureau next to the captain's station. Secure locks had never been a high priority, considering the supertanker's limited crew and long voyages. Connor diddled with the lock, using the screwdriver in his pocket. He slapped his palm against the handle of the screwdriver, and the drawer popped open.

Connor dug through the manila folders, finding his own file: Connor's hiring record, Uma's incident report, and an arrest order. His face darkened. He had to be long gone before everybody stopped running around in circles.

Connor yanked out more of the files, shuffling them— anything to gain a little more time when they started hunting him down. Maybe he could slip off the ship without anyone seeing. Glancing out the bridge window, he saw the fog-dimmed lights of the approaching city. It seemed very far away. He had to hurry.

Connor turned to get out of there. The captain would know by now that the fire alarm was a hoax, and he would have no doubt who had done it. Dailey remained stone cold on the floor next to his broken glasses.

Time to haul ass.

He pulled the metal fire door shut behind him as he left the bridge and twisted tight the wheel lock. During the entire four-day trip down the West Coast, Connor had never seen the bridge door closed. Bracing himself against the wall, he kicked viciously at the wheel lock with his heavy work boot. The wheel bent, jammed.

The grin returned. "Try explaining that one, Captain Butthead!" They would need a blowtorch to get the door open again. Connor sprinted to the long cargo deck. This just might work out after all.

Fire alarms screeched. Cabin doors slammed open as groggy, off-duty crew members scrambled into the corridors. Seamen shouted to each other, wanting to know what was going on. Instinctively three crewmen stumbled into the brisk night to man the water cannons, but they saw none of the crude-oil cargo burning.

On deck two, Captain Miles Uma found no sign of fire. Cramming his cap down on his frizzy hair, he stood by the alarm on the wall, saw that it had been pulled intentionally. Realization fell into place as a wave of cold anger coursed through him. His skin prickled. "I'm going to kill Brooks!"

Uma's stomach soured with dread as he suddenly realized his mistake. Brooks had not followed him down the stairs. The slimeball must still be up on the bridge with Dailey. Even with such a small crew, Uma knew he should have locked the bastard up.

They were close to the narrow and treacherous Golden Gate. Too close. And Brooks was pulling some stupid stunt. Uma bounded back up to the bridge deck.

The door to his own bridge stood shut against him, the wheel lock bent. Uma strained against the wheel, but it remained jammed. He hammered with a fist. "Open this door right now!"

He received no answer. Listening, he could hear the automatic collision-avoidance radar beeping a warning. His mind whirled, and his stomach tangled in impossible knots. Of their four-day, two-thousand-mile journey, this was the most crucial point, "threading the needle" through the deep channel under the Golden Gate Bridge to Oilstar's North Bay refineries. Dead Man's Curve.

Uma was appalled at his own stupidity, his overconfidence. Captain Joseph Hazelwood had done the same thing on the *Exxon Valdez*—left the command post at a critical moment. Uma angrily slapped the bulkhead; his hand stung. Stupid!

Uma stepped back and kicked as hard as he could. The thick metal door did not give.

A crewman panted up the stairs, followed by two others. Uma briefly wished they had given him a few more moments to get through the door; now everyone could see his helplessness.

"What is it, Captain?" asked the crewman. Uma did not turn to look at him.

"The door's jammed." He kicked again, hard enough to send a sharp pain through his shin. Uma threw his shoulder against it. His voice suddenly turned hoarse. "Help me get in there now!" He shoved the crewman forward. Another man joined him, but the three of them slammed against the door in vain.

Uma turned and pointed at the crewmen in the stairwell. "Get me a battering ram—anything. Move it!"

Muffled through the door, the collision-avoidance alarms kept beeping.

Out on the vast, cluttered deck, alarms bleated into the night. Connor wondered if Captain Butthead had made it back to the bridge yet. He wished he could be there to watch Uma's expression as he tried to cope with the jammed door.

Connor hurried out to the storage shacks, pump control banks, and water-cannon valves. Everything was wet with spray, slimy with oil residue. He crumpled the incriminating papers as he faced the stiff ocean breeze and tossed the wad overboard. The white ball glimmered in the moonlight, then vanished forever. If he could just hide until the ship docked at the terminal, then slip off . . .

He looked across the ship, the twelve tank hatches, the catwalk down the center of the deck, the pressure and vacuum relief valves. The *Zoroaster* was so long the crew had to take bicycles from one end to the other. He would have little trouble finding a place to lie low for a few hours.

He couldn't jump and swim to shore; years ago, maybe with a wetsuit and surfboard, he would have tried. The cold, fast-moving waters of the Bay were notorious—and even fully loaded, the tanker rode six stories above the water. He should have thought of that part before setting all this in motion, but Connor hated to waste time overplanning. He did what he needed to do, then tried to be flexible if the details didn't work out right.

The alarms suddenly ceased, plunging the ship into an echoing silence. Off in the distance, he heard the asynchronous hoots and chimes of foghorns around the Golden Gate. Through sparse fog, the coastal cities lit up the shoreline like Christmas lights. Connor was glad to be approaching civilization again.

The twinkling outline of the Golden Gate Bridge seemed very, very close.

Using a pipe as a battering ram, the crew finally broke through the bridge door, letting it hang on one twisted hinge. Uma kicked the door aside, allowing access. He spotted second mate Dailey on his knees, groaning and trying to pull himself up.

The Golden Gate Bridge was much too close.

Uma ran three steps toward the controls, then stopped to stare across the *Zoroaster*'s sprawling deck at what lay ahead. The Golden Gate loomed, a narrow opening into the calm waters of the Bay. The bridge hung across their path with a flickering necklace of automobile headlights. Rocky headlands crouched in the surf, where lighthouses sent their beacons out to sea.

Uma knew the north tower of the bridge stood on rocks extending from the Marin shore; but the south tower rose straight out of the sea on the San Francisco side, built on a shelf of rock fifty feet deep and a quarter mile from land.

For a fraction of a second, Uma froze. His career was over. He could never save the ship in time. His mind numbed, unable to grasp the disaster about to happen in front of his eyes, all because of his stupidity.

The supertanker took about a mile to turn, and she'd had four days to build up speed. But he couldn't just stand there.

He slapped at the intercom. "Full reverse!"

The grinding hum from the engine room sounded strained and uncooperative. The *Zoroaster* shuddered with the sudden change as the engine responded.

Collision-avoidance radar bleeped, a sound that frightened him much more than the fire alarms. He scanned the screens at the navigator's station. Red danger circles overlapped the tanker's silhouette and the south pier of the bridge. Over the radio, the voice of a Coast Guard operator kept calling for a response.

At the radio station, he switched channels to the Coast Guard frequency. "Mayday, mayday! This is *Oilstar Zoroaster*. We are headed for the Golden Gate. Declaring an emergency and prepared to abandon ship!"

Uma squinted at the radar, watching the tanker's projected path. The ship headed straight for one of the two great towers that supported the Golden Gate Bridge. He grunted, moving the rudder as far to port as the electronic control would allow.

He might be able to make the great ship swing just enough. Just by a fraction. Uma sounded the whooping general-quarters alarm. He wondered how many of the *Zoroaster*'s crew would assume it to be another false emergency and go back to their bunks.

He held the rudder hard to port. His body felt drained, exhausted. Behind him, one of the seamen muttered, "Come on, we'll make it . . . we'll make it."

Uma stared out the windows. The bridge came at them like a giant pillar. Momentum would carry the *Zoroaster* through, and all he could do was sit and watch.

The *Zoroaster* almost missed her doom.

But with a two-hundred-thousand-ton ship as big as the Empire State Building, "almost" is not good enough. The tanker struck the concrete fender surrounding the south tower and crushed it.

Slowed but not stopped by the impact, the *Zoroaster*

scraped her starboard side against the jagged concrete and steel. The double hulls offered protection against minor grounding and maritime accidents, but not a monstrous impact such as this. The inertia ripped open both hulls like so much paper. The *Zoroaster* hung up on the wreckage of the concrete fender, settling downward to the deep shelf of rock.

Five of the supertanker's twelve holds immediately split; within minutes, metal fatigue breached three additional holds.

The *Zoroaster* held more than a million barrels of oil—42 million gallons. Most of which began to pour into the San Francisco Bay.

Crude oil gushed like black blood.

TWO

HOOKED ON A FEELING

The phone rang again.

Alone in his stables, Alex Kramer tended the two horses. He insisted on ignoring the ache, no matter how much the leukemia tortured him. He had plenty of experience with pain.

The telephone extension he had wired out to the barn sounded tinny, invasive. He hated it.

Alex looked up, but didn't move. The ringing phone seemed to cut through him. He didn't want to talk to anybody. In happier days, Jay or Erin would have rushed to grab the call—Jay expecting his college buddies, Erin a high-school boyfriend. If his wife, Maureen, hadn't gotten the phone first. Alex had never had to worry about answering it before.

But in one disastrous year, he had lost his entire family—Maureen and Erin killed when a gasoline truck slammed into them on a winding road, Jay a casualty of the latest Middle East conflict. Cocking his head to look behind him at the large, empty ranch house, Alex wondered why he bothered to stay behind in such a hollow place.

Because I don't ever want to leave those ghosts behind.

The phone kept ringing. Let the answering machine in the house get it.

Finally, after four rings, the phone fell silent. The only noises were the restless stirring of the horses, the morning breeze rustling through the live oaks and pines, and the birds in the wooded hills of Marin County, California. Alex turned back to the horses, feeling numb relief. Dealing with people, even on trivial matters, was too much effort. Too much effort.

He gathered the tack for his ritual ride. Moving cautiously from the pain in his body, and reverently with his memories, he saddled his daughter's mare, Stimpy, a chocolate quarter horse with a blond mane. Tomorrow he would take Ren, his own horse, for a ride. The two horses loved their exercise, and Alex needed the excuse to get out.

Holding the bridle, Alex hooked an arm between the horse's ears, then slid the bit into Stimpy's mouth. After settling the headstall, he buckled it. Lifting the bulky Western saddle required most of his remaining strength, but the horse waited graciously. Alex rested a moment, holding himself up by the saddle horn; it even hurt to breathe. He reached under Stimpy's belly to tighten the cinch strap. Finally, brushing himself off, he levered himself up into the saddle.

Without prodding, Stimpy walked out of the stables into the sunshine. In the fresh air, Alex's lethargy cleared. For longer than he could remember, he had used the unpaved fire roads in the wooded hills north of San Francisco for morning rides; he and Erin had explored them years before, racing, picnicking, eating the sloppy "secret recipe" peanut-butter-and-jelly sandwiches she always made before a ride.

Under the stands of oaks, surrounded by an ocean of rustling grass, Alex found it quiet, peaceful . . . a far cry from the nightmarish hell of the Oilstar refinery where he worked. He drove to his office three days a week—management's concession "until you recover from your grief," as if that were possible.

Oilstar had forced him to go for five sessions with their "psychological fitness and health" counselor, a flinty-eyed young woman with short blond hair that seemed a mass of cowlicks. She had tapped a red-enameled finger-nail as she explained the stages of severe grief to him: shock, then disbelief, anger, and finally resignation. Alex had listened to her politely, contributing as little as possible. Each time he left a session, he felt no different, understood no more about why his family had been taken from him, and felt no more fit for work. At least it proved that Oilstar considered his bioremediation research valuable.

As Alex rode out, the morning was so bright and fresh, it mocked him.

At noon, Alex returned to his echoing house, drawing the curtains to shield him from the cheery sunlight. He noticed the blinking red light on the answering machine, but decided he didn't want to deal with it at the moment. He went past the living room and wet bar, down the hall where the kids' rooms stood empty and silent, to the master bedroom. He showered, turning the water hot enough to scald away his body aches for a while, then dressed carefully as if his clothes were made out of glass. He thought about eating lunch, but his stomach wasn't ready for it. He finally played the telephone message.

Resting one elbow on the tile countertop, he listened to the voice of Mitchell Stone, his deputy project manager in the microbiology lab. "Alex, where are you? Don't you watch the news, for God's sake! With the *Zoroaster* thing, the execs are scrambling for any way to save their butts. Maybe we can pull Prometheus out of the closet. Give me a call and get in here as soon as you can, okay?"

As the message ended, Alex frowned at the machine, annoyed at the intrusion. No, he did not watch the news, and it surprised him that Mitch assumed he did. He hadn't even turned on the TV in a month. *Prometheus?* That work was over a year old, merely a precursor to the bacterial strains they were developing now.

Oilstar had funded Alex's work as a showpiece, their nod to the popular "green" movements. Bioremediation was the catchword, cultivating natural microbes that had an appetite for the swill man wanted to destroy. Already, many companies were developing microbes that would digest toxic wastes, PCBs and PCPs, even break down garbage.

When his daughter Erin turned seventeen and suddenly awakened to political causes, she had first railed at Alex about working for a big oil company, spouting phrases she had memorized from leaflets; but then Erin had beamed with pride and relief when she learned he was attempting to get rid of the tons of Styrofoam and nonbiodegradable plastics clogging the nation's landfills.

"Prometheus" had been just a step along the way, a strain that could metabolize certain components of crude oil, primarily octane and a few aromatic ring molecules. Not terribly useful, according to Oilstar.

What could Mitch have in mind now? And what on Earth was a Zoroaster? He clicked on the dusty television, but saw without surprise that his cable service had been cut off. The only stations he could get through the surrounding hills showed a soap opera and a grainy image of talking heads.

Resigned, Alex tried calling in, but the lines were busy. He listened to the buzzing signal, then returned the phone to its cradle. He felt like telling Mitch to solve his own damned problems and then hanging up on him. By the time he finished the long drive to the refinery, maybe his thoughts would have cleared.

He slowly tugged on an old jacket against the spring chill and started for his four-wheel-drive Ford pickup.

Out in the corral, the horses nickered at him, and several crows rattled at him from up in the pine trees. He paused for a second, just breathing the air and thinking nothing, before getting into his truck. He drove along the winding road toward the freeway and the Richmond bridge.

He rode in silence, but then he switched on the radio to see if he could find out what Mitch had been talking about. *Zoroaster*. Thumbing the dial, he found only stations that had music or advertisements at first, but National Public Radio had a long discussion about the aftereffects of the *Exxon Valdez* spill, the *Torreycanyon*, the Shetland Islands spill, and other tanker accidents. Alex wondered why that had become so topical after all this time. Must be an anniversary of one of the disasters or something. He moved along at exactly the speed limit, other cars passing him regularly.

Alex was primarily an idea man at the bioremediation lab, leaving Mitch and the others to take care of bothersome details with management and record keeping. Mitch panicked about deadlines at least once a month.

Half an hour after leaving home, Alex exited the freeway and turned toward the sprawling Oilstar refinery. As he approached the chain-link fence, he saw a crowd of protesters in front of the guard gate. TV camera crews stood on the sidelines. The demonstration seemed orderly; Oilstar had brought in extra rent-a-cops, along with a handful of California Highway Patrol officers.

Alex raised his eyebrows. One group or another found reason to rail at Oilstar several times a year, but whenever somebody planned a protest, they usually informed Oilstar in advance, along with the local media. He was so tired of all this, angry at the demonstrators for tossing more unpleasantness in his lap. He just wanted to sit at home and rest.

As his pickup crawled past the protesters, he saw the usual signs depicting oil-covered seabirds and otters, the skull-and-crossbones; the word *Zoroaster* was repeated over and over. Well, he thought, maybe it was something important after all. Maybe there had been another spill somewhere. He had worked for Oilstar long enough to know there would always be oil spills . . . and the oil companies would always swear that it would never happen again.

At another time, his daughter Erin might have been among the protesters. Erin had become outspoken whenever she found a cause, "Save the Whales" or "Don't Use Colored Toilet Paper." Though he had not always understood Erin's drive, he had never been scornful or disdainful. She was a smart girl and full of questions, many of which Alex had not been able to answer. He was just glad she felt such a passion for things.

But Erin would never grow up to join these demonstrators at the Oilstar gate, and he felt inexplicably annoyed at the protesters for that.

He drove past the crowd without incident, then worked his way across the refinery grounds, beyond a wasteland of pipes and tanks, fractionating towers and steam, with huge oil-storage tanks riding the surrounding hills. The place looked like an Escher industrial nightmare, amplified by hissing noises and foul smells.

Eventually, he found himself by his office on the second floor of Oilstar's research annex. Fumbling with his keys, he opened the door and went inside, ignoring the yellow telephone messages taped to his door. His office looked too clean, too neat. He had never taken the time to be tidy when he was swallowed up in work; now he did little else but rearrange his papers into neat piles.

A picture of Alex's family sat on the desk, all four of them smiling, a frozen moment from the past. His own image faced him, wire-rimmed glasses and graying hair above a neat peppery beard; beside him sat Maureen, strong and slender. Jay, twenty-one years old, reddish hair cropped short since entering the army, his sparse mustache all but invisible against his skin; petite Erin with strawberry-blond hair, striking dark eyebrows, and flawless skin, a beauty that was lost on the high-school boys. Erin would have shattered hearts had she lived to enter college.

"About time, Alex!" Mitch Stone leaned on the doorframe. "I've already set up a meeting for us tomorrow morning with Emma Branson and the other mucky mucks. We've got to move on this right away."

At twenty-eight and rising fast, Mitch concerned himself with dressing impeccably. He got his hair razor-cut every other week, wore stylish clothes, even sported a tie in the *lab*. In public, Mitch toed the Oilstar party line and talked fast. He didn't try to annoy Alex, but his skewed priorities, office politics, and constant "emergencies" had drained away Alex's respect for him. Alex remembered when he himself had been filled with so much ambition.

Mitch ticked off points on his fingers. "The engineering folks are getting lightering operations underway to pump the rest of the oil out of the cargo holds. The tides are playing hell with the wreck. Boat teams are rigging booms around the spill, but there are pleasure boats and protesters up the wazoo, maritime rubberneckers in everyone's way. Best estimates are that a quarter of a million barrels have already dumped into the Bay and it's still gushing out. *Zoroaster—*"

Alex held up a hand to stop the other man. He noticed his fingers trembling. "Mitch, I don't know what on Earth you're talking about. Tell me what a Zoroaster is before you go on."

Mitch goggled at him. "You mean you don't know? Oh, come on!" Tugging on Alex's sleeve, Mitch marched him down the carpeted halls into the lunchroom.

A sour, burnt smell drifted up from a puddle of coffee in the bottom of the pot. Washed coffee cups—no two alike—sat upended in wet spots on brown paper towels between the sink and microwave oven. The television was turned on and loud. Four people straddled uncomfortable plastic chairs at the wood-grain tables, watching CNN. Alex had not seen such rapt expressions on viewers' faces since the coverage of the first Gulf War.

"Could be the biggest spill ever," Mitch said. "Far bigger than the *Exxon Valdez*. Only this time it's not up in Alaska, it's right here in the San Francisco Bay!"

From a helicopter, the TV camera looked down at the wreck of the *Oilstar Zoroaster*, its side ripped open by the southern tower of the Golden Gate Bridge. A montage of shots, beginning with pictures at dawn, traced the growth of the spill during the day. Boats hovered on the edges of the slick.

Alex's knees went weak; he was appalled at himself for belittling Mitch's reaction, the protesters' outrage. The sharp thorns of pain in his bones felt suddenly overwhelming.

The broadcast showed seagulls blanketed with tarry residue, floating corpses of sea otters. Crowds stood anxiously on Fisherman's Wharf, staring out at the approaching oil. Alex's breath quickened; his head ached, starting with a pressure in his temples that wouldn't go away. The program played a long sequence of archival footage from the 1989 *Exxon Valdez* disaster.

Mitch clapped a hand on Alex's shoulder. "The bozos over at Admin Gardens are in a state of panic. They're willing to try anything for some positive publicity. We can cash in on it if we get approval to release Prometheus to help the cleanup efforts!"

Mitch didn't seem affected by the images on the television. He lowered his voice. "We'll be heroes even if it doesn't work!"

Alex shook off Mitch's hand and stared at the oil spilling across the water, the thick liquid lapping against the shore. He remembered the times he and his son Jay had spent days hiking on the rocky headlands. Especially the time when Jay had told him he wanted to drop out of college and join the army . . .

"What's the matter, Alex?" Mitch frowned. "Don't you see what an opportunity this is?" He pressed closer.

"An opportunity?" Alex said in a voice that came out as a low growl. Time and again, since the death of his family, he had shielded his emotions behind a wall of weariness and apathy; at rare times, though, the wall cracked to expose a furnace blazing inside. He had never been a violent man, but he had been walking on the thin ice of intensely charged emotions for months.

Alex flexed his right hand; the pain inside made his breath like ice knives, and Mitch stood just *too damned close*. Suddenly lashing out, he shoved Mitch backwards—not hard, but enough to knock the other man over a chair, sprawling to the floor.

"You're right, Mitch," Alex said, "but you don't have to be such an asshole about it."

THREE

GOOD DAY, SUNSHINE

Spencer Lockwood shielded his eyes from the glaring sun. The wasteland around White Sands, New Mexico, looked more like the surface of the Moon than a restricted national preserve. Bleak gypsum sand stretched to the horizon, broken only by scrub brush, yucca plants, and lava rock. The rugged peaks of the Organ Mountains shimmered like a mirage. The heat made the dusty air smell like gunpowder.

Numerous rocket and guided-missile systems had been tested at the White Sands missile range in its half century of existence. Mountains in the east stood over Trinity Site, where the first atomic bomb had been detonated in 1945. To the north, the five-mile-long ramp of a prototype railgun launcher ran up Oscura Peak, where a month earlier it had accelerated its first test satellite to low Earth orbit. History, plenty of history.

Spencer was determined not to add just a footnote to the story of White Sands; he was after an entire chapter.

For now he devoted his attention to the small metal antennas that dotted the compound. Thousands of whiplike microwave receivers blanketed a circular patch of desert two kilometers in diameter, making it look like a huge pincushion. A barbed-wire fence surrounded the "antenna farm."

Spencer knelt by one of the frail-looking antennas and fingered the flexible wire. *Work for me today, baby!* He had cobbled the whole project together on a shoestring budget, and he dreaded that his experiment might fail because of a stupid glitch. A preventable glitch. Then the bureaucrats would shut down the whole circus.

"Hey, Spence!"

He jerked his head up. Surrounded by the small wire constructions, he seemed to be standing in the center of a field of metallic cornstalks. Shading his eyes, he saw a gangly woman wearing an Australian hat walk toward him. Rita Fellenstein was a technical whiz, but she had taken it upon herself to be a combination den mother and butt-kicker for the solar-satellite group—including Spencer.

"It's gonna work," Rita said. "Stop hovering over it."

"Just checking the connections one last time." Spencer wiped his hands against his pants.

Rita stepped around the wires. "Well, don't get all anal retentive about it. You're starting to act like Nedermyer."

"He could get you fired for a remark like that," Spencer said.

"Fire a national lab employee? Get real. Come on, let's get back to the command trailers. The reporters want to talk to you."

Spencer felt a tug at his gut. "Uh, I've got to check this stuff." It seemed that every time they got the array hooked up they lost contact with one of the antennas, usually due to a kangaroo rat gnawing through the cables.

"No you don't need to check it. You've already done it. I've already done it. And the technicians have already done it. Now go talk to the newsies before first light comes down."

"I just hate it when they ask stupid questions." He realized he was not sounding much like a history-making visionary.

Rita put her hands on her narrow hips. "Well, Nedermyer doesn't mind talking to the press. He'll come across as an important Department of Energy watchdog over us brash young scientists. And if you don't get back there, they'll be quoting *him* instead of you. Do you want them to get a Washington bean counter's view of the project?"

Spencer detected a smile beneath the shadow of her hat. "Okay, okay. I give up. He always tries to rain on my parade."

Of all the bureaucrats who had visited the solar-antenna farm, Lance Nedermyer was the most difficult for Spencer to understand. Nedermyer had built a fast-burning reputation during his younger days, with a promising future ahead of him in research. But a White House Fellowship had lured him to the Washington political scene, and the spark of his scientific curiosity had fizzled. "Potomac fever," they called it. Nedermyer had thrown away his chance of doing real research in favor of gaining political influence.

Spencer started toward the battered U.S. Government truck at the periphery of the antenna farm. He stepped over the spaghetti web of wires on the ground, connecting hundreds of whiplike antennas. The setup didn't have to look pretty to work—nor did it have to cost an arm and a leg. That was the beauty of it.

Spencer had to trot to keep up with Rita's long-legged pace. "I lost track of time," he said. "When's the next flyover?"

Rita answered without checking her watch, still striding along. "Alpha One is due in forty minutes. It's got a dwell time of five minutes, with Alpha Two and the rest of them right on its heels. It'll be another twenty-four hours before the Seven Dwarfs are in place again."

The "Seven Dwarfs," a cluster of small solar-collection satellites, circled Earth more than three hundred miles up, spaced in different orbits, appearing overhead one after the other. Spencer marveled at the simple concept. He couldn't claim total credit for coming up with the idea, but he had been instrumental in getting the project off the ground.

The satellites converted raw solar energy into microwaves. Once the first satellite popped over the horizon, it would beam focused energy down onto the field of antennas, not unlike the millions of telephone conversations comsats already beamed to Earth. The key was to use a lot of little, low-orbiting satellites instead of a single big one.

Spencer had spent years fighting for his project, trying to convince uninterested politicians or military types of the best way to tap the power of the sun. Low-efficiency passive solar arrays on Earth could generate only minimal power, enough to run a few local farms. Only by deploying enormous solar panels in space, then beaming the power through the atmosphere, would solar energy pay off in a way big enough to make a difference.

But other technical experts hawked their own ideas to the same committees; since the decision makers knew little or nothing about the subject, they were swayed by razzle-dazzle presentations and good public speakers rather than by solid technical content.

Spencer's test had finally come down to the wire, and today was the day he would blow the other guys out of the water. He hoped his smallsat program would be as simple in practice as he made it sound in his sales pitches.

Rita slammed the door of the old gray pickup, then roared across the rutted temporary roads. The infrequent New Mexican rain fell two inches at a time, then dried the ground hard as cement. Spencer ducked to keep his head from hitting the roof of the truck as they bounced toward the cluster of buildings. He tried to talk, but his teeth clicked together as the truck jounced. He kept quiet until they reached the command center.

He brushed aside his usual revulsion at the substandard quarters the government had allotted his project. Maybe the TV reporters wouldn't shoot too much footage of the facility itself. The "blockhouse" was a bank of three revamped 1960s-vintage trailers that had been used for various experiments at White Sands. A mesh of chicken wire completely surrounded the trailers, making the blockhouse into a giant Faraday cage, safe from stray microwave beams if the satellites missed their mark.

The rattling hum of portable air conditioners buzzed outside the white aluminum-siding walls. A fist of twisted fiber-optic wires ran from the distant microwave farm to a switchboard inside.

"Get your badge on, Spence," Rita said. "Look nice for the newsies."

He pulled his laminated badge out of his pocket and clipped it to his collar. Awful ID photograph, on a par with the one on his driver's license. Brown hair that wouldn't stay combed, blue eyes open a little too wide, prominent sunburn, and a thin face wearing an expression as if he had just swallowed a grape whole. Spencer wondered if it was a requirement that photo identification had to be embarrassing.

The cool, musty-smelling blockhouse felt good after baking out on the desert. The only light inside the trailer seeped through closed miniblinds or shone from computer screens. The overhead fluorescents had been switched off. A jukebox purchased from an old café in nearby Alamogordo sat dormant in the corner.

The news crew from Albuquerque had their equipment set up in a small alcove walled off by portable room dividers. Spencer had hoped for a bit more media, but the big San Francisco oil spill monopolized most of the prime-time broadcasts.

Spencer's people chattered in a precise staccato drone, verifying readings from the antenna farm, calibrating the solar smallsat. "DOE's on the line, Spence. They told us to call them when you got here."

Spencer dismissed it with a wave. He had more im-

portant things to do than to chat with Department of
Energy paper-pushers. "Tell them I'm tied up. What's
our time?"

Rita Fellenstein glanced up from a computer monitor.
Colors from the CRT display reflected off the sheen on
her thin face. "Twenty-three minutes until Alpha One
comes into range. Go ahead and kiss up to DOE—they
have a psychological need to give you a pep talk. That
way they can take credit for our success."

Spencer ignored the suggestion. "Any air traffic?"

"Sky's clear, verified by El Paso control."

"Data link?"

"Echo checks are error-free."

A decade ago the operation would have taken ten
times the people and a thousand times the budget.
Spencer looked around in quiet satisfaction, content that
his project had succeeded against "conventional" DOE
wisdom. The bureaucracy of Big Science added thousands of unnecessary corners that could be cut if you
weren't brainwashed into believing they were necessary.

He raised his voice over the murmur in the blockhouse. "Okay, you guys, all green on the diagnostics.
Everyone knows the drill—any reason to call for a hold
takes precedence. Problems?"

The trailer remained silent except for the background
hum of equipment and air conditioners. The reporters
stood around, shuffling their feet, adjusting their pin
mikes, not understanding the details but sensing something important about to happen.

"All right, signal DOE we're going hot," Spencer said.

Activity filled the dim trailer. Excitement raced
through Spencer's veins, the anticipation of seeing his
project come on-line at last. A voice interrupted him,
sounding as if it had taken years to perfect its nasal
resonance. Spencer's stomach dropped.

"I don't like your 'negative response only' policy, Dr.
Lockwood. Statistics prove that a checklist methodology
eliciting positive acknowledgments has an appreciably

higher percentage of success. DOE would feel more comfortable if you adopted this procedure, as the rest of the civilized world does."

Lance Nedermyer's fleshy torso filled most of the walking space in the crowded trailer. Though the block-house was cool, beads of perspiration dotted Nedermyer's flushed forehead. At the moment, he was probably the only man on the entire White Sands installation wearing a suit and a tie. Spencer wanted to say: *My people know their jobs, Lance! Teamwork sometimes proves more effective than checklists.* But, much as he wanted to, Spencer could not afford to embarrass or ignore the man. "Thanks for your input, Lance. I'll be sure to include your suggestion in our post-test assessment comments."

"I'd be more pleased if you'd make them part of your operating procedures, posthaste."

"Thanks, Lance." But Spencer had already hunched down in front of a communications workstation operated by Juan Romero. Romero, with his long black hair and drooping mustache, looked like a bandit from a cheap Western—and Romero intentionally played the part to the hilt.

Romero expanded a portion of his screen to show a televised view of the antenna farm, taken from the top of a hundred-foot tower outside the blockhouse. The image of the metallic receivers wavered in the heat, making them look like thousands of fingers reaching up to grasp the invisible radiation.

"Sixty seconds," said Rita Fellenstein.

Spencer wet his lips; the desert dryness seemed particularly piercing now. "Jukebox plugged in?" he whispered.

"That was the first thing on the *checklist*." Romero raised his voice loud enough for Nedermyer to hear; then he grinned broadly out of sight.

Spencer felt Nedermyer's eyes on him. The news crew hushed. TV cameras pointed at the techs constantly updating the system status.

"Folks," Spencer said, raising his voice, "we're about to catch the first solar energy ever beamed directly from space. Keep your fingers crossed."

At the top left corner of the workstation in front of him, numerals flashed the countdown. Spencer wondered if he should voice the numbers out loud for the benefit of the DOE bureaucrats in D.C. He joined the faint whispering as everyone counted down to first light. "Three . . . two . . . one . . . bingo!"

The televised view from the desert didn't change. Romero and Spencer stared at the screen. They saw no indication that millions of joules of energy were raining down from space into the waiting arms of a thousand microwave antennas.

The news crews probably wanted to see a dazzling green death beam streak down from orbit. The trailer fell silent as everyone held their breath. Nothing.

Click!

Bright light filled the trailer, then a whirring hum. The sound of the Beach Boys singing in harmony swept through the air. Spencer smiled as the strains of "The Warmth of the Sun" drifted from the jukebox. Everyone laughed and started clapping. Spencer broke into a wider grin; Romero slapped him on the back.

Nedermyer scowled at the jukebox. The music grew louder until it blared out of the speakers.

Spencer reached left and right to shake hands. His crew congratulated him, pounding him on the back. "Hey, somebody notify DOE!"

Rita waved an arm and held up a portable telephone. "Spence, the Assistant Secretary wants to talk with you."

"Tell her I'm monitoring the test." A champagne cork popped, and Spencer was doused. Breaking free of the revelry, he made his way toward the reporters. Now he didn't mind talking to them. Over the din, he could hear voices shouting performance figures.

"We're showing a thirty-five-percent conversion efficiency! With this baseline, we've already exceeded the design specs!"

Nedermyer stood with his arms crossed, lips drawn into a tight line. Nedermyer's foot tapped, but it didn't seem to be moving to the beat of the song. The ruddy color that crept into the bureaucrat's cheeks was far darker than a sunburn.

Spencer motioned with his head to the jukebox. "Well? Are you satisfied, Lance?"

"At what? This . . . stunt?"

"We could have used anything for a load. We thought this would be a bit more . . . memorable than an oscilloscope."

"There's a purpose for all the diagnostics equipment your group has purchased, Dr. Lockwood. They convey much more information for competent analysis than this boom box of yours."

Spencer lowered his voice. "What is your problem, Lance? Can't you see it worked? Give us a little credit."

Nedermyer's whisper had the edge of a bayonet. "I spend all year long trying to crowbar money out of the trenches for your pet projects, and you screwballs turn it into a comedy routine! We had to can a dozen other equally worthy proposals to get your funding, Dr. Lockwood, and look what kind of impression you've just made. Imagine the headlines: Government Wastes Millions of Dollars to Turn on Jukebox from Space! Are you too young to remember how the public howled when the Apollo astronauts were having too much fun on the moon? You're supposed to act *respectable* in situations like this. Can't you grow up for a few minutes, golden boy?"

The jukebox song changed to "I Get Around." Chuckles rippled through the trailer. Rita's voice boomed over the background noise. "Quiet! Switchover in one minute. Alpha Two coming up."

Spencer turned to Nedermyer, trying to get back to neutral ground. "Ready for the next satellite. Care for a closer look?"

Nedermyer kept his arms folded. "I can see—and hear—from where I'm standing."

Spencer kept a straight face as he went over to Rita's area. Three telephones and two laptop computers lay jumbled next to her workstation. Even sitting, the gangly scientist was nearly as tall as the reporter hovering over her shoulder. Rita pointed to a graphic on the screen for the reporter's benefit. "Alpha One is about to go over the horizon. We'll lose contact soon."

The reporter pulled his microphone back and spoke into it. "I thought these satellites stayed overhead the whole time."

"To do that, we'd have to put the satellites up so high that their beam would spread out too much by the time it got down to Earth. Our beam from low-orbiting satellites stays tight enough for us to milk it. But the downside is that each satellite is overhead for only five minutes."

"Does that mean your antenna farm will only generate electricity for a few minutes a day?"

Spencer rolled his eyes and wondered if the reporter hadn't done his homework, or if he was just playing dumb to clarify things for his viewers.

"No, we've got seven satellites in four different planar orbits for broader coverage," said Rita.

"The Seven Dwarfs," the reporter said, grinning.

"Right. We were fairly certain we could lock the microwave beam from the first satellite. The real trick is to see if we can turn on the next satellite when it comes into view *without interrupting the power*. If there's enough overlap between the beams, the electrical network won't even notice the difference."

A shout erupted from the front. "Two, one . . . transition! Alpha Two is locked on!"

Spencer noticed no dimming of the lights, no jitter in the jukebox. The party started all over again.

Rita kept talking, giving the canned speech every member of the project knew by heart. "At least one of the Seven Dwarfs is within view of White Sands forty-six percent of the time. But they may be at too low an angle to do any good. Eventually we hope to get a continuous ring of satellites over the Earth so we never lose touch—at least in daylight. We also need to build more antenna farms along the path, so that as soon as a satellite loses sight of one farm it can switch to another."

The reporter recorded all the information, but Rita didn't slow down. "Once we get them up there, all that energy is free. Since the cost of sending up smallsats is decreasing, it'll become economical and a lot less polluting than any form of Earth-based power system. Twenty more satellites are sitting in sealed storage at the Jet Propulsion Lab right now. We'll eventually need about seventy for a complete system, but the strategy is to first show they work. Solar satellites don't wear out, you know, they just keep going and going and going—like that pink bunny."

Another cheer went through the trailer a few moments later. "Alpha Three overlap and switch-on is successful. Three down and four to go." The celebration was more subdued this time. After the first milestone, every other event seemed less significant.

"What about the *Zoroaster* spill?" the reporter asked.

Spencer interrupted the interview; he had hoped for a question like that. Rita looked relieved. Spencer stepped too close to the microphone, then awkwardly backed away as he talked. "The pictures speak for themselves. Until we develop alternative energy sources like this one, we're going to keep having accidents like that one." He felt warm inside as he said it. The words came out like a perfect sound bite, and he had no doubt the broadcast would use it.

Before long, the seventh satellite passed over the horizon. The lights dimmed and the jukebox stopped. Spencer was suddenly exhausted.

Like an addict craving another hit, he looked around to keep the thrill going just a little longer. He spotted Lance Nedermyer standing in the corner, alone, talking into a telephone. Nedermyer loosened his tie, then turned his back on the party.

Spencer set his mouth as he realized he had to do some damage control; he reached Nedermyer as the bureaucrat hung up the phone. "Looks like a total success, Lance," he said. "We're having a quick-look briefing in ten minutes to go over preliminary data."

Nedermyer smiled tightly. "I've seen all I need to for now."

"Too bad the Secretary couldn't make it out."

"No need to, that's why I'm here." He turned for the exit. "If your test is over, I'll be heading back to Albuquerque. It's a three-hour drive."

Spencer followed the man out the door, growing angry as Nedermyer brushed off his accomplishment. Outside, the sunlight seemed to explode with brightness. With an effort, Spencer kept his voice friendly. "Albuquerque, already?"

Nedermyer pulled off his tie and strode toward his rental car. The ground crunched beneath his feet. "That's what I said."

"Well, is there anything else I can show you?"

"I said I've seen all I need to see—"

Spencer's patience snapped and he reached out to grab Nedermyer by the elbow. The man's arm felt as fleshy as it looked. "Lance, you can't deny that what happened here today marks a new era. When all the satellites are up—"

Nedermyer shook off Spencer's hand. Squinting in the harsh sunlight, he fumbled in his pocket for a pair of sunshades to clip onto his eyeglasses. Spencer saw himself reflected in the lenses. Nedermyer said, "You just don't get it, do you, Lockwood?"

Spencer stopped. "Get what?"

Nedermyer waved a hand at the trailer, then toward the antenna farm. "All this is just a game to you. A stunt. You might have captured the public eye this afternoon, but I have to deal with the flak back inside the Beltway.

What am I going to tell Congress when they ask why DOE is spending money playing surfin' music?"

Spencer narrowed his eyes. "Why are you doing this, Lance? You *can't* be that dense."

"I was just on the phone to headquarters, Dr. Lockwood." He started to walk toward his car, but he took off his sunglasses and pointed them at Spencer. "I've recommended that the National Academy of Sciences review your program before we spend any more money on your operation."

"That will take half a year! We've got smallsats waiting at JPL. They're already built—"

"I'll be back in a month with the panel to see your full-scale test results. And there'd better be some good science out of it. Play by the rules, Spencer. Everybody else does." He jammed his sunglasses back on his face and strode to the car.

Spencer watched the cloud of dust dissipate as Nedermyer drove away. He didn't know how long he stood there before the door to the trailer opened and Rita Fellenstein called, "Hey, Spence! The reporters want to talk to you again."

Still in shock, Spencer kept watching the road where Nedermyer's car vanished into an unpleasant mirage.

Someone had plugged the jukebox into the main power. The strains of "Don't Worry Baby" drifted out the door.

FOUR

SYMPATHY FOR THE DEVIL

Alex Kramer drove toward the ocean, following memories more detailed than any map. In the morning fog, he passed down narrow roads in the Marin headlands, where craggy rocks met the sea near the foot of the Golden Gate Bridge. At "vista point" turnouts showing postcard views of the bridge and the San Francisco skyline, rubberneckers stretched for a glimpse of the spreading blackness below. It made him sick.

All night long, Alex had been transfixed by news of the spill, sitting with one light on in the empty ranch house and watching the same footage over and over again. It seemed like a parallel to the disaster that had smothered his own life.

Out on the Bay, smaller tankers pulled beside the *Zoroaster* and tried to off-load oil in desperate lightering operations; boats wrestled to deploy booms around the slick as it spread. Hundreds of people scurried about with equipment, but it seemed futile. Most of Oilstar's effort seemed to be directed at telling people the spill wasn't as bad as it looked, that they had everything under control.

Alex passed old Fort Baker and Fort Cronkhite with their crumbling batteries and gun emplacements high on the bluffs. The landscape was a drab but striking range of colors, from the deep green of the stands of flattened cypress to the dry yellow-brown of gasping grass and brilliant orange of wild California poppies.

He and his son Jay had spent some of their best times hiking out in the headlands. He had thought never to come here again because of the ghosts he might find along the trails; even the water reminded him of the time he and Jay had sipped from the same canteen and splashed barefoot in the rocky surf. The Coast Trail had been their last decent outing together before Jay followed his unit to Saudi Arabia.

Now Alex drove downslope to the end of the road in Rodeo Cove, an isolated section of coastline just north of the Golden Gate, with rough surf suitable only for wet-suited divers and daredevils. He parked on the cracked asphalt and got out of his pickup, unable to tear his gaze from the shore. He held the truck's open door for support. Foul hydrocarbons permeated the air, masking the salt-and-iodine smell of the ocean. His eyes and nose burned.

The current of the outgoing tide had sucked the *Zoroaster*'s crude oil back out to sea, where it had spread farther. Then, with the tide's returning flow, the waves had splattered the dark ooze against the coastline in an ever-widening stain.

Alex wanted to turn from the horror. His stomach rippled with the leaden weight of brewing nausea. But his feet moved of their own accord, stumbling toward the beach. Five people, dressed warmly in jeans and flannel shirts, stared and said nothing to each other.

Hastily erected DANGER NO SWIMMING and CONTAMINATED WATER signs dotted the beach. Normally rich brown, pebbled with black and tan rocks, the sand was slathered with an opaque slime of crude. Viscous waves licked the shore.

Oil-smeared seagulls chased the waves, looking for something to eat; they circled in confusion at the strange new consistency of the ocean. Farther out to sea, buoys clanged. Normally, fishing boats would have bobbed with the swells—but not today, and not for a long time. At the tide line, algae clustered against the rocks among other shellfish, already dying.

A few years before, Alex and Jay had started a long backpacking trip here. The Coast Trail wound along the headlands for miles, and the two of them walked in the cool air all day, looking down at the crashing surf from the crumbling edges of horrendous cliffs.

Jay had labored for a year at the University of California, San Francisco, though he had little interest in school. During their three-day hike, Jay finally broke the news to Alex of his decision to join the army. Jay had rubbed his short red hair, looked at Alex, then away, then back at him again. His pale skin had flushed a deeper red as if he was embarrassed to be changing his mind about what he wanted to do with his life.

"I know it's not what you wanted me to do," Jay had said. He took a nervous sip from the open canteen, offering it to Alex, who shook his head. Jay looked away again as he screwed the metal cap back on. "But college just isn't what I want to do, at least not right now. I want to challenge myself in a different way, and I think the army can do that for me."

Alex had been surprised, but not unduly upset. He and Maureen tried to keep a light hand on the children. Both Erin and Jay were intelligent and sensible; they made their own decisions. "If that's what you think will work best for you, Jay. It's better to change your mind than to keep going along with what you know is a bad decision."

Jay, who had not hugged his father since eighth grade, clapped an arm around Alex's shoulder, gave a brief squeeze, then struck off down the trail at a greater speed, embarrassed. . . .

Alex still remembered the visit from the two army officers, informing him that Jay had been killed in a nighttime skirmish on the Saudi border in one of their oil wars.

Now the roar of the surf sounded like distant, booming gunfire in his ears.

Alex stood unmoving at the tide line. Dark blobs clumped on the beach. The waves had churned the crude and water into a frothy, gummy substance, "mousse," that stuck to everything.

A seagull flew overhead, its mouth wide open. The waves crashed in, bringing the oil closer, and Alex skittishly stepped back.

Cold wind blew in his eyes. The same oil slick would smother the Bay, wrap around Alcatraz Island, Angel Island, Fisherman's Wharf, the Embarcadero. San Francisco had been called the most beautiful city in the world—and it had just been brutally raped by the *Zoroaster*. Seeing the effects up close, Alex felt the walls surrounding his anger and despair rattling, crumbling.

Right now, Oilstar officials were desperate for any public-relations coup. They would leap at any hook Alex Kramer could offer, though the barbs were plainly visible. Panic removed all common sense.

Alex breathed deeply, trying to ignore the pain in his chest. Mitch Stone was probably correct in thinking the Prometheus microbe could help clean up this spill. This was a wound that could not be ignored.

Trembling, Alex squatted and dipped his fingers in the blackish brown ooze on the shoreline. His fingers came away soiled and greasy, covered with a stain that looked like blood.

Blood and oil. In his life, the two had so much in common.

FIVE

SLIPPERY WHEN WET

The wreck of the *Oilstar Zoroaster* lay like a corpse on the Golden Gate Bridge's south tower, canting downward at a drunken angle. On the span above, cars crawled by as people craned their necks to gawk.

Coast Guard boats, Oilstar barges, and private fishing boats descended like vultures to continue massive lightering operations. Riding choppy waves beside the *Zoroaster,* a smaller tanker—the *Tiberius*—lashed up to the hulk. Straining pumps attempted to pull crude from *Zoroaster* faster than it could leak into the Bay.

As its cargo holds emptied, the wrecked supertanker rode higher in the water. Pumps replaced ballast with Bay water to keep the *Zoroaster* from floating up and losing its precarious balance.

Hung up on the bridge's south pier, the *Zoroaster* had been ripped by the same submerged ledge the steamer *Rio de Janeiro* had struck a century earlier; the *Rio* had dragged over half of its passengers and crew to the bottom, and now the *Zoroaster* rested against the same ledge, groaning against the six-knot ebb tide.

Standing on the deck of the *Zoroaster,* Todd Severyn jammed a broad, aching shoulder under one of the massive transfer hoses cast across from the smaller *Tiberius.* Other men from his lightering crew fought with the hoses, hoisting them over the deck rails and swinging the hose derrick to align them with cargo hatches. Todd tried to bellow orders, do at least as much work as his best man, and keep from puking all at the same time.

Todd planted his big feet on the slick deck, keeping a delicate balance with his heavy work boots. The stinging hydrocarbon fumes burned his eyes, his nose, as volatile petrochemicals roiled into the air. But the slant and rocking motion of the wreck in the choppy sea nauseated a Wyoming man like Todd more than the smell of crude.

He had worked oil for most of his life, getting his start in the oil-shale processing plants near Rock Springs, before Oilstar had sent him to Kuwait, Burma, Alaska, the North Sea. They had assigned him to an offshore rig off New Orleans for his first big job—but he had never before been in charge of a hellish job like off-loading the *Zoroaster.*

"Come on, kids!" he shouted into the noise of the pumps, the wind, the gurgling oil far below. His throat was raw from yelling, and his crew staggered about in exhaustion mixed with panic. Overhead, helicopters branded with TV station logos circled to get dramatic footage. Spectators looked through the crisscrossed superstructure of the Golden Gate Bridge. It felt like a three-ring circus; Todd wished he were back in Wyoming. The last time he had taken off by himself with nothing more than a horse, mess kit, and bedroll on the plains seemed like a million years ago. Well, a few months at least. But it sure beat this crappy work.

Out on the water, absorbent booms along the greatest concentration of floating oil filled up and clogged. Skimmers tried to draw in the oil but lost ground quickly in the face of the gushing flow. Cleanup tugs struggled to deploy nylon containment booms, long draperies that hung under the water, lassoing the oil for pickup by recovery boats. A barge anchored near Alcatraz Island received the recovered oil from containment vessels. Privately owned fishing boats and small pleasure craft added their efforts, scooping five-gallon buckets of foul-smelling crude directly from the surface.

At the stern of the *Zoroaster,* the wall of the four-story deckhouse admonished in large, mocking letters: NO SMOKING, PREVENT ACCIDENTS, and SAFETY FIRST.

Todd worked with three men to clamp the transfer hose into the hatch of cargo hold 7. He moved in a barely controlled frenzy, like the rest of his team, and they ended up getting in each other's way. The clamorous racket, the foul fumes, and the treacherous deck made conditions worse.

Todd pulled a wrench from a deep pocket on his greasy slicker and tightened the seal. "Start the pumps!" he yelled, raising a gloved hand.

Farther up the deck, the Oilstar helicopter pilot waved an acknowledgment, then spoke into the chopper's radio. A few moments later, the hose shuddered as *Tiberius* started another pump. More crude began to flow out of the *Zoroaster*'s hold.

Todd stumbled to the deck rail. The weather slicker hid much of his big-boned frame, but he had managed to smear oil over his craggy face and brown hair. He coughed and spat over the rail.

Below, brownish black oil continued to bubble out of the torn hull like a vile potion in a cauldron. The oil lay two feet thick on top of the water. If it were up to him, he'd just as soon toss the tanker captain overboard into the mess; the idiot should have at least gone down with his ship, like a real captain, after causing a disaster like this.

With the outgoing tide and turbulent weather, there was a very good chance the *Zoroaster* would slip off and plunge into the deep channel. If that happened, the tanker would drag with it the 800,000 barrels of oil still on board. Its cargo holds would leak into the Bay for years.

But Todd had a job to do, and he would bust his back cheeks to accomplish it. He couldn't turn back the clock and prevent the wreck from happening. He had to ignore his disgust at seeing the massive damage grow worse every second. The whole dang world was watching, but he had to focus on the job at hand. Keep cool. There would be time to get pissed later—get good and drunk, maybe even look up that captain and kick some butt. While other people spent all their time yakking and complaining, Todd Severyn waded in and started *doing* something about it.

He yanked off his thick gloves, stuffed them in his pocket, and reached inside his slicker. Hauling out his walkie-talkie, he clicked the channel to his counterpart over on the *Tiberius*. "Glenn! Give me an update. How much have we off-loaded so far?"

The radio crackled after only a moment's pause. "Close to fifty thousand barrels. Pretty good for a day's work—"

Todd scowled. "Darn it, that's only a few percent of what's still inside."

He heard shouting in the background of the *Tiberius*. Glenn snapped back, "Then shut up and keep pumping! We're doing everything we can."

The transfer hoses had been pumping for less than fifteen minutes, throbbing as they sucked barrel after barrel out of the *Zoroaster*'s holds—when the wind picked up. Todd froze, wondering what else could go wrong. Lightering operations were tough even under good conditions, but now the sea grew rougher. The fog had cleared, but the sky turned gray, like a smoke pudding.

The deck began to creak, and the ship suddenly lurched to the side, increasing the slant.

Todd scrambled to grab the rail as panic welled up in him. He heard the other six men on the tanker shouting. He hated to leave a job unfinished, hated to run away when conditions got worse—but he wasn't stupid. He knew when to make the call. He pressed the Talk button on his walkie-talkie. "Getting unstable, Glenn. Start thinking about closing up shop." He looked at his watch. It was getting close to high tide, the greatest danger, when the supertanker rode highest on its unsteady balance against the bridge pier.

The *Tiberius* responded. "They're going to crucify us if we abandon this puppy, Severyn. She's still gushing thousands of gallons a minute."

Todd wanted to smash the walkie-talkie on the deck. "If the *Zoroaster* goes down, none of my people are gonna be on it. I'm ordering the chopper to start shuttling people back over to you."

"We'd better check with Oilstar—"

"It's my call, and I'm making it." If Emma Branson didn't like it, she could come out of her high-and-mighty Oilstar office and do the work herself.

He switched off the walkie-talkie and raised a hand to get the attention of his crew. He pointed toward the helicopter, then held up four fingers. Seeing this, the first team of four broke away from their work and struggled up the slick, sloping deck toward the helicopter, which seemed about half a mile away. The pilot started the engine while waiting for them; two minutes later the blades began to rotate.

The walkie-talkie crackled. "Oilstar okays it, Severyn. But the minute the weather turns better, we come right back."

Todd's stomach twisted with the thought of how much oil still remained in the unbreached cargo holds. He shouted as the wind picked up again, "After the chopper takes the first load of my people over, we'll unlash the two ships. Stop pumping from cargo hold 3. We'll disconnect right now. Three of us will stay here to get the transfer hose ready when it's time."

He turned to see the four men clamber aboard the helicopter. The blades became a blur, and the craft lurched from the deck, heading toward the adjacent *Tiberius*.

As Todd watched the copter land on the other tanker,

the *Zoroaster* groaned under his feet, listing and settling deeper. He fell back against a metal supply shack mounted to the deck. *Keep cool,* he reminded himself, but the thought of the tanker sliding off the submerged ledge and plunging to the bottom filled him with a terror that he tried to stomp out before his men could see.

Jimmy Mack, a wide-eyed kid just days with the company, started yelling about stupid risks. Todd staggered over to help him disconnect the transfer hose from cargo hold 3. "I keep my word—no one's going down with this ship!" He bent over and used his wrench on the transfer-hose connection.

Two men detached the hose from the hold and hauled it toward the deck rail. Black oil gushed from the end, splattering the deck. Todd radioed for the *Tiberius* to shut off the pumps to cargo holds 7 and 8. "Start unlashing the ships," he said. The words sounded like failure to him, and it made him angry. "Get ready to disengage these other hoses."

On the deck of the smaller tanker, the helicopter lifted off and began its journey back. Working two men at a time, Todd and his companions threw off the heavy hooks securing the *Zoroaster* to the *Tiberius*. The thumping vibrations of the helicopter grew louder as it approached the supertanker's landing pad.

"Disconnect those hoses," Todd shouted. "Move it!"

As a large swell struck, the *Zoroaster* lurched, tumbling them backward into the water cannons. Todd smashed his elbow against a large red pipe, but managed to grab the rail of a foam-monitor station. Everything was going wrong. Todd felt as if he were standing in the path of an avalanche. One of the men smacked his helmet on a release valve, and water began to spray from a nozzle.

No longer lashed together, the two tankers drifted apart by a few more feet.

The transfer hose at cargo hold 7 sheared away, spraying oil in all directions. With a loud pop, the hose

connected to cargo hold 8 tore off. The *Zoroaster* began
to tilt sideways, away from *Tiberius*.

"She's going down!" Todd shouted. For just a moment
he wanted to run in blind panic to the empty chopper
pad, but he had to get his crew off. He shoved Jimmy
Mack toward the landing platform. "Go! Now!"

"Yes, sir!"

All three men began a scramble for the helicopter pad
near the stern deck. They were covered with petroleum
slime; the rough metal deck plates were slick with crude.
Jimmy Mack stumbled to his knees, disoriented with
panic. Todd reached out a big hand and helped him up.
"I told you I keep my word!"

The helicopter came in and tried to land, but the
Zoroaster tilted fast. Todd grabbed a rail to keep his
balance. Just as the second team of three made it to the
landing circle, the copter rose up and circled back
around, leaving Todd and the two others to yell for it to
come back. The tanker lurched again.

Over the side of the ship, the black petroleum looked
like a vile quagmire, bubbling like lava. Fumes burned
Todd's face and eyes like acid. He couldn't imagine a
death worse than drowning in several feet of crude oil.

The helicopter wheeled overhead and landed with a
skid, bouncing across the deck. Without waiting for the
rotors to slow, Todd and the others ducked their heads
and scrambled to the open door. They tumbled into the
back in an oil-stained pile of bodies. The last one on,
Todd still hung halfway out of the hatch as the copter
took off. "Yeeee-hah!"

The pilot flew without speaking, his jaw clenched, as
they lifted up and away from the *Zoroaster*'s tilting
superstructure. Todd struggled to a better position to
watch through the scratched Plexiglas cockpit window.

Below, the *Tiberius* pulled away from the sinking
Zoroaster. Sliding down, rolling sideways as it lost its
slippery grip on the Fort Point ledge, the *Zoroaster*
toppled in a slow-motion avalanche. Todd's stomach

sank with it. Water and oil foamed gray in the churning violence of the plunge. The supertanker's hull yawned open wider, geysering black crude into the waters.

Before his eyes, the disaster became a thousand times worse.

Despite the desperate lightering operations, nearly fifty million gallons of crude oil remained in the breached cargo holds. Cold, dark water swallowed the doomed supertanker in less than fifteen minutes.

Todd watched, sick with disgust. From inside the *Zoroaster*, oil would continue to gush upward for years . . . and now there was no way to stop it.

SIX

NOWHERE MAN

The *Zoroaster* spill was a shit-storm in a small room, but Speaker of the House Jeffrey Mayeaux had to cover a smile as he faced the audience for the news conference. He took grim pleasure in knowing he had arrived on the scene a full three hours before the Vice President was due. The rooster-faced VP didn't even know he had been upstaged yet.

A techie wearing jeans and a faded yellow T-shirt scurried stooped over like a hunchback, checking leads to the microphones on the podium. Mayeaux walked in, flanked by his chief of staff Franklin Weathersee and a Secret Service mastodon. He fixed his eyes on the reporters; they looked like crawfish in a bowl, and he was about to have them for dinner. He wore his gravest "I'm from the government, I'm here to help you" expression.

The Honorable Jeffrey Mayeaux would do his best to witness the concerns firsthand and say the necessary words to foster hope. He was good at that. Yes, the government would do everything possible to help the San Francisco area cope with this crisis. You betcha.

The Executive Branch would be pissing Tabasco sauce by this evening.

Mayeaux had skipped out on his Acapulco "conference" early for the sole purpose of stealing the VP's thunder. Unannounced, Mayeaux was the first high-level government official to respond to this serious disaster—and the bozos at 1600 Pennsylvania would not get the credit this time. Mayeaux would shake the hands and kiss the babies; Vice President Wolani—Miss Congeniality—would get the tough questions a few hours from now. The whole escapade should add at least another ten grand onto Mayeaux's lobbyist salary after he retired from Congress in a year.

A half-dozen video cameras jockeyed for position as he turned to expose his best side. He eyed a cute brunette gripping a microphone bearing the letters KSFO. Watching the way she wrapped her fingers around the shaft of the microphone, holding its head close to her red lips, Mayeaux thought how deliciously erotic it looked. Admiring the swell of her bodacious breasts against her silk blouse, Mayeaux made a mental note to have Weathersee offer her an off-the-record interview, "inside sources," before he had to jet back to the East Coast. Often enough, promotion-hungry lady reporters were willing to go to extremes for a scoop. And you wouldn't know unless you asked.

Like a few other Louisiana politicians, Mayeaux didn't give a coonass's damn about scandal. His constituents watched it with the fascination of spectators at a car accident—but as long as they knew some of Mayeaux's obvious weaknesses, they didn't dig too deep for hidden flaws. The old saying went that every person owned the same total allotment of vices . . . so the folks who looked squeaky clean usually had some very twisted skeletons in their closets. According to that theory, a Holy Roller like VP Wolani probably got off by pulling legs off live frogs.

Mayeaux straightened, pulling himself to his full

height of five and a half feet. For his opening statement, he spoke slowly, careful to smother his leftover Cajun accent, as he always did in public speeches.

"Incredibly devastating," he said. "This could set back the advances we've made in environmental management by decades. I have personally contacted the Federal Emergency Management Agency to encourage their best efforts here. I also advocate calling out the National Guard, but of course that's up to the administration, whenever they get here. I understand the Vice President is on his way, so you can ask him yourselves. He'll be along any time now."

"Mr. Speaker, Mr. Speaker!"

He scanned the crowd until he caught the brunette's eye. He raised his eyebrow a fraction before nodding to her. He didn't give a rat's ass for her question, but he kept his public face on autopilot. He wondered how much of a challenge she would be. "Go ahead."

"How will this affect the proposed new gasoline tax? Will the administration back the House's legislation calling for a majority of the tax to be used for cleaning up the environment?"

He pegged her: tough reporter type, arrogant and driven, looking for the big story. Willing to do just about anything for it—and he bet his Louisiana homegrown hot link would satisfy her. "I don't see how the president could refuse to sign the bill, especially now, with this mess right in America's lap."

"But do you anticipate a fight? Could this be a big test of your abilities as Speaker?"

Mayeaux put on his "grave and understanding" expression to mask his utter scorn for this test of his abilities. He was in this for the ride and the perks, and by next year he could say goodbye to all the bullshit.

"We all try to work within the system, ma'am. I've been in close contact with Vice President Wolani, who is making time in his busy schedule to personally view this disaster." Mayeaux squelched a smile before it could form on his face. "I'm sure when he returns to Washington, he'll convince the president of the necessity for this legislation. If not, then I'll have to twist a few more arms." He flashed the brunette a warm smile and turned to answer other questions.

Before long, he glanced at the clock at the back of the pressroom. He had been talking for ten minutes. Good enough. Short and sweet. The reporters would remember the "zingers" more than the message; he'd have to personally thank that cute new speechwriter who'd come up with the lines on the jet up from Acapulco.

Excusing himself, Mayeaux smiled one last time at the brunette, then answered a final question over his shoulder as he was led into the anteroom. Weathersee, a stable but joy-killing anchor through Mayeaux's entire career, bent closer and spoke quietly. "Emma Branson is waiting upstairs in a private suite."

"You make a good den mother, Franklin," he said.

The chief of staff ignored the comment. "She needs to speak with you."

Mayeaux glanced around and saw no one dangerous in view; the media was gone, and with no one listening, he let his annoyance show. "That old bitch? I can't afford to be seen with her, especially now. Oilstar connections are going to be extremely bad for my reputation right now."

"I thought you were planning to work for her," Weathersee said calmly.

"That's *after* I retire, and you know it, Franklin!"

"She came in through the back entrance. No one saw her. She says it's urgent," Weathersee said. "She's in a hurry and is calling in a few favors."

Mayeaux allowed himself to be guided toward the elevators. "Yeah, yeah." He knew who had spearheaded the donations that bankrolled his campaign. Even though other big oil companies had stayed away from direct contributions, Emma Branson and Oilstar had played too important a role to ignore.

They emerged from the elevator. Weathersee waited

outside the penthouse door as Mayeaux entered, somehow managing to stand for impossibly long periods without fidgeting.

Mayeaux smiled broadly at Branson as he padded across the beige-carpeted floor to kiss the lizard-faced woman on both cheeks. He thought he might get frostbite on his lips—God, he knew she had once been married, but Mayeaux couldn't imagine anyone willingly fucking the old hag.

He flashed her his warmest grin. "This is like old home week, *cher,* defending the environment, running into old friends." He stroked his hand up and down her arm. She looked so much like a mummy. "How've you been? Damn tragic about that tanker!"

Emma Branson smiled, but her eyes looked as hard as a diamond-tipped oil drill. She wore a necklace of small pearls over a throat that was wattled like an iguana's. A television set in the back of the suite recapped Mayeaux's live interview; she did not seem pleased about it. Branson picked up a decanter of Scotch and poured two fingers' worth into a pair of glasses; she thrust one at him.

"This is no time for bullshit—my corporate board is waiting for me. This spill will hurt the economy a great deal more than it will hurt the environment, Jeffrey. We'll get this mess cleaned up well enough in a few months, but the oil business will be paying forever. We're going to be in court over this one for the next half century."

Branson placed her glass on the counter without sipping from it. Mayeaux didn't say a word; whatever the old iron maiden wanted from him, it wouldn't involve small talk. Branson came straight to the point. "I'd hoped to speak with you before the press conference. You sounded rather enthusiastic about this new tax of yours—how hard are you going to push it?"

Mayeaux took a measured sip of Scotch. It had a smoky, peatlike flavor. Very pure. It had to be a single malt—even he had to admit that everything about Emma Branson was first-class. He paused long enough to make her think his answer wasn't spring-loaded.

"It's scary, Emma. This spill provides the catalyst for the new tax, and there's nothing I, or the back-room boys, can do to prevent it. There's too much momentum behind the bill. Every TV in the country is flooded with *Zoroaster* images, and people are demanding a scapegoat—they want to string somebody up by the balls, and they don't care who. The tax will be a way to ensure 'it doesn't happen again.' You know, like 'the war to end all wars.' Propaganda bullshit, but there you have it."

Branson shook her head. "Do you really think you could use that money to buy more efficient equipment or make better tankers? Do you think even triple hulls would be safer? Smaller tankers means more tankers, more traffic means more accidents. Simple statistics. You don't gain anything."

Mayeaux swirled his drink and took a final sip. He might as well have been wrestling with an alligator. Emma Branson was personally responsible for bringing in over five million in contributions, and even at that, he had been lucky to get reelected this time. If every other state besides Louisiana hadn't had term limitations, Mayeaux would never have gained enough seniority to be elected Speaker this year. Pure unadulterated serendipity, a *fait accompli* before the new selection rules could grind their way through the system. With his track record, he would never rise higher—but with Branson's backing, he'd make a fine lobbyist for the oil industry. Damn fine, with his connections.

He sighed and placed his drink on the counter next to Branson's still-untouched glass. A shame to waste good Scotch. He looked her in the eye.

"Emma, as always you have a point. Sometimes I get so wrapped up in politicking that I forget my roots, not to mention my friends. Tell you what—when I get back to Washington, I'll bury this legislation in subcommittee. I'll throw my staff into patching together a compromise solution." He reached out and squeezed her hands.

Branson pulled her hands away, but she did not argue with him. As he reached the door, Branson's raspy voice said, "I'll be paying close attention to the *Congressional Record*, Jeffrey. Just remember those future plans of yours. Don't bite the hand that feeds you." She paused, then smiled. "Or *I'll* be the one to string you up by the balls."

Mayeaux forced a chuckle, keeping a grin plastered to his face. "I'm heading back to D.C. right now to work on it."

Outside the door, Weathersee steered him to the elevator. "The VP's plane is due in another hour. Did you want to join the welcoming party?"

Mayeaux's grin melted as soon as he was away from the penthouse door. "Hell, no! I've already upstaged the bastard. I don't want to be seen fawning over him. It's bad enough I promised Emma Branson I'd look for an alternative to the energy tax bill." He raced through the options—there had to be a way to not piss off the oil industry.

Weathersee raised an eyebrow, then looked at his watch as they waited for the elevator. "I didn't think you'd want to stay. I've booked you back on a direct flight that leaves in less than an hour—" He fell silent, glancing around as the elevator door opened; when no one came out, they stepped in. "Unless you have other plans? I did keep your suite at the hotel."

Mayeaux sighed and smiled. "Offer that brunette KSFO reporter an exclusive deep-background interview with me tonight. Order room service. Champagne. I'll leave tomorrow morning. And call my wife—tell her I've been held over."

"Should I start the staff researching gas tax alternatives?"

Mayeaux shook his head, waving dismissively. "And

have Huey Long roll over in his grave? There's no way to stop it, no matter what I promised Branson. I'll throw it back into negotiations and let it build up its own momentum—as long as I don't go on record for it, that should keep Branson happy. I'll call for a voice vote so she can't pin me on anything."

The elevator bumped to a stop. When the door opened, a crowd surged toward him. Speaker of the House Jeffrey Mayeaux put on his smile and started shaking hands, offering reassurance. He spotted two sweet young things straining to get a glimpse of him.

He hated the work itself, but God, he loved being a congressman.

SEVEN

FAIL-SAFE

But are we following our contingency plan?" Emma
Branson said, glaring at her deputies in what had to be
the most claustrophobic meeting room on the entire
Oilstar site. "Can we at least say that much? We have to
find some kind of positive spin for Oilstar."

"Uh, we rescued the crew of the tanker—how about
that?"

"What kind of positive spin is that?" Branson snorted.
"We rescue a captain who blames the whole mess on
some mysterious crewman who's disappeared? The public wants to see every member of the *Zoroaster* crew
shot."

Charlene Epstein, a deputy with severe gray-blond
hair, slapped a stack of thick books that no one had ever
bothered to read before. "We think we adhered to all the
legal requirements, but the plan is eight volumes long.
Six thousand pages of convoluted sentences and flow
charts that nobody ever thought about needing to
follow!"

Branson shook her head, disgusted instead of surprised. The arguments had continued all morning. Arriving from her brief meeting with Mayeaux after his grandstanding news conference, now she was ready for some shouting. She counted off names on her fingers. "The Petroleum Industry Response Organization signed off on it, the Departments of Transportation, Interior, Energy, the EPA, the Coast Guard Pacific Area Strike Team, the American Petroleum Institute. Didn't anybody *read* the damned plan?"

"Everybody's passing the buck, Ms. Branson," Henry Cochran said. "No one ever really believed a million-barrel spill would happen."

"Lucky us, to witness it in our lifetimes!" Charlene snapped. All of Branson's deputies began arguing at once.

She tolerated only a moment of the chaotic shouting, enough to let them blow off some steam; then she slammed her hand down like a schoolteacher. The deputies shut up.

"So," Branson said, her voice rattling, "we wrote all this documentation to cover ourselves, but nobody even knows what we committed to. We've got an army of demonstrators outside the gate. People are making death threats on me, and not one of you has a clue about what Oilstar is supposed to be doing."

"It's not that simple—" Cochran interrupted. Sweat covered his bald head and florid face, making his fashion-frame glasses slide down his nose.

"Cut the bullshit, please," Branson said quietly. "What about the lightering operations? How much did we pull off before *Zoroaster* went under?"

Walter Pelcik squinted at his figures, running pudgy fingers through his beard. "Seventy-five thousand barrels. That's a damned good amount, I might add." He grabbed another piece of paper. "The skimmers are recovering some of what's floating on the surface, but for all intents and purposes we've got an inexhaustible supply down there inside the hulk, and it's going to keep leaking for years."

Charlene Epstein shuddered. "We already have a spill that's four to five times greater than the *maximum* estimates of the *Valdez*—and it's not way up in No-wheresville, Alaska. It's in downtown San Francisco."

Cochran shook his head, then yanked off his glasses. "They are going to string us up. We might as well all change our names and move to Argentina."

"Enough of that, Mr. Cochran," Branson said. "Oil-star will accept responsibility for this spill, and we will make our absolute best effort to clean it up. Is that clear? Have we requested all available skimmers worldwide? Do we need more booms? What else can we do to mitigate this disaster?"

Walter Pelcik folded his hands over his paunch. "We've ordered everything. The other oil companies are pitching in, mostly for the PR value."

Charlene slid one of the heavy books off a stack. "What other options do we have? They won't let us do controlled burning. The Bay Area Air Quality Management people would rather smell stinking petroleum fumes for a decade than have a few days of black smoke."

Branson tried to recall everything she knew about their own preparations. "How about dispersants? We've got a whole stockpile—why don't we use them?"

"No chance!" said Pelcik. "The environmentalists are all singing the same song on that one, and you know how powerful those groups are when they actually *agree* on something!"

Cochran leaned over the conference table. "Disper-sants break the oil up and suspend it in the water. Right now the crude is floating on top. Dispersants would mix it with the water, make it look great from above—but the suspended oil would still be killing fish and damag-ing the food chain."

Branson sighed in exasperation. For the first time in her life, she felt like giving up. "You mean we've got nothing else? What do you suggest we do, roll over and die? I won't believe there are no alternatives."

"Well, there is Argentina," Cochran said, smiling weakly.

At the doorway, a tall young man cleared his throat. "Excuse me?" He wore a tie and expensive clothes. Beside him stood an older man in jeans and a flannel shirt. "I'm Mitchell Stone and this is Dr. Kramer. We have a meeting with Ms. Branson?" He looked at his watch and smiled before any of the startled deputies could answer. "Looks like our timing is pretty good, because we're going to offer you something that might solve this crisis."

For a strange instant, Branson recalled the story of Faust; she wondered if Stone would offer her a magical solution to the *Zoroaster* spill . . . for the mere price of her soul.

Cochran glanced at both of their badges, then turned to flip through an appointment book. "Oh. Bioremediation people."

Branson heaved a weary sigh. Dr. Kramer hung behind Stone, who seemed too full of himself. She decided which one to trust on the basis of her first impression. Kramer looked tired and listless, with a simmering fire behind his eyes. She recalled a memo that had mentioned Kramer's name, something about losing his family in an accident, an Oilstar fund to send flowers. She had even signed the form letter herself.

"What can we do for you, gentlemen? We're in the middle of an important meeting."

Stone flinched a smile. As he stepped into the room, the strong smell of his sweet cologne mingled with the haze of cigarette smoke thickening the air. "We need you to listen to us for a moment. What you decide after that is up to you."

The deputies frowned at the interruption. "We'll be brief," Dr. Kramer interjected, looking very uncomfortable.

Mitch strode toward an overhead projector in the corner of the room. He pulled a set of viewgraphs from under his arm and slapped one on the projector, punching the button that turned on the lamp. The title stood out against the blue-and-gold Oilstar logo: THE PROMETHEUS PROJECT.

Branson sighed. "Is a canned presentation really necessary? I get so much plastic flipped at me that I don't believe my people can think for themselves anymore. Just talk to me and get it over with."

Stone faltered, then flicked off the projector. "Of course." He drew a breath. "In the Bioremediation section, we've been searching for a way to use natural microbes to break down substances in the environment, toxic wastes and so forth. Dr. Alex Kramer, here, and myself head up a team studying ways to break down long-chain polymers in landfills. You know, plastic garbage bags, beverage containers, Styrofoam cups and packaging. Waste products of such polymers deteriorate very slowly. We're trying to find ways to get rid of it."

"Excuse me!" Walter Pelcik said, raising his voice. His bushy brown beard stuck out in all directions. "But we've got an oil spill to deal with here."

Stone raised his voice a notch higher and continued without acknowledging the interruption, speaking directly to Branson, as if she was the only one who counted. Smart guy. But he had better get to the point in the next few seconds.

"As the first step, we developed an organism we called Prometheus. This little microbe has an appetite for octane—the eight-carbon molecule in gasoline . . . and *crude oil.*

"At the time, we didn't see any use for it, but we applied for an FDA license just in case. Why would anyone want to decompose crude oil? Well, now it seems you might have a use for our little miracle." Stone looked at the others. Dr. Kramer hovered beside him, fidgeting but not interrupting Stone. The conference room became quiet as the information sank in.

"Let me get this straight," said Branson. An unexpected sensation twisted inside of her. Hope. "You've come up with some kind of germ that *eats* crude oil?"

"Not all of it," Dr. Kramer answered, stepping forward, moving in front of Stone, "only the octane component and some of the ring hydrocarbons."

Branson got right to the point. "So what does it leave behind? What kind of toxic mess are we going to have to deal with? Will we be in worse trouble than we are now, like with dispersants?"

"No." Dr. Kramer shook his head vigorously. "Octane is just carbon atoms and hydrogen. When the Prometheus organism metabolizes the octane, it leaves behind CO_2 and H_2O, carbon dioxide and water, with maybe a little hydrogen sulfide—like rotten eggs—from sulfur contaminants in the mix. Nothing toxic whatsoever. It'll work."

Stone picked up the thread. "From our studies, we know that twenty-five percent of the *Zoroaster* crude is lightweight hydrocarbons that will evaporate off in a few days all by themselves. The rest of it, though, will be broken down slowly by photooxidation and natural microorganisms in the water. That part will take years."

His eyes gleamed. "What we're offering is a way to get rid of all the *octane* in the spill. That, plus the evaporation effects, will decrease the amount of visible oil on the Bay by something like sixty-five percent in a few *days*—and it will leave no pollution behind."

Dr. Kramer cleared his throat. "We need to make clear, though, that Prometheus does not attack longer-chain hydrocarbons. That's been our problem in fighting Styrofoam and plastic waste. You'll still be left with the tarry residue they keep showing on the news."

Branson's heart pounded, and a flush rose in her face. "But from the public's point of view, over half the spill will disappear? That's a dramatic and obvious effect."

"You said you applied for an FDA license—why don't you have it? And what if this microbe spreads?" Cochran said. "How are we going to get rid of it when we're done?"

Dr. Kramer shook his head. He spoke confidently, as if daring them to disbelieve him. "That's not unusual. It takes *years* for the FDA to process those things. Anyway, we should be able to get a waiver in an emergency. The other problem will take care of itself. These microorganisms are not indigenous to the area. We got them out of the ocean, near volcanic vents deep beneath the Gulf of Mexico. We crossbred them with some of the other oil-eating strains from samples along the beaches in Prince William Sound in Alaska. They'll flourish for a while, feasting on the spilled crude oil, but they'll die out quickly. They can't handle this climate, and their food source will disappear as soon as the spill goes away. They can never become airborne."

"We've demonstrated that several times in laboratory tests," Stone added. "We can show you the reports. Dr. Kramer has all his lab books."

"Well, we have to do something," Branson said, tapping her nails on the table. She looked around the smoky room. "And this could look very, very good for Oilstar."

"It's not a cure-all," Dr. Kramer said.

"We're only interested in a short-term solution for now," she retorted. "I need something spectacular to confirm that Oilstar is doing all it can. Once the press is satisfied, they'll turn to some other problem." She tapped a pencil on the table. "How soon can you have it? When can we try it?"

Stone flipped through viewgraphs to double-check information he should have known perfectly well—unless he was just putting on an act to appear overly conscientious. "Prometheus has been successfully tested. We generated piles of reports out of it. We've already started making a supply, and the strain reproduces quickly. That's one of its advantages. Once we get the waiver from the FDA, we can start spraying the spill in a day or so."

"I'm not sure about this microbe stuff," Cochran said. "I can just imagine people complaining even louder about genetically engineered organisms than they are about the spill itself."

"Excuse me," Dr. Kramer said, as if he had anticipated the question. "Don't let anyone raise those objections. These microorganisms are crossbred strains of naturally occurring microbes. No genetic engineering."

Branson waved aside the words. That part didn't matter, and she had heard what she needed to know. "If the people stonewall our every effort to clean up the spill, we can take the moral high ground because we offered a solution *and they didn't want it.*"

She beamed at Stone and Dr. Kramer. "We'll call a press conference for tomorrow morning, a regular town meeting. We can let the public decide—and Oilstar wins either way."

EIGHT

CIRCLE FOR A LANDING

Emergency override! Eagle One, this is Albuquerque tower. I say again, emergency override!" The squawk of the walkie-talkie jerked Brigadier General Ed Bayclock out of a tedious Friday interview in his base office. Time to leap into action.

David Reinski, the young-and-trim mayor of Albuquerque, somehow didn't notice the emergency call and kept chatting. "General, this White Sands agreement could benefit Albuquerque as well as Kirtland. Could you point that out in your dinner speech?" Reinski addressed Bayclock as if they were equals.

"Quiet, please!" Bayclock said, holding up a hand as he strained to hear the radio voice.

"Guzzle Thirty-seven on approach," the walkie-talkie said. The voice sounded tight and high-strung. "Five souls on board with an ETA of five minutes. An emergency has been declared."

In an instant, Bayclock became a different person, shoving trivial business matters to the back of his mind:

the agreement he had just signed with the White Sands Missile Range and the upcoming awards dinner, at which Mayor Reinski would introduce him. No time for that baloney right now. God had given different people different skills, and not everyone was as good at coping with emergencies as he was.

He lurched forward in his overstuffed chair. The warm leather creaked as he snatched the clunky old radio from its recharging stand. "Tower, this is Eagle One. Give me details." From his window, Bayclock looked out over Albuquerque International's thirteen-thousand-foot runway out in the desert, but saw no sign of the approaching aircraft.

"KC-10A unable to retract their boom, sir," the tower voice answered. "Their controls were inadvertently scrambled by a high-power microwave test at Phillips Lab. Main pump has failed, and they are unable to dump fuel. They're coming in from the east and are cleared to the desert where the crew will eject—"

"Belay that!" Bayclock said. The KC-10 was a wide-body jet outfitted as a flying fuel tank, and it would explode like a bomb if it crashed. "Foam up the runway and have them do a slow pass."

Dammit, he'd hang those Phillips Lab scientists later.

"A *flyby?*" The tower voice sounded incredulous. "General, we are following the emergency checklist!"

"You heard me," he said. He didn't have time to explain to some snot-nosed airman. "Bring them low enough so I can spot the damage. I'll watch them at the break-to-final point, three miles from the runway. Then you let *me* decide what to do. That's what I'm paid for, son."

Waiting for a response, Bayclock glanced at his office walls, at the framed photos of fighter aircraft, at the memos and reports stacked on his desk. He longed for the days when he had been in the cockpit himself, "kicking the tires, lighting the fires," and blasting off into the stratosphere. Not chained to a desk.

Desk job. The words soured his mouth. It was the one

thing he had disdained throughout his thirty-year Air Force career. *Real men don't fly a desk.* Yet Bayclock had been offered a star, the chance to serve as a general officer with command over a large number of people, more responsibility. He was not power hungry, but he firmly believed a man should serve to the best of his ability. And few people had the *ability* to do the job Bayclock did every day. He could not shirk the tough assignment just because he would miss flying.

"What's taking so long, dammit!" he said to the silent radio. He could feel the cold, exhilarating sweat prickle beneath his clean uniform.

"Uh, we're getting flak from the crew, Eagle One. We told them your plan, and they insist—"

Bayclock strangled the Transmit button. "Tell them to do the flyby, or they're going to wish they crashed with their plane! They're not qualified to make this kind of decision." He took a deep cold breath. He didn't question orders from above, and he didn't like it when others did it to him.

"Rog," came the stiff reply from the tower.

Keeping the old-model walkie-talkie in one hand, Bayclock reached for his dark blue flight cap. He snapped at Reinski as he started for the door. "If you want to come along, Mr. Mayor, you'll have to *move* it."

Reinski jerked to his feet, but Bayclock left without waiting for an answer. The general clicked past officers and enlisted people, who moved out of his way. He paid them no attention—he had his body set on autopilot, intent on getting to the staff car.

He burst out of the air-conditioned headquarters building, feeling the sudden dry heat slam him like a baseball bat. He trotted to his staff car parked in the reserved space, then turned to see Reinski tripping down the steps after him. "You coming?"

"Yeah." Reinski wheezed, out of breath.

The general's driver was nowhere to be seen, but Bayclock could damn well drive himself. "Hurry up, Reinski, but don't get in my way."

"Shut up and drive, General. There's an emergency here," Reinski said as he scrambled into the car. Then, with an uncertain grin, he added, "Sir."

Bayclock snorted at the young mayor, then let out a guffaw. Flicking on his lights as he screeched from the parking lot, he barely missed an oncoming car. Out of the corner of his eye he saw Reinski frantically trying to fasten his seat belt.

Bayclock fumbled at the dashboard and brought up a microphone. "Tower, Eagle One. I'm heading to the break-for-final. What's the status of Guzzle Thirty-seven?"

The radio crackled. "We're foaming the runway now."

"Is that plane going to crash?" asked Reinski. His voice seemed to carry a mixture of dread and anticipation.

"Maybe." Bayclock shot a glance at the scrawny mayor fidgeting in the front seat. "But not if I can help it."

When they reached the runway, Bayclock jumped out of the car, leaving the door rocking on its hinges. He held a hand up to his eyes, searching for the incoming plane in the bright desert sky. The smell of hot asphalt rose up from the tarmac. The overtaxed staff car made ticking noises as it sat under the sun.

When Reinski joined him, Bayclock spoke without turning. "There's a flying fuel tank up there with a gas hose they can't pull in. The problem is the hose isn't made out of rubber—it's a twenty-foot-long hollow steel pole that juts down. The crew thinks it'll be like lighting a fuse if it scrapes on the runway. They can't dump their fuel, so they want to bail out."

"And you're not allowing them?"

"Hell no!" said Bayclock. "Not without seeing for myself. People in situations like this tend to panic and overreact. It's *my* call, and I'll make it. What is this, twenty questions?"

Reinski's eyes were wide as he stared into the sky. He was looking in the wrong place. "But if those men die because of—"

Bayclock glared. "I'm not going to let them do anything stupid, Mr. Mayor. Once they fly over our position, I'll tell them what to do." He didn't want to be distracted right now. He had to concentrate—be ready to change his mind in a flash. "My people trust-me."

Reinski kept scanning the sky for the crippled tanker aircraft. Bayclock could hear stuttered transmissions over the radio as the tower communicated with the tanker. Three miles behind them, trucks crisscrossed the runway, spraying fire-retardant foam. Ambulances, emergency trucks, fire engines, and Kirtland AFB police vehicles waited at the edge of the runway.

Bayclock patted his pockets, looking for a cigarette, a pack of gum, anything to keep him busy. He picked up the microphone. "Tower, Eagle One. Give me an update."

"No change, Eagle One."

"Patch me directly into the cockpit."

Tower sounded reluctant. "Ah . . . Rog."

Bayclock fingered the microphone. "Guzzle Thirty-seven, you there?"

The reply came back in irritation. "Rog, rog, Eagle One. You sure you know what the hell you're doing, sir?"

"Affirmative," said Bayclock. "Listen, I'm three miles east of the runway—you bring her down to five hundred feet and I'll give you a reading. That's plenty of time to either land or keep going to the desert if I wave you off. You copy?"

The voice over the radio sounded clipped and tired. "That's a rog, Eagle One."

Bayclock spotted the plane coming low over the Manzano Mountains, east of Albuquerque. He felt a sudden rush as he focused his attention even more on the problem. He knew he could do this. Bayclock had never been wrong in an emergency before. Never. "Got you, Guzzle—looking good." The enormous KC-10 moved so slowly it seemed like a zeppelin in the air.

The giant wide-body roared past, low to the ground. Bayclock would have to make a decision fast. His heart pounded. He knew the crew of the tanker would be white-knuckled up there, praying, counting on him. The import of the situation buoyed Bayclock. Beside the staff car, Reinski was saying something, but Bayclock shut the distraction out of his universe.

. He squinted, taking a split second to spot the refueling boom. He glanced quickly away, then back again to confirm what he had really seen. He spoke rapidly into the microphone. "Guzzle Thirty-seven, your boom is rigid and extended so low it will snap on landing. Bring her in—I say again, bring her on in."

The shrill reply came immediately from the lumbering tanker, now less than two miles from the runway. "If the boom doesn't snap, it'll skid and light us up!"

Good thing I'm making the decisions, Bayclock thought. "Bring her down!" he commanded.

The pilot gave no confirmation other than two rapid clicks over the radio. Bayclock watched as the tanker descended through the remaining five hundred feet. The last few seconds seemed to take forever. "Come on, come on!"

The jet flared with its nose up in the air, wheels reaching out to grab the runway like a bird of prey. The long boom struck the foam-covered tarmac. A brief flash of light gave Bayclock the sudden sick feeling that he had made the wrong decision, and the fuel tank would go up in a Nagasaki-class fireball.

But the boom broke off and tumbled into the barren scrub. The aircraft wobbled from side to side, then finally touched down. It skidded; then the tires kicked up foam that enveloped the plane. All Bayclock could see was a huge ball of dust, foam, dirt, and debris as ambulances and emergency vehicles raced down the runway.

Bayclock slammed his hand on the staff car, leaving a small dent. "Shit hot!" Jumping inside, he took off for the runway, barely giving Mayor Reinski time to climb in. He didn't care if the mayor had to walk.

As they pulled up to the KC-10 hissing and cooling on the tarmac, Bayclock saw long streaks of water and dirt along its fuselage. The crew staggered out of the plane down a long aluminum ladder, and an ambulance whisked them away. He felt vindicated as emergency personnel stepped up to the tanker and sprayed fire retardant over the fuselage.

General Bayclock's perfect track record had yet to be broken.

NINE

ANGEL

In the middle of San Francisco Bay, the volunteers gathered on forested Angel Island to meet the oncoming black tide. Standing on the rocky shore, they looked like desperate defenders pitted against an overwhelming force.

On the pier in Ayala Cove, Jackson Harris fought to keep despair from crushing him. Three days, and the job still seemed immense, impossible—but if he let himself start believing it to be a hopeless task, he wouldn't be able to go on. His stomach felt watery and knotted from his anger.

While corporate cleanup crews concentrated on the Golden Gate Bridge, Fisherman's Wharf, and other high-visibility areas, Harris was outraged to learn that they had written off one of his favorite spots in the Bay Area. He and his wife Daphne had worked the phones nonstop to bring a team together on the secluded island state park in the middle of the Bay. Together, they had plugged into their own activist network and mustered volunteers to protect Angel Island. The group received equipment from a handful of Oakland industries, which had donated dozens of dumpsters and tons of plastic garbage bags to hold the oil-stained rags and other debris from cleaning the shoreline.

Acrid chemical fumes mixed with the stench of decaying bodies of birds and fish. Staring across the foul water, Harris spoke into his radio to the boats out on the slick. "Keep to your search pattern. Pick up all the birds and sea otters you can get." They would try to save the live ones, but even carcasses were important for the lawsuits to be filed against Oilstar.

Harris lifted his thumb from the Talk button. He scratched his scraggly beard, still frowning. He hadn't showered in days, not that primitive and isolated Angel Island had such facilities; he hadn't slept much in the past three days either.

Off Point Stuart, the edge of the island closest to the spill, Harris's group had sunk fifty-five-gallon drums filled with cement to anchor a long string of buoys in an inverted V. Between the buoys, they strung heavy plastic fabric as a diversion boom to split the flow of thick crude and deflect it around the island. Yesterday when the spill struck, the V bifurcated the oil . . . but not enough. Now the black flow curled around to slop against the shore.

Harris left the pier and crunched down the crumbling, poorly maintained road. At the charcoal picnic grills, groups of volunteer kids cooked an endless supply of hot dogs and hamburgers for the famished workers. Harris stretched his aching arms, but decided he could stand some more heavy work. No time for rest. Never any time for rest. The spill would keep moving, keep destroying, and only he and his volunteers stood in its path.

At the water's edge, people in rubber wader boots stood in the oozing crude. They dunked five-gallon buckets to scoop thick oil from the surface, passing each bucket to the next person in line. Once again dredging deep inside himself for just a little more energy, Harris slipped into the brigade line, relieving one of the brothers who looked ready to drop. The man nodded his thanks, then staggered to the grassy picnic area and collapsed onto a weathered picnic table.

A loud radio boomed music from a San Francisco Top 40 station, but few of the volunteers seemed to hear the tunes. Harris loved music, but in the last few days it seemed like his capacity to love anything at all had been smothered by the spreading blanket of crude.

The fire-brigade line skimmed oil, one bucket at a time. It would take his people *ten million* buckets to remove all the oil spilled by *Zoroaster*. Harris refused to admit it was a hopeless task, because that would pop the fragile soap bubble of stamina that kept him going.

After dragging another heavy bucket partway up the beach, Harris handed it to the next person in line, who lugged it to the reservoir tanks. Harris looked down at his thigh-length rubber boots, yellow rain slicker, and canvas gloves, all smeared with sticky brown oil darker than his skin.

The walkie-talkie at his side crackled again. "Jackson, this is Linda. We have to come back in. Boat's overloaded."

He handed off another bucket and stepped out of the brigade line, pulling off his gloves and grabbing the walkie-talkie. "All right, man. We'll get another crew to take over."

A few minutes later, a fishing boat puttered toward the dock. Harris yelled for another group to help off-load the cargo of carcasses and surviving animals the rescue crew had scooped up. Among the other volunteers, his wife Daphne ran up to help.

Trim and wiry, with very dark skin, she looked beautiful even in frayed overalls with oil smeared on her face and sweat trickling down her neck. When Daphne had studied law at Berkeley under a scholarship, she probably never imagined herself in a place like this. But Daphne wanted to help needy people, help the environment, taking a job in a small firm in Oakland so she could work in the volunteer legal-aid clinics.

She gave Harris a weary smile, bent toward him for a

kiss, smudging him with oil, then laughed. On his lips, the oil tasted like vile medicine. The humor lasted only a moment before they both turned to help transfer the stricken animals to the pier.

They carried the live ones first—sea otters, terns, and gulls soaked in oil. Three people stood together, straining to haul the first sea lion from the boat. It panted, squirming in a slow-motion effort to escape. Its wide brown eyes were encircled by the red that indicated hemorrhaging.

Harris knew what the oil was doing to the internal organs of this struggling creature. Its kidneys would fail, unable to filter such massive amounts of poison from the bloodstream; its intestines would be immobilized, preventing the absorption of nutrients. He felt bile rise in his throat. He remembered hundreds of sea lions sprawled on Fisherman's Wharf, sunning themselves and bellowing their contentment.

Most animals, even the ones "rescued," would probably die from the spill anyway. Oil-soaked pinfeathers or fur no longer insulated the animals from the cold waters of the Bay. Many could not float, and would drown in the sludge-covered water.

Daphne and the others took the animals to hand-pumped shower stations, where they squirted soapy water and used brushes to scrub off the oil. Daphne worked quickly, waving her hands out of the way of a doomed seagull, alarmed by the movement but too exhausted to struggle, as the panicked but stunned bird tried to peck any object that came near it.

The team worked in silence, unable to manage the usual banter of volunteers engaged in a large job. Even if the animals survived to be released again, they would simply return to the Bay, where they would get contaminated once more. Seeing the animals' plight tore at Jackson's heart; he could not just leave the creatures to die a variety of slow, cruel deaths. The odds were against them, but that wouldn't stop him from trying.

The boom-box radio announced a spill update, and

gave a short human-interest story on the heroic volunteer efforts on Angel Island, which drew a scattered but lukewarm cheer. Then the reporter said, "Oilstar Public Relations Officer Henry Cochran claims their efforts to clean up the spill are being hindered by environmental restrictions that prevent them from mounting an all-out response."

A man's slow, reedy voice continued, speaking for the oil company in what sounded like a prepared statement. "We have well-researched and innovative solutions for coping with this problem, but the government says we need *weeks* of study before taking this action. That is ridiculous! Look out in the Bay—how can we just sit around, knowing that we have a possible cure? Tomorrow, Oilstar will hold a 'town meeting' to discuss a crucial plan to decrease the spill by forty percent within a four- to five-day period, leaving no toxic residue. We may be restrained—again—by bureaucracy and finger-pointing, but we *have* a solution. If the state and federal governments won't let us use it, don't blame Oilstar."

Jackson Harris stared across the water toward the northern part of the Bay. He could see where the Richmond–San Rafael Bridge terminated near the Oilstar refinery. How could they make such preposterous claims? Forty percent of the spill gone in a few days? No toxic residue? Did they have some sort of magic wand?

He did not trust the big oil company, but they wouldn't make such wild claims unless they had *something*. And after seeing the relatively minor success of his volunteers' efforts, he was just about willing to give Oilstar a chance.

TEN

NINE TO FIVE

Heather Dixon fixed her eyes on the set of plane tickets in her new boss's hands, trying to control her frustration. Albert "You can call me Al" Sysco tapped the tickets against his palm as he sat on the corner of her desk in an attempt to make himself look taller.

"Sorry, Heather," he said. "Boston changed their mind and wanted me to go at the last minute. They think people will be more receptive to dealing with managers instead of the worker bees."

Bullshit, she thought. *Surety Insurance knew he'd take this trip as soon as he got the promotion instead of me.*

Sysco tucked the tickets in the breast pocket of his polyester suit. Heather knew the itinerary: a small plane to Phoenix from the Surety Insurance western headquarters in Flagstaff, Arizona, then a jet into San Francisco International. Sysco would be traveling with four other Surety middle managers, all male, none of them more qualified than she was.

Ambulance-chasing lawyers were descending on the

Zoroaster spill like locusts, sniffing for lawsuits. The insurance industry was orchestrating a defense, gearing up to fight the claims. The main Surety headquarters in Boston had already announced plans to argue that damage caused by the oil spill should be classed as the result of an Act of God or a terrorist action, neither of which would be covered by most policies. Sysco would fly to San Francisco and stay in fine hotels, leaving the "worker bees" back home in Flagstaff.

"What am I supposed to do while you're gone?" Heather asked, knowing damned well what he was going to say.

"Take over my desk."

For months Sysco had dropped unpleasant innuendos about Heather Dixon's incompetence, about her lack of dedication to Surety and ability to be a team player. If it hadn't been for Sysco's self-serving maneuvers, she would have gotten the job of auto-claims section manager herself.

Heather decided not just to hope, but to actually *pray* that his plane crashed en route. Not a big fiery crash— just one so that Sysco would never be found, where he could survive for a while in the Arizona desert and spend a long, slow time dying of thirst. Maybe the other middle managers would have to eat him for sustenance . . . but then they'd probably die of food poisoning.

"Gee, I'll do my best, Mr. Sysco." She batted her eyes like the brain-dead bimbo he had implied that she was.

She had never learned how to wear a dress with feline grace; she was tall and well built, yet not graceful enough to be a model. Her mother called her "clunky." Her reddish brown hair hung perfectly straight. In her thirty years, Heather had tried dozens of different styles, long and short, even once with a punkish scarlet streak. No one seemed to notice.

Albert Sysco didn't catch the sarcasm in her answer. "I'll be back in three days. Try not to screw up too much." He turned, a medium-sized man on the outside, remarkably small on the inside.

Heather gave him the finger under her desk. She heard a quiet snicker and whirled to see Stacie, the other claims-resolution assistant, watching from her desk. As Sysco slipped into his cubicle, Stacie flipped him off too.

Heather smiled. She had worked at Surety for seven years, but she couldn't say she enjoyed her job.

The phone rang, but Stacie ignored it. "At least he'll be out of our face for a few days," she said.

Heather nodded. "I guess that's a better vacation than going with him."

ELEVEN

IMAGINE

Everybody screwed up. Everybody insisted it would never happen again. No one learned the lesson.

Alex Kramer felt numb, standing in the eye of a storm of shouting and accusations at Oilstar's "town meeting." He wanted to shout back, to wring a few necks at the insanity of the entire situation: full of sound and fury, signifying nothing. More than anything, he wanted to be at home, alone, searching for peace.

He had known Oilstar's public meeting would be a circus, but he hadn't thought he himself would be thrust at the center of it. The bedlam in the room drowned his words. Standing at the podium, he closed his eyes and took a breath, trying to ignore the pain from the cancer chewing at his body.

Mitch Stone, at first disappointed at not being Branson's chosen spokesman, now sat in the front row—in a new suit and tie, of course—grinning support for Alex.

The audience murmured like a torch-bearing mob ready to storm the scientist's castle. Alex gripped the sturdy podium with stiff hands, using it as an anchor. *Just get it over with,* he thought.

Out in the room, the spectators fidgeted on folding metal chairs that creaked as people sat down. Tripods with cameras stood in the corners. In the back of the room a silver coffee urn crouched above flickering blue Sterno flames, flanked by stacks of Styrofoam cups. Alex could smell the fear, feel palpable anger rising in waves from the audience. It strengthened his resolve.

It'll never happen again. I promise.

Alex saw two factions in the audience: "Luddites" and "Techno-Nazis." The Luddites feared change, arguing that industry had caused the disaster in the first place. They would tear up experimental pest-resistant crops because they had been "tampered with," only to complain later about the use of pesticides; or they would "liberate" animals from medical labs, and later complain about the lack of progress in AIDS and cancer research.

On the other side, the Techno-Nazis believed that science could solve every problem, that researchers could scribble on a blackboard and whip up a miracle cure, given a few sleepless nights and a lovely lab assistant. They would wave aside checks and balances and safety regulations and argue that "natural" solutions were too slow, too late, and too ineffective.

Alex flinched but stood like a statue against the public outcry. Once he dropped the first pebble to start the cleansing avalanche, Alex could collapse and let the events bury him. But not until he succeeded in setting it all in motion.

The earsplitting squeal of an air horn shocked everyone into silence. Alex jerked around.

Sitting in a chair toward the edge of the stage, Oilstar CEO Emma Branson held up the air horn. Her wrinkled, powdered skin was pale with controlled anger. She raised her voice beyond any need for a microphone. "Stop this nonsense!"

Near the stage, two security guards shifted, readying

themselves. Their presence made Alex uneasy. Someone had taken potshots at Branson's house the night before, blasting out her downstairs windows. The Oilstar refinery had received two separate bomb threats in less than twelve hours, and demonstrators blocked the refinery gates. Before entering the packed meeting room, everyone in the audience had stepped through a metal detector.

The night before, Mitch had helped Alex put his presentation together. Branson had insisted that Alex be the one to speak at the press conference, implying that Mitch looked too young, that an older researcher like Alex had more credibility. "These people have seen too many slick fast-talkers," Branson had said. "So we're going to give them Pa—Lorne Greene—instead."

Now Branson stepped to the edge of the stage, smoothing her dress and looking down at the quieted audience like a sour high-school teacher announcing detention for the entire class. "If you let Dr. Kramer finish speaking, you'll hear how Oilstar wants to solve this problem! Why argue before you have any information?"

Alex tried to remember what he meant to say next. Glancing down at his notes, he pushed the Advance button and turned to look at the slide on the screen.

The picture showed an Alaskan shore, gray sky, steel-colored water. Rocks studded the beach, and thick oil covered everything. This had been the start of it all. "Here you see part of the shoreline in Prince William Sound after the *Exxon Valdez* spill. Looks familiar to all of us."

He realized he was mumbling his words, and cleared his throat before clicking to the next slide. A rectangle of the shore, thirty meters by twelve meters, had been cordoned off. Men and women in yellow rain slickers stood outside the ropes.

"As part of the cleanup, Exxon spent ten million dollars to test bioremediation work similar to what Oilstar is proposing. They sprayed a fertilizer called

Inipol to encourage *natural* bacteria in the environment to break down the slowly volatilizing alkanes and simple ring hydrocarbons in the spilled crude."

He clicked to the next slide, showing the same test plot. This time the rocks inside the ropes showed little of the black stain. He let some of the pent-up anger and defensiveness leak into his voice. "Within ten days, the concentration of natural bacteria in shore soil samples had increased a hundredfold, and you can already see the benefits. It's obvious that this sort of treatment has a substantial effect."

Alex took a sip of tepid water, then continued through slides showing the progress of the oil-eating bacteria. "Neither Exxon nor the EPA investigated which bacteria were doing the most work, but Oilstar has had an aggressive bioremediation program under way for years. We've researched Alaskan bacteria and samples from deep under the ocean near natural oil seeps. We think we have something that can radically reduce the effects of this spill."

"But what if it gets loose!" said Jake Torgens, a well-known "eco-terrorist" who had organized rallies and vocal protests. The police already had him under investigation about the bomb threats to the refinery.

Branson stood to answer. "The only way to let Prometheus work is to let it loose—but only on the oil spill. We can't put an airtight dome over San Francisco Bay, can we? The Food and Drug Administration has followed the development of this microbe from Day One, and they've expedited their licensing process to grant us a waiver. Besides, the microbe cannot become airborne, isn't that correct, Dr. Kramer?"

"Our tests show it's perfectly safe—" Alex began.

Someone said, "That's what Oilstar said about supertankers!"

At a long table to the left of the podium, one of the government representatives pulled a microphone toward himself. In front of each representative lay a stack of reports that Alex and Mitch had coauthored, internal memos, and copies of peer-reviewed journal articles. Alex doubted that many of the reps understood even the titles, like "Expression of Transposed Plasmid DNA Segments in Natural Microorganisms to Specify Hydrocarbon Degradation."

"I appreciate Oilstar's innovation," the government rep said, "and I think we should strongly encourage thorough testing and perform a detailed study."

A short-haired woman in the front row of the Techno-Nazis leaped to her feet. "They've already done the tests! Read the reports—what more do you want? The damned FDA even says it's safe! The damage is getting worse and worse every second while you all just sit around arguing!"

Branson smiled with exaggerated patience. Her look seemed to say, *See who the reasonable people are?* "You don't throw a cup of water at a burning house to test whether it'll stop a fire."

Alex thumped the microphone to draw attention back to himself. "I should point out that a test application on a cordoned section of the spill, as was done with the fertilizer in Prince William Sound, won't work here. Prometheus is not intended to stay behind barrier tape, but it is a self-limiting organism. Our laboratory tests were successful. The woman from the audience is absolutely correct—every second we delay increases the ecological cost of the spill. We have to make our best attempt and see if it works."

"And what if it doesn't?" a woman from EPA asked.

Alex shrugged. "Then we try something else." He turned at the sound of a scuffle outside the auditorium entrance.

A bearded black man wearing an oil-smeared raincoat pushed his way past two security guards, slapping their hands away. "I passed through your metal detector and I'm not carrying any weapons!" he shouted, as if intending to make the audience hear every word. "Let me in!"

On stage, Branson stiffened. The guards tightened near her.

Alex thought he recognized the intruder from one of the news clips he had been watching obsessively since the day after the spill. *Harris.* Jackson Harris, the man leading the volunteers on Angel Island. In one hand Harris carried a large plastic garbage bag; stains of crude oil covered his boots and pants. His nostrils flared as he marched to the stage. One of Branson's guards unsnapped his holster.

Harris stepped to the bureaucrats' table, casting his gaze across city council members, designees from the Coast Guard, the Petroleum Industry Response Organization, the Fish and Wildlife Service, the Food and Drug Administration, and the EPA. Then he reached inside his garbage sack.

The representatives shrank back, as if Harris was going to pull out an Uzi. Instead, he lifted a dripping black mass that might once have had feathers. As he held it in his hand, the shape sprawled out, letting long wings loll down. Thick oil spattered the table, staining the stacked reports.

Harris let the bird drop on the wooden table. A pelican. Its long, rapier beak gaped, as the bird slowly drew its dangling wing back toward its body. It was still alive, but not for long.

"What is this!" An outraged councilman from Sausalito slid his chair back.

"This is what's really going down out there, man. This bird is one of thousands," Harris said. "If you'd get off your fat political asses and get your hands dirty, you might understand why we're so worked up!" He raised his voice to a shout directed at all of them. "Stop fucking around and *do* something!"

He turned toward Alex hiding behind the podium. "You're not talking any germ warfare or genetic-engineering shit, are you, Mr. Big Oil Company?"

Alex barely shook his head. "No," he whispered. "These are natural bacteria." Though not exactly naturally *occurring* bacteria, he left unfinished.

Harris turned to the audience. "Oilstar got us into this

mess, and we can sue their asses later—but right now, if they got a solution, how can you *not* try it?" He crossed his arms over his slicker. "I'll do it myself, right now, if Oilstar gives me some of their magic oil-eating shit. You red-tape lovers can arrest me, but at least something'll get done!"

Branson returned to the podium. Alex stepped aside to yield the microphone. The Oilstar CEO seemed determined to show some progress, as if that would be enough to quench the outrage directed against her.

"Thank you, sir, but it's our responsibility," Branson said. "I appreciate the urgency of your concern—we have been forgetting the real effects of this disaster." She took a deep breath. "Oilstar will take the risk . . . and accept the legal consequences. On my authority, Oilstar *will* deploy the Prometheus option, using our helicopters, our pilots, our equipment. And we will do it at the earliest possible moment."

Branson pointed at the dying pelican on the table and frowned at the representatives. "If we encounter any interference from the government in trying to clean up this mess, I personally guarantee you will find the biggest lawsuit in California history right in your lap." Accompanied by her guards, Emma Branson walked with self-assured dignity off the stage and out the rear exit.

Before attention could return to him, Alex climbed down from the stage. Mitch clapped him on the back. "We got it!"

Alex felt the world growing fuzzy. Branson had set the wheels in motion; he had fooled her as thoroughly as he had everyone else. He closed his eyes to shut out the hubbub in the room—but he was left with only the emptiness inside him.

It'll never happen again. That was certain.

TWELVE

DESPERADO

Oilman Todd Severyn crushed a blob of dried seagull dropping under his work boot, then paced up and down the Oilstar pier that extended into the deep channel in the North Bay. Tankers such as the *Zoroaster* would hook up to transfer pipes and off-load cargo into storage tanks that dotted the hills around the refinery.

The early morning was calm, perfect flying weather. The fog seemed to dissolve in front of Todd's eyes, but he could smell the sour stench of oil on the water long before he could see it.

The Oilstar corporate helicopter, specially outfitted for spraying a fertilizer solution swarming with the Prometheus microbe, waited on the weathered dock. The copter pilot sat in her seat, legs dangling out of the cockpit. She looked bored behind mirrored sunglasses; she was getting paid by the hour, even on the ground.

Todd had orders to spray the oil-eating microbe this morning—but if the darned state inspector didn't arrive before the court injunction did, they'd all be hung out to dry. *Probably attending a séance or checking the stars to see if the karma is right,* Todd thought. *Prissy California sprout-eaters!*

The "suits" were locked in a push-and-shove legal battle over the Prometheus bug. Oilstar insisted on using an observer from the state office of Environmental Policy and Inspection; the EPI in turn had retained a microbiology expert from Stanford University. Getting EPI approval for the fiasco seemed like covering their butt with a postage stamp, but Todd wasn't paid to make Oilstar's decisions—just to implement them.

At the land end of the long pier, Dr. Alex Kramer sat inside a metal control shack, which now served as a field command post for the spraying operation. The scientist didn't talk much; with his glasses, neat gray beard, and thinning gray hair, Alex reminded Todd of his father back at the ranch.

Todd looked at his wristwatch again and ambled back to the helicopter. His down vest and new jeans felt hot and stiff and uncomfortable. "Jeez, I wish we could get this show on the road!"

Oilstar had leaked false locations for the staging area of the spraying operations, which would temporarily fool the reporters, environmental nuts, and regulatory agencies—but they would soon figure it out. Todd wanted to be long gone before then. Never ask permission, as his dad always said; easier to apologize later.

Sometimes he wished he had never left Wyoming, where he could see snow-capped mountains in the distance, blue sky overhead; where he could drive a pickup down endless dirt roads and not see another person for days. He could have made a decent living running his parents' ranch, but he had chosen to go into petroleum engineering instead.

His work for Oilstar took him places no sane person wanted to go: the wasteland of Kuwait, its featureless sand broken only by smoking fires and war wreckage; the cold North Sea, with biting winds and battleship-gray clouds, the ocean whipped into a rabid froth; or the

jungles of Indonesia, with bugs the size of rats and
humidity thicker than the oil pumped out of the ground.

For some reason the skewed oddness of California
bothered him more than any of those places. At first
Todd thought his leg was being pulled when somebody
told him to wait until the "phase of the Moon" was right
for spraying Kramer's microbes. Todd talked around in
circles until he finally discovered that the official simply
meant that the *tide* needed to be in. What a bunch of
wackos.

It made no sense that Branson would thumb her nose
at the law by going ahead with the Prometheus spraying
. . . and then force Todd to wait for a single inspector
and some Stanford observer. Why couldn't they just
spray Kramer's little buggies and be done with it? Why
make things worse by further delay? People had no
common sense in the granola land of "fruits, nuts, and
flakes."

At least Todd saw the light at the end of the tunnel,
knowing his Oilstar contract would end soon. That was
the nice thing about being a consultant. You came in, did
the job, raked in the bucks, and got the heck out of
Dodge. There might be a lot of crap to put up with in the
meantime, but he could always go back to Wyoming to
clear his head.

In the crisp morning air, the crunching sound of
wheels on gravel made him turn to see an old mid-sized
sedan toiling up the narrow patchwork road along the
water's edge. He noted with relief the poop-brown color
of all State cars, then spotted a round, intricate seal on
the side door. Environmental Policy and Inspection.
Shock absorbers creaked as the sedan jounced in pot-
holes, pulled up to the open gate in the chain-link fence,
then edged slowly over the bump onto the Oilstar pier.
The driver seemed overly cautious. Todd strode out to
meet the car.

The passenger door popped open, and a petite young
woman stepped out. With long jet-black hair and soft,

strikingly attractive Asian features, the inspector was not at all what Todd had expected. He had been prepared for a dumpy business-suited bureaucrat; instead, the woman wore white tennis shoes, jeans, and a comfortable sweatshirt. At least she hadn't arrived in a dress-for-success dark skirt and blouse.

He had the state inspector pegged before she even noticed him: recent liberal-arts graduate from some eastern college—Mary Washington, Amherst, Bryn Mawr. . . . She probably wanted to make her mark by uncovering some toxic waste scandal; then she'd move to Washington, D.C. Being Asian, and a woman, this one would keep the Equal Opportunity clowns in ecstasy for years.

She probably hated country and western music, too.

But Todd forced a neutral expression onto his face, ready to do the necessary duty dance, and determined to get the helicopter off the ground. He tipped his cowboy hat. "Excuse me, ma'am. I'm Todd Severyn, test director for Dr. Kramer. We've got everything prepped here, and we've been waiting for you. As soon as the state inspects the equipment, we can get going." He tried to sound gruff, no-nonsense.

Her back to him, the young woman pulled a briefcase out of the car. She straightened and took one long appraising look at his cotton shirt, down vest, cowboy boots, and hat. She seemed to form an assessment of Todd as quickly as he had made up his mind about her. "You've got the wrong person, Tex."

Tex? Todd frowned. "Excuse me?"

"You're looking for Mr. Plerry."

The driver emerged, straightened his suit, and stepped forward. "Ah, Mr. Severyn?" he said with a faint lisp, extending his hand. The man was paper-thin, mustached, and had immaculately slicked-back hair. "Glad to meet you. I'm Francis Plerry, director for environmental policy. Emma Branson asked me to come here personally—she's an old acquaintance of mine." Plerry cleared his throat and turned to the helicopter for the first time. Todd wanted to wring his neck—this wasn't a tea party.

"Sorry we're late, but I had to swing by Stanford to pick up Dr. Shikozu. She has graciously volunteered to accompany you when the microbes are released. Iris, have you introduced yourself?"

Shikozu cut off more conversation with a quick, impatient gesture. "We don't have time, Mr. Plerry. Judge Steinberg already signed a restraining order, and we need to get up in the air before somebody can get here to deliver it. Let's go, Tex."

Todd narrowed his eyes at the sharp-tongued woman. It wasn't *his* fault they were still sitting on the ground. "Well, we've been waiting for *you*, ma'am." He drew out the "ma'am," knowing it would annoy her.

"Pleased to meet you, too, Tex," she said, taking him aback. The glint in her eye made him wonder if she was intentionally jerking his chain . . . and enjoying it.

Plerry smiled thinly and continued. "Dr. Shikozu is an assistant professor at Stanford, specializing in microbiology and polymer chemistry. Her expertise will be invaluable in reassuring the public that this is a safe and well-considered action." Shikozu and Todd both looked at him, wondering who Plerry thought he was kidding.

"But getting down to business—?" Shikozu said, crossing her arms over her sweatshirt. Plerry looked flustered at being rushed.

Todd had a difficult time hiding his reflexive grin. "My feelings exactly," he said. "The microbes are in a canister under the cockpit. We'll start spraying once you give the word. We estimate it'll take a few hours to cover the entire spill." He directed them to the helicopter. The pilot sat up and climbed back into her cockpit.

Shikozu looked Todd in the eye as they stood by the helicopter. "I've tested a frozen sample of Alex Kramer's original microbes as a control back at Stanford. Not having second thoughts, are you?"

Todd felt suddenly warm. "No second thoughts, ma'am. I just work here, and it's my job to get the spraying done."

"All right." Shikozu bent under the helicopter. "Let's check out the dispersion equipment. Then we can start our work." They squatted under the helicopter's belly as Shikozu studied the apparatus. Todd had no idea what she was looking for.

He glanced up quickly when he heard a pandemonium of cars approaching. A convoy of vehicles honked their horns, winding along the narrow shoreline road. A gravel truck from the nearby quarry rumbled to a halt, momentarily blocking the stream of cars.

"Start the rotors!" Todd yelled to the copter pilot. She scrambled with the controls, but he saw nothing happening. Todd threw a glance behind him. The gravel truck ground its gears, but the cars wouldn't stay stopped for long. "What's the problem?"

The pilot kept her head down, running through a checklist. "Give me two minutes and I'll have you in the air."

"Can't you get us up any quicker?"

She reached up and to her left, flicking a switch. "I'll burn out the units if I go faster." A low whine came from the engines.

Todd turned back to Iris. "You'll have to make a decision mighty quick, ma'am."

"I think all the dispersal systems look adequate." Shikozu straightened. Todd grudgingly gave her credit for sensing the emergency. "Don't you agree, Mr. Plerry?" Her almond eyes widened, and she looked back to the road as the cars drove across the loose gravel outside the chain-link gate. Car doors slammed.

"Uh, yes," Plerry said, stepping back from the helicopter. "It looks fine." He nodded again as if to reassure himself. The helicopter blades began to rotate slowly.

The vehicles in the convoy were old and battered, Volkswagen beetles, Chevy Novas, Ford vans, many covered with bumper stickers: EARTH FIRST! and SPLIT WOOD, NOT ATOMS!

Iris pulled herself into the helicopter from the passenger side, scrambling to the backseat. The rotors made a whirring sound like the world's loudest fan. She stuck her head out of the side window. "Hey, Tex! They're not here to sell you Avon products! Get your butt inside— you can gawk all you want from the air."

Todd's cheeks burned that someone else was telling *him* to hurry! He clambered in.

On the pier, Alex Kramer stepped out of the corrugated metal control shack, looking with blank, astonished eyes at the approaching group of people. He seemed startled at the interruption, then raised his hands as if to surrender.

"Go!" Todd shouted at the helicopter pilot. His pulse raced, as if this were as big a threat as the time he had leaped into a chopper to escape the sinking *Zoroaster*.

The pilot popped her gum, eyes invisible behind her mirrored sunglasses. "Okay, you're paying for it if I burn anything out. Buckle up."

One man ran ahead of the others on the pier, weaving his way around the debris and equipment piled there. In one hand he gripped a folded piece of paper like a weapon. It was that wacko Jake Torgens, known for pounding spikes into trees to stop lumberjacks. Torgens's words vanished in the increasing roar of the helicopter's rotor. Todd leaned over the side and mouthed, *I can't hear you!* and pointed first at his ears, then at the helicopter blades.

The pilot pulled back on the control stick, and the copter wobbled as it lifted off the pier. It hung for a moment like a bumblebee before darting higher.

Torgens, clutching the folded paper, put on a burst of speed; for a moment Todd thought he was going to make a leap for the landing strut, like a scene from a James Bond movie. But he pulled up short, shaking a fist at them.

The copter soared away from the Oilstar pier, turning south to fly under the span of the Richmond–San Rafael Bridge.

Todd turned to Iris. "I just don't get these guys. They scream at Oilstar to clean up the spill, then they scream when we try to do it." He shook his head. "If we listened to people like that, we'd still be in caves arguing about the dangers of fire."

Iris looked at him with one uplifted eyebrow. He had never seen eyes as dark as hers. "Interesting you should use that analogy when we're about to disperse a microbe called *Prometheus*."

"Right." Todd tried not to show that he didn't know what she meant. "Well, I wish those people would *disperse* too."

The helicopter headed toward the heart of the spill, where they would begin spraying.

THIRTEEN

TRAFFIC

As Spencer Lockwood's plane descended toward San Francisco International, he watched the tiny, glimmering traffic crawl along the freeways below. Sunlight skated across iridescent rainbows on the oil slick sprawled across the Bay.

He didn't want to be here. He felt like a politician with all the smiling, handshaking, and logrolling he would be required to do with his colleagues at Sandia National Lab in Livermore. "Networking," Nedermyer called it, but it didn't have much to do with actual working. Spencer wished he were back in New Mexico, refining the solar-satellite experiment—they had so much analysis and so many refinements left to do! He was wasting his time.

He mentally slapped his hand for maintaining such a bad attitude. *Chin up! It'll all pay off in the end. Right . . .*

The other passengers craned their necks to see through the scratched double glass of the jet's windows. Spencer grimaced at how far the oil had spread across the green-blue water. With a satisfied smile, he wished he could go up and down the aisle, whispering the words "Think solar!" into everyone's ears.

He rubbed his eyes and wished the flight attendants would bring another cup of coffee. Spencer hated flying in early, but otherwise he had to give up an extra day for traveling. And whenever Spencer was gone, Rita Fellenstein tinkered with the equipment at the antenna farm. Even though her modifications worked like a charm—most of the time—Spencer didn't like to discover them after the fact.

He heard a whirring thunk beneath the fuselage as the landing gear locked into place. Flight attendants strolled by, snatching napkins and plastic cups. Spencer tucked his briefcase under the seat, holding it with his ankles. Inside were viewgraphs detailing the resounding success of his smallsats over the antenna farm. He couldn't wait to show them off, win a few more supporters, and get back to White Sands.

Sandia, one of the nation's Big Three national laboratories, had a huge primary facility in Albuquerque on Kirtland Air Force Base; but much of Sandia's alternative-energy work took place in their smaller facility in Livermore, California, about an hour's drive east from San Francisco. With discretionary funds, Sandia had paid for part of Spencer's smallsat test bed, as well as the miles-long electromagnetic launcher that ran up Oscura Peak in White Sands.

Spencer's request to speak before the energy gurus at Sandia Livermore seemed an inspired idea. After working as a grad student at Caltech under a Nobel laureate, then successfully filing several moneymaking patents of his own, Spencer considered himself a whiz kid, flaunting his success in the face of stodgy committees. But after Lance Nedermyer's unreasonable skepticism, Spencer decided to become more visible among his colleagues. Working on his own, on a shoestring budget with a bunch of Young Turks, he needed *validation* more than anything else.

Spencer sat back in his seat and went over the canned talk in his head. The wreck of the *Zoroaster* had provided the world's biggest visual aid against dependence on oil.

Car horns blared, tires screeched—

Spencer jammed on the brakes, nearly standing up in the rental Mazda. A sudden flash of cold sweat burst over his body. The woman in a blue Mercedes behind Spencer gave him a one-finger salute after she too squealed to a halt.

He took a moment to compose himself, then looked up and down the line of stopped cars. Traffic wasn't moving on the San Mateo Bridge. Cars, camper trucks, flatbeds, vans, and motorcycles had come to a halt in both directions.

Spencer had driven from the airport over the second longest of the five bridges spanning the Bay. While the western end of the San Mateo Bridge rose high to allow large ships passage, the rest of the span lay only a few feet above the shallow water, like a road floating on the Bay.

Spencer rolled down his window, but the breeze smelled like a mixture of rotten eggs and burning tires, foul odors from the volatile components of crude oil. Crinkling his nose, he quickly rolled the window back up. He turned up the radio and tapped his fingers on the steering wheel. He couldn't find any music. News announcers kept talking about the "*Zoroaster* Disaster," using the rhyming phrase like a slogan; no doubt it would show up on the next cover of *Newsweek*.

Spencer hated traffic, idiot drivers, honking horns, exhaust fumes. At times like this, he appreciated the long, straight highways in New Mexico, where you could rip open the engine and fly by at a hundred miles an hour, never seeing another soul.

He got out and climbed on top of his white Mazda Protege to see if he could tell where the traffic was held up, but he saw only stopped vehicles. He looked at his watch, wondering if he would ever make his noon meeting at Sandia National Lab. Dammit, he had cut his schedule close, but he should have had enough time—if only he had remembered to allow for traffic snarls.

Other people stepped out of their cars, giving up on waiting. Children ran to the edge of the guardrail, looking down at the oily water; parents shouted for them to come back. Spencer stared with a mixture of awe and disgust at the thick stain like gangrene on the Bay. By contrast, White Sands and the array of gleaming microwave antennas seemed so pristine, so silent, so clean. . . .

Thousands of people had driven to get a glimpse of the largest oil spill in history. Some shimmied down to the water and bottled a souvenir, like Mount St. Helens ash. He drew in a deep breath of air, then choked on the stink.

A low sound of chopping filled the air. Probably a police helicopter checking out the traffic jam. He imagined a voice blaring from a loudspeaker, "All right down there! Everybody into their cars and start moving at the count of three!"

As the whirring grew louder, a low-flying copter bore down on them from the north. Painted bright green, the machine obviously belonged to no police service. The helicopter flew quite low, spraying something onto the water surface. Spencer frowned. Some kind of dispersant?

He looked up as the helicopter doubled back, making an overlapping pattern on the water. Spencer shaded his eyes as it swooped low over the bridge. He ducked into the car as a fine mist drifted down onto the stopped traffic. Although he couldn't smell anything over the petroleum fumes, he hoped the spray contained nothing toxic. As the craft passed overhead, he could see an enormous drum slung under the fuselage.

Several of the spectators standing on the bridge were sprayed; they jumped for cover, but the helicopter continued southward. Spencer used the windshield wipers to smear the droplets on his windshield, spreading it like translucent fingerpaint across the glass. Before long, the moisture evaporated, leaving only a faint residue, a thin gummy film. He waited for the cars to start moving again.

Finally, long after the helicopter had disappeared from sight, the tops of trucks far ahead of him crept forward. With a sigh of relief, Spencer started the engine, glanced at his watch one more time, then began the crawl toward Sandia lab.

FOURTEEN

ON THE BEACH

Two hundred feet above the water, Todd Severyn couldn't decide which was worse: the jolting, earsplitting throb of the helicopter . . . or the pilot's radio blasting out "We Built This City." At least the ride was a bit more comfortable than the crazy takeoff from the deck of the sinking *Zoroaster* a few days earlier.

He had long since stopped trying to carry on a conversation with Iris Shikozu, who sat behind him in the cramped passenger compartment. Between the pilot's radio and the streams of cold air blasting through the open window next to him, he couldn't hear much anyway. He thought wistfully about riding across the Wyoming grasslands, and concentrated on waiting out the test. Sitting here, he felt as useful as a middle manager.

The pilot nudged her mirrored sunglasses against the bridge of her nose, then prepared for another run. Momentum pulled Todd against the cold, hard metal cabin wall as she wheeled the helicopter around like an old-time barnstormer. She gripped the spray lever that released a fine mist of the nutrient solution swarming with Prometheus microbes. Their first pass had cut straight down the middle of the slick; overlapping flights followed in a classic mosaic coverage pattern.

Todd turned to stare out the window. He could make out the discolored mud flats of the South Bay. Black film from the oil slick outlined sandbars in the shallow water.

He watched Iris as she looked past him to the water below. It was obvious she didn't share the same enthusiasm for Kramer's little buggies, but she didn't voice any direct skepticism when he asked her directly. Maybe she was one of those folks who always looked on the bad side. A glass was half empty instead of half full. But Iris had to believe *some* good would come of the spraying, or she wouldn't be here in the first place.

She leaned forward to yell in his ear, startling him. "You're certain of the initial canister temperature?"

What does that have to do with anything? "Absolutely. I made sure we followed Doc Kramer's checklist to the letter. The buggies were kept near freezing. Now they're awake, and it's time for breakfast."

Iris said, "*If* this works."

Todd frowned at her attitude. "It will." He'd done his part of the job, and so had everyone else. As far as he was concerned, it was all over but the waiting.

Todd sat back in his vibrating Naugahyde seat, glancing at Iris. The hint of a smile tugged at her lips. It flustered him not to know whether she was intentionally pushing his buttons. He turned away to cover his confusion.

On the next pass, they came upon the oil suddenly as they sped across the water, not more than ten feet above the surface. The helicopter bounced in turbulence. Strangely enough, Todd felt more at ease flying low—it reminded him of roundup time, when he had ridden in his dad's chopper to herd some of the cattle from the open range in Wyoming.

The pilot clenched her grip on the spray control lever. Behind them they left a trail of fine mist drifting down to the water. The helicopter soared low over the San Mateo Bridge, where thousands of cars jammed the narrow strip of concrete. Todd looked down at the people staring up at them. The spectators probably didn't have any idea what was going on.

The radio crackled. The pilot grabbed the handset without easing up on the controls. She acknowledged the speaker. "Yo! For you, Mr. Severyn," she said. "Mr. Plerry, back at the pier."

Todd glanced at Iris, who only shrugged. Any contact from the pier could only mean trouble, and Todd was in no mood to stop now. Not in the middle of a job. He sighed and reached forward to take the handset. "Severyn here. What is it, Mr. Plerry?"

After a short squawk, Plerry's feathery voice burst from the radio. "Mr. Severyn, things are getting a bit out of hand here. This group does have a legitimate court order, and I'm afraid they are insisting that you cease immediately and return to the pier."

Todd rolled his eyes. No frigging way! He had a job to do and he was going to get it done, for the good of the whole country. "What's that? I can't hear you." He had read about similar things during the *Exxon Valdez* cleanup—serious cleanup attempts stopped in midstream by bureaucratic bickering. He pushed the microphone out the open window, allowing the outside air to blast over it. He pulled it back in and shouted, "Getting some interference here, Plerry. We must be flying too low."

"Mr. Severyn," Plerry continued, sounding panicked. "I can read you the court order over the radio. They don't have to hand-deliver it to you. I think it best that you stop your spraying operations. A gesture of good faith on our part."

Todd shoved the microphone out the window again, this time giving it a good thump against the side of the helicopter. "All I'm getting is static, Plerry. You're fading fast. We'll have to check out the radio systems when we get back. Severyn out."

He tossed the microphone back to the pilot. Both she and Iris looked at him. He shrugged. "What? You can't close the barn door after the horses are loose."

"That's rather unethical, isn't it, Tex?" Iris said.

Todd clenched his teeth. *Unethical?* Didn't anybody understand priorities? "Look, I told Oilstar I'd get this done—and I'm a man of my word. I'd rather apologize afterward than get bogged down asking permission from those wackos in the first place. I plan to get this oil spill cleaned up the best way I know how. That's exactly what I'm doing."

She shrugged. "For better or worse."

On the Oilstar pier, trying to stay away from other people, Alex Kramer monitored the test from the metal storage shack. A flutter of dread and nervousness kept his stomach taut. His joints felt like they were gliding on ground glass.

Outside the protesters swamped Plerry, who had given up trying to answer their questions. Two minicam vans from local TV stations pulled up. Alex ducked inside the shack. The wolves would push their way through the door in a moment. He could imagine the ghost of Erin among them. He closed his eyes and drew deep breaths. All the brutal attention he had endured in the last few days had taken its toll, but he only had to hold on for another hour. Then there would be no stopping Prometheus.

Since the spill, Alex had begun to wonder if fate had intentionally backed him into a corner, making certain that he had nothing to lose. Nothing at all. It had been an enormous decision; but now that Prometheus was deployed, he had nothing to worry about. Cool relief washed over him.

Todd Severyn had managed to complete the spraying run, and the helicopter was even now returning to the pier. Soon all hell would break loose.

Someone pounded on the door of the shack. Before Alex could answer, the door rattled open. "Dr. Kramer, would you step outside please?" The man wore a T-shirt beneath a hooded sweatshirt. "The police are here to arrest you and Mr. Severyn."

Alex blinked as he stepped into the sunshine, walking like an automaton. The bright green Oilstar helicopter chattered its way across the sky toward the pier. Jake Torgens, the bearded man who had charged through the gate waving his court order, shooed people away so the copter would have a place to land. Plerry sat all by himself on the hood of his car, staring at his loafers.

After the helicopter settled onto the wooden pier, several protesters pushed forward, ducking low. Torgens shouted, "Just wait a minute!"

When the helicopter's passenger door popped open, Todd swung out. Torgens came forward with his court order, accompanied by a uniformed police officer. "You should have stopped!"

"Mr. Severyn, I have to place you under arrest," said the police officer.

"Yeah? On what charge?" Todd asked.

"Reckless endangerment of human life and property. Dispersing a possibly hazardous or toxic substance."

Todd made a rude noise. "Bogus charges, and you know it. I'm doing this to help people and property by cleaning up the whole danged mess. It would be a crime *not* to use Dr. Kramer's stuff if it can get rid of the spill."

The policeman shrugged. Alex came up to stand next to Todd. For the first time in months he felt light on his feet, freed of an enormous weight. He could let go. The hard part was over. "Will you need to use handcuffs?" he asked.

The policeman looked surprised. "No, I don't think that'll be necessary."

Todd shook his head and spoke to Alex. "Don't worry, Doc. Oilstar will bail us out in a few hours."

"I know," Alex said. "What's done is done."

Todd laughed, ostensibly talking to Alex, but raising his voice loud enough for everyone to hear. "Isn't it funny that these wackos didn't show up until they knew it would be too late? They want to have it both ways. If your Prometheus bug doesn't work, they can press charges. If it does clean up the spill, they'll just keep their mouths shut. They can't lose. But at least *we* did the right thing, regardless!"

"Yes," Alex said, "yes we did."

They moved toward the police car. As he climbed into the backseat, Alex felt a calming resignation. He had never been in a police car before.

The door thumped shut, sealing him next to Todd in the warm, stale-smelling car. He didn't feel like a criminal. He really did have nothing left to lose. He had given the Earth a legacy.

Nothing like the *Zoroaster* spill would ever happen again. Guaranteeing that was worth sacrificing everything.

FIFTEEN

QUESTION

Straining to see through the smeared windshield of his rental Mazda, Spencer Lockwood followed the signs to Visitor Parking in front of the Sandia Lab administration building. He grabbed his briefcase and ran into the lobby. He was half an hour late, which meant his tour of somebody's lab was going to be cut short. He hoped it didn't tick off one of the colleagues who might support his smallsat project.

He signed in at the visitor's desk while the receptionist paged Moira Tibbett, his Sandia contact. Tibbett, a deputy leader of one of Sandia's energy programs, had agreed to give Spencer the standard tour. She had faxed him a preliminary agenda—but he had lost it on his cluttered desk at White Sands.

Sipping bitter coffee from a Styrofoam cup in the reception area, Spencer fidgeted. He glanced at the colorful technical brochures on display, all of which described how Sandia would solve the nation's energy problems for the next century.

Not a good sign, he thought, since he was an outsider

with a competing concept. Sitting down, he flipped through his viewgraphs again, balancing them on his knees. He wondered if he should take the clip-on necktie out of his briefcase and wear it. This might be laid-back California, but Sandia had a reputation for being more formal than the other national labs.

When Moira Tibbett came through the gate, Spencer stood to shake her hand. "Sorry about being late. The traffic . . ."

Tibbett was tall and straight-backed, dressed in an uncomfortable-looking plaid suit. "Don't worry about it. We know all about traffic out here." She led him to the chain-link gate and handed the uniformed guard the pink copy from an escort request form. "We appreciate you coming up to have a look, Dr. Lockwood. Are you familiar with our energy programs?"

"A little." Spencer already felt his muscles tense. He'd come here to promote his *own* program, maybe scare up some support. Sandia's "exchange of ideas" sounded like a one-way filter.

That afternoon, discouraged to the point of surrender, Spencer entered the Sandia auditorium, trying to haul his spirits up by his bootstraps. He had put on his tie after all.

In tour after tour, researchers had soapboxed about their projects, strongly implying that everyone else was wasting the taxpayers' time and money. Busy enough battling their coworkers, they had no room to endorse some outsider's solar-power program. Maybe this whole trip wasn't such a good idea.

The auditorium was already half filled. The room had three hundred seats, each covered with deep blue cushioning. Moira Tibbett stood tall and severe at a podium at the center of the wooden stage. The sounds of gathering people made a white-noise murmur. Spencer made a mental note to project his voice, even though these people didn't seem to be in a listening mood.

Below, waiting for his cue, Spencer shook hands with

some of the scientists, muttering appropriate words about how he had enjoyed touring their laboratories; in response, they expressed eagerness to hear his talk. Sincerity seemed as scarce as extra funding, though. He found it difficult to keep up the act.

Tibbett tapped the microphone to quiet the crowd. *Showtime!* Spencer thought. He reconsidered his viewgraphs, trying to pick a better slant for his talk. Nothing felt right.

"The Director's Colloquium Series is pleased to present Dr. Spencer Lockwood." Tibbett pulled a few index cards out of the pocket of her plaid suit and glanced at her notes. "Dr. Lockwood is a Caltech 'hat trick,' having received his bachelors, masters, and doctorate in physics there—very unusual for Caltech. He worked under Dr. Seth Mansfield in particle physics, helping to lay the foundation for Mansfield's Nobel Prize."

Spencer smiled tightly at the scattered applause. He always downplayed his contribution; he had been only an assistant, a second author on three of Mansfield's papers.

". . . his power-beaming experiment, for which he won last year's E.O. Lawrence Award. Dr. Lockwood has expanded his initial microwave work to incorporate dozens of small solar-power satellites, recently completing a series of groundbreaking tests on which he'll now report. Dr. Lockwood?"

Spencer looked out over the crowd. Placing the first viewgraph on the projector, he picked up the laser pointer and prepared for the worst. He could handle it. He had faced skeptical audiences before.

He felt like a shipwreck survivor being circled by sharks.

Forty minutes later, the coldly polite comments kept coming. Spencer's last viewgraph, a bulleted list of CONCLUSIONS, shone on the screen, but no one looked at it. His colleagues asked questions phrased as springboards for discussions of their own projects, rather than reflecting any interest in Spencer's work.

"—much less efficient than geothermal—"

"—what about impact ionization effects, which are of course not present in fusion-power concepts?"

Spencer answered each comment as precisely as he could; in the back of his mind he thought of Galileo defending his findings to the Inquisition. Out of the audience's view, he gripped the podium, digging his fingernails into the fake wood. He found himself repeatedly sipping his glass of water, knowing it was a nervous gesture but unable to stop. The water tasted bitter.

"—isn't it true that artificial ethanol is easier to access?"

"—now that the inherently safe TRIGA nuclear plant is cheaper to make—"

The rebellious "young hotshot" part of Spencer was amused at their behavior—how different from the popular stereotype of cool, logical eggheads. He had heard it said that scientists were the only army in the world that killed their own wounded.

Finally, he had enough of the bullshit. Spencer snapped off the viewgraph projector and gathered his transparencies. "Thank you for your time," he said. *Numbskulls,* he wanted to add, but gave them a tight smile instead.

As a wave of hypocritical applause rippled through the auditorium, Spencer tried to let the tension wash off of him. These people were not looking for results, or even alternative answers. Each person was responsible for a different solution to the same energy crisis, and each person wanted to validate only one individual area of research. If Lance Nedermyer enjoyed this political game back in Washington, he could have it.

Moira Tibbett led him out the side door of the auditorium. "Dr. Lockwood, I must apologize." Her eyes downcast, she looked beaten. "Everyone views this as a zero-sum game. There's only a fixed amount of money to go around, and if anything new gets funded, something has to die. It's not that they disagree with you on a scientific level—"

"I understand." Spencer forced a smile to soften his abrupt reply. He unclipped his guest badge and handed it to her. "If you'll escort me back to the gate, I can find my rental car."

"Of course," she said, taking the lead with brisk steps. "I can recommend some local restaurants, if you'd like."

"That won't be necessary," he said. Though his return flight did not leave until noon the next day, Spencer had no intention of staying a minute longer.

SIXTEEN

PRETTY WOMAN

The pile of papers from the "To Be Signed" stack fell off the conference table and scattered over the plush carpeting in the Speaker's office. Jeffrey Mayeaux was too preoccupied with getting his hands up the young speechwriter's dress to notice.

She slid back on the polished wood grain of the table, spreading her legs and finding purchase for her feet on the heavy padded chairs. The fabric of her skirt hissed across the surface. Mayeaux's fingers stroked her waist—she was firm and muscular, no flab. Probably worked out at the Hill health club, running around in Spandex, sweating, jiggling her bodacious gazonkas. He closed his eyes and grinned at the thought. Time for some different aerobic exercise.

She remained silent, without the usual cooing, gasping sounds he expected. Rather than letting it deter him, Mayeaux took it as a challenge. What was her name? Tina . . . *Tanya*. Great name. It made him as horny as a fallen priest just thinking of it.

He hooked his fingers around the waistband of her pantyhose and slid them over her hips, her buttocks, lingering on the warm skin with his fingertips. He felt sweat tracing a damp line up his spine, in his crotch. She arched herself, giving him room to work with his hands.

Tanya wore a slick peach-colored dress that slipped up nicely. Mayeaux pushed it out of the way and rubbed his fingers on the mound between her legs, rapidly growing impatient with the fabric of her pink cotton panties. He slipped a finger under the panties, tickled the crisp pubic hair for a moment, teasing her. The strong musk of her arousal drifted to his nostrils, bringing back a memory of that first time he'd ventured into the French Quarter. His pulse felt all watery with excitement. He slipped his middle finger inside.

"Oh!" she said. *Finally.* The young speechwriter glanced at him, then looked away.

This was a lot different from when Mayeaux had been much younger in New Orleans, cruising down Bourbon Street alone at night, gawking at the whores and the transvestites. He remembered screwing a dozen different women in humid and musky upper-level apartments, with the drapes open and the sounds of competing jazz bands drifting in from the street. Back then, he had to do a lot of work to get laid, but now the women came to him. One of the little bonuses of being the senior member of the House. He had to be grateful to a system that could do this for him, simply because he came from a state with no term limitations. And the best part was, his own wife let him get away with it. It was part of their agreement.

Tanya arched back on the table, closing her eyes and tilting her chin in ecstasy. Stretching her arms above her head, she ran a tongue tip in a slow circle around her lips. She had fawn-colored hair, long with subtle curls held back by barrettes. Her crotch hair was full and tan.

"Hold on for a Louisiana hot link with the works," Mayeaux said, chuckling. Tanya didn't seem to notice, and he didn't give a coon's ass. He had powerful constituents; he had already set himself up for life with enough pork-barrel projects in Louisiana that he could ease into a lobbying job at the end of his term. He did not intend to get reelected; he just meant to get his well-deserved reward before he left office.

Unbuckling his belt, he pushed his pants and underwear down to his knees. He grabbed Tanya's hips, positioned himself, and pushed inside her without further foreplay. He had a meeting in ten minutes.

Mayeaux began pumping, and Tanya raised her legs further, opening herself wider for him. They both breathed harder. Her bare skin squeaked on the polished wood surface of the table. He grinned to himself, knowing that the Joint Chiefs would sit down at the same table in another hour. If they asked, he could convince them that the damp stains on the table were doughnut frosting. He wondered if they'd be able to smell the sex.

Mayeaux kept himself in shape, and he did a good job in bed—or on the floor, or on the conference table. . . . But none of these sweet young things would look twice at him if he had been an insurance salesman, a grocery store manager. The women in the Beltway knew how to advance their careers.

Power was such an aphrodisiac.

Out of the corner of his eye, Mayeaux noticed a brief, odd expression on Tanya's face, a hint of boredom. She knew how to play the game—he had explained it to her in perfectly clear terms; it was part of the post–Anita Hill era. He just hoped Tanya didn't give him some disease. At least after his vasectomy he had no worries about being slapped with a paternity suit.

His escapades were becoming legendary, like JFK's. He kept trying to push the limit, but somehow the boundary moved one step farther away for each indiscretion he committed. The media liked him, too; they seemed amused rather than outraged.

Thrusting over and over again, Mayeaux ground his hips against Tanya's, holding tight to her waist to keep her from sliding across the table.

The door to the Speaker's office popped open. His chief of staff, Franklin Weathersee, stepped inside. Mayeaux cursed himself for forgetting to lock the door. Weathersee glanced at the spectacle on the conference table, then calmly stepped back out of the room.

Tanya gasped in shock and scrambled away, rolling off the table. Mayeaux fought back the urge to laugh. She snatched her pantyhose, pulling them up, and yanked the smooth peach fabric of her dress back into place. As she brushed back her hair, Mayeaux thought he saw a look of relief on her face.

Mayeaux buckled his pants and turned to call through the door. "Dammit, Weathersee, couldn't you knock?" But he could never be angry at Weathersee—the man had saved Mayeaux's butt too many times in the past.

The door inched open. "Sorry, sir." Weathersee dropped a stack of papers on the floor. "These are the briefing materials you wanted in preparation for the trip to Kirtland Air Force Base. It's for the Tech Transfer Act." Poking his head into the room, he glanced at the speechwriter, then back at Mayeaux. "And whenever you're finished here, sir, Vice President Wolani is on the phone for you."

Without a word, Tanya fled past him. Mayeaux scowled, but looked admiringly at her ass as she went out. He wondered when they would be able to finish what they had started. Or, if not with her, he'd get somebody else.

For now, he'd just as soon have kept the vice president waiting.

SEVENTEEN

CELEBRATION

After spending the morning in jail, Todd didn't mind the long drive to Alex Kramer's house, as long as he could keep the window rolled down and the fresh air blowing in his face.

A load of crap had come down since that morning, and the rolling Marin foothills calmed him. He turned up the radio, tapped on the wheel, and sang along with an old Willie Nelson song. He was ready to unwind at the Oilstar "victory party" at Alex's home. By spraying Prometheus, Todd had turned on the light at the end of the tunnel.

As expected, Oilstar bailed Todd and Alex out after only a few hours in the Contra Costa County jail. Oilstar lawyers had been prepared and waiting. By early afternoon, Emma Branson had gone on TV, railing at the interference from do-nothing government agencies.

Todd had never been in trouble with the law before, and having an arrest on his record really ticked him off; once the charges were dropped, his sheet darn well better be clean. He'd placed an awful lot of confidence in Kramer's microbes.

Unexpectedly, he came upon Alex's ranch house, half-hidden in the tall trees; he braked quickly in his Ford pickup, coming to a dead stop in the road before turning right into the long gravel driveway. None of the cars parked on the lawn and in the drive looked more than three years old, and there were more foreign cars than American ones. He shook his head. These same mineral-water-drinking lamebrains complained about America's economy and then handed their buying dollars to some German or Japanese car company.

Getting out of the truck, he settled his cowboy hat on his head. As he crunched up the driveway, he glanced at the split-rail fence extending along the one-story ranch house; a small barn stood just around the corner. He took a deep breath. The familiar damp, musty smell of manure told him Alex kept horses. Not what he expected from the quiet scientist.

One of the secretaries from the bioremediation offices answered the doorbell. Not a secretary, he corrected himself; in California, the women called themselves "administrative assistants." She wore lots of makeup and was dressed to kill. He wondered what she would look like in jeans.

Todd didn't have time to say anything before she waved him inside. "Hey, everybody, our other convict is here!"

Pianos and violins played snooty classical music on the stereo. People milled around the main living room near a small wet bar where they served themselves. Prepackaged hors d'oeuvres sat out on a table: crackers, cut vegetables, cheese. A sliding glass door stood half-open, leading to a patio and the backyard. Other people chatted and laughed in the kitchen, leaning against the tile counters. From their dress, Todd supposed the guests had stopped by on their way home from work.

He hadn't yet seen the host. He wondered if Alex lived

alone in such a big place. Somehow, this did not strike
him as a bachelor pad. Even with all the gathered people,
the sound of the music, the conversations, the house felt
. . . unused, as if it had been closed up for a long time.

Todd got himself a bottle of Coors from the small wet
bar and stood nursing it, sloshing the foamy taste around
in his mouth. He stood by himself in between other
conversations, looking at all the people he didn't know.
He tried to smile as he shook hands, accepting congratu-
lations for getting the work done and for bucking the
system. Trying to escape further conversation, he wandered down a narrow hall.

Someone squeezed past him to the bathroom. Poking
around, he opened the door to a closed room. Medals,
newspaper clippings, and a battle streamer hung on the
wall, just above the photo of a young man in a starch-
ed army uniform. Other pictures surrounded the memorial—Alex himself standing by the boy in hiking
gear, the boy crouched by the ocean holding an abalone
shell.

An adjacent wall featured a young girl. Photos of her
at various ages were arranged in a circle: a ballerina, a
Pioneer girl, a high-school cheerleader next to her
mother—everything a proud and loving father would
put together. . . .

Todd's musings were interrupted by a loud voice and a
slap on the back. "Cowboy Todd! Come on, loosen up,
celebrate!"

Todd turned to see Alex's bigmouthed deputy, Mitchell Stone. "Mitch, how are ya?" He wondered if Mitch
had gone to some expensive eastern college to learn to be
such a horse's rear end.

"Just friggin' great." Mitch hung an arm around
Todd's neck. A fruity wine-cooler smell surrounded the
man, mixed with the aroma of cheese dip. Mitch took a
sip from the glass he held in one hand. "You know, the
way things are going, we're going to owe you a lot more
than that consulting fee."

"How's that?"

"You made us heroes!" Mitch roared. Todd couldn't figure out what was so funny. "It's a great day for the future!"

Todd squirmed out from under Mitch's arm and steered him into the hall, closing the door behind them. He wondered about the pictures—who were those people? The displays of Alex's . . . children? . . . made him uncomfortable. He wanted to protect Kramer's privacy.

"Give the bug time to work, Mitch, before you—"

"Hell, I saw it with my own eyes. It *can't* fail." He raised his glass to Todd; it held a peachy drink with tiny bubbles rising to the top.

Todd held up his half-full bottle of beer. "I think I'll get a refill. See ya!" He escaped before Mitch could articulate a reply. He hurried down the hall back to the crowded room, hoping to lose himself among the fifteen or so people. Todd wished for some Outlaws, or Charlie Daniels, or any country music, but the foot-stompin' beat might stir things up too much.

He thought about going to the patio, maybe take a look at the horses, when he spotted Alex Kramer standing alone outside, leaning on a porch rail and holding a drink. Alex had a bemused look, holding his folded eyeglasses in his hand as if pondering a secret joke. Squinting into the distance, he studied the rolling hills behind the house. He barely seemed aware of his own party.

Todd started toward the sliding glass door when he bumped into someone backing away from the bar. A plate fell to the floor. "Gosh, I'm sorry!" Todd said, looking at the petite woman stooping down to pick up spilled munchies. She wore a bright red blouse and black pants.

"I didn't expect you to be a ballerina wearing those cowboy boots," Iris Shikozu said, stooping to snatch her glass from the floor. "But I would hope for a little bit of coordination."

Todd glanced down at his large boots with a mixture of embarrassment and anger. "Who backed into who?" he asked, bending to help her.

Iris brushed a hand across her face to move the strands of jet-black hair that had fallen across her eyes. "I think I can handle the massive task of picking up these crackers by myself." Then, as if reconsidering, she gave a slight smile. "You could go get me another plate of food."

Relieved to do something, and also to be away from further sarcasm, Todd made his way to the food table. He set down his half-empty bottle of Coors, picked up a paper plate, and started to grab potato chips, salami, dill pickles, olives. He suddenly stopped. Iris did not strike him as a potato-chip-and-salami type of person. In consternation, he looked at the food, trying to think of what she might prefer—he didn't have a clue as to what tofu looked like. Well, how about olives? No, probably too much salt. He settled for fresh carrots, celery, cauliflower, and broccoli; looking at the other selections, he picked a few crackers—those must be safe, they looked like whole-wheat—a deviled egg, and an artichoke heart.

He took the plate back, but Iris was nowhere to be found. The thought crossed his mind that she might have ducked out, just to make a fool of him. Then the plate was taken from his hand.

"I'd better get this before you spill it," Iris said.

Before he could stop himself, Todd growled, "What did *I* do to put a chip on your shoulder? And where were you hiding?"

Iris recovered from her surprise with remarkable speed; a grin spread across her face. "Well, well. The cowboy can think for himself. But I believe you're jumping to conclusions." She held up a damp dishrag in her free hand. "I was just getting something to wipe up the mess on the carpet."

As she bent down, Iris knocked over the white wine

she had set on the gray-blue rug. "Oh, crap." She picked up the clear plastic cup and dabbed at the seeping damp spot. Todd grabbed a handful of paper napkins and knelt to help her blot up the stain.

"You wouldn't make much of a ballerina yourself," he said.

She gave a low laugh. "Touché."

When they had mopped up as much as they could, Todd straightened. Iris brushed back her hair and was silent for a moment before she finally said, "I'm going to get another glass of wine. Want a beer?" It seemed to take an effort. "Then you can help me eat some of these carrot sticks."

Todd blinked. "Sure."

They went to stand by the sliding glass doors to the patio. A panoramic view of the Marin hills spread out in the late afternoon. The horse corral took up most of Kramer's backyard. A thicket of Ponderosa pine started fifty yards from the house and spread up the hills.

Iris spoke first. "You know, before this oil spill people would have lynched you for even suggesting the idea of spraying Prometheus microbes in a populated area."

He shrugged. "You do what you have to do. In an emergency, you can't just sit around and wait for committees to sort everything out." He nodded toward her. "I appreciate your help."

"I wasn't there to help you. I was representing the state's interests."

"Right." He sipped his beer and looked around. After a moment he said, "Know anybody else here?"

Iris shrugged. "I recognize a few of the scientists, but I don't really pal around with oil-company employees."

The silence was awkward for some seconds before Todd spoke again. "So what do you people see in California? You don't really like it here, do you?"

She seemed to think over her answer. "I enjoy my work."

"I didn't ask about that."

She glanced up. "In my line of work, you go where the jobs are. We can't all live in Texas, you know."

"I'm from Wyoming, not Texas. But we wouldn't want the crowds, anyway."

They spent the rest of the hour talking. Although she attempted to come across as tough as nails, Iris opened up once Todd steered her away from talking about academia and her Stanford connections.

By the time he finished his third beer, many people began drifting away from the party to get home for dinner, as if at some secret signal. Todd didn't want to leave, but he began to grow more self-conscious as he saw others departing, calling goodbyes to Alex until he and Iris were the only two left. Outside, the sunset flashed diffusing colors across the sky.

Alex stepped back through the glass patio doors, looking around as if checking to see whether it was safe. Todd and Iris both looked up at him. "Excuse me." Kramer smiled sheepishly. "I'm not usually fond of cocktail parties, but my wife hosted them sometimes. She must have been better at it than I am—people never used to leave before midnight."

Iris drew herself up. "Well, I've got quite a drive back to Stanford. Thank you for inviting me, Dr. Kramer. Glad we had a chance to talk, Todd."

"Me too." He was quiet for a moment. "Uh, look. How about grabbing some supper? All I've eaten is rabbit food tonight: celery, carrots—"

"I've really got to get back to the lab before heading home." She hesitated. "Some other time?"

"Right." Todd tried not to let his disappointment show, but at least she hadn't blown him off completely. He didn't know any of the restaurants out here anyway —and if he found one, they probably served only California cuisine, where a plate of diced eggplant and bean curd next to a boiled new potato and a sprig of steamed broccoli passed as a meal. He'd like to show Iris a good steak house, but then she probably didn't eat meat.

Todd wasn't sure why he felt drawn to her. She was at least fifteen years younger than he, shorter by over a foot, and had a sharp tongue—nothing like the women he was used to dating, who were impressed by rough-and-tumble oilmen. He stared at her as she gathered a black sweater and waved briefly at him. Todd watched her open the door, and debated following her. He knew he was bad at picking up on signals. Maybe if he asked again—no, she would probably just turn him down. She closed the door behind her, leaving Todd feeling awkwardly alone.

Alex looked at him, then glanced away. He struck Todd as a lonely old man. "Come on outside, Todd," Alex said, "and I'll show you the stable." He drained his wineglass and struggled to his feet from the sofa. The sound of horses came through the open patio doors. Everything seemed serene and peaceful out here. It reminded him of his parents' ranch.

Todd thought about the horses, but not wanting to invite himself, he controlled the eagerness in his voice. "Thanks, but I've overstayed my welcome. I ought to get back to my condo—"

"Nonsense," said Alex. "It's not like there's anybody around here for you to bother." He brushed his hand over his neat iron-gray beard and gave a weak smile. "You helped me a lot today, so stay awhile. Let's go check the horses."

"Are you going to ride?"

Alex thought for a long moment. "Why not? It'll be dark before long, but they know their way around here. It'll only take a minute to saddle them up."

Todd followed him out of the house to the corral. Dry grass crunched beneath their feet. Alex held open the gate, but as he tried to yank it shut, he hung his head as if he had just felt a wave of sadness. Todd pulled the gate shut himself. "You okay, Alex? You don't look so hot."

"I'm fine." Alex shuffled to the stable, as if embarrassed that Todd had noticed his momentary lapse.

Wiping his hands on his jeans, Todd approached the two horses. Who would have thought the scholarly introvert kept horses? "How long have you had them?"

It took a moment for Alex to answer. "My daughter Erin was wild about horses. Got her a pony on her eighth birthday, and when she was fourteen I gave her that chocolate quarter horse over there, Stimpy. I guess it's been four years, now. We used to take them out a couple times a week."

"I didn't think of you as the riding type."

Alex fumbled in his pocket for a sugar cube and approached the nearest horse, the palomino; he held a bit and bridle in his other hand. "This used to be a large part of my life, but I haven't had much time lately. The horses probably need the exercise as much as I do." The palomino nuzzled Alex's hand, and the sugar cube disappeared. Alex quickly bridled the horse and held the reins out to Todd. "This is Ren, my horse. Go ahead."

"Do your kids still ride much? I think I saw their pictures in one of the rooms."

Alex froze, then answered in a hollow, curt voice. "Both Erin and Jay are dead."

Todd squirmed, feeling as if he had shoved his cowboy boot into his mouth all the way up to the heel. "I'm really sorry. I didn't know."

"It's all right. I'm over it now," Alex said in a controlled tone that contradicted his words. "I'm just glad you're here to help exercise the horses."

They saddled the two mounts in awkward silence; then Todd swung up onto the palomino. Alex seemed protective of his daughter's mount.

Ren felt poised beneath Todd's legs, ready to respond. The feel of the horse beneath him awakened memories. He had spent much of his younger years riding, comfortable with his own horse, working hard on the ranch. He had forgotten how much he missed it, how little time he had to do what he liked while he ran around the world fixing Oilstar's emergencies.

He let Alex take the lead. The two rode across the sprawling back fields and along a path into the trees. With the approaching dusk, everything shone with a soft glow. The air carried a heady, damp smell of grass and pine. The horse made soothing noises as it breathed, rustling through the grass.

"This is nice, Todd," Alex said. "I haven't gone out for a ride since this *Zoroaster* mess started."

The horses were familiar with the terrain, slowing as the grade got steeper. It took twenty minutes to reach the top of the hill behind Alex's ranch; from the crest Todd could see lights dotting the valley, houses separated by acres of land instead of the endless crowding of San Francisco.

Todd broke the silence. "I could almost settle down here. You can't tell we're so close to the city."

Alex's expression was unreadable in the failing light. "If you'd like, Todd, you can come up and ride the horses whenever you want. You'd take better care of them than I do."

Todd sat upright in the saddle, and for a moment the words clogged in his throat before he finally said, "Really? That would be great!" His voice sounded high-pitched with excitement. He felt a big grin spreading across his face.

"Only if you promise to treat the horses right, though. I'm no good at it anymore."

"That's an easy promise to keep!"

Alex's shadowy face wore a lost smile. "Erin and I spent afternoons riding after I got home from work, then we used to race back to the house, even at night. She loved playing the daredevil." His words faltered.

Todd waited for Alex to continue, but when Alex spoke again, he changed the subject. "I was in grad school before I ever got close to a horse. Maureen, my wife, talked me into taking her on a riding picnic." He laughed for the first time all night. "I was a real green-horn, and the horses knew it. As soon as we were out of sight of the stable, my horse halted and started eating grass. Wouldn't move no matter what I did."

Todd let Alex talk, beginning to see the man in another light. He wondered how much time Alex spent moping around the house feeling sorry for himself and what had happened to his family.

Todd remembered times in his life when he had dwelled on things he couldn't change. When his high-school sweetheart Kelly had dumped him for some guy joining the navy, he had spent months frustrated and hurt, constantly reminded of happier days, finding emotional land mines in scrapbooks and old junk drawers. But Todd also knew bad times could be wrapped up and put away, for a little while at least. He had let loose, riding off and doing stunts on his horse at his parents' ranch, until his dad had threatened to ground him. Alex needed to let loose too.

Shaking the reins and kicking his mount with his heels, Todd caused Ren to rear up suddenly. A stupid idea with a strange horse, he knew, but just being on horseback again exhilarated him. He felt the power in the horse's muscles, and a flash of delight surged through him. He held on and felt the joy of life tingle from his head down to the heels of his boots.

Alex looked over his shoulder, startled at the commotion, and his horse backed away.

Todd pulled back on the reins. "Come on, Alex. Race you back!" He didn't wait for an answer. Todd slapped Ren's side with an encouraging yell. "Yeeee-hah!" The palomino took off, as if remembering an old game.

Todd could hear only the sound of his horse crashing through the brush, galloping through the tall dry grass. His eyes had grown used to the evening light. Todd clucked at Ren, but he had left Alex behind. The older man must be in no mood to be reminded of the past.

The grade leveled, and Todd slowed his horse. Immediately, the sound of another horse galloping came from behind him.

Todd urged Ren into motion again, but Stimpy bore down to overtake Todd's horse. Alex crouched low over the saddle, urging the quarter horse to greater speed. Todd saw a focused expression on the man's face.

The two of them rode faster through the clearing, charging toward the stables in the home stretch. Both horses ran full-out, filled with exuberance. By the time they crossed the clearing and reached the corral, Alex was three lengths ahead of Todd.

Acknowledging his defeat with a laugh, Todd reined the horse to a halt, swung down, and patted Ren on the neck. He laughed again, feeling warm inside. He panted. "What a ride!"

Alex brought Stimpy around, chuckling for a moment. "That was dangerous, you know."

"Ren knew the way." Todd reached out to grab Stimpy's bridle for Alex to dismount. "Like you said, this wasn't the first time these guys have raced in the evening." He patted Stimpy. "You're pretty good in the saddle, Alex. I took you for a gentleman rancher— the type to keep a couple of horses, maybe ride them once in a while without really knowing what he's doing. I guess I was wrong."

Alex shook his head and stiffly swung down from the chocolate-brown horse. His face looked stormy with sudden doubt, as if something had collapsed inside of him. His shoulders drooped, and he held on to the saddle horn as if to steady himself.

Todd scrambled down from Ren. "Hey, Alex! You sure you're all right? You look like something's really bothering you. Worried about whether your Prometheus bug is gonna work?"

Alex shook his head as he turned to lead Stimpy back toward the stable. "No, that's not it at all. I . . . I was just enjoying myself, and I didn't know what to do with the feeling. It's been a long time." He fidgeted, keeping himself turned away from Todd. "I think you'd better go. I've got a lot of cleaning up to do and . . . and I've got a lot of things to think about."

Todd scuffed his boot in the dirt. "Sure, Alex. Thanks for letting me stay awhile."

"No, Todd. Thank you." Alex turned back to him, gripping the bridle of the chocolate horse. "You come up here again soon to ride these horses. Promise." Behind his glasses, Alex's pale eyes fixed on him. "I mean it. That's important to me."

"Sure," said Todd. "I promise. I always keep my promises."

EIGHTEEN

THE LONG WAY HOME

Spencer Lockwood fumbled through the glove compartment and pulled out the map of California from the rental-car packet. It didn't show many details, but he needed only the major highways to find his way back home.

His return flight to Albuquerque did not take off until the next day, but Spencer had no intention of waiting in Livermore. He would only sit in a stuffy hotel room and read a few of the journals he had brought with him, go to bed early, fight traffic back to the San Francisco airport, then fly on to New Mexico.

Or he could *drive* most of the way back in the same time. It looked like a straightforward trip, a long, peaceful drive.

At Caltech in his grad-student days, Spencer and his buddies would hop into the car and take a road trip for the weekend, heading for the San Gabriel Mountains, Palm Springs, or Tijuana. It had been years since he'd done that.

Spencer relished the prospect of having no distractions, being able to think things out. Driving refreshed him, and the hum of the wheels on the highway gave him a sense of freedom.

He'd cancel his flight, then return the car at the Albuquerque airport. He'd even make that Tech Transfer ceremony in plenty of time. Grinning, Spencer checked the gas gauge—still three-quarters full. He cycled the radio through its Seek mode twice, searching for surfin' music, and finally settled for an oldies station. He turned the car east onto Interstate 580.

The broad landscape seemed to open its arms to welcome him. The five-lane highway wound upward into a line of grassy hills that rose like battlements on Livermore's eastern flank. The Altamont range held something special, one of his favorite sights each time he came to Sandia in Livermore. Stretching for miles across the mountains stood thousands of wind turbines, row upon row. The world's largest wind farm captured gusts whipping over the range, spinning white aluminum blades and generating power.

As he cruised along, he craned his neck to stare at several different types of windmill, the standard sunflower shape, three-bladed wind turbines, whiplike two-bladed propellers that spun around in a blur. Vertical-axis Darrieus wind turbines stood near the freeway like giant eggbeaters stirred by the breeze.

Tax incentives for alternative-energy development had made most of the Altamont windmills feasible during the Reagan administration; when the tax credits ended, many investors sold their windmills, and some of the turbines had fallen into disrepair. The sprawling wind farm still generated a great deal of power, though, which was sold to the state electrical grid.

The windmills were set up much the way Spencer's microwave antenna farm would work in White Sands. Windmills in the east; solar-power satellites in the southwest. *Oil spill to the west.* Spencer smiled: the future would have its way, sooner or later.

The car raced onward, leaving the windmills behind.

*   *   *

The Central Valley lay like a swath of the Great Plains down the middle of California.

Without a panicky chaos of cars around him, Spencer liked to drive and let his mind wander. He enjoyed daydreaming while racing down a desert highway, surrounded by the sprawling horizon, wide-open spaces. It was how he brainstormed, throwing out crazy ideas to himself until he found something that made sense.

And he wasn't going to let this road trip go to waste.

He thought of his smallsats orbiting over the antenna farm. The technology of the collectors was nothing new. Silicon photovoltaic cells had been around since 1954, when the prototypes achieved only a six-percent energy conversion from direct sunlight. The energy crisis in the 1970s turned an enormous research effort toward developing "clean and inexhaustible" solar power, pushing photovoltaic cells up to twenty-percent efficiencies. In 1989, a concentrator solar cell used lenses to focus sunlight onto the cell surface, yielding even higher efficiencies. Gallium-arsenide and other types of photovoltaic materials also showed promise. Unlike electric generators, solar cells had no moving parts and could operate indefinitely if they were protected from damage. And they produced no pollution.

But widespread application of ground-based solar energy had always been hindered by its cost—up to a thousand times more than electricity generated by oil, coal, or hydroelectric plants.

Now that he had successfully demonstrated the technique of staggering focused microwave beams from low orbit, though, Spencer's team had solved that problem. But there were practical considerations as to how many smallsats they could loft, and how many antenna farms could be scattered across the landscape.

The only way to convince people was to complete the experiments, get the facility providing real power for real people. It wouldn't be difficult to hook up to New Mexico's main power grid.

Spencer's team had operated on shoestring budgets before. Life in grad school, even with Professor Mansfield's generous help, had taught him how to make do. Thanks to the lukewarm review from Lance Nedermyer, Spencer's gang back at White Sands would retain only the minimum amount of money to keep going—"maintenance budget," the Department of Energy called it. Just enough to keep the lights on and the custodians employed. But ingenious use of resources could always counterbalance budget cutbacks. They could even *sell* electricity to the Public Service Company of New Mexico.

Spencer intended to keep calling his own shots, performing the research he could afford. It was the type of challenge he enjoyed.

He pushed down on the Mazda's accelerator, listening to the engine hum louder, but the landscape was so vast it crawled by. He couldn't wait to get back to White Sands.

NINETEEN

TEACHER, TEACHER

Pretending to study from a stolen calculus textbook, Connor Brooks sat at an open-air table at the Stanford student union and looked for his next mark. Campus was easy pickings.

He shook his shaggy head. *Serves the rich bastards right! Teach them a lesson they won't learn in their snooty classes.*

In the first few hours after the *Zoroaster* wreck, Connor had thought himself doomed. His original plan had been to hide on the gigantic tanker and then sneak off when it reached the Oilstar terminal; but that lunatic Uma had rammed the ship into the bridge. Then the Butthead had tried to blame everything on him!

But the Coast Guard and the news media saw right through that flimsy excuse. A captain was responsible for his ship. Uma never should have left the bridge, fire alarms or no fire alarms, and he never should have been such a fascist in the first place—it was only a matter of time before his crew rebelled. Besides, tankers like the *Zoroaster* should carry better safety mechanisms, collision-avoidance systems so that some Captain Butthead couldn't ram into a bridge. *Some people just never learn.*

He kept his gaze moving, scoping the various groups of pimply-faced kids. The meaningless equations in the math book blurred under his eyes. People really made sense out of this crap? The students relaxed under red-and-white–striped umbrellas, drinking beer and eating pizza. Some sat alone. He kept an eye on one kid with long, limp brown hair and a sorry attempt at a mustache. The kid shot down one imported beer after another as he read a fat classic-looking novel. Sooner or later the kid would have to get up and head for the bathroom.

About one time in five, the idiots left their backpacks unattended. Connor enjoyed giving somebody else a few hard knocks for a change.

After another fifteen minutes, the kid spread his paperback novel out on the table, squashed the spine with the palm of his hand to make sure it lay flat, then stood up. He rubbed the small of his back, scratched his shoulder blades, then shuffled toward the glass doors leading inside to the rest rooms.

He left the backpack sitting at his place.

Connor shook his head at the kid's stupidity. Feigning a yawn, he stood up, leaving the calculus book on the table. Someone would eventually pick it up. Looking as natural as could be, Connor strolled in one door of the union, then out another door, circling back to the abandoned table as if it were his own. *Don't look at me. I just forgot this stuff.*

The fat book facedown on the table said *Anthem* by Ayn Rand. Gee, just the type of light fluff everybody wanted to read while sitting out on the union patio on a sunny late-spring afternoon. With a glance around, Connor shouldered the kid's pack; then, as an after-thought, he lifted up the book, flipped a few pages to lose the kid's place, and set it back down again, smiling.

Moving quickly, but not hurriedly, he walked away. As he moved, Connor fondled the backpack; the slick nylon fabric slid across his fingertips. Mom and Dad probably bought it for the kid just before the semester started.

He sauntered around the side of the building, past a stained concrete loading ramp by the cafeteria and two dark green dumpsters surrounded by the cloying sweet-sour smell of old garbage. Sometimes it was fun to sit and watch the expressions of loss and confusion when the suckers came out to find their belongings gone, but Connor didn't feel like it today. He'd been hanging out at Stanford for days, and the campus cops would catch on to his game sooner or later. He wanted to get out of the Bay Area as soon as possible.

He sat down on the tile lip of the dry fountain and unshouldered the pack. From this vantage point, Connor glanced up at the wandering students going in and out of the union to use the photocopy machines and the pay phones. Still no sign of the kid. Maybe he had to take a crap.

Connor unzipped the pack and found three new spiral notebooks with white covers and a red Stanford Bookstore logo. Inside, the kid had taken crisp, meticulous notes about Melville's use of metaphors. Connor dropped the notebooks on the ground.

In the front pocket Connor found a chocolate-chip granola bar, which he stuffed into his shirt pocket. He rummaged among a handful of pens and pencils, two pizza coupons, and just at the point of giving up, he found a twenty-dollar bill taped to the fabric in back. It wasn't the kid's wallet, probably "emergency cash" that worried parents insisted their son keep "in case something happens." Well, Connor needed it more than the kid did. Twenty bucks was twenty bucks.

Abandoning the pack, he got up and wandered down the mall, past poster vendors, jewelry makers with their wares displayed on rickety tables, someone selling cassettes from the Stanford Men's Choir. He smelled new-mown grass in the air.

People milled about, but none of the college babes returned his looks. Although he kept himself reasonably clean, Connor was starting to look homeless. He had found a few dorms with open showers, and—like everything else—if he looked as if he knew what he was doing, nobody thought to stop him.

Connor had set his sights on going back to northern Arizona. His parents lived in Flagstaff, but he hadn't spoken a word to his mother and father in twelve years. But he could walk in with a toothsome Prodigal Son grin on his face. What was the old saying? *Home is where, when you go there, they have to take you in.* He wanted to settle down for a while, figure out where to go next.

Connor found a kiosk with bulletins advertising student films playing in auditoriums, religious campus crusades, roommates wanted, tutoring services. He scrutinized the displays when something caught his eye. A flyer stood out, on vibrant pink paper with a handwritten message photocopied onto it:

DRIVE MY CAR TO ATLANTA FOR $500

Connor drew in a deep breath. Finally, something he could use! Glancing at the address, he yanked off the flyer.

The dorm was called Roble Hall—pronounced "Row-BLEE" by the person who answered the phone—and Connor Brooks found it by wandering around campus for an hour.

The three-story dorm was a towering sandstone edifice covered with ivy, like something straight out of the movies. The doors were painted white; the inside smelled like a damp old attic; the olive-green carpet was worn and threadbare. He went up the wrong staircase, came back down to a lounge filled with beat-up sofas that looked like they had been stolen from the Salvation Army, then backtracked until he found the room he was looking for.

"Yo!" the student said, opening the door. "You the guy who wants to drive my car? I'm Dave Hensch."

What a prick. Hensch looked like a cut-out from the Mystery Date Game: V-neck sweater over a spotless white shirt, tan slacks, loafers. His mouse-brown hair was cut short, and his face had a baby-pink flush that suggested he still scrubbed behind his ears.

Connor offered Hensch his best smile, stroked back his lank blond hair, and extended his hand. He tried not to show his scorn for this preppie idiot. "Hi, I'm Connor. Nice to meet you."

Hensch led him into the small room with rickety wooden furniture painted a sticky brown, a single bed with a red ribbed bedspread. "I'll be flying back to Atlanta at the end of the summer, and I need to have my car waiting for me. It's a long drive—you sure you're up to it? No classes this semester?"

Connor sat down on the hard wooden chair by the narrow desk, looking comfortable because that always put the suckers at ease. In the metal trash can, an old banana peel masked the nursing-home smell in the room. "I'm taking a break this semester. And I've got relatives in Atlanta I haven't seen in years. Besides, seeing the country is the best education."

Hensch nodded. "Yeah, I know. My parents made me spend a summer in Europe for the same reason."

Connor stifled a snort. He started to feel impatient. "So, Dave, what kind of car is it?"

"An old AMC Gremlin." Hensch looked embarrassed. "Don't laugh. It's probably the crummiest car on campus, but it was my first set of wheels. I've spent more on repairs than the car ever cost me but, hey, I'm attached to it. Can you drive a stick?"

"Sure thing. I'm ready to leave at any time." He put a concerned tone in his voice. "You sure you can get by without your car for the next few weeks?"

Hensch dismissed the thought. "I can always just rent one if I need it, right?"

"I suppose." *Rich bastard. Serves you right.*

Hensch turned to the window. "Yesterday a few buddies and I took the car up to look at the oil spill, sort of as a going-away bash. We wanted to be able to say we saw it firsthand, you know? Have you been there?"

"Yeah, I saw it up close." Connor rubbed his hands together. "Now, you'll pay the money up front, right? That's the way these things usually work. I keep receipts and get reimbursed for my actual expenses of gas and lodging and stuff when I get to Atlanta?" He was making this up, but it sounded reasonable.

"That doesn't give me much security," Hensch said, looking doubtful. Bright points of red appeared on his skin, as if it embarrassed him to be negotiating money. "I understood that it's usually done half and half. You get the rest of the cash when you deliver the car."

Connor shrugged, then decided to press his luck. "That's okay by me, if it makes you feel more comfortable. But could you at least loan me a hundred against the expenses? You know how much I'm going to spend just on gas to drive across the country, and it would be a hardship to do it all out of pocket."

Hensch paused, then pulled out his wallet, sliding several bills out, flipping through as if he was used to counting fifty-dollar bills. "How about three hundred? That's half plus an extra fifty. Good enough?"

"You got a deal, my friend." Connor reached out to take the cash and shake Hensch's hand.

"Oh, and I'll need to see your driver's license for ID. Got any accidents on your driving record?"

Connor froze for just a moment. This would be the test. He had a driver's license, of course, but his name had been plastered around the papers ever since he had skipped out on the *Zoroaster* wreck. What if Hensch recognized him?

But to hesitate now would ruin everything. He flipped out his wallet and removed his license. "No accidents since I was in high school. I got a speeding ticket last year, but I went to traffic school and had it taken off my record. I think I'm a pretty safe driver."

Hensch barely glanced at it, noting the credit cards in Connor's wallet but certainly not guessing they had been stolen. "That's all. Just wanted to make sure you had one."

Connor was too shocked to feel immediate relief.

Hensch fiddled with the keys on the ring and pulled off two. "I'll take you down to the car. I've got my folks' Atlanta address, with detailed directions, plus some phone numbers for emergencies. I really appreciate this."

Connor squeezed Hensch's outstretched hand. "No, Dave. Thank *you.*"

Connor had been driving for more than an hour and a half, escaping the South Bay and cutting across to Interstate 5, the main traffic artery down California's monotonous Central Valley.

The battered old AMC Gremlin looked like a scrunched artillery shell that had failed to detonate on impact. The body was bright lavender with a wide, curving white racing stripe. The old vehicle was probably worth little more than the five hundred dollars its owner was paying to have it driven across country.

It was a gas guzzler, too.

As the engine whirred and rattled, bringing the car up to a maximum speed of 53 mph, Connor watched the gas gauge drop. Other cars passed by him like spawning fish swimming upstream, but he struggled along. When he reached the crossroads town of Santa Nella, he pulled off at one of the gas stations.

Santa Nella had a clot of fast-food restaurants, a giant motorized windmill advertising pea soup, and a few motels—though why anyone would want to stay in the middle of the empty Central Valley, Connor could not fathom. Cars pulled in and out in a confused tangle of too many drivers who had been behind the wheel for too long in one sitting.

A vehicle sat beside every pump at the gas station, as

the owners shoved gas nozzles into their tanks. Connor waited in line behind a bronze Chevy pickup. He thumped his fingers on the dashboard. Ahead of him, an old man wearing a dark blue cap sporting a fertilizer logo moved with the speed of growing grass. "Just squeeze the handle and the gas'll squirt out, grandpa!" he muttered to himself. "That's the way it works."

When it was finally his turn, Connor pulled up and got out, leaving the creaking door to hang half open. He opened the Gremlin's gas tank and grabbed the fuel-pump nozzle. A sour, rotten-egg smell drifted up to him from his car. He wrinkled his nose. "Smells like some-one farted in there!"

He inserted the gas nozzle and began pumping, keep-ing his face down so as not to attract attention. The black rubber vapor sheath wrapped around the nozzle like a condom. Gasoline rushed into the Gremlin's tank, and sharp gas fumes swirled all around.

He went to the outside cashier window, paid the attendant in cash, then drove off again.

Another car pulled up as he left. The driver took the pump nozzle, and slid it into his own gas tank, sniffing at the residual sulfur odor.

Connor intended to drive all night to reach Los Angeles, then hook east toward Las Vegas, and from there head to Arizona. He'd never driven the distance before, though he guessed it could be done in a straight day or two on the road.

But fat with the cash the Stanford clown had given him, Connor decided to spend the night in a nice motel, get a good shower, shave, make himself look presentable.

The Gremlin started acting up an hour or so before he expected to reach LA. He had just passed the crest of the Grapevine, the line of mountains blocking the Central Valley from the outer fringes of the Southern California metropolis. Around him, rugged shoulders of mountains rose high above, spattered with bright freckles of orange, purple, and white wildflowers, now turning into dark shadows against the deepening indigo of the sky.

The engine stuttered as he climbed the pass, wheezing along as even loaded semi trucks crawled past him uphill. The car chugged as if in great pain, then caught again. At the crest, when the grade shifted downhill, Connor eased off on the accelerator.

The gauge showed his tank to be at least a quarter full. He tapped on the dashboard, but the needle hovered in the middle. Dammit! That crummy service station in Santa Nella must have watered their gas. The Gremlin sounded as if it had indigestion.

He kept wrestling with the steering wheel, fluttering his foot on the gas pedal. Angrily, he snapped the emergency flashers on and crawled along. Full night had fallen. If the car died now, he would be stranded in more ways than one, because he sure as hell couldn't call Triple A, and he couldn't wait for a CHP officer to pull up and help. The moment they found out Connor's name, they'd snap on the cuffs.

He had just passed the exits for a middle-of-nowhere clot of gas stations and fast-food restaurants when the car died for good. It wheezed and gave a death rattle, allowing Connor just enough freedom to wrestle it to the side of the road.

In disgust, he climbed out of the car and slammed the door. Traffic soared past him on the freeway. A truck blatted by, rumbling downhill. He saw the stream of headlights and wondered why, of all those cars, *he* had to get one that didn't last more than a few hours.

He lifted the hood, and the rotten-egg smell rose in a cloud all around him. He wished he had some effective way of venting his anger, like maybe throttling Dave Hensch. How had Hensch expected him to get all the way to Georgia in a junk heap like this? No wonder the preppie hadn't wanted to drive it! Connor began to wonder if the kid and his snotty Stanford buddies were laughing it up, wondering where their patsy would be stranded. He walked around the Gremlin and kicked the tire as hard as he could.

Grumbling, Connor abandoned the dead car and hiked along the side of the road. One car honked at him, and he flipped a finger in response. He headed back toward the last exit, trying to figure out how to find some other form of transportation.

TWENTY

WHITE RABBIT

Iris Shikozu's lab at Stanford was like any other research lab, set up to fit the eccentricities of the lead scientist, without regard to how bewildering it might be to anyone else. Iris felt right at home; she knew where everything was, and didn't care whether anyone else could find it.

Like a rat making its way through a high-tech maze, she moved past PCR systems, sequencers, film readers, an electrophoresis setup, log books, and image analyzers. The air seemed flat as she breathed it, the dulling metallic and plastic smells of new equipment mixed with old.

The lab's stereo system played a live comeback CD from the rock group Kansas. Her colleagues couldn't figure out how she could concentrate with the stereo blaring, but the cheering audience and the music charged her with energy. She loved concerts. Competing with the music, a diffusion pump chugged as it kept the microbe-containment vessels at low pressure; cryogenic pumps at the far end of the room added to the background noise.

Holding a Styrofoam cup of potent black coffee, Iris stood in front of a whiteboard that ran the length of one wall. Chemical-rate equations were scribbled in blue, green, and black dry-erase marker. Some of the reactions were circled in red; some had exclamation points. A Polaroid camera sat on top of a filing cabinet; several instant photos balanced on the marker tray, recording important equations that had once been scribbled on the board. Iris rarely took the time to copy her work into a lab notebook; the Polaroids were faster.

Pacing, she studied the symbols, tapping her fingers against the desktop with the music. She needed to understand why her predictions based on the control sample of Kramer's Prometheus organism were so different from actual measurements out on the spill. The reaction rates equations circled in red were orders of magnitude too small. The tiny organisms were supercharged somehow, like the coffee that kick-started her brain. But Iris couldn't find the catalyst driving the little buggers. It worried her when she didn't understand something.

The Prometheus problem had sunk its claws into her, grabbing her focus so that she noticed little else. She took another sip of coffee, not caring that it was lukewarm. Iris had long since lost count of how many cups she had downed that morning.

She leaned back against a black laboratory table and tried to make sense of what she knew. She thought she understood how Prometheus worked. Prometheus had an appetite for octane—eight carbons and ten hydrogens in a straight chain—metabolizing it into water and carbon dioxide. But no organism would eat *only* one food, and with the myriad components of crude oil, the microbes should be munching shorter-chain hydrocarbons and some of the aromatic-ring molecules.

Since the spraying, multispectral imagery from high-flying NASA planes showed a marked decrease in oil density around the spill. Prometheus was metabolizing the spilled crude more than a hundred times faster than expected. TV and print journalists had begun running feature stories about Kramer's "miracle."

It pleased Oilstar to no end—but Prometheus wasn't supposed to be behaving that way.

Iris had taken samples from the surface of the spill where it had been treated with Prometheus. She detected plenty of carbon dioxide as waste product, as expected, but she also found substantial traces of sulfur dioxide and sulfuric acid.

Alex Kramer and Mitchell Stone had delivered the original control sample of microbes only last week. Kramer claimed the sample had remained in a cryogenic container for over a year. "The microbes we'll be spraying are identical, but one generation removed," Stone had assured her.

After running simple tests on the control, Iris established microbe reaction rates, temporal densities, and localized activity, everything neatly pigeonholed in its own statistical universe. Routine stuff, but she took pride in her work. All of her predictions for Prometheus had been grounded on this baseline.

Were these latest anomalies happening because she had somehow goofed up her initial test run? A screwup causing this much variance could cause a genetic laboratory to lose its license, and Iris knew she wasn't that sloppy. Her parents had imposed a rigorous work ethic and study regimen on her; Iris had hated it while growing up, but it had proved very useful once she got into Stanford. Now she was damned good at what she did, and she knew it. She had reviewed her work and found no errors—and so, logically, the problem must come from somewhere else.

The microbes Todd Severyn had sprayed on the oil spill just didn't match the baseline. Nowhere close. The rates were all wrong. And that, in her opinion, was impossible.

Unless she had been given a fake control sample.

Her insides twisted with a rush of cold uneasiness,

disbelief, and anger at being jerked around. Kramer did not seem the type to play practical jokes, nor did he seem so careless. She had read and admired some of his published papers on the Oilstar bioremediation work.

But a difference of this magnitude couldn't possibly be a mistake.

The only way she could tell the two organisms apart was through a genetic check. It was tough enough tracking down minuscule differences in genetic structure without a devoted team and dedicated equipment. She had tried to use Schaeffer's Autotrans 700 down the hall, but he had just upgraded his GeneWorks software and had not yet reconfigured the system. And she couldn't pay for an outside service, either, since the state Environmental Policy and Inspection department had frozen its support of her work with Oilstar and a dozen regulatory agencies in the middle of their legal battles.

Besides, if Prometheus cleaned up the *Zoroaster* spill much faster than expected—that was terrific, wasn't it?

Wasn't it?

Iris drained the rest of her coffee and turned from the whiteboard to pour herself another cup. On the stereo, Steve Walsh, the lead singer for Kansas, urged her to "Carry On."

She'd been in her teens when the *Exxon Valdez* had slathered the Alaskan coast with crude oil. Since then, certain microbial strains had been researched for various bioremediation applications, from plastic in landfills to toxic waste. Wall Street had seen enormous potential in startup bioremediation firms; even the White House had established a major initiative in biotechnology.

As she reached the bottom of her next cup of coffee, Iris started to feel a tingling buzz as her system became saturated with caffeine. Good. It helped her think.

Todd Severyn would have told her not to worry about the reaction rates. *It doesn't matter if everything fits with predictions, as long as it works!* She didn't know whether to scowl in annoyance or be amused at his ridiculous posturing. She couldn't decide what she disliked most, his defensive reaction to her or his straightforward naïveté.

But Todd had surprised her by bulldogging his way to get the spraying job done, and by sticking to his word even to the point of being arrested. It was a far cry from the whitewashing and polite lies that permeated faculty politics here at Stanford.

Iris found herself staring at the whiteboard. Turning, she poured the remainder of her coffee down a chemical disposal. Time to make a new pot.

The expected anomalies—the so-called "known unknowns" such as bacterial infection—were a cinch to account for because they had some kind of logical explanation.

But Prometheus had too many "unknown unknowns."

TWENTY-ONE

RUNNING ON EMPTY

For the first time since the spill, Jackson Harris woke from a sound sleep in his own bed, instead of in a sleeping bag on Angel Island. He blinked bleary eyes at the glowing green numbers on his digital clock on the nightstand next to his glass of water.

Daphne shook him awake again. "You're gonna miss your interview, Jackson!" She was already up and dressed. He never understood how he could have been crazy enough to marry a genuine morning person.

Jackson and Daphne Harris had returned from Angel Island to their house in Oakland to prepare for several media interviews about their volunteer work. His stunt with the oil-covered pelican at Oilstar's town meeting had been melodramatic, calculatedly so, but man did it make for great television! And there had been plenty of cameras to record it. No way did he mind media attention, not if it served the cause.

In an hour, he was scheduled to be interviewed in the San Francisco National Public Radio studio for their morning "Forum" show; then he would go to the KRON-TV studio to tape a human-interest spot for the evening news on Channel 4. TV stations liked Harris because he was actually doing something about his convictions, getting volunteers to work, putting his money where his mouth was. And these interviews worked like magic, stirring up donations to keep the brothers and sisters going.

As he crawled out of bed, Harris smelled coffee brewing, a rich aroma that smelled good enough to have wafted off a commercial. He listened to the morning city sounds of Oakland: the traffic, the neighbors, the radio that sounded too loud after days isolated on the island. He flinched with guilt, knowing his volunteers still had to make do with the primitive facilities available in the state park.

Harris was convinced that the Prometheus microbe had made progress. The oil had a rotten smell now, and the globs of crude were thicker, as if the lighter hydrocarbons had dissolved away. But the volunteers had not lessened their efforts. As a warm shower pounded his body, Harris stood in a daze. His body had never ached like this in his life.

In his years working with the Sierra Club and Greenpeace, or fighting for city funding dollars, Harris had become outspoken. He had learned how to talk in front of an audience, how to drop sound bites so the reporters would quote exactly what he wanted them to, how to get them to ask the right follow-up questions.

Daphne handed him a cup of coffee and turned up the stereo as Harris dressed in his interview clothes, one of the rare times he dragged the suit and the tie out of the back corner of the closet. He loved good music, but being at the mercy of the too-much-talk Top 40 radio stations on the boom box out on Angel Island had made him grumpy. Humming to a classic Jackson Browne song, he tried three times to knot the tie evenly; Daphne finally had to straighten it for him.

He took a sip of coffee, then glanced at his watch; he had to split. He considered taking the cup in the car, but he would probably spill it all over his shirt during the commute. He gulped the rest instead, kissed Daphne, then headed for the door. She raised her eyebrows and gave him a thumbs-up as she stood on the porch. As soon as he left, she would start making phone calls, hunting down additional supplies or volunteers.

Outside, the morning was brisk, clear. A faint tracing of dew highlighted dusty streaks on his windshield. He felt refreshed, ready to take on any interviewer. At another time he might have felt nervous, with the beginnings of stage fright in his gut, but the *Zoroaster* spill had made him so angry that he couldn't keep quiet.

Their home had a small yard and low property value, located too close to the BART mass-transit tracks—but it was home. He and Daphne had chosen to live there in the thick of things, among the people they wanted to help. The lawn was losing its battle against the thistles and weeds, which looked greener than the drying grass. A faint, sour odor of pesticide drifted over from his neighbor's lawn, but the other grass didn't look any better off. Gang graffiti was scrawled on some of the brick walls nearby, but street kids left him alone, especially since he had taken some of them on day trips out to state parks.

Normally, he would have taken BART into San Francisco, jostling and standing among all the other commuters, but neither the TV nor the radio station was close to the BART line; it would take him all morning if he worked his way through the labyrinth of MUNI bus service. Instead, he'd drive his own green Pinto station wagon, which had served him faithfully for 200,000 miles now.

When Harris sat behind the wheel, the springs creaked under him. He put the key into the ignition and tried to start the engine, but the Pinto groaned and coughed like a cat trying to spit up a furball. Something smelled rotten, worse than the burnt-rubber smell of the old vinyl seats. He frowned and twisted the key again. He hadn't been having any trouble with the car. The engine struggled, but would not turn over.

Harris slammed his palm on the steering wheel, eliciting a thin peep from the horn. He couldn't miss his interview. "Why today, of all days?" The car didn't answer. Daphne peeked out at him from the small kitchen window and ducked away. He tried the key once more, with no better luck. He looked at his watch again.

Harris ran inside the house. Daphne was already on the phone, trying to call emergency road service. The line was busy. She hung up and dialed again. Frustrated, Harris grabbed the thick Oakland telephone book and flipped to the yellow pages.

"I don't have time for this, baby," he told her.

"I know you don't."

She called one emergency service listing after another; most of the lines were busy. She mimicked one recording with a sarcastic, old-biddy voice, "Sorry, but all of our personnel are currently out on calls assisting other customers."

"What am I supposed to do?" Harris asked. "This is the dumbest excuse I ever heard of for missing a big interview! When was the last time we drove the car?"

"Yesterday. It sounded kind of ragged then."

"It always sounds ragged."

Daphne finally got through to the last place listed, but after she cocked her head and listened for a moment, she slammed the receiver down. "Fifteen names ahead of us," she said, "at least a two-hour wait."

"Why on Earth are all the emergency vehicles already out on calls? What the hell is going on?" Harris muttered.

Daphne waggled her finger at him. "Bitch about it later, Jackson. Right now you get your ass down to the BART station, then get a cab inside San Francisco."

"A cab! We can't afford that!"

"You can't afford to miss this interview either. This is important. Now go!" She swatted him on the butt as he sprinted out the door.

In his best clothes, Jackson Harris began to run toward the BART station.

TWENTY-TWO

COMMUNICATIONS BREAKDOWN

In the early-morning rush hour, Todd Severyn joined three million other people trying to stampede into the city, bumper to bumper. By now he hated downtown San Francisco and wanted desperately to be back in Wyoming.

His arraignment hearing was set for 10:00 A.M.

Crawling across the Bay Bridge, expensive foreign cars surrounded him, BMWs and Mercedes Benzes with conservative paint jobs, Porsches in blazing tasteless colors. They all kept a car length from Todd's heavy Ford pickup, which could squash them in a second. He rolled up the windows after choking down some of the noxious fumes. Toward the horizon, even the air had a gray-brown tinge.

Wearing new polyester slacks—bought for the impending arraignment—instead of his usual jeans, Todd was hot and uncomfortable. He hoped he would make a good impression; he had even polished his boots. He seemed to squeak when he moved, and he had nicked himself shaving.

He wasn't supposed to do anything but stand and look innocent—and get there on time. Oilstar's lawyers would handle the rest, but that didn't put him at ease. He'd never even met them.

Through gaps in the bridge guardrails, he caught glimpses of the glittering water underneath. Oil still shone on the surface, but it seemed sparse now, clumpier. Dozens of recovery boats dotted the black lake, nibbling at the perimeter. Alex's little Prometheus bugs seemed to be working.

The traffic inched ahead. Todd had the urge to pound his fist on the loud horn of his truck, but that would make him look as bad as the other city jerks. A charcoal-gray Mercedes in front of him belched bluish smoke from its diesel engine; in the car beside him he could see a woman squinting into her rearview mirror, applying makeup; behind him, a man read the newspaper while driving, casting an occasional glance at the road.

Todd leaned forward and turned up the radio. The country & western DJ spent more time jabbering than playing music. He wished the guy would just shut up and get on with the tunes.

"—unusually high number of breakdowns, making traffic on all Bay Area freeways a real mess. Two cars stalled or out of gas on the Golden Gate Bridge, one on the Bayshore Freeway, three on the San Mateo Bridge. Dumbarton's clear—so far. You cowhands must have had one rough weekend to forget to fill up your cars! The rest of you all, be prepared for a long ride into the city."

Finally, the DJ played a new Ray Stevens single, "The Wreck of the *Oilstar Zoroaster*" to the tune of an old Gordon Lightfoot song. Todd slapped the steering wheel and guffawed.

He glanced at his watch; in Wyoming it would have taken him less than twenty minutes to cover twice the distance. He tried not to let it get to him. Short of ramming the car up front, there was little he could do about it.

Another ten minutes passed before he moved far

enough ahead to see the amber, blue, and red lights of a
CHP cruiser. Three new vehicles cluttered the right-
hand lane: a wine-colored Lexus, a Honda Accord, and a
Mitsubishi Something-or-other. What the heck was going on here—nails in the road? A pileup? New cars
didn't just break down by themselves, all at the same
time. Smiling to himself, he muttered, "Next time, buy
American!"

Traffic muscled its way past, like an arm-wrestling
match between aggressive drivers. Todd moved his big
truck into the gap and gritted his teeth. Other cars
moved out of his way, and eventually traffic accelerated
to its normal hectic pace.

The confusing maze of exits off the bridge came up
soon, shooting streams of traffic in every direction like
silver balls in a pinball game. Todd got the panicky
sensation of not knowing where he was going, with too
many cars around him to forgive mistakes. He finally
spotted a green-and-white sign directing him to the Civic
Center turnoff, and he sighed in relief. He craned his
neck and noticed two other cars—a van and a VW
Beetle stalled on the exit ramp. Must be a good day for
towing services.

Once off the freeway, he began fighting stoplights,
crazy intersections, and idiots double-parked right in the
lanes of traffic. He kept glancing down at the folded map
on the passenger seat, trying to find his next turn, but he
could barely keep track of all the streets he passed. At
each forced stop, he rechecked his route. He looked at
his watch, a solid Timex he had owned for ten years,
helplessly watching the minutes tick away. Jeez, he
thought he had left himself plenty of time.

In one intersection, two business-suited men pushed a
car out of the street toward a gas station. Todd wondered
if everyone had gone wacko . . . or crazier than usual.
Maybe the fumes from the oil spill were causing brain
damage.

When he reached the courthouse, an imposing white

structure that looked exactly like a movie-lot version of a hall of justice, Todd found a place to park with surprisingly little difficulty. He wondered if part of the workforce had stayed home; was today one of those weird government holidays celebrated only by banks, post offices, and nobody else? He checked his Timex again; his hearing was scheduled to start in six minutes.

Todd and Alex had separate hearings, separate lawyers, all paid for by Oilstar. The Oilstar lawyers were probably pissing their pants right now waiting for him. Todd had no desire to show up late and be slapped with contempt charges. He slammed the door of his Ford and began jogging along the sidewalk to the large judicial building. His cowboy boots clomped on the concrete.

Inside, striding down an echoing courthouse hallway that had dozens of doors on each side, he turned the wrong way before he managed to locate the hearing chamber. People were lined up in the halls, arguing with various officials and guards. Some seemed incensed about sudden cancellations. Todd self-consciously combed his sweaty hair, swallowed, and hurried through the swinging door. When he stepped into the room, he paused, breathless and puzzled.

Bare beige walls, theaterlike seats, and pale wood accented the chamber. The judge's desk was empty, though, and even the lights were not fully turned up. Two security guards spoke in low tones at the front of the room; one wore a blue turban. An old man slouched in the back of the chamber, wearing a tan trenchcoat and working on a crossword puzzle.

"Where the heck is everybody?" Todd said. He remembered the ominous words in his arrest warrant: "Reckless endangerment of human life and property; illegal dispersal of a possible toxic substance; disregard for public safety." Had his hearing been canceled, or rescheduled? Why hadn't anybody let him know? Where were the Oilstar lawyers?

The guards looked up as he approached. "Can I help

you?" The blue-turbaned towel-head was dressed in a crisp brown uniform, a gold badge, and a nametag that read ORENIO.

"I'm here for the hearing. What's going on?"

Orenio shrugged. "A lot of cancellations this morning, sir. Didn't you see what is happening on the streets?"

"I thought you all would be used to traffic by now."

"Never been this bad, no," Orenio said. He looked Todd up and down, taking in the cowboy boots, polyester slacks, and bolo tie. "It is a mess out there."

Todd frowned. "What about my arraignment?"

"It will certainly be rescheduled. No judge. Where is your own lawyer, sir?"

Todd shook his head in bewilderment. "What a circus!"

Orenio nodded quickly, as if his chin were having a spasm. "Judge called from her car phone to cancel this morning's hearings—we have had a bulletin out for the past half hour on all stations. Something is very strange out there. Very strange."

The other guard rolled his eyes as if it were an old argument between them.

Todd wondered if he should fill out a form, leave some sort of record that he had come to the hearing, but the clerks at the windows were swamped, and he had no intention of waiting in line. He hated lines. He just wanted to leave. . . .

Back in his truck, Todd tried to navigate his way to the Bay Bridge as he drove, counting seconds until he could escape from the noise and the smell and the chaos. He had a splitting headache, and he wanted an ice-cold Coors. He passed a young dark-haired man parked in a loading zone, hunched over the steering wheel as he tried and tried to get the engine of his delivery truck to turn over.

Flicking on the radio, Todd caught a fragment of a sentence. The DJ was *still* talking! Someone had accused Oilstar—oh, brother!—of releasing a bad batch of gasoline that was causing all the cars to stall at once. He supposed that made a certain amount of paranoid sense, since people always wanted a handy, simplistic explanation for all the world's ills. Maybe ghosts or space aliens had contaminated the gas. Ever since the *Zoroaster* spill, Oilstar bashing had been a popular pastime for the media.

When the DJ kept talking, Todd switched off the radio and drove in silence toward the Oilstar refinery to check in.

TWENTY-THREE

CROSSROADS

The Manzano Mountains, at the northeastern end of the Kirtland Air Force Base, did little to block the desert wind. Behind the scrubby foothills on a conical volcanic rise, the 11.5-foot-diameter telescope was just a blob in the dust storm. Brigadier General Bayclock thought how ironic it was that they were trying to show off a far-seeing observatory, when they could barely see a hundred feet themselves. But the weather didn't see fit to cooperate with the general's orders.

On the mountaintop, Bayclock stood stiffly for the cameras, hating every second of the bullshit. No marching band, no sunshine—it was turning out to be a crummy ceremony. Albuquerque Mayor David Reinski and a Department of Energy rep, Lance Nedermyer, hovered behind him.

The star of the show was Speaker of the House Jeffrey Mayeaux, who had flown from Washington, D.C., to observe the ceremony, since technology transfer was one of the Speaker's pet projects. Mayeaux seemed to be in his element, not bothered by the weather and making the best of the cameras; his attitude impressed Bayclock.

The piss-poor visibility disappointed him. He had overhauled the base, working all personnel double-time to pick up every scrap of litter, straighten every bush, repaint every building, wax every floor for Mayeaux's visit—and this damned dust storm had ruined everything.

Mayeaux's comments for the cameras had sounded as if they were scripted. Bayclock had seen plenty of that rah-rah bullshit in print before. The Speaker somehow managed to shake hands with anyone who passed within striking distance. He smiled so much his teeth were probably getting sandblasted.

The tech-transfer ceremony at the air force telescope facility was over, and the dozen official participants, wearing dust-spattered uniforms and suits, shielded their faces. Nedermyer fiddled with a pair of clip-on sunglasses. Local reporters hung around like overgrown puppies.

"This way, Mr. Speaker," Bayclock said, gesturing toward the minivans that would shuttle them back to the headquarters building. Mayeaux was the highest level government official Bayclock had ever hosted at the base. The Speaker of the House wasn't directly responsible for Bayclock's orders, but reporters fell over themselves to follow the Louisiana politician like circus spectators. He let scandals wash over him as if they were silly challenges.

Lance Nedermyer stood between Bayclock and Mayeaux, looking out of place in his dark suit and wing-tipped shoes. His tie flapped in the wind. He raised his voice much louder than necessary. "The new-technology telescope will be an indispensable part of our research down at White Sands tracking the smallsats with the University of New Mexico. I apologize that the project director, Dr. Lockwood, couldn't make the ceremony. Apparently he had other priorities."

The tracking and logistical support for the solar-power receiving station down at White Sands fell under Nedermyer's purview. *Scientists and jerkoffs,* Bayclock thought, *all talk and big ideas and never anything tangible to show for it.* "The Air Force is also cooperating fully in this venture," Bayclock added.

"Yes," Mayeaux said, turning a shrewd glance toward Bayclock. "I was very interested to read about that in the briefing materials, along with some of the top-notch defense work you're doing here at the base. Your people are concentrating on directed-energy technology now, General? I was most impressed to read about that drone plane you shot down in the 1970s."

Bayclock tried to hide his embarrassment. Mayeaux must have flipped through the briefing materials and memorized an item or two just so he could drop appropriate comments in conversation. Bayclock wished he had picked a different example, though. Long before Kirtland had been put under his command, propellerheads at the base's research arm had tested a laser to shoot down aircraft—and decades later he still didn't have a working laser weapon in any of his planes.

"Uh, yes sir," Bayclock said. "We're developing another laser to fit in an aircraft that can fly above most of the atmosphere and destroy ballistic missiles. We're also researching high-power microwaves. They held an interesting test the other day." *And damn near shot down a fuel-tanker airplane.* "We've even got a bunch of doomettes working on Star Trek-style plasma weapons —compact toroids, they call them."

Nedermyer bent closer as he pushed into the conversation. "Uh, bear in mind, though, Mr. Speaker, that the R-and-D phase of new concepts is sometimes rather prolonged."

Bayclock himself held no hope that the Buck Rogers weapons would work within the next fifty years, but he didn't say that. He couldn't get excited about anything he wasn't able to strap onto an F-22 today.

Mayeaux nodded. "Even though results sometimes seem a long time forthcoming, we must continue to invest in basic research for our own survival as a nation." He smiled and shook Bayclock's hand with a grip that was as firm and dry as an adobe brick. Impressive. Bayclock's previous experience with career politicians had been that their handshakes were sweaty and slimy, and the lack of pressure was equaled only by their lack of trustworthiness. Mayeaux wasn't afraid to meet his gaze.

"Without fundamental weapons research, we wouldn't have even a breech-loaded rifle, not to mention the latest high-tech weapons. Our jet fighters are the best in the world, thanks to scientists like yours pushing the envelope. Let them know we appreciate it."

Bayclock narrowed his eyes as he grudgingly considered the point. Without the techno-nerds, Bayclock himself would never have been able to pull a fighter into a nine-gee turn, to keep a bandit in his sights with a night infrared tracker/pointer, and pull off a supersonic air-to-air kill. That was worth something, wasn't it? Every man had his job to do; as much as he hated to admit it, Bayclock had no problem with that.

Mayor David Reinski accompanied them to the waiting shuttle van. He had come ostensibly to represent the University of New Mexico, but he seemed cowed by the Speaker's presence. Nedermyer, on the other hand, couldn't stop talking. As they climbed into the back of the minivan, Nedermyer took off his glasses and brushed his florid face. His lacquered hair stuck out in stiff chunks from the whipping wind. His midriff had started to go to fat, probably from baby-sitting too many desks. The driver, a young Hispanic lieutenant, slid the van's heavy door shut with a thump. The sudden silence sounded loud in Bayclock's ears.

"Glad that's over," Mayeaux said with a smile. "I've enjoyed visiting your facility, General, but you can keep your desert wind. I'm getting on a plane to San Diego instead. I've requested the naval-base commander there to arrange for pleasant weather, along with a little New Orleans–style hospitality."

They all chuckled. The armed forces often provided free flights to high-level government types for on-site "research," if they agreed to stop by the bases for a bit of PR. Bayclock said, "Too bad your family couldn't come with you, Mr. Speaker."

Mayeaux shrugged. "Damn shame, isn't it? They're spending some time back home. My wife keeps herself so busy with social causes she rarely gets a chance to accompany me." They buckled their seat belts as the lieutenant swung up into the driver's seat. The wind rattled the windows.

Mayeaux turned to Nedermyer. "From what I've heard, that solar-power experiment at White Sands could have a big impact. My staff tells me this Lockwood fellow is quite the miracle worker."

Nedermyer smiled tightly. "Don't believe everything your staff tells you, Mr. Speaker. Between the microwave farm and the railgun satellite launcher at White Sands, DOE has some hard funding decisions to make. You of all people know we can't throw money at everything."

Bayclock raised an eyebrow. A DOE person who was not afraid to speak his mind? He nodded to himself, making a mental note. "I've received orders from high up to logistically support the White Sands operation. It seems to have top priority."

Now Nedermyer turned to him. "People and priorities change, General." Bayclock wondered what Nedermyer's private agenda might be.

"We all have our own priorities, gentlemen," Mayeaux said in a voice as smooth and hard and cold as polished granite. "And now that we've met, I think we'll be able to work well together in the future . . . whatever might come up."

TWENTY-FOUR

WE MAY NEVER PASS
THIS WAY AGAIN

After driving for hours in the rental Mazda, Spencer Lockwood passed the bleak, low hills rimming the Central Valley and headed east into oil country. The arrow-straight roads across the flatlands reminded him of rural farm lanes, with crops on either side and clods of mud on the pavement left behind by lumbering farm machinery. He kept the air conditioning turned up high, rolling up the windows to seal out the thick farm smells.

Spencer grabbed a fast-food hamburger in Bakersfield for a late dinner, then checked into the least expensive room he could find. He didn't care about TV or telephones or adult movies. He flipped through the yellowed Gideon material in the nightstand drawer and went to bed early, stretching out on the lumpy mattress, listening to the rise and fall of traffic noises outside, and feeling tension drain from him as he let his mind wander. He had wanted the road trip to think, and so he concentrated on what next to do with his project, now that his Sandia excursion had failed miserably.

Twenty more completed solar-power smallsats sat in storage at the Jet Propulsion Lab in Pasadena. Scheduling their launch aboard one of the shuttle flights had always been problematic, as was using a Delta Clipper or even one of the Pegasus rockets.

Sandia's prototype railgun on Oscura Peak seemed a viable alternative for launching smallsats, but the rails needed to be extended so the satellite could reach a proper orbit. Unlike delicate space probes or megachannel communications satellites, the smallsats were simple energy collectors with microwave transmitters. They could withstand the huge acceleration of an electromagnetic catapult. Perhaps the railgun people would be interested in teaming up for a test case, once they upgraded their equipment; but that might take years.

He finally drifted off to sleep without coming up with any new ideas.

Spencer woke up refreshed, though a bit stiff. Unfolding the road map of California, he saw that it wouldn't take him much out of his way to cut through Death Valley National Monument—a place he had always wanted to see. He would never make the trip otherwise, and he'd always resent never taking the time if he skipped it now. "What the heck," he said, "I'm doing the rest of this road trip on impulse."

He made a quick call to Rita Fellenstein to inform her he was going to be a little later than he thought; she knew better than to bring up any business and just left him alone.

The previous night had been chilly, and the white Mazda chugged and grunted as he tried to start it. When the engine finally caught, Spencer sniffed a sulfurous odor, muttered to himself about the "Bakersfield stench," then drove off.

He wound past grassy hummocks studded with an arsenal of oil pumps toiling away. The road plunged through Kern Canyon, sheer cliffs covered with wild-flowers rising on either side. The river boiling with spring thaw and the rugged rocks made for spectacular scenery, but horrific driving conditions. Other trucks and cars took the curves wide, usually not bothering to check if someone might be in the oncoming lane. He hugged the cliff wall as he drove, sitting bolt upright.

Despite the challenging road, Spencer found his thoughts returning to his high-school days when a girl named Sandy—an odd name, considering that her hair was coal black—had taken the bright nerdy kid under her wing as a social-welfare project.

Sandy was the older sister of one of Spencer's equally nerdy buddies. She talked Spencer into trading his black-rimmed glasses for hard contact lenses. She convinced him to go to a hairstylist to get his hair cut, rather than having his mother do it. She ruthlessly went through his closet like a guard weeding out prisoners; she paid no attention to his protests as she tossed out threadbare plaid shirts he had worn since junior high, corduroy pants that rode too high above his ankles, shirts with pen-stained pockets—and then she took him shopping.

Spencer rapidly developed a crush on Sandy, but she had no romantic interest in her "project"; she just wanted to see if she could turn an ugly duckling into a swan. He was content to wait, knowing that someday that special girl would come into his life. Newly charged with self-confidence, he entered college as a different person. From that point on, he had Sandy to thank for his success in life as much as his mentor Dr. Seth Mansfield. Now, if he could just find the girl with the sunburned nose. . . .

After about an hour of mountain driving, Spencer approached a gas station with a house trailer behind it. A sign at the side of the road announced DICK MORGRET'S LAST CHANCE GAS STATION. He glanced at his fuel gauge, surprised to see he had only about a quarter of a tank left. He had filled up in Bakersfield the night before, and he had been traveling only a few hours. "Stupid rental car!" he muttered. Or had someone siphoned his tank?

He decelerated swiftly and pulled into the station's gravel drive. A breeze kicked up dust, obscuring a Marlboro sign rocking back and forth on metal feet. The place looked abandoned, but as soon as Spencer stopped the car, the plywood door of the house trailer creaked open, and an old man in coveralls clunked down the metal steps. The man—Morgret himself?—raised a hand in greeting, then picked up a bucket and squeegee next to the cigarette sign.

Spencer glanced at the pumps, saw no SELF-SERVE sign, and waited for the old man to come over. He popped the gas tank.

"Morning," Morgret said. "Fill her up? Or are you just one of those piss-heads wanting directions?"

Spencer couldn't keep himself from laughing. "No, give me all the gas you can fit in the tank."

Morgret grinned again, exposing brown teeth. "For that, you get your windshield washed. You're going to have plenty of bugs splattered across it once you get down to the desert. It's butterfly season, and the air is full of them."

Morgret yanked the hose from the pump and slid the metal nozzle into Spencer's gas tank. His weathered face puckered up at the rotten smell. "What you got in there, son?"

Spencer shrugged, distracted by the surrounding mountains and the isolation. "It's a rental car." Horses ambled across a scrubby clearing in the distance, and he wondered if it was a wild herd. He hadn't had a chance to look at the scenery without risking driving off a cliff. "Is this really the last gas station before you get out of the mountains?"

Morgret chuckled. "Nah, there's another one twenty miles down the road, before you hit Highway 395. The sign makes for good business, though."

"I bet."

Morgret left the pump while he grabbed the dripping squeegee and slathered the windshield. "Nobody reads close enough. Sign says *Dick Morgret's* Last Chance.

This station is *my* last chance—I got nothing but this house trailer, squatter's rights on this land, and a pretty damn shaky line of credit with the oil company. If this place goes belly-up, I might as well do the same." He finished the windshield, then went back to squirt a few more cents into the tank to round out the dollar. "Twenty-one bucks."

As Spencer paid him, Morgret said, "You get that car checked, you hear? Don't like that funny smell. Something's wrong with your catalytic converter, I bet."

Spencer nodded. "I'll report it when I turn in the car."

As he drove off, Spencer saw the old man sniff the nozzle on his pump, then shuffle back toward his house trailer.

Only a few hours later, Spencer stared at the gas gauge in disbelief, then managed to work the dying Mazda Protege off the road to the gravelly shoulder. For the last ten miles the rental car had sounded like it was gargling gasoline. He wondered if there was a slow leak in the gas tank.

Feeling as desolate as the landscape around him, Spencer opened the car door and stepped out onto the road, shading his eyes against the afternoon sun.

It was the worst place in the world for a car to break down.

He had driven out of the Sierra Nevadas into the expanse of the Mojave Desert, past forests of gnarly Joshua trees. Some of the towns on his map were no more than rusty signs, boarded-up houses, and abandoned motels.

The car expired as he reached the intersection of Highway 136, coming from the Lone Pine Indian Reservation. The two roads met at a stop sign, but Spencer could not imagine two vehicles being on the road at the same time. He was totally alone.

He stood beside the open car door and peered into the distance. Nothing. The surrounding stillness swallowed all other background noise. He saw the volcanic Inyo

Mountains in front of him. Swirls of caustic white powder whipped up into dust devils from breezes over the dry lake bed to his left. He saw no blade of grass, no living thing other than a few mesquite bushes and cactus.

And he was stranded there. Spencer hoped someone would come by sooner or later. He listened to the wind. He popped the hood, listening to the faint sounds of gurgling and wheezing in the engine. The Mazda was a rental car, after all, but he could see nothing obviously wrong, no snapped belts, no loose hoses. The radiator had not overheated. The rotten-egg smell clung to everything, but he could not imagine where it came from. He sighed, feeling his stomach churn. This was supposed to be a relaxing trip, a way to get away from it all. Perhaps he had gotten too far away from it all. . . .

Ten minutes later, he was decidedly uneasy. Still no cars. Could people die out here because their cars broke down? Chances of a highway patrol cruising this section of road seemed slim. He realized with a sinking feeling that Rita Fellenstein had only a vague idea where he was. How long would it be before anybody started searching for him? Or would they?

He suddenly felt thirsty. There was no place for shade, and he did not want to leave his car. He had to stay there, just in case somebody came.

Just in case.

Fifteen minutes more. His shirt clung to him. How long would he wait? The desert silence was maddening.

Finally Spencer heard a throbbing in the air, a distant hum, and he snapped to alertness. He wondered if it might just be a plane flying overhead. He squinted down the road, watching the liquid heat make the air ripple over the blacktop like gasoline fumes rising from a tank. In the clear, empty air, Spencer heard the engine much sooner than he made out the shape of the approaching vehicle. As soon as he could discern a Jeep clipping toward him at ninety miles an hour, Spencer stood in the middle of the road waving his hands.

What if the driver passed him by? Spencer didn't usually stop to help people with car trouble. He redoubled his efforts and shouted, "Hey!"

The pitch of the oncoming engine changed as the driver downshifted. Spencer stepped back to his car, trying to figure out what to say.

His rescuer drove a black Jeep jacked up for high clearance and off-road driving. The Jeep slewed in a partial doughnut, spraying sand and gravel from the road shoulder as it stopped. The canvas top flapped from a loose snap, showing tools, a cooler, and rumpled clothes tossed in the back. Spencer walked toward the Jeep as the driver's door popped open.

The young man's face was sunburned. The size of a football player, he looked clean-cut and friendly. He wore tattered jeans, a T-shirt with NAVY emblazoned on the front, and a broad grin. "Boy, lousy place for a car to break down."

"You're telling me!" Spencer said. "Could you lend me a hand? I think I've got a leak in the gas tank—I just filled up a couple hours ago, but I'm on empty already. You don't happen to have a spare can with you, do you? A gallon or two would get me to another town where I can dump this hunk of junk."

"Take more than a gallon to get to a town where you can trade in a rental car." He stuck out his hand. "I'm Bobby Carron. I don't have a spare gas can, but I do have a hose. We could siphon some of my gas into your tank. That should get you to Lone Pine, about twenty miles back on 136."

"All I need is a phone."

"Then that'll do ya. Ridgecrest is where I'm heading, China Lake Naval Weapons Center. A lot bigger city, but that'll take you an hour. If you got a leaky gas tank, I wouldn't chance it."

Bobby Carron rummaged around in the back of his Jeep, finally pulling out a length of narrow hose. "I do a lot of off-roading in this puppy. Need to be prepared for most anything."

From the dust and caked mud on the sides of the Jeep, Spencer could imagine some of the places Bobby Carron might have taken his vehicle. "Anything I can do to help?" asked Spencer.

"Yeah, pop your gas tank," Bobby said, sliding one end of the hose into his own tank. He got down on his knees, put the end of the tube in his mouth and sucked, puckering his cheeks as he drew gasoline out of his tank.

When fuel finally gushed out, Bobby grimaced and spat, then jammed the other end of the hose into Spencer's tank. The spoiled reek drifted out of the rental car's gas tank. "Problems with the catalytic converter, I think," Spencer said, repeating Dick Morgret's diagnosis.

Bobby sniffed. "I smell like that myself when I've had too much Mexican food."

Bobby let a few gallons flow into Spencer's car, then pulled out the hose, letting the gas trickle back into his Jeep's tank. "That should take you far enough to get some decent help. Sorry I couldn't do more, but I gotta get back to the base."

"You're a lifesaver, Bobby. Thanks a million!"

Bobby made a dismissive gesture. "No problem. Glad to be of service." He rolled up the hose and tossed it in the back of his Jeep. "Let's prime your carburetor so you can get going."

Spencer let Bobby tinker under the hood for a few moments. "All right, try it!" Bobby said.

Spencer started the car, heaving a sigh of relief to hear the engine rumbling. If his tank did indeed have a leak, he would lead-foot it to the next town. He'd had enough of this supposedly relaxing side trip. It was time to call an end to this vacation, and just get himself back to White Sands.

Bobby Carron honked the Jeep's horn as he spun around, then peeled off on the desert highway toward the China Lake Naval Base.

TWENTY-FIVE

THE SONG REMAINS THE SAME

The coffee at Stanford's Tressider Union wasn't any better than the stuff from Iris Shikozu's own pot—but sometimes she just had to get out of the lab, smell the morning air, and watch the other students going about their business.

When she had only light teaching duties to muddle her postdoc work, she took a break each morning to sit under one of the red-and-white umbrellas at Tressider, sipping coffee as she read the student paper. But today she took a large cup to go and tucked a copy of the paper under her arm.

A shocking picture of a scrawny, grime-smeared black man holding an oil-smothered pelican dominated the front. An old photo of herself, oversized glasses and all, appeared in the lower right-hand corner. The article said that Stanford researcher Iris Shikozu had overseen the Prometheus spraying. The reporter made Iris out to be a patsy for the big oil company, while Todd Severyn and Alex Kramer, not to mention Oilstar management, were the bad guys. Some students, irate at her involvement, had made crank phone calls to her lab, but Iris just snapped back at them.

On the kiosks she had seen flyers announcing a rally against Oilstar that morning, but the turnout of protesters was much lighter than Iris expected—only a few people waving banners and attempting to pass out leaflets to other students, who had no interest. Their noise seemed insignificant in the laid-back flow of students in the mall.

Stanford hadn't experienced a real protest in years, but she thought that frustration over the *Zoroaster* spill would have brought the demonstrators out screaming. Maybe everyone wanted to see if Prometheus worked before they complained—and although thick crude continued to gurgle from the sunken tanker, the spreading slick was shrinking measurably.

A few people claimed a connection between Prometheus and the rash of car breakdowns supposedly caused by a "bad batch" of gasoline from the Oilstar refinery. To disprove those rumors, Iris herself agreed to perform a quickie analysis for one of the TV stations looking for a scoop, just to prove that the two couldn't be linked. She had even shipped blind samples via overnight mail to a few of her colleagues.

Now, as she took her Styrofoam cup of coffee and made her way across campus, dodging bicyclists and skateboarders, Iris barely noticed the groups of students playing tag football, Frisbee, or just lazing in the sun. By the time she returned to her lab, the combustion-product spectrograph analysis of the bad gasoline would be complete.

The door to her lab was unlocked. Refilling her cup from the coffeepot at the table, Iris listened to the answering machine. After a message from the TV station querying about her analysis, Todd Severyn's twangy voice came on, stuttering in an attempt to ask her to return the call. She smiled. It must have been hard for the old cowboy to ask her to do that. *I wonder what he'd be like in bed. . . .*

Sipping the coffee, Iris strode around the gas chromatograph hooked up to the experimental chamber, then slid into the chair and tapped on the keyboard. This would prove once and for all that there was no connection between the breakdowns and Prometheus.

A long string of numbers appeared, highlighting an array of expected parameters. Frowning, Iris clicked on an additional data file and compared the two in silence. It didn't make any sense.

She put down her cup, intently watching the screen. The jagged trace of a spectrograph jittered across the monitor, exactly matching the first.

She ran back her analysis of the Prometheus microbe eating the spilled oil and a sample she had obtained of the supposedly bad gasoline.

No difference.

The Prometheus microbe had infected the gas tanks in the cars that had broken down.

They can't *be the same!* she thought. There was no vector. How did the microbe find its way into the gas tanks?

Her hands shook as she ran through her computerized Rolodex to find Kramer's number at Oilstar. First the Prometheus reaction rates were drastically different from what she had observed with her control specimen. Now the organism seemed to have gotten into automobile gas tanks. Had it found a way to go airborne? Before giving her unofficial OK to the spraying operations, Iris had run numerous tests on the control sample—none of this should have been possible.

Unless Kramer had used two different microbes: one for her initial tests, and a more voracious one to be sprayed onto the Bay . . . where it would cause all sorts of havoc.

After six rings, a computerized voice instructed her to leave a voice-mail message for Dr. Kramer. She hung up and tried again. Who could she call if Alex wasn't around? She tried to remember—there was that jerk at the party . . . what was his name, Mitchell Stone? She dialed again, asking the Oilstar operator to connect her. Iris waited impatiently for him to answer, then finally slammed the phone down.

Damn! She brushed her black hair with a quick swipe and reached for her coffee. Draining the dregs, she paced, thinking of Mitch Stone, then Kramer's party . . . then Todd Severyn.

It *would* be an excuse to call him. Otherwise, that Wyoming cowboy would keep bugging her until she went out with him, saying "ma'am" and "aww, shucks" every chance he got. Normally, she wouldn't allow herself to be distracted by personal affairs, but there was something about him . . . was it his honesty that attracted her to him, or his naïveté?

She decided to wait before calling Todd to see if he knew how to reach Alex Kramer. She would recheck her work. First order of business. Drawing in a breath, she turned back to the spectrometer. She vowed to watch over every incubation period, recheck every procedure until things turned out right.

Things didn't turn out right.

Iris watched the screen, at a loss for words. Being overly meticulous, she had taken three hours to go through the two-hour checklist. In the meantime she placed cautious calls to the labs where she had Fed-Exed blind samples the day before. Her colleagues confirmed her analysis, but she gave them no details.

Kramer's microbes were breaking down the oil spill, and now they were in the gas tanks. Eating gasoline.

Another quick call to Oilstar confirmed that Kramer was still out. Frustrated, she hung up the phone just in time to have it ring again, startling her. She grabbed the receiver, but it was only the TV news crew bugging her about the analysis. She put them off by using multisyllable technical jargon and saying she needed to recalibrate her results. If she talked now, she would send them into a panic!

Her mind started to reel with the implications of what she had discovered.

No use putting it off anymore; Todd might know how to reach Kramer. Plus, he probably had more common sense than most Oilstar people. Or anyone else, for that matter. She tapped the black lab table for a moment, then returned to the phone.

Rewinding her answering machine, she listened to the message again and dialed Todd's number.

TWENTY-SIX

FREE RIDE

Just off the exit ramp Connor Brooks could see the colored lights of BP, Union 76, Shell, Chevron, Texaco, and Oilstar gas stations. If Connor was going to rip anybody off, he decided it should be Oilstar. No question about it. They had already done enough to him.

He had hiked in the breakdown lane from the dead hulk of the lavender Gremlin as traffic whooshed past. Though it was ten o'clock at night, cars pulled in and out of the gas stations clustered at the exit-ramp oasis in a steady stream.

He glanced at the cars at the pumps, but did not see what he was looking for, nothing he could use. The tile-roofed station looked too quaint to be real. He went inside the Star-Shoppe convenience store and, using some of the money Dave Hensch had given him, bought one of the three-foot-long ropes of jalapeño beef jerky. The overweight clod running the cash register looked about as interested in his job as an army doctor checking a thousand new recruits for hernias. All the better,

Connor thought. Then he went out to stand at the pay phone.

Connor chewed on his beef jerky, picked up the phone, and pretended to talk into it as he watched the cars come and go.

A mustard-yellow Volkswagen bus, a silver Honda, a red Nissan pickup, a Chevy, another Honda, a Toyota, a big black Caddy, a rusty pickup piled high with old furniture and cardboard boxes, a low-rider El Camino, three Winnebago campers in a convoy. He saw college students in the cars, families with kids, Grandma and Grandpa with a poodle barking behind a rolled-up window, a group of college girls coming back from a skiing trip.

But Connor saw no opportunities. Still, shit would happen, if he waited long enough.

He hung up the phone, walked around the building, then went back to his vigil. He had eaten all but four inches of his beef jerky by the time he made his move.

An ancient station wagon with fake wood sidewalls pulled up; it had only one man inside. The driver opened the door and clambered out, dressed in old jeans and a plaid flannel shirt, needing a shave, and stumbling as if he had been driving for the last four years without a break. Like a horse with blinders on, the gangly man headed for the rest room. He left the station wagon's lights on, the engine running. Perfect.

Connor strode toward the car. Hesitation only wasted time.

By the time the driver had slipped through the battered gray door of the men's room, Connor had reached the station wagon. Not the type of vehicle he would have preferred, but he wasn't picky.

He opened the driver's door and slid inside. Connor's heart pounded. No one had seen anything yet. Maybe this would teach the jerk to be more careful next time.

The seats were worn, and the interior smelled like burned garbage. The ashtray overflowed with crushed-out cigarillo tips. Connor scowled. Slob! But he didn't care, as long as the car could take him to Flagstaff, Arizona. He adjusted the seat, gunned the engine, then put the station wagon into gear. "Ready or not, here I come!"

Just as the station wagon started moving, the gangly driver walked out of the rest room. He stopped for a moment, as if astonished to see someone stealing his car. Then he jumped in front of the station wagon, waving his hands for Connor to stop.

What? Does he think I'm stupid?

Connor jammed the gearshift into reverse and lurched away from the driver. The man had stringy black hair, dripping wet, as if he had just gone in to splash cold water on his face. His flannel shirt hung unbuttoned over a grimy T-shirt, flapping like wings as he flailed his arms.

Before Connor could put the car into gear again and drive in the other direction, the driver snatched at the door handle. "Asshole! Get outta my car!"

Connor used his elbow to shove down the door lock, then reached behind him to lock the back and the passenger side doors. The driver shouted, pounding on the windows, yelling for help.

Connor gunned the engine again and began to move. People turned and stared at the scene. For God's sake, Connor thought, did the whole world get extra points for causing him trouble?

The driver threw himself in front of the car, hammering his fists on the hood. Connor tried to swerve, but in a split instant he realized that even if he did get away, the driver would call the police, give the license number of his car, a description of the thief—and the highway patrol would be crawling all over the interstate looking for him in no time. What a mess!

It would be better if this guy couldn't say anything coherent for a while, Connor thought. Just a little while.

Without spending a lot of time checking it out with his conscience, Connor yanked the steering wheel to the side and brought the station wagon around into the shouting driver. Beside the gas pumps stood a black oil drum with a plastic liner. Connor swerved to knock the man into the trash barrel.

He didn't notice the concrete support pillars holding the barrel in place. The station wagon crushed the driver into the barrel and then the reinforced concrete pillar. Instead of toppling the trash can out of the way, the car smashed the man with a loud, sickening crunch. The front bumper of the station wagon struck him at the hips, ramming into the unyielding cement. The oil drum buckled.

A flower of blood burst out of the driver's mouth, accompanied by a scream that Connor barely heard. He pulled the shift into reverse, backing the car away.

The man fell to the pavement. The crumpled oil drum rolled on top of him. Other gas station customers began shouting, running toward him.

"Oh, shit!" Connor said. "Why didn't you get out of the way?" If he stopped to help the crazy bastard, he'd be caught red-handed stealing the car. When the cops ran his ID check, they would find the outstanding *Zoroaster* charges. All because this jerk felt his crappy old station wagon was worth dying for? Of all the stupid things! *No thanks.*

The car's owner lay bunched against the gas pumps as two people bent over him. Blood streamed from his mouth and nose. The fat kid swaggered out of the Star-Shoppe to see what the fuss was about, then turned so pale his pimples faded.

"Forget this!" Connor said, then stomped on the accelerator pedal, spinning tires and squealing out of the parking lot.

He could get back on the Interstate, hook east on the 210, then north on I-5 to I-40, which would take him to Flagstaff. If he didn't stop, he could make it in six or seven hours.

It would take the cops an hour to figure out what had

gone down at the gas station, even longer if the driver wasn't in any condition to talk. Connor could sail right past them. And the highway patrol would expect him to try to vanish into the sprawl of Los Angeles, not head east to the state line.

Besides, it wasn't his fault.

Connor roared up the entrance ramp, flowing into the relentless stream of traffic. Behind him, the lights of the gas station oasis dwindled in the distance.

Now he was home free.

TWENTY-SEVEN

WORKING FOR A LIVING

In her small cubicle, surrounded by identical cubicles in the Flagstaff offices of Surety Insurance, Heather Dixon wondered why the receptionist kept forwarding calls to her. She stared at the pile of insurance claims on her desk. Even though she had worked one claim after another without taking a break all day, the stack of papers waiting to be processed grew two inches every hour.

She was working harder than an administrator. Funny they weren't willing to pay her for it.

She punched a button on the phone to pick up the call, then held the receiver between her shoulder and ear as she filed proof-of-loss forms. "Surety Insurance Company, may I help you?"

"I hope so," said the thin male voice on the line, "you're the eighth person I've been transferred to."

"Sorry, sir. We've been unusually busy, and—"

"I understand," the man said, at the ragged end of patience, "and I'm normally a laid-back person. But if you will just take my information and promise it'll be straightened out, we can both be done in a flash. Deal?" He had a no-nonsense voice that might have been pleasant if he hadn't been pushed to the edge.

"Yes, sir. Let's see what we can do."

"I've given my name a dozen times. Could you please punch it up on your computer? I'm Spencer Lockwood, spelled just like it sounds. I was driving my rental car, a Mazda Protege, and it broke down near Death Valley, California." He rattled off the words as if he had memorized them. "I couldn't get a replacement from the rental car company, so I was forced to rent another one on my own. Now that I'm back in New Mexico, I'm calling to ask if the emergency road service on my own policy will cover the new rental, because the rental company refuses to pay."

"How can they turn down a request like that?" she asked, scowling. "Did they give you any reason?"

Lockwood said, "They told me I should have just waited a day or so—by the side of the road, presumably —and they would have had a new car delivered to me. Since I refused to wait for them, they claim they're not obligated."

Heather sighed, then yanked her reddish-brown hair back behind her ears—one of the most unflattering ways she could wear it, but she was too harried to notice. The young college students manning the receptionist desks refused to deal with anything out of the ordinary, especially on a horrendously busy day like this. They input only the routine claims and let the computers bump the questionable ones higher in the system.

"You really should discuss this with your own agent," said Heather.

"My agent's been gone for a week, and I'd just as soon get this taken care of. I don't have time to chase down errors once they get lodged in your computer's brain."

Heather took down the pertinent data on a form. Lockwood was trying admirably to be nice, so she made an effort on his behalf. "All right, Mr. Lockwood. I'll do what I can. It'll take a week or so before you get confirmation of our discussion and Surety's decision, but I won't let it get lost in the shuffle. Promise."

"Thank you," Spencer said. "You deserve a promotion for this!" He laughed.

"Yes I do," she agreed, but she wasn't laughing.

She held on to Lockwood's form for a few moments, pondering where in the pile it should go. Suddenly, Albert "You can call me Al!" Sysco was there, slapping his palms on her desktop.

"So this is where the holdup is! Paperwork's piled on your desk, and you're sitting around daydreaming. Shake it, Heather!"

She wanted to take a baseball bat and "shake it" on his head. But she went back to work without voicing any of the retorts that popped into her head.

She sorted through the stack of papers. They would all need to be keyed into the computers before the claims could be processed, and Lockwood's form would have to be vetted by someone in authority, someone like Al Sysco. Heather glared at him as he stormed away; then she stamped APPROVED on Lockwood's claim.

Smiling, she filed it in the box of completed forms.

TWENTY-EIGHT

DAZED AND CONFUSED

When Todd reached Alex Kramer's office in Oilstar's bioremediation facility, he found the door locked. Yellow phone-message slips were taped to his door, one over another until they made a stack. Todd flipped through them. A note from Iris was on top; the bottom one was dated three days earlier. Two days after the victory party. He frowned. He could see why Iris couldn't track him down.

Most of the other offices seemed empty as well, as if Oilstar had declared an employee holiday. Mitch Stone's office also stood closed; a handwritten note was stuck with a red pushpin into the wall above his name plaque. WORKING AT HOME. CAR TROUBLE.

Around the Bay Area, cars were breaking down right and left—the "bad gasoline" from the Oilstar refinery had hit far too many vehicles, and now fingers were pointing at other area refineries, as well. A few people suspected deliberate sabotage of the gasoline output.

Frustrated, Todd got the division secretary to waddle down the hall and open Alex's office for him. Todd followed her, as if he could herd her into greater speed. "He called in sick a few days ago," she said. "Haven't seen him since."

Todd stared into a dark empty room. Concern gnawed at him. What if some radical protester like that Torgens guy decided to go after the scientist responsible for the Prometheus microbe?

Inside, the desk was neat, all the papers filed, as if Alex knew he wasn't coming back. A part of him expected to see sheets draped over the furniture. "You haven't heard from him since, when, Tuesday?"

The secretary shrugged. "I don't know, Mr. Severyn—we've got so many people out with the traffic snarls and breakdowns that I can't keep track. I'm not their mother, you know."

"Never mind." He opened his wallet and dug out Alex's unlisted phone number as he walked into the office. Picking up the desk phone, he asked out of the corner of his mouth, "What number do I use to dial out? Nine?"

"Eight."

He punched the number while the secretary watched him suspiciously.

Alex's phone rang, but no one answered; even the answering machine was disconnected. That was odd. Alex had not looked well after their wild horse ride. What if he was alone at home, too sick to answer the phone?

"You're sure he didn't call? Wouldn't somebody call in sick if they weren't going to come in for work?"

She sighed, pushing her lower lip out at him. A thin smear of lipstick had deposited itself on her teeth. "Usually, but a lot of these scientists live in a different universe. We had one guy who never managed to button his shirts right, and another one who had to be reminded to take lunch every day. They're on flex time. They work late into the night sometimes, and other times they don't come in at all. Especially with Dr. Kramer's . . . uh, personal problems, we don't see a lot of him."

Todd listened to ten hollow rings before hanging up.
Remembering the victory celebration, he recalled the
closed room filled with treasured pictures of lost family
members. Alex Kramer lived alone. No one else would
worry about him if Todd didn't check. Besides, he'd
promised Iris to see what he could find out. "I think I'm
going to drive over there."

Grabbing his cowboy hat, he waved it at the secretary,
said, "Er, thank you, ma'am," and clomped out of the
office, leaving her to lock up behind him.

Out in the parking lot, his own truck started right up. He
breathed a sigh of relief, then wound his way through the
cluttered, narrow roads inside the refinery. He drove
past the usual batch of yelling protesters, then headed
for the San Rafael Bridge and Marin County.

Todd had no problem until he got on the freeway.
Weaving past stalled vehicles—more than he had ever
seen before—he found that the far left lane was open.
Traffic crawled along, but at least it moved. He felt his
stomach rumble with anxiety and impatience, worried
about Alex but also growing more dismayed as he passed
a van hauling a motorboat stalled off to the side of the
road, then a motorcycle, then a Toyota, and finally a tow
truck itself abandoned in the breakdown lane. He turned
his head, preparing for the worst.

When Todd finally made his way through the hilly
backroads, he was relieved to see Alex's four-wheel-drive
pickup in the gravel drive. The brown Chevy sat parked
next to Alex's ranch house, which looked closed-up and
abandoned. Alex must be home—but why hadn't he
answered the phone? Could he be out riding one of the
horses?

Todd's truck bounced in the driveway as he pulled up.
Swinging down from the cab, he ambled to the door,
trying to look calm but growing more uneasy with each
step. He rang the doorbell. Nothing. He rang again and

shouted, "Hey, Alex, you in there?" Impatient, he tried the doorknob, then pounded on the door—still no answer. The grassy hills and nearby forest smothered all sound.

Muttering, he walked around back, his boots crunching in the dry grass. He heard neighing as he approached and smelled the bright, fresh odor of the stables. The two horses trotted to the fence as he approached. Todd held out a hand as the palomino, Ren, nuzzled him, looking for a sugar cube or a carrot. He noticed that the back corral gate was wide open, but the horses had remained next to the stable.

Todd scanned the backyard, then went to close the gate. The horses followed him like lonely puppies. "Hey, Alex!"

When no one answered, he ran a hand along Ren's neck. The crisp animal smell made him long for Wyoming. "Sorry, buddy. I'll get you some sugar later." He swung over the wooden fence and walked across the corral. The horses followed, even to the point of nudging Todd with their velvety noses. He half expected to see Alex come out of the stable, but the place was vacant. Worse yet, the feeding trough was empty. Ren whinnied.

"Hold on," said Todd. He slipped into the barn and returned with a rustling armload of hay, which he dumped into the trough. The dry, weedy scent clung to his shirt. Todd found the smell pleasant. The horses pushed toward the food and ignored him. As they munched, Todd rubbed the sweaty back of his neck.

Obviously the horses had not been fed for a day or two. No one had seen Alex since the party. Something terrible must have happened to make him neglect his horses. From what Todd had noticed on their ride, Alex doted on the animals.

Something must have happened to him.

Despite their empty smiles and bubbly "Have a nice day!" comments, Todd thought Californians were particularly callous to their neighbors. They never checked on each other or watched each other's homes, barely managing to wave when they went to get the mail. If some tragedy had happened to Alex, the other residents would turn a blind eye until somebody else took care of the problem.

Well, Todd wasn't from California, and in Wyoming people watched out for each other.

Todd strode to the rear of the house, around flower beds gone to weeds. A picnic table out back sat streaked with caked dust, and the blue-and-white overhead umbrella had been rolled down for some time. At the back door, he pulled open the screen and rattled the knob on the white-painted door, but it was locked solid with a deadbolt.

He didn't give much thought to calling for help. Who was Todd to file a missing-persons report anyway? He had spoken to Alex after the celebration, gone on a brief horse ride with him, but he could not claim to be a longtime friend. Did Alex *have* any longtime friends? The police would probably tell Todd to wait a few days, check back, maybe something would turn up.

But Todd kept imagining Alex unconscious or dead on the floor inside his house. He would rather pay for some broken glass than leave the microbiologist inside.

Besides, he could always apologize later.

Todd spotted the smallest window he could crawl through, the laundry room by the mudroom in the rear hall. He jiggled the window frame. It was locked, but loose.

He jogged back to his truck for the tool kit, rummaging and clanking around until he found a large wooden-handled screwdriver. Returning to the back window, working quickly but carefully, he jimmied the frame open without breaking the pane. He supposed that living in the country gave Alex a sense of security, enough that he didn't have sophisticated locks. On their ranch in Wyoming, Todd's parents rarely bothered to lock their doors.

Crawling through the window, he found himself in a clean hall back by the washer and dryer; he smelled the lingering perfume of laundry detergent, but saw no clothes in the plastic baskets piled on top of the dryer.

"Alex?" He hurried through the house, looking from side to side. All the lights were off, the curtains drawn, leaving the place in gloom. He kept expecting to find Alex crumpled on the floor, perhaps bleeding. Moving from room to room, he hastened his search. Nothing.

Alex's truck was here, the doors were locked, the horses had been left unfed for days, but they were both here. . . . Alex did not seem the type just to wander off.

Todd stood in the large living room next to the wet bar and looked out the bay windows in back. He debated saddling up one of the horses to go search the riding paths. What if Alex had gone out after dark, after Todd left, troubled by the horse ride and the conversation, the resurrected memories? In the dimness, Alex could have stumbled and broken his neck, or fallen into a ravine, or had a heart attack.

But the house seemed to be holding secrets, shadows hiding around corners. The air felt cool and sluggish around him, as if it had not been disturbed for some time.

A faint, gritty odor made him look at the fireplace, to see a rumpled pile of papers and ashes, a solid stack of lab notebooks with burned edges. The crisped, bubbled outline of a blue-and-gold Oilstar logo adorned one of the cardboard covers. He brushed aside the metal mesh screen. Black flakes of ash curled up from the consumed papers.

A gnawing sensation intensified at the pit of his stomach. On the phone Iris had told him she suspected something terribly wrong with the spread of Prometheus, but she wanted to talk to Alex before she raised any alarm. Why would Alex burn a pile of old notebooks, when he could just throw them away?

Unless he didn't want anybody to find them.

"Alex?" Todd called again, then swallowed a lump in his throat. His stomach fluttered, then sank as he grew more certain he would not find the microbiologist. At least not alive.

He walked down the narrow hall to the bedrooms, past the bathroom, which smelled of mildew and old soap. The floorboards creaked under his cowboy boots as he continued to the back rooms. The bed in the master bedroom was made, but the bedspread looked rumpled and the pillow dented, as if Alex had lain on it for a while before getting up and going somewhere else.

On the nightstand, next to a clear glass half full of water, lay a bulky old Smith & Wesson double-action revolver. Todd recognized it as one of the older models, 1930 or 1940, but it had been recently cleaned. He could smell the hard metallic aroma of the firearm.

Todd went cautiously to the bedside and picked up the weapon, wrapping his palm around the handle grip. The Smith & Wesson felt slick, but Todd realized it was his own sweat. He sniffed the barrel, but smelled no acrid gunpowder that would tell him it had been fired recently. He couldn't understand why Alex had taken the gun out, then left it lying around the house. Had he lost his nerve over something? Todd wet his lips.

When he turned back to the hall, Todd saw that the door to the other bedroom stood shut, as if closed against prying eyes. Todd gripped the cold doorknob and hesitated.

"Alex? Are you in there?" he said, then knocked lightly.

After a moment of silence, Todd took a deep breath, then pushed the door open slowly, expecting it to creak, afraid something might jump out at him.

The miniblinds had been drawn, leaving the muffled room awash in murky gray light. Before Todd's eyes could adjust, his nose caught a dry, sour smell of wrongness, the lingering pit-of-the-stomach twist of death, the stench of decaying flesh.

Alex sat on a padded kitchen chair in the middle of the room, slumped and motionless, as if gravity had slowly sagged him.

"Alex!" Todd said, then snapped out of his sluggish shock. He slapped the wall twice before he found the light switch. Sharp yellow illumination sent the shadows and gloom fleeing. "Awww, jeez, Alex!"

Todd took two steps forward and stopped. Alex Kramer rested in a rubbery position, as if his joints had turned liquid for a moment, then frozen into place with rigor mortis. His skin had the grayish, mottled appearance of someone who had been dead for a day or so.

His head was cocked forward on his neck, resting his chin and his neat peppery-gray beard against the base of his throat. His eyes were squeezed shut, surrounded with the cobwebs of wrinkles.

He wore comfortable clothes, faded jeans, a work shirt, no shoes, and grayish white socks. In his lap he clutched his folded eyeglasses in one hand. The other hand gripped a picture frame, turned facedown against his jeans.

Todd stepped forward, feeling clumsy like an intruder, but driven. He had just reached out for the picture frame when the pointed toe of his boot kicked something that rattled hollowly on the floor under the chair.

He bent over and picked up three dark-orange prescription pill bottles. Todd didn't recognize the names of the drugs, but they sounded like high-strength painkillers. Under a strip of yellowing cellophane tape, the date on one prescription label had expired five years before.

The pieces fell into place, rattling like bones in an empty cup. Todd pictured Alex taking out the revolver in the master bedroom, lying restless on the bed, agonizing over his decision to kill himself, and then eventually choosing another way, a method that was not so violent. But ultimately just as effective.

Todd stood on creaking knees, blinked his stinging eyes several times, and touched the picture frame in

Alex's lap. He lifted, then pried the photograph free of the dead man's grip. It showed a handsome woman, classy-looking, with short hair and subtle, careful make-up. She wore a secret smile that seemed to slide right past Todd, as if she had directed it at someone else.

"Why the heck did you have to do this, Alex?" Todd whispered, squeezing the brim of his cowboy hat in his left hand. "Nothing could have been that bad."

On the walls in the memorial bedroom, the other photographs, certificates, documents, seemed to hum with background noise, ghosts and memories, frozen moments that Alex had trapped in this room and had refused to set free. Now he had burned all his notes on Prometheus and gone to join his family.

Todd stood up, his head spinning, his body barely able to move. Finally, with one last glance at Alex, he went to find a phone so he could call the police, Oilstar, and Iris Shikozu.

TWENTY-NINE

FINAL COUNTDOWN

Iris Shikozu felt as if she were stuck on the *Titanic,* knowing it was doomed to sink but unable to do anything.

Aside from the muted chugging of the vacuum pumps and the air-conditioner in her lab, she heard no students out in the hall, no clicking of shoes as people walked by, not even the distant sound of a professor droning on in a lecture room. She hadn't even bothered to turn on the stereo, not since Todd had told her that he was going to Alex Kramer's house. She wished he would call, if for no other reason than to confirm what she had uncovered about Prometheus and the transportation breakdowns.

Genetic assays had proved that Prometheus was destroying gasoline as well as devouring the *Zoroaster* spill. And the actual microbe Alex Kramer had provided for the spraying operations was very different from the innocuous control sample he had given Iris for initial testing and verification.

Through Francis Plerry at Environmental Policy and

Inspection, Iris had urged a drastic crackdown on gasoline sales and transportation beyond the Bay Area, at least until they could determine how far the Prometheus organism had spread. But the governor had refused to take an action that might cause a panic.

Iris passed the word anyway, hoping someone would refute her results; but every one of her colleagues came up with the same answer. Several of the other researchers immediately saw the implications, and everyone started making phone calls.

Random samples of gasoline were infected with Prometheus hybrids. Unexplained breakdowns were reported across the state, and the contamination was spreading exponentially from gas tank to gas tank, filling station to filling station. On the news last night, Iris had seen a story about rashes of mechanical failures popping up in Chicago, Denver, and Dallas. It was a plague, plain and simple. *A petroleum plague.*

In a fit of panic, she went to the small lab sink next to the coffeepot and scrubbed her hands three times with a bar of harsh pumice soap. If this microbe metabolized octane so voraciously, it might eat the shorter-chain hydrocarbons in her own body. She looked over the instruments she had touched. The organism might start breaking down other polymers.

She grabbed her Styrofoam cup, dumped the cool brown dregs into the sink, and poured herself more steaming coffee, sipping it black as she fought to keep her hands from trembling.

The phone shrilled at her. Nearly spilling her coffee, she wove her way around the cluttered equipment and grabbed the phone on the third ring, breathless. "Hello?"

"Iris, this is Todd." He sounded too serious.

"Can I talk to Dr. Kramer? This is really important!" Todd hesitated. "He's dead."

"Dead?" She stopped, unsure of what to say. "How can he just drop dead and leave us with this mess?" Iris set her small mouth, then sat down in the creaking old office chair behind her desk. She knocked papers aside to clear a spot to rest her elbow. "Todd, you have no idea how serious this is! Kramer did something to his Prometheus—"

"I know. Alex burned his notes at home, then . . . he killed himself. Whatever he did, it's spreading like crazy! You should see all the cars breaking down on the roads. I thought he promised it couldn't become airborne."

"Right now," Iris said, a thick lump of panic rising in her throat, "I don't believe much of anything Dr. Kramer promised." Trying to remain calm, she picked up a pen and tapped it nervously on the surface of her government-surplus desk. "I'm pretty sure Prometheus is being spread from gas station to gas station. As a contaminated car fills up, it leaves some of the microbes on the nozzle. Everyone else who gets gas there picks up the infection."

Todd paused, as if digesting this information. "Holy cow! So what do you suggest we do?"

"Right now we need to quarantine the area, the whole state of California if necessary. And the faster we act, the sooner we can stop it from spreading. Cars can't run very long if their gas is infected, so that puts an upper limit on how far they can transport it. If we can get the police to close down the state borders—"

"What about airplanes, or ships?"

"Prometheus is fairly specific in only attacking octane," said Iris. "I've got to go, there's too much to do, too many people to contact. This is going to be rough."

Todd was silent for a moment. "I'm at Alex's place, and I've got to wait for the police and the coroner. I think . . . I think he's been planning this. He asked me to take care of his horses a few days ago." He hesitated. "How else do you need me to help?"

Her mind raced ahead, prioritizing which agencies to contact. She found her hands shaking—with excitement, or fear? She had too many things to do. "Uh, I have to get through to Oilstar management. There's really no one I can depend on. . . ."

"Do you need me down in Stanford?"

"Yeah, sure." Her answer came too fast, and she realized that she *did* want him there, if nothing more than to provide comfort while she was trying to sort through this emergency. If only she had more time!

Then she focused on what he was saying and interrupted him. "No, wait. No telling how long any of our vehicles is going to last. You might have a hard time getting all the way down here."

"You just start coordinating how we can go after this thing. I'll worry about me," Todd said. "And hey, if you need a contact at Oilstar, I'll march right into Emma Branson's office even if I have to knock over the receptionist. Don't you take any grief from anyone either."

"Do I usually?"

A pause, then a chuckle. "No, I don't suppose you do."

As she hung up, Iris was already going over the details of what had to be done. If this was truly a plague, there had to be contingency plans at the Centers for Disease Control, the National Military Command Center, the Federal Emergency Management Agency—dozens of places that should be able to offer her guidance.

Francis Plerry. She had to go through him again. He wouldn't be much help, but he could set a few wheels in motion. At the very least he should have access to the governor in Sacramento. Iris looked for her Rolodex, found it behind her mammoth-sized *CRC Handbook* of chemical data, and fumbled through the white cards until she pulled out Plerry's number. The first time she dialed she got a busy signal. Damn!

Picking up her cup of coffee, she took a big gulp that stung her tongue and dialed again. The ringing seemed to go on forever before a brusque female voice answered and put her on hold.

She reached for her coffee again. Seconds ticked away. How long would it take for the governor to impose a vehicle quarantine that would make the medfly incident look like a joke?

"Hello?"

"Mr. Plerry? This is Iris Shikozu, from Stanford—"

As she started to speak, the white Styrofoam of her coffee cup turned spongy, as if melting. Then it sloughed over her fingers. Warm liquid splashed down her blouse. Iris jumped back, shaking her hand and staring at the cup.

The coffee wasn't *that* hot anymore. What could make the cup melt like that? Something that broke down Styrofoam . . . *hydrocarbon polymers.* . . .

She felt her knees turn watery.

Plerry's voice came from the phone, now on the floor. "Hello, Dr. Shikozu? Are you all right?"

Iris stood transfixed, staring as the cup turned to frothy white foam with a faint, muffled crackling sound in the puddle of coffee on the floor. She slid off the chair and fell to her knees. "Oh, no."

"Dr. Shikozu?"

Iris dipped her fingers in the gooey remains of the cup and plucked at the white, fizzing strands. The Prometheus vector was no longer confined to direct physical contact.

The microbe now attacked petroleum plastics as well as gasoline.

And it was airborne.

PART TWO
BREAKDOWN

THIRTY

EIGHT MILES HIGH

Navy Lieutenant Bobby Carron stepped out of the Bachelor Officers' Quarters and craned his neck, looking into the crisp, cloudless sky. A perfect day for flying. In a few hours, he and his wingman would be strapped into their identical F/A-18 fighters, blasting off from the China Lake Naval Weapons Center in the bleak California desert, and roaring across the country.

In the early morning light, Bobby stretched his arms to toss off the last remnants of sleep. The flat military base opened up to a panoramic view of the cracked, dry lake bed—"beautiful downtown China Lake"—that spread out undisturbed for miles, white and dazzling. Chemical plants around nearby Trona scooped and processed the powdery wastes, but the U.S. Navy had claimed a chunk of the desolate landscape for its own use.

Bobby felt rested and ready for the cross-country mission. He had a few hours until "wheels up," but he had errands to run before his weeklong absence from the base. The scheduled time was the latest they could leave and still be cleared all the way to Corpus Christi, Texas.

If they took off early, so much the better—more time for beach, surf, and babes.

Overhead, an experimental aircraft lit up its engines to break the 6 A.M. silence; flames shot out twenty feet behind the distant jet's engines as afterburners kicked on.

A door opened down the hall. Bobby saw a head crowned with a shock of red hair. Bobby grinned. For once he wasn't going to have trouble getting his buddy Ralph "Barfman" Petronfi out of bed. Ever since they had been roommates at the Naval Academy, Petronfi could sleep through anything—except on a flying day.

Bobby whistled. "Hey, Barfman." Petronfi's propensity for tossing his cookies while flying was legendary.

Barfman turned sleepy eyes to Bobby. "Hi, Rhino. Ready for the beach?"

"Soon as I clean up my Jeep. Gotta grab some breakfast."

"I'll file a flight plan. Want to leave early?" Barfman said.

"If I can get everything done."

"I'll preflight us at the squadron."

"That's a rog." Bobby ducked back into his quarters to pull his gray flight suit from the narrow closet and put it on, patting down his many pockets to check that each held its appropriate map, keys, wallet, pen, chewing gum. Bobby went out again, hiking to the Officers' Club to gulp down a breakfast of eggs, warmed-over steak, and powdered orange drink—a breakfast high in protein so he wouldn't need to take a crap during the day's flight alone in a cramped cockpit. Barfman usually fasted before a long flight, which kept him from puking into his oxygen mask if they encountered any clear-air turbulence.

Bobby grabbed his nylon flight bag on the way to the mud-spattered Jeep. He had packed the night before—swim trunks and two changes of jeans and cotton shirts. The naval training base near the Texas beach was a favorite roost for cross-country crews, complete with surf and bikinis. Bobby had a nice life, flying every day, living on flight pay, no kids, no alimony. Once in a while he missed playing football, but flying made up for it.

Parked in the weedy gravel lot, his black Jeep was plastered with muck from a weekend of four-wheeling around dry Owens Lake. He loved doing doughnuts out in the brackish standing water and spraying salt and powder in a rooster-tail behind him. He didn't want to waste time washing the Jeep right now, but he knew how much damage the alkali mud could do to his paint job. With a little time until the preflight briefing, Bobby decided to use the base's self-service wash three blocks down the street.

Bouncing into the driver's seat, he poked his keys into the ignition and tried to start the Jeep. The engine barely turned over, and when it caught, the Jeep rattled as if it were running low on gasoline. The gas tank read full; he had filled it up after returning late last night. Bobby frowned. He smelled a faint odor of rotten eggs.

Bobby nursed the chugging Jeep along the street lined with old barracks buildings and a small BX. He parked in the service station lot crowded with the hodgepodge of other vehicles. He swung out of the Jeep and jogged inside the station. A female captain and two men out of uniform stood in line at the service desk; another two women—wives of enlisted men—sat in chairs in the waiting area.

Bobby listened to the mechanic taking information from the first customer. The phone rang, but the attendant ignored it. Bobby glanced at his watch. The two women sitting in the plastic chairs looked impatient and surly, as if they had been here a long time. He sighed. He would have to leave the Jeep here and walk the couple blocks to base operations for the flight. He regretted not being able to wash the mud off, but it was only a Jeep, not a Jag. Jeeps were supposed to get dirty.

The service attendant looked harried. "Got five people ahead of you, Lieutenant," he said with surprising courtesy. "Don't know if we can get to it this morning."

"Can I leave it? I'm gone for the week."

The attendant shoved a triplicate repair sheet across the desk. "Sure. Fill it out on top and sign here."

Bobby scribbled his name and details about the Jeep. "Looks like you're pretty busy. What's up—two-for-one special?"

"You tell me. Started this morning. If I didn't know better, I'd think we got some of that bad batch of gasoline, but our gas comes from Bakersfield, not the San Francisco refineries."

Bobby dug into his flight suit for the keys. He tossed them across the counter. "I'll be back on the ninth."

Outside, he retrieved his flight bag from the driver's seat, pulled the canvas cover over the top of the Jeep, and started walking down the street. The way his luck was going, Corpus Christi would probably be hit with a hurricane when he was halfway there, and he'd have to divert to Del Rio instead. . . .

Squadron headquarters was a long one-story building painted white to reflect the sun. The squadron mascot, a Tasmanian Devil with an arrow through its head, was painted on the cinder-block outside walls. Inside, photos of old F-4s taking off from a wooden-decked aircraft carrier, a lumbering P-3 flying patrol over the ocean, a pair of F-14 Tomcats launching missiles hung on the walls. At the end of the hall a set of doors led to the ready room, weather unit, orderly room, and the CO's office.

Entering the preflight area, he saw Barfman in a gray flight suit hunched over a chest-high table, drawing with a red Magic Marker. Maps, computer listings, and Notes-to-Airmen covered the bulletin boards.

"Just finishing off the flight plan, Rhino," Barfman said. "I want to go before the hunger pains start. Ready to head out?"

"Yeah," said Bobby. "My Jeep conked out on me, had to leave it at the service station."

"From what I heard in the ready room, you're lucky they even put your name on the waiting list. Base motor pool is backed up, and they're refusing to take any more vehicles."

The memory of that guy running out of gas in the Death Valley desert raced through Bobby's head. "Is there some sabotage going on around here or what?"

"Yeah, it's some new Commie secret weapon. Magically exchanges the engines of American-made cars with top-of-the-line North Korean jobs. That's why everything's breaking down."

Bobby swung his flight bag to the foot of the table. "Thank you for explaining. Now let's book out of here before they cancel our flight."

"Hey, I've waited three months for this cross-country. No way am I going to let a bad batch of gasoline put a hold on my vacation." Barfman pushed a sheaf of lined papers over to Bobby, folding open to the right page. "Log in the flight plan and I'll check with Weather."

Bobby looked over the route Barfman had outlined in marker. They were set to make the trip with an intermediate stop at Nellis AFB in Nevada, just outside of Las Vegas. They probably could have stretched the hop to El Paso, but if they broke down, spending time in Las Vegas was preferable to the Texas border town any day. . . .

"Ah, Rhino, got a little problem here." The sound of Barfman's voice crackled through the white-noise roar of the jets.

It took Bobby a second to snap away from a daydream of sea breezes, warm sand, and a Gulf shrimp dinner. They were no more than an hour out of Las Vegas, heading across the blistered barren desert of central New Mexico. Cramped in the cockpit of his one-man fighter jet, Bobby bent to pick up the handset. He clicked the radio, using the frequency he and Barfman had agreed on.

"What's up, Barfman?" He spotted his partner's F/A-18 Hornet two miles ahead of him. Frosty white contrails streamed from the engine in the cold thin air.

"I show a faulty pump indicator. Doesn't look good."

"Try Emergency Repair Procedure Number One," Bobby said.

"I already tapped the damned dial. It's not a faulty reading."

"How's your flow rate?"

"Next to nothing. I got a sluggish response on the controls. Something's not hooked up the way it should be."

Bobby scanned his own instruments in the cockpit. Everything looked fine. "What do you think?"

"Well, I'd say I was running out of fuel—but we just tanked up at Nellis. Can you zoom up here and give me a once-over? Is one of my tanks leaking?"

Bobby squeezed his transmitter twice to click off an acknowledgment, then pushed the throttles. He felt an immediate surge as the engines gulped more kerosene-based fuel. Pulling back, he slowed to match Barfman's velocity and inched toward the F/A-18. He circled the fighter, craning his neck to inspect it. "Negatory, Barfman. Can't see anything wrong." He started to move behind his partner's aircraft when he glanced at the altimeter. "Hey, watch your altitude."

"I'm losing airspeed," said Barfman, his voice grim.

"You ready to declare an emergency?"

He waited, listening to the static. "Ah . . . not yet," Barfman said at last. "But we'd better find someplace flat to put this baby down."

"Rog," said Bobby, feeling a mixture of relief and deeper concern. "You keep her flying, I'll check things out." He eased back on the throttles.

Bobby reached into the leg pocket on his flight suit and pulled out an airfield map of the southwestern states, unfolding it against the cramped front panel of the cockpit. Smoothing the map, he scanned it for the nearest runway, but saw nothing close. He clicked the radio. "Doesn't look good, Barfman. I'm calling the cavalry." Bobby glanced at his INS—the Inertial Navigation System—before calling. On their routine flight path, they had been handed over to the Albuquerque regional FAA control center some minutes before.

Barfman acknowledged only with two clicks on the radio, no words at all. Bobby swallowed. Barfman must be having a much harder time than he realized.

Bobby changed the frequency to pick up the FAA control center, keeping his voice calm and firm as he called in. "Albuquerque control, this is Navy Zero Sixer out of China Lake. We're approximately a hundred thirty miles southeast of Four Corners. Request immediate location of the nearest airfield."

"Navy Zero Sixer, this is Albuquerque. Do you have an emergency?"

The option raced through Bobby's mind. It was one thing for Barfman to try and bring the fighter in all by himself—if nothing was really wrong with the jet, they'd just refuel, hop back in and zoom to the beach. No problem, no worry, no messy paperwork. But if they declared an emergency, then all hell would break loose—at the very least they'd have to appear before an inquiry board.

Bobby wet his lips; the high-altitude air was bone dry. "Ah, Albuquerque, we've run into some difficulty but are not ready at this time to declare an emergency. Please advise ASAP on the location of the nearest airfield."

"Roger, Navy Zero Sixer. You may divert to Santa Fe or Los Alamos to the north or keep coming in for three airfields in the Albuquerque area. Please inform of your situation."

Barfman's jet continued descending. Barfman's voice came over the speaker, clipped with tension. "Getting kind of hard to handle, old buddy. Not sure I want to try to bring her down in the mountains around Los Alamos—"

Suddenly, large gaps appeared in Barfman's contrails, as if the jet engines had been turned on and off in quick succession. Bobby gripped the control stick with his sweaty hand as icepicks of cold sweat stabbed up and down his back.

"Barfman, you all right?"

His partner's voice sounded tight, under control. "I'm fighting engine-out, Rhino. This thing wants to shut down. Do you think somebody watered the fuel at Nellis? That damned Air Force JP-4—" Barfman's voice cut off entirely and white noise filled the airwaves.

"Barfman, do you read?" Bobby waited a second, hoping and praying that something would improve. It didn't. When Barfman didn't answer, Bobby pushed his throttles to the max; the fighter leaped through the air. Barfman's jet dropped like a rock. Bobby clicked his mike. He felt helpless, unable to do anything but watch. "Barfman, do you copy?"

Bobby nosed his craft over to follow Barfman's descent. He peered through the transparent canopy of his fighter. The contrails had vanished from Barfman's jet; there was no flame in the engine—he must have had a complete power failure. But what about the backup? That should have kicked in. Without power, the electrical system would not work, making the radio inoperable. The rudders and stabilizers could be moved through hydraulics, so Barfman had some control; but with no thrust, the fighter would fall one foot for every ten it moved forward. Barfman didn't have much time to eject.

Bobby clicked to the emergency guard frequency. "Mayday, mayday. Navy Zero Sixer calling for help, southeast of Four Corners. We have a flameout and are rapidly descending. Request emergency equipment immediately."

He skinned close to Barfman's jet, almost wingtip to wingtip. He breathed sharp cold air in staccato gasps. Bobby could see his friend's helmet through the cockpit, his head down as he wrestled in vain with the unwieldy hydraulic controls.

Bobby knew of no way to stretch out the inevitable

crash—at this rate, Barfman would impact the ground at five hundred miles an hour. Bobby glanced at his altimeter; they were passing through fifteen thousand feet and still accelerating downward.

Albuquerque control came over the radio. "We've lost your squawk, Navy Sixer. Do you copy?"

"Come on, Barfman—punch out!" Bobby slid the jet off to the side to give the other pilot room to eject—but nothing happened. The altimeter continued to run down. "Come on!"

Barfman didn't have a chance in hell to land, even if he regained total control. Bobby glanced out his cockpit; rugged brown terrain swooped up to meet them.

"Navy Zero Sixer, do you read?"

Ignoring the ground controller, Bobby jerked his stick to the right, rolling until he was beneath Barfman's jet, accelerating down faster than the F/A-18 fell. He had to get Barfman's head up out of the controls! Holding his breath, Bobby shoved the throttles forward; when he was under Barfman, he kicked in the afterburners with a sound like a bomb blast. The sudden acceleration shoved Bobby back in his seat.

Barfman appeared to be struggling with his ejection handles. Bobby cut off the afterburners and pulled back on the stick. He felt the gees build up and squash him into his seat.

Pulling his jet into a loop, Bobby searched for Barfman's fighter. The sky wheeled around him, the desert looked like brown scabs below him with baking sands and lumpy weathered lava outcroppings. "Barfman, where are you!"

A moment later, he saw a flash of light. A massive brown cloud rose from the desert floor where Barfman's fighter had slammed into the ground. Bobby winced for just a second, but he couldn't let himself believe his buddy had been trapped in the cockpit. Making an animal sound through his teeth, he wrenched the control stick to pull his fighter over. He scanned the sky for a parachute, an eject seat. "Come on, come on!"

Then he felt a shudder run through his own plane.

He found the fuel indicator—his pump appeared to be malfunctioning. The flow rate from the tank to the engine started dropping. Something had blown, just like in Barfman's jet. "Oh, shit," he said.

The speakers crackled to life. "Navy Zero Sixer, we have lost your squawk. We are standing by. Please engage your transponder. Estimate has you northwest of Double Eagle Airport in Albuquerque. Do you copy?"

Bobby shook his head to clear the shock that gripped him. Adrenaline flushed the cobwebs from his system, making him sharp. His altimeter showed that he had climbed back up to twelve thousand feet, and aside from the faulty reading on the pump flow indicator, there was nothing to show he was in any trouble. Not yet. He knew he should be doing something—trying to land his craft so he wouldn't be taken by surprise like his friend. He still saw no sign of Barfman's parachute.

Life or death. He squelched the fear, the helplessness. No time for that now. Bobby shoved the throttles to full, kicking in the afterburners. As the surge of acceleration hit him, he realized he might have only minutes to find a place to land, especially if the sudden plague of breakdowns hit his own F/A-18.

He keyed his transponder and spoke into the mike. "Mayday, Mayday, Albuquerque control. Navy Zero Sixer declaring an emergency. Attempting to reach Double Eagle Airport. One plane in our flight is down, approximately thirty miles behind me. My flow pump reads faulty, and if I lose engine power I will not be able to transmit. Request immediate emergency assistance, foam, and emergency vehicles—"

"We have you fifteen miles out, Navy Zero Sixer. Please be advised there is no emergency equipment at Double Eagle. I say again, no emergency equipment available."

"Great," muttered Bobby. From what he had seen on the map, he'd have to fly over the city of Albuquerque to reach the municipal airport, which meant putting thousands of people at risk if he couldn't nurse his plane all the way to the runway.

He pushed the aircraft as fast as he dared, hoping to reach the Double Eagle Airport before everything crapped out on him. He tried to keep a balance between altitude and speed, knowing that he could trade off one for the other; but he also didn't want to fall into the same trap as Barfman, and lose stability while wrestling with the hydraulic controls.

The humped line of the Sandia Mountains loomed in the distance. Below him the ground smoothed out, leaving the rugged terrain behind. He might make it.

"Navy Zero Sixer, please be advised—" The speaker went dead leaving the cockpit weirdly silent except for the rushing wind. At the same instant he felt a gigantic sagging as the engines died and the A/F-18's electrical systems shut down. What the hell happened to the backup? The system was isolated from the main engine —this couldn't happen!

Adrenaline and split-second fear switched off the questions in his mind. Deal with them later. Bobby immediately pushed as hard as he could to lower all flaps to extend the camber in an attempt to increase his lift.

He spotted Double Eagle Airport off to the left; he had vectored in too far south. Cursing under his breath, he inched the fighter's nose to the left, trying not to do anything that would send the already precarious craft out of control. He had to punch out—no way could he bring this fighter in. No way.

But what had gone wrong with Barfman? Had he tried to eject, only to fail for some unknown reason? Or had Barfman simply waited too long, kept his head buried in the controls?

He saw a long stretch of green in front of him—the Rio Grande. What a place to run out of gas! He frantically tried to turn the craft, but felt a growing wobble.

The craft would lose it any second now. Slamming his helmeted head against the back of his seat, he reached down and grasped the ejection handles. He'd crash through the canopy if it didn't blow open, but better that than staying with the jet and digging a crater in the desert. He looked straight ahead, closed his eyes, and pulled up as hard as he could.

An instant later he felt the shock of cold air, a sound that overwhelmed him—wind, crashing, tearing. His right leg and mouth felt torn apart. He was thrown from the seat, twisting. Attached to the parachute, a line snaked out in front of him, ripped into the howling wind.

He felt himself tumbling. The parachute started to open. He had to clamp his mouth shut to keep from vomiting.

It was going to be one mother of a hard landing. Bobby gritted his teeth and tried to stay conscious. The parachute tugged him upward in an effort to slow his plunge.

Below him, he watched his jet explode into the desert floor.

THIRTY-ONE

DON'T CALL US, WE'LL CALL YOU

Iris Shikozu's portable phone no longer worked, but the clunky old model in the bedroom of her apartment still functioned. She knew it must be because different plastics broke down at different rates. The plague was spreading like a flood, submerging the entire city.

She carefully pushed buttons, hoping the equipment wouldn't fall to pieces as she dialed. She had to talk to somebody. The world seemed to close around her as everything broke down. On her bedroom wall, posters of middle-aged rock groups stared down at her, offering silent sympathy for her predicament.

In only a day the news had become intermittent. The plague had been spreading quietly since the Prometheus spraying, infecting numerous items, metabolizing gasoline first and then attacking other polymers, until components began to break down all at once. All at the same time.

The radio news told stories of riots in South Africa, a major stock-exchange crash in Tokyo, communications blackouts from various parts of the world. The President himself was stranded out of the country, and now the Vice President had been stuck in Chicago when all aircraft were grounded. Everything was happening too fast.

She listened to the buzzing ring against her ear as she waited for someone to answer. More often than not, the phones had been out of order. She suspected that plastics in the various telephone substations had dissolved, but the phone company had managed to reroute most of the calls. So far.

Francis Plerry, her contact at EPI, answered the phone; Iris launched into her rehearsed speech before he could hang up on her.

"I've been waiting for you to return my calls, Mr. Plerry. I called five times yesterday. I have some information regarding the spread of the Prometheus plague and how it is attacking plastics." She sat down on her double bed, pulling the phone after her, calmed now that she could finally speak to someone. "I need to be put in touch with the other research teams addressing the issue. Have you even established other teams?"

"Miss Shikozu," Plerry said, "I received your messages, and I'm sorry I haven't gotten back to you. This place has been a zoo since rumors of the plague started. Er . . . I'm sure you understand that a lot of these people don't want to talk to you."

Iris felt like he had slapped her in the face. "No, I don't understand that at all. Why wouldn't they want to talk to me?"

"Well . . ." Plerry sounded flustered. "*You* were the one who inspected the Prometheus microorganism and deemed it safe. Obviously, few people are interested in your theories after you so grossly misinterpreted the data."

"That's bullshit, Plerry! Dr. Kramer gave me a bogus control sample to analyze, then sprayed something completely different on the oil spill—"

Plerry kept right on talking. "There may actually be certain charges of criminal negligence and endangerment of public health when all this blows over."

Iris rolled her eyes. *When all this blows over? Right!* Todd Severyn had Plerry pegged from his first impression: this guy was out of touch with reality.

"Yeah, Plerry, we'll talk about that later. For now I've got some information for the other teams. The Centers for Disease Control, the NIH, the Department of Defense, and the petroleum industry all better throw their research muscle into this."

Plerry hesitated on the other end of the line, and she could picture his Adam's apple bobbing up and down. "I assure you, Miss Shikozu—"

"That's *Dr.* Shikozu, and I'm damned tired of you 'assuring' me!" she said. "Listen to me. Most of the equipment in my lab is already shot, so I can't run any analyses, but I have been able to piece together some of my own results. I know why Prometheus is going after plastics.

"The microorganism primarily dissociates the octane molecule, which is made up of eight carbons in a chain, surrounded by hydrogen atoms. Most petroleum plastics are just longer polymers made up of shorter hydrocarbons, interlinked. Kramer engineered the new strain of Prometheus to break out eight-carbon chains from longer polymers, as well as some ring hydrocarbons. It can reach into heavy petroleum molecules and snip out bite-sized molecules. That's how it breaks down plastics! Any plastic that doesn't have eight-carbon segments should still be safe—"

Plerry cut her off. "Thank you, Dr. Shikozu. The working teams have already come up with that independently. But it's not always true. We have not been able to come up with a simple explanation for why Prometheus attacks certain plastics and leaves others alone. Nylon seems to resist the plague, and so does polyvinyl chloride, PVC—which *should* be one of the most easily affected plastics. But even that may change, as the microorganism adapts to new food sources. We just don't know yet, but we are working round the clock to look for answers."

"Have you gotten in touch with Kramer's assistant Mitch Stone?" Iris persisted. No one had ever given her such a cold brush-off before. She deserved a little more respect and consideration. "He might know something."

"The research teams have already commandeered Dr. Stone and his expertise. He is working with Oilstar to interpret Dr. Kramer's notes right now."

Iris felt exasperated. She was never good at sitting still, and she couldn't just wait for somebody else to work on the problem. She wanted to be involved. She wanted to be somewhere she could put her hands on the problem. She stood up again and brushed her hand across the bedspread to smooth the wrinkles. "Maybe I could assist them."

Plerry's voice was as smooth as hemorrhoid ointment. "Thank you for your interest, Dr. Shikozu. I'll take that under advisement and pass it along to the appropriate people. We'll get back to you if anything turns up." He hung up on her.

Iris stared at the receiver. "Good thing the petro-plague doesn't eat pure slime, Plerry." She slammed the handset back into the cradle. She paced her apartment, desperate for something to do. This was worse than being forced to go on vacation.

Iris padded over to the stereo. She didn't know how much longer she'd have electricity, so she might as well do something constructive. The power had flickered out earlier in the day, as she sat at the kitchen table trying to go over chemical equations without the aid of her computer. She figured all the wiring in her apartment would be affected; the electrical substations must be insulated with plastic, though natural rubber seemed to resist the plague, but the generating stations would fail before long.

She flicked on the amplifier, cranked the volume knob, and went to select a CD. Tom Petty? Talking Heads? Yeah, "Burning Down the House" sounded particularly appropriate.

She plucked out the jewel box, but it had a cloudy, frosted appearance. When she lifted the compact disk, it sagged in her hand, the plastic substrate gone limp like a floppy computer diskette.

"Oh, dammit!" Iris said, tossing the jewel box and CD across the room—the same Talking Heads album that featured the song "Making Flippy Floppy." Appropriate.

"This is really getting annoying. The fall of civilization is bad enough, but do I have to face it without my music?"

THIRTY-TWO

TAKE THIS JOB AND SHOVE IT

The moment Heather Dixon dragged herself into the offices of Surety Insurance, her supervisor shouted at her. "Where the hell have you been, Heather? Damn it all, this place is going crazy! Boston's been calling since six o'clock this morning."

She blinked at Albert "You can call me Al" Sysco, already exhausted from her ordeal of just getting to work. After her car wouldn't start, she had to walk nearly two miles in her high heels, red plaid business skirt, and itchy pantyhose.

Al Sysco, the water-cooler Napoleon, lorded it over the women in the office as if it were his due, breathing down their necks until they couldn't do their jobs—and then he reprimanded them when productivity dropped. Heather decided it was because he had a tiny penis, but she had no intention of finding out for sure.

She wanted to tell him that Headquarters knew full well there was a two-hour time difference between Boston and Arizona. She wanted to tell him that her calves were sore from walking in clothes that were meant to be admired, not exercised in. She wanted to know what in the world Sysco had been doing in the office at 6 A.M. anyway.

Most of all, she wanted to go to the coffeemaker, yank out the filter basket, and stuff a steaming wad of coffee grounds down the front of Al Sysco's pants.

Instead, she went to her desk. "My car wouldn't start, and the streets are a war zone." The city seemed much worse than the local radio news described it, though for two days the broadcasts had been growing more panicked as reporters tracked the progress of the "petroplague."

"You've got a hundred forms to process already. I've made some follow-up phone calls, but you'll have to do the rest of them. I'm going nuts! The phone connections break off half the time anyway. Keep trying until you get through." Sysco wiped his palm across the sweat in his porcupine hair. In the background, a few telephones continued to ring. The air smelled stuffy and held an aftertaste of turpentine.

Two women bustled down the hall, arguing about something, then split down two separate paths among the cubicles, still shouting over the metal-rimmed cloth office dividers. Heather noticed that half of the office cubicles were empty. Pale green ferns poked over the top of the nearest barrier. Her own wood-grain desk was strewn with pencils, cute Post-it notes, two coffee cups, and clippings from the comic strip Cathy.

Before Heather could get to her desk and slip her canvas purse into the bottom file drawer, Sysco came by with a six-inch stack of paperwork. Heather ignored him as she turned to switch on her terminal.

"Don't bother," said Sysco. "They're falling apart from that gasoline plague. What a mess. I can't get Surety to give me a decision on how we're going to cover all this. Use the telephone, but for God's sake don't tell anybody the computers are down! Say that we're, uh, 'unable to access that information at this time' or some such nonsense."

Heather blinked. If Surety's networked computers were down, they were in big trouble. If plastic components were falling apart across the country, then why the hell had she come to work at all? People resisted changing their momentum, moving from their daily routine. Tabloids had screamed about the end of the world for so long that everyone seemed numb to the possibility. But maybe . . .

"Stacie has an old Selectric typewriter under her desk," said Sysco. "You'll have to type things by hand."

Heather glared at him as he turned back to his own work area. His shoulders hunched with spring-wound tension. Sysco was such a little man, harried and suffering. At the moment, she didn't particularly envy him the promotion.

She walked over to Stacie's desk and stooped to find the old gray-brown Selectric underneath the desk. The thing felt like an anchor as she slid it out along the worn carpet. Tiny broken carpet fibers sprayed out as the nap crumbled. Her left foot snagged on a burr, and the pantyhose ran from ankle to knee. "Shit," she mumbled, then hefted the typewriter, waddling with it back to her own desk.

She kicked off her heels and wiggled her toes on the hard plastic chair mat to get the circulation back. The mat felt tacky against her feet.

Not even 9:30 in the morning, and she already felt sweaty and uncomfortable. Why had she worn one of her nicest business skirts today? Why did she keep playing the game?

Claims poured in by the thousands as panic spread. She shuffled through the paperwork, seeing a marked change from simple car breakdowns to damage caused by disintegrating plastic components in machinery.

She swallowed, overwhelmed but still unwilling to believe the magnitude of the disaster. Such things couldn't *really* happen. Someone would figure out how to stop it soon, and then they could pick up the pieces, pay off the claims, and get back to normal.

But all this was too much, getting worse every hour. She had seen the changes in Flagstaff just in the last couple of days, when the first breakdowns occurred. It reminded her of weather in the mountains, when a bright day could knot with ugly thunderheads within an hour. Maybe an even worse storm gathered right now, and she had come to work like an idiot instead of running for shelter.

Not concentrating, Heather let her fingers tangle on the Selectric's keys—it had been years since she had used a typewriter, and she found herself backspacing and using the correction key every other word. The keys stuck repeatedly, and the machine made odd *clunking* noises when she typed; Heather supposed there were just as many small plastic parts in an electric typewriter as there were in the computers. For the time being, the carbons would be screwed up, and she would have to use white-out. Then somebody would have to rekey everything into the database whenever the computers got up and running again. If they ever got running.

"What are you doing, Heather?" Sysco said. "Don't bother with the typing now, for Chrissake! You can stay late to catch up on that. Pick up the phone and get these people off my ass! I think the lines are up now."

She stared at the typewriter. "You *told* me to type these, Al."

He rolled his eyes and sighed at her. His face reminded her of a llama's. "You're doing it again, Heather: thinking. Just do what I tell you to do. You don't need to think."

She was thinking all right, thinking about jamming a metal wastebasket down on Al Sysco's head and doing a tap dance on his temples.

Stacie finally staggered into the office a little after noon. She had ridden her bicycle on the rims of two flat tires. "Crazy people out in the streets. Nobody knows what to do!" Heather took no consolation in listening to Al yell at Stacie.

When she pulled out her lunch sack to unwrap a tuna

sandwich, the plastic bag had turned into goo, seeping into her bread. Heather stared at it. The plague was working its way through the office, floating through the air, attacking anything it could eat.

She looked at the fake wood-grain coating on her metal desk, at the plastic pens in her cup, at the plastic knobs on her office chair, at the plastic buttons on her clothes. *What next?* At any moment, some key support component in the Surety building itself might fall apart, causing the walls and ceiling to crash in.

She did not want to stay here another minute.

She picked up the phone in a reflex action as Sysco charged back to her desk. "Heather, take over my station. I have to meet with the crisis team. Might take me an hour."

Heather straightened in her seat, still clutching the phone. As her anger simmered, her pastel-pink fingernails made deep indentations into the softening plastic of the telephone handset.

"Sorry, Al, but I'm not qualified to do that kind of work. I might botch it up. I don't dare touch it." She stood up, cold and calm inside. The eye of the storm.

"What did you say? I don't have time for this, Heather!" Sysco's eyes looked as if they might pop right out of their sockets. "This is important—"

Heather snatched her lunch sack and handed it to him. The dissolving plastic had made a creeping stain on the brown paper bag. "Here, Al—have a tuna sandwich." She turned to Stacie. "I wouldn't put up with this creep any longer than you have to, Stacie. See ya."

She wanted to watch Sysco's expression turn splotched and livid as she strode to the stairwell, but she did not dare turn around. Her legs shook as she hurried down the echoing concrete steps. Her shoes felt strange, as if they no longer fit right. Great. Her heels would probably dissolve before long.

She left the Surety Insurance building, doubting she would ever set foot inside it again.

Out in the parking lot, she marched onto the hot pavement, forcing herself not to run, ignoring the ache in her calves, giving no thought to the long walk facing her before she reached the safety of home. The world might be falling apart, all right, but she didn't feel any particular attachment to the old order of things. She could leave it behind with no regrets. Screw them all. It was time to take care of herself.

Sitting in the reserved parking space, Al Sysco's silver Porsche gleamed in the sun. He had owned it less than three months, and he still washed and waxed it every weekend. He had bought it to celebrate stealing her promotion, and she knew it.

She stared at the Porsche. It looked like a snarling metallic insect. Insects were for squashing, weren't they?

Heather opened her canvas purse and pulled out the nearly full bottle of pastel-pink nail polish. She hated the color, hated nail polish in the first place; she wore it only as part of professional dress in the insurance company. Now she had a better use for it, if the plague didn't somehow dissolve the enamel first. She twisted off the softening cap and dribbled the enamel in swirls over the driver's-side windshield. Once the nail polish baked a few hours in the hot Arizona sun, Albert "You can call me Al" Sysco would need an ice pick to get it off.

"You can call me *vindicated*, Al," she said, then set off for home, on foot.

Al Sysco fled Surety Insurance at seven o'clock that evening. Everyone else had left hours before, but he was in charge. He was the responsible man on the job. The entire day had been hell. The California gasoline plague kept getting worse, showing up in all parts of the world, according to the reports. Industry was in a panic, big cities were in turmoil—and it seemed as if every human being on planet Earth wanted to take it out on him.

Dusk had fallen, and the streetlights stood dark and dead. The power had flickered on and off all afternoon, and Sysco wondered if dissolving electrical insulation would end up starting fires. One more thing for the insurance company to worry about!

Heather Dixon had walked out in the middle of the day, and Al vowed to see her fired as soon as all this was over with—but right now he prayed she would come back.

Stacie was a slow and plodding worker, and Candace was just a trainee. They couldn't do anything right, and Candace had spent half the day in tears. He had physically shaken her by the shoulders, yelling that they were in a crisis situation, dammit! It didn't do any good. He could not survive another day like this one. He wished somebody would start solving this plague problem.

He stopped in front of his Porsche, and his mouth dropped open. In the dim light, it looked like a gigantic glob of bird shit had splattered his windshield. He looked closer. "Nail polish! Sweet as an armpit! Gawd!" He tapped it with his nails, but the opaque pink coating could have been electroplated on.

Sick to his stomach, he climbed behind the steering wheel. He just wanted to go home and work his way through every beer in the refrigerator, then start on whatever else he could find in the liquor cabinet.

But when he turned the key in the ignition, his car refused to start.

THIRTY-THREE

BACK IN THE SADDLE AGAIN

Todd moved through Alex Kramer's empty house, not quite sure what he should do now. He had been here for days, flustered to be in a situation where the plan of action was not obvious, and the most sensible thing seemed to be just sitting tight. He wanted to get off his butt and do something.

Bending down in front of the cold fireplace, Todd riffled through the ashes, pulling out the scorched chunks of Alex's Prometheus notes. A handful of pages were intact.

Todd paced the floor. It was deceptively calm and peaceful here, but he knew the chaos was growing in the cities, on the clogged freeways.

When he had called the ambulance to report Alex's suicide, it had taken them five hours to reach the home out in the Marin hills. Todd had yelled at the harried-looking blond man in grimy blue-and-white paramedic uniform, but the man snapped back that only one of their vehicles worked, and that they had answered dozens of calls. The paramedics covered Alex's body and carried it out to the ambulance, slamming the back doors. The driver pulled out, spraying gravel from the rear tires as Todd stood speechless on the porch.

With nothing else to wait for, Todd had left Alex's house, locking the front door behind him. But when he had tried to drive to Stanford to meet Iris, his Ford pickup broke down after only five miles. He had stared at the ticking, motionless hulk parked on the side of the road, tires wrenched in a sharp angle. He had shaken his head, turned around, and started the hike back, angry, confused, and afraid. His cowboy boots crunched on the road's soft shoulder, and not many cars passed him.

What a day!

Letting himself back in through the jimmied laundry-room window, Todd had gone to Alex's phone and called fifteen emergency road service numbers, finally getting one that told him to wait.

He paced through the house again. He found a set of keys on the dresser in Alex's bedroom, and with a bright but uncertain thread of hope, he jogged out to the front driveway and climbed into Alex's pickup. He fiddled with the keys until he found one that fit in the ignition. The starter cranked, but the engine just made grinding, chugging noises.

Todd scowled, but really wasn't surprised.

Unless he took the horses, he was stuck here, unable to get down to Stanford. Iris needed to see whatever was left in Alex's notes—but *riding* down to Stanford? Even he wasn't that crazy.

He slept restlessly on Alex's sofa in the family room, stripped down to his underwear and wrapped in a blanket he found in one of the closets.

The next morning, when he picked up the phone to call Oilstar, to yell at the tow service, to talk to Iris, the line was dead. "What the heck?" He slammed the telephone down.

He had promised Iris he would come down to see her

as soon as possible, and he always kept his promises. Besides, she had to have those notes. He stewed in the living room, muttering to himself, looking through the glass patio doors, still trying to figure out what to do.

He wondered if Iris was worried about him. Her personality made him think of an injured bobcat, but he couldn't shake the feeling that she was testing him, toying with him. Todd knew he was hardheaded, too, so he might be attracted to her because of her spunk—a challenge?

There were two types of women in the world—those that stood steadfast, and those that jumped from bed to bed. Iris seemed the steadfast type, but if something ever did happen between them, he wasn't sure if he could put up with the rest of her ways. He sighed. He must be awfully bored to let his mind wander like that!

By midmorning, the power flickered and went out, leaving the house dark, cool, and stuffy. He caught a whiff of stale beer and cheese he had missed before, probably left over from the party. He stepped into the family room and scanned the carpet, but he saw no sign where Iris had spilled her wine.

He looked at a stack of plastic wineglasses on the corner of the bar, saw them sagging under their own weight. Todd touched them with his fingertip, saw his nail make a crescent-shaped indentation. When he lifted his elbow from the padded edge of the bar, the indentation remained smashed, stretched out of shape. The air carried a volatile, oily smell of dissolving plastic.

He stepped away from the bar and turned to go down the hall, stopping in front of the closed door of the "memorial" bedroom where Alex had died. Braving the chill inside himself, Todd opened the door and stepped in. Daylight slanted through the half-opened blinds, glinting on the framed photos of Alex's family. One of the frames had fallen apart as some sort of plastic binder gave way, and an army photo of Jay lay on the floor among large pieces of broken glass.

Todd scanned the memorabilia again. After the suicide, all the faces seemed more intense now, more sharply defined. A certificate and medal bearing the name Jay Kramer. A snapshot of the young girl, Erin, standing by a pony. Todd had fed her horse, Stimpy, ridden the trail that she had loved to explore. He felt he had gotten to know her somehow.

Alex had left the ranch, his life's work with Prometheus, and now there were only pictures, ribbons, and cold medals—artifacts meaningless to anyone who did not know Alex Kramer.

Todd backed out of the room.

Alex had been a family man, something Todd himself didn't relate to. Consulting in the oil business, Todd couldn't afford to put down roots. The women he met expressed no desire to follow him around, to pick up everything on a moment's notice and move across the world . . . not that he was ready for that baggage yet.

Todd remained close to his parents, and he visited their ranch as often as possible. Ranch hands came and went, but the family would always be there. He wondered how his mom and dad were doing with the spread of the petroplague, but they were basically self-sufficient out on the Wyoming plains.

In the dark refrigerator Todd found leftover party hors d'oeuvres, cheese, stale rabbit-food vegetables, beer, and some open bottles of wine. Some of the plastic wrappers looked wet and runny. He didn't touch them.

He grabbed some cheese and scraped the rest of the old food into the garbage. He took a can of Coors and drank it down fast, then selected another one for sipping.

Okay. What the heck was he supposed to do now? What was he even doing here?

Part of him wanted to get roaring drunk, to sit on the sofa and listen to some C&W songs on the stereo. But the power was out, and Alex's music library didn't have much besides classical stuff anyway. Several radio stations had already dropped off the air, including the one that allegedly played country-western music but spent most of the time yakking instead.

Wiping his hands on his jeans and taking the beer with him, Todd stepped through the sliding patio door and surveyed the backyard. The horses wandered around the corral. Ren whinnied and stepped up to the fence.

Todd didn't like impossible situations, never had, never would. He'd discovered early on that the quicker he figured out a plan of action, the less he'd worry. He ran over his options, and he kept coming up with the same answer.

"Time to get the hell out of Dodge," he muttered.

He tried the phone one last time, and to his astonishment found a static-filled dial tone. He dialed Iris's number, praying for the phone service to last long enough for her to answer. The phone rang, then rang again. He suddenly realized he didn't know what to say to her. When Iris answered on the fourth ring, the connection was scratchy, intermittent. Her voice had a strange echoing quality.

"Tex! Where are you? I didn't know the phones were still working. Have you seen what's happening all around the city?"

"Iris!" he shouted into the phone. "Are you all right?"

"Me?" She seemed shocked that he would ask. "When I go outside I can see smoke in most directions, like fires burning out of control. It's hard to tell what's going on. I thought I could just hole up at home, but things are getting worse by the hour. I . . . I need to get out of here. Head east toward the Central Valley, I think, where there's a better chance to survive."

Todd felt another gush of urgency. He had been cut off here at Alex's, relatively safe, while Iris was in the middle of a potential bonfire. "Can you stay safe for another day?" he interrupted. "I'm at Alex's house now, but I'm going to ride out on his horses. I'll come get you. We can travel cross-country together."

It took a moment, but she answered slowly, with an uncertain humor, "Are you asking me out, Tex?"

"Pick you up at eight," he said, then paused. "Or as soon as I get there."

Her voice grew more serious. "I'll believe that when I see it. Security is getting pretty grim about who they let on campus. People are starting to realize how tight the food situation is. Just stay where you are, Todd."

"People have called me boneheaded before and just plain stubborn. I'll make my way to Stanford. I promise."

"Are you crazy?"

"Probably. Just wait for me."

"Todd!"

He hung up before she could say anything else. Even if he could get Iris to come along with him, he didn't have a clue where they might go. But he knew it was insane to remain in the city.

Moving with a new sense of determination, glad to have a goal again at last, he rummaged through the house, gathering supplies: first-aid kit, dusty sleeping bags, camping utensils, and dry food from Alex's cupboard. The last item he packed was the old Smith & Wesson he had found on Alex's nightstand. In a drawer he found four boxes of ammunition.

He considered waiting until morning and getting off to a fresh start. But that didn't feel right—he could travel through the afternoon, into the night, keep away from people or traffic.

Besides, he had always wanted to ride off into the sunset.

THIRTY-FOUR

RUNAWAY

Jackson Harris sat across from his wife Daphne at an old Formica dinette table in the kitchen, trying to digest the phone conversation he'd just had. Sure, it would be easy to just pack up a few things and run out to Altamont and stay with Doog—but then what would they do? Harris and his wife had obligations to their people, the kids they had taken to state parks, the volunteer army that had worked so hard on Angel Island, Daphne's church group, his own inner-city cleanup work. He couldn't just abandon all that.

Running away didn't seem feasible. He looked at Daphne. She had pulled her frizzy hair back with a blue hairband, and her strain-tightened face looked more angular in the uncertain light.

He could still taste the onions and spices from the quick meal of canned vegetarian chili he had warmed in an old pan on the gas stove. They had about a week's worth of canned soup, beans, and vegetables in the pantry. Many of the grocery stores had already been looted.

"We can't stay here, Daph," said Harris. "No way." Overhead, the lights flickered, then stayed on.

"All right," said Daphne, straightening up and managing the no-nonsense expression she did so well. "But how we gonna keep ourselves afloat and help as many folks as we can?"

All afternoon, he and Daphne had taken turns attempting to make calls from the phone hanging on the kitchen wall, begging favors, trying to borrow supplies, but panic and confusion had spread faster than the plague. Phone service was intermittent, and it probably wouldn't last much longer. The city of Oakland had started to break down, not just automobiles, but random items made of plastic. Though the plastic-eating phase had not yet struck their home, the Harrises' own battered Pinto had not coughed to life for days, and their neighbors were similarly trapped.

It could only get worse.

The BART trains had stopped running, and the bus system ground to a halt. Traffic on the streets was less than a third of what he was used to seeing; a few vehicles still managed to chug along, but they would probably succumb to the petroplague before long. Police cars, ambulances, and fire trucks couldn't respond to emergency calls.

Harris rapped an old pencil on the side of the table in a nervous, sporadic drumbeat. "We can round up some people and head out to the Altamont commune. Doog won't mind so long as we work."

Daphne snorted. "Doog and work don't belong in the same sentence!" She had no quarrel with Doog's politics, but Daphne resented him for not sticking with the battle in the inner city.

Doog and a group of aging hippies had fled into the isolated hills between Livermore and Tracy years ago when they saw their John Lennon world fading into yuppiedom. When "liberal" became a dirty word, Doog had just shaken his head at Harris. "Man," he said, "has the world gone off the deep end, or what?"

Harris flipped the pencil down on the table and met Daphne's gaze. "Doog is doing just fine out there, Daph. He's only forty miles away. He's got the aqueduct for water and windmills for power. They grow most of their own food. They've been living off the land for years. You got a better place in mind?"

Daphne shrugged. Sweat glistened on her cheeks. She had not put on makeup that morning, but Harris didn't think she had ever looked more beautiful. "Okay, it's a good enough spot to hide out for a while. I got no desire to be here to defend our home when the mob comes through."

Harris grabbed her hand and squeezed. "This is going to be a hell of a lot worse than the Rodney King riots. It's not just a public temper tantrum. People are going to be starving before long, and they won't have soup kitchens. Come winter, they'll chop up anything that burns just to stay warm. If we want to save any of our people, we got to go someplace else, and soon."

"Rats leaving a sinking ship," Daphne muttered.

"Pilgrims heading for the promised land," he corrected.

Three buses sat in different states of decrepitude in the parking lot of the Holy Grace Baptist Church. Rusted cans and junk-food wrappers littered the chain-link fence against the red-brick church building. Two basketball hoops sat unused on either end of the lot; it had been years since a chain net had graced either hoop, and the painted court lines had long since worn off the pavement. Despite the security fence, gang graffiti was spray-painted in black and bright blue on the sides of the buses.

The Reverend Timothy Rudge handed Daphne Harris the keys to the vehicles. He was a stocky man with strange spindly arms and legs, dressed in worn jeans and a maroon sweatshirt. He pursed his full lips. "I haven't gone anywhere for days. They might not work, you know."

"They probably won't," Daphne said, clutching the keys. "But one of them just might, and we only need one. That plague is spreading, but it can't eat everything at once. We might get lucky." She paused and looked at his face, weatherbeaten from years of preaching on the streets. "Sure you won't come along?"

He shook his head. "Somebody has to stay behind. Might as well be me. You and Jackson been working with these people on your wilderness-experience programs. You know what they can do if they let themselves believe in it. They deserve a chance."

Reverend Rudge turned wearily and watched Jackson sweating as he pulled another load of blankets and supplies from the church shelter. Daphne rattled the keys in her hand. "What about you, Reverend? If things get bad—"

"When things get bad around here, we'll call the congregation to the church. Make a stand."

"You'll never be able to protect yourselves," Daphne said, a lump in her throat.

"We can try. We just may be able to keep an island of stability here downtown. Have faith."

"I hope so," she said, knowing as she spoke that her words were false. From the Reverend's fatalistic expression, she knew he understood it too. She turned away, unable to look at him any longer.

She went to the newest of the three buses and climbed into the bucket seat. Daphne had driven this bus often when they took their volunteer groups. She tensed in a combination of hope and dread as she jingled through the key ring to find the proper key. Her fingers were slick with sweat as she jammed the key into the ignition and twisted hard, as if to show the vehicle who was boss.

But the engine refused to turn over. She tried four times, without success. Jackson stood in the parking lot, watching her. He shrugged and pointed to the next vehicle. Sighing, Daphne climbed out and went to the second bus, an older model with two broken windows.

Jackson continued to haul supplies for the trip. Volunteers from the Harrises' recent crusades gathered in the church, people who were willing to work for a cause, people who didn't have anything else to lose in their daily lives. Of course, if none of the buses started, the whole expedition would never happen. Daphne couldn't allow herself to admit that possibility.

The second bus protested, but Daphne gritted her teeth and kept grinding the starter. The engine finally coughed to life and rumbled like a tiger with a stomach ache. Blue-black diesel exhaust, already smelling foul from the first attacks of the petroplague, spat out the rear. She raised her fist in the air, and Jackson set down his paper grocery bags on the pavement and mirrored the gesture.

"Okay, everybody! Get the stuff on board the bus," Jackson Harris shouted. "We got to drive out past Livermore, and we don't know if this bus is gonna last. I hope you're all wearing walking shoes."

"Yeah, right, Jackson!" said Lindie, a whip-thin single mother with five children. "We bought two-hundred-dollar Nikes with the leftovers from my check this month!" Harris felt abashed, knowing she'd probably had enough trouble just finding shoelaces for all her kids.

A young couple walked to the bus: the large-eyed boy sixteen years old, the tired-looking girl no more than fifteen and very pregnant. They had been sticking together, trying to scrape together enough money to eat. The offer of leaving downtown Oakland to live out in the country seemed like paradise to them.

Denyse, a pouty thirteen-year-old girl, boarded alone, mastering a haughty expression. Harris had a high opinion of her; she was intelligent and headstrong—but her mother was a hooker, and Denyse would probably end up on the same dead-end path unless someone rescued her.

The group of refugees included two vacant-eyed homeless men, Clint and Albert, who had given up on a system that had no interest in giving them another chance; now they looked on Jackson Harris as if he just might be as good as his word.

A short fourteen-year-old boy hung on the other side of the chain-link fence and snickered, as if trying to look bigger. "Hey, fuck this Boy Scout trip!"

Harris crossed his arms over his chest and walked up against the fence, staring the kid down. Harley acted as if he'd always wanted to be in a gang, but had never actually joined. Instead, he tried to look tough, making loudmouthed comments but backing off whenever he was challenged. Harris had seen it happen a dozen times before.

"Suits me fine, Harley. We don't want chickenshits along. We need real tough dudes, not hot air and stuffed jackets."

Harley bristled. "Who you talking about? I'm guarding my turf!"

"Look at yourself, man. There ain't gonna be any of your turf left in a month, and we're going to be sitting warm and happy out by the windmills." He made a gesture of dismissal at the young man and turned away. "Anybody too stupid to see the change coming is bound to get stomped on."

Harris had managed to get the kid to come help them on Angel Island, putting him to work on the charcoal grills cooking hot dogs and hamburgers. Before that, Harley had complained about a "stupid road trip" to Yosemite National Park, which Harris and Daphne and the Reverend Rudge had also staged—but the kid had spent most of the day staring slack-jawed at the towering granite rock walls and the gushing waterfalls.

Now their eyes met, and Harris smiled at him. He knew Harley wouldn't survive another week as the turmoil exploded in Oakland and all around the Bay Area.

"And what would I want with you Boy Scouts, huh?" Harley sneered. "Go out and mow some cracker's lawn?"

"No." Harris shook his head, grinning. "They got cows for that. Think you wanna be a cowboy?"

"Bullshit!"

"Yeah, and cow shit. Probably horse shit, too. We got it all. But it's gonna be hard work, not for dumb fucks. You better stay here, Harley." He walked back to the bus. "Go ahead and guard your turf."

The young man postured and scowled at Harris. "I know what you're trying to do, man! You're fuckin' with my mind. You're crazy!"

Harris shrugged. "I been called crazy by white people before—but I usually pull it off anyway. Just remember that."

He brought the last box of supplies, a grease-stained, ragged cardboard box, and climbed aboard the bus. Daphne gave him a quick kiss, then yanked the bus door shut, as if this would be another one of their day trips to a state park. Harris looked out the broken side window to see Harley standing by the chain-link fence, a troubled expression on his face.

Then the bus shuddered and died.

The people on the bus gave a simultaneous groan, and Daphne struck the horn with her fist in frustration. It peeped weakly. Reverend Rudge stood at the door of his church, hanging his head. He kneaded his thin hands in front of his waist. Lindie, the woman with five kids, said, "We can't walk all that way!"

Harris stood up. "Hey, let's try the last bus before we all start bitching! And if it starts, you need to haul ass and get the supplies transferred. We could have gone five miles in the last few minutes we sat here in the parking lot."

Daphne opened the bus door and swung down, keys in hand. She did not look optimistic about the third vehicle, which sagged on weak suspension. Bullet holes scarred its olive-painted sides, and a great spiderweb crack blazed across the windshield. It had only one wiper blade—in front of the driver's seat, luckily—but the other had been snapped off.

Bumping each other, the passengers piled out, kids laughing or crying or punching each other. The grown-ups carried grocery bags, boxes, blankets, pillows. Harris grabbed a second load, setting up a fire-brigade line from one bus to the other. He looked up and paused. Harley had left his heckler's spot at the fence and begun to help.

"Holy shit, look who's got a brain after all," Harris said.

"Fuck you, man."

When Daphne turned the key in the ignition, the engine chugged, then miraculously caught; it sounded as if it had a few more miles left in it. "Come on!" Daphne shouted. She hauled back on the lever that swung the door shut even before Harris had climbed the steps. She jammed her foot on the clutch and fought with the stick, ramming it into first gear. The bus lurched forward.

Harris held on to the bar, expecting to hear the bus stall out, but the engine kept up its chugging, indigestion sound. Harris and Daphne both waved at the Reverend Rudge through the cracked windshield.

The bus crawled out onto the city streets, avoiding stalled cars and walking people. Two dark-skinned businessmen thumped on the side of the bus as it rolled by. A Volkswagen Beetle putted across an intersection ahead of them. Traffic was sporadic enough that Daphne ignored the streetlights, afraid to risk idling the bus's engine.

Throwing her arms and shoulder into the effort, Daphne wrestled with the steering wheel, fluttering her foot on the gas pedal, trying to keep the vehicle moving by sheer willpower. They crawled out of downtown Oakland and onto the freeway network, easing through intersections and not daring to stop at corners. Occasionally a stalled car blocked one of the lanes. The shoulder looked like a parking lot with abandoned automobiles.

She turned her head to watch them as the bus moved by; she wished she could offer them a hand, but it would be impossible to help all the crowds, all the lives affected by the spreading disaster. She and Jackson couldn't do everything.

The bus engine popped, as if it had begun missing on one or more cylinders, but Daphne kept driving eastward, away from the city. She squeezed the grip of the steering wheel, adding her own willpower to the engine. Every mile brought them closer.

In a weak attempt to dilute the anxiety and tension, Jackson and the other passengers broke into a few verses of "99 Bottles of Beer," which degenerated into silliness and nervous laughter. But even the songs faded into a subdued quiet.

Daphne looked up in the bus mirror, seeing two dozen glistening or averted eyes, passengers biting their lips, making fists in their laps, gripping the seat backs. They could not pretend this would be another exhilarating day trip. They were leaving their lives and everything they knew behind.

Forty miles and two hours later, the battered church bus passed Livermore and exited the freeway onto a narrow road that led into the rural Altamont hills. Daphne expected the bus to die at any moment, but they had escaped from the city. Before long, Oakland would probably burn to the ground in an unchecked firestorm much worse than the fire that had leveled the hilly, rich part of the city a few years earlier.

Their group would be safe out among the windmills.

Daphne coaxed the bus past ugly, out-of-the-way auto-wrecking yards and gravel-supply lots alongside railroad tracks, which reminded her of the more desolate sections of downtown Oakland. She also saw a sign for the Sandia and Lawrence Livermore National Laboratories, government research centers that sat quietly near the foothills. With all the funding they stole from human-works projects, Daphne hoped they could come up with a solution to this petroplague crisis.

By now, the engine gasped and burbled, as if every

minute would be its last. The passengers had started talking to each other again with relief and excitement. Some of the kids kept their faces plastered to the windows, though the grassy, hilly landscape offered nothing particularly exciting to look at.

Jackson sat up front next to her, staring out the windshield. "It's gonna be okay, Daph," he said. It sounded like a mantra. He rubbed her shoulder. "We can walk from here if we got to."

"I know it."

The bus toiled up the narrow, winding road, filling most of the width of the pavement. Steep dropoffs fell away to her right; the road had no guardrail, only a line of drooping barbed wire partway down the slope to fence grazing cattle. They saw few houses.

Daphne turned her entire body at the steering wheel to wrench the bus around a sharp curve. The engine belched and stalled out, but she was able to flutter her foot on the gas pedal, coaxing it back to life for just a few feet more.

Up ahead, a sign said ROAD NARROWS. "Great," she muttered.

At the crest of the hill, the engine died for good. Momentum carried them forward a few feet more, and Daphne jammed the gearshift into neutral. The bus kept rolling until finally gravity helped them along.

"We can coast downhill for a while," she said.

Jackson was grinning. He squeezed her shoulder. "We've only got another mile or so anyway. We made it!" he shouted, and the others joined him in the cheer.

As they came out of the shadow of the hills around a corner, the panorama of the Altamont range spread out. The passengers looked out the left side of the bus, talking among themselves.

The rolling, grass-covered hills seemed to go on forever. Covering the range were thousands and thousands of windmills like a mechanical army, their blades turning in the clean breeze.

THIRTY-FIVE

SEALED WITH A KISS

MEMORANDUM FOR THE PRESIDENT

FROM: ASSISTANT TO THE PRESIDENT
            FOR SCIENCE AND TECHNOLOGY

SUBJECT: MATERIAL AFFECTED BY "PETROPLAGUE"

The following list of items has been compiled to help assess the scope of the spreading "petroplague." Because of the uncertain nature of the microorganism and the varying compositions of many plastic formulations, all or some of these items may be compromised by an attack from the plague.

For a complete discussion of the suspected chemistry and decomposition analysis for 72 representative petroleum-based polymers, please see Appendix F (attached).

    Styrofoam cups and packing materials
    Food packaging
    Vinyl car seats
    Shampoo and toiletry bottles

Electrical wire insulation (NOTE: natural rubber seems
    to be excluded)
Shoe components/soles
Shoelace tips
Automobile gaskets
Plastic plants
Soda straws
Balloons
Pens
Acrylic display cases
Linoleum
Carpet fibers
Polyester clothing
Acrylic coatings
Weather stripping
Magnetic tape substrates
Compact disc substrates
Circuit boards
Some paints and sealants
Computer monitors
Certain components of furniture
Telephone handsets
Medical hypodermic syringes
Eyeglass frames
Soft contact lenses

THIRTY-SIX

LAST CHANCE

Up in the mountains, the house trailer's old kerosene heater had stopped working. Fumbling in the dimness, Dick Morgret tried a fourth time to light it, without success. He kicked the piece of junk with a rattling metallic clatter, then tossed the wooden match stub on the floor. Groggy with sleep, Morgret stumbled around the cramped trailer, trying to remember where he kept the extra blankets.

An early-summer rainstorm swept over the California mountains, drenching the Last Chance gas station out in the middle of nowhere. Morgret had awakened shivering on his cot. He listened to raindrops hammering on the metal roof; trickles of water leaked inside, soaking his possessions. He grumbled, but didn't waste breath on any of his really good obscenities, since no one else was there to hear him.

He yanked one of the ratty quilts from the storage cubicle under the dinette table. The heavy cloth smelled of mildew, but the rest of the trailer had plenty of strong odors to mask it.

As he lay back on the cot, waiting for his body heat to warm the blankets, water dripped through new leaks in the walls. Every inch of insulation had turned to toothpaste, letting water seep in from all corners. Earlier that evening he had tried stuffing rags into the cracks, but then gave up and just draped canvas tarps over the furniture. The whole friggin trailer was falling apart, just like his life. What else was new?

His bed remained cold, as if his body couldn't spare any heat for the blankets. He'd slept alone for close to sixteen years now. He had buried three wives already and had no interest in making it four. All of them had been beefy and bossy—but sometimes he missed the simple pleasure of someone else making noise in the house, or keeping the bed warm. Now the only sound he heard as he finally drifted off to sleep was the patter of rain leaking through the widening cracks in his home.

By morning the air had cleared. Morgret glanced out the window. The creek winding down from the mountains had swelled from the rainstorm. In the distance, he could see a few wild horses trotting around in the meadows.

He got up, stepped in a puddle of cold water, and sat down on a card-table chair to peel off his soggy, threadbare socks. After using the crapper out back, he shuffled to the two gasoline pumps under the rickety aluminum awning. He had nothing better to do than spend the day waiting for customers who would never come.

Highway 178 wound through the mountains, descending into the great desert basin of dry lake beds, military testing ranges, and Death Valley. Morgret hadn't seen any traffic on the road for two days, and the last car had not stopped by. No traffic, no customers. No customers, no income. No income, nothing to pay off the creditors.

The gas—both regular and unleaded—smelled awful even to him, and worse yet, it wouldn't burn. Some environmental shit, probably, and that frightened him. If the government found out, he'd probably have to rip out his buried tanks and install new liners. In that case, Morgret would just up and abandon the gas station, leaving it for the crows.

The Oilstar tanker truck had not come up from Bakersfield with his delivery this week—but Morgret had no money to pay the driver anyway, and his credit was as good as wet toilet paper. Morgret wondered if he was liable to the oil company for contaminated gas.

He laid an old newspaper on the seat of his lawn chair to keep his pants from getting wet. The morning remained cool, but he sat in the shade because the air was bound to get warmer and he wouldn't feel much like moving in an hour or so. Morgret lounged back to watch the world go by.

Except the world wasn't going by. No traffic. Nothing.

Toward midmorning he heard a hollow, clopping sound coming down the road; it took him a moment to recognize the sound of shod horses, not the roaming wild herd. In a moment, three riders came around the curve. They wore canvas ponchos dotted with dark splotches from leftover raindrops. All three had long hair; the smallest, youngest-looking man had a thin mustache, but the other two were clean-shaven. Morgret recognized the broad-shouldered Hispanic man on the black stallion at once. Morgret struggled to get up from his folding lawn chair by the time Carlos Bettario rode up to the gas pump.

Years spent outdoors had given Bettario's skin the look and feel of well-worn leather. He tied his long, pepper-colored hair in a ponytail that hung behind a flat-brimmed Clint Eastwood hat.

They nodded nonchalantly at each other. "Howdy, Carlos," said Morgret. He looked at the stallion, then at his gas pump. "Fill 'er up?"

The other two riders, ranch hands he supposed, chuckled. Bettario patted the stallion's muscular neck, and said without the slightest trace of an accent, "No thank you, sir, I think this one still has a full tank."

"Just another piss-head who doesn't want any gas! What brings you down from the dude ranch, Carlos? Inviting me to a church social?"

Bettario owned and operated Rancho Inyo, a popular tourist ranch near Lake Isabella, where the idiot vacationers could pretend to be cowboys. It had made Bettario a rich man.

"Hell, if you had any gasoline, I'd buy every drop. But I don't expect you're better than anybody else in the country." Bettario laughed. "No, I came to rescue you, my friend."

Morgret scowled at him and sat back down in his creaking chair. How had Bettario known the gas pumps had gone bad? "Rescue me? What are you talking about, Carlos?"

"From the plague, man. What're you going to do with yourself now? Your station was barely surviving before." With a gesture of his chin, Bettario indicated the dilapidated house trailer, the sign that still said LAST CHANCE.

Morgret narrowed his eyes. "What plague?"

The ranch hands exchanged glances. Bettario took off his hat. "Man, you must be kidding me! Don't you watch the news?"

"Gee, Carlos, I must not have paid my cable TV bill for the month. I've been thinking about getting one of those two-thousand-dollar satellite antennas—but it wouldn't do me much good, since I don't even own a damned television! I ain't got a newspaper that's less than a month old."

Bettario shook his head. "Man, a plague is wiping out all the gas, and now plastic too. People are going nuts. We're lucky we live up here away from the chaos." The stallion snorted, as if he disagreed with Bettario's opinion of "lucky." "Me, I'm smart enough to realize that we're going to have to pull together and work our *cojones* off to make it through the first year."

Morgret squinted at him, but Bettario wasn't the type to play practical jokes. And it did explain the bad gas, the total lack of traffic, the week-late gas tanker. "So, you're coming to rescue me, huh?"

The stallion nosed around for something to nibble on. Bettario jerked the reins to raise the horse's head. "We got rid of the tourists at Rancho Inyo, and I have room for a few people who know what they're doing. You've been around a long time, Dick. You're full of bullshit, but you've also got a lot of common sense, and you know how to work. I need men to help keep the larders stocked, which means hunting and fishing and working with the livestock. We're going to round up the wild horses, because without automobiles, horses will be worth more than gold.

"You also know how to fix things," Carlos continued. "Rancho Inyo gets its power from the hydroelectric plant by the reservoir. Even without oil to burn, I suppose a dam and a waterwheel can keep working—if we figure out a way to keep them lubricated."

Bettario smiled down at Morgret standing in his coveralls. "Come with me back to the ranch, Dick. My boys here will help you pack up whatever you want to take along."

Morgret raised his eyebrows, then gestured expansively toward the leaking trailer, the fouled-up gas pumps, the empty highway. "Let me get this straight, Carlos. You want me to leave *all this* just so I can hunt and fish the whole day long? Round up some horses, chop some wood, for free room and board at a place where the city slickers pay a hundred dollars a night?"

"Three hundred fifty, last year." Bettario nodded. "Yeah, sums it up pretty well."

"Sounds better than getting jabbed in the eye with a sharp stick." Morgret glanced around the small patch of land he owned by virtue of squatter's rights. He had grown roots here, but somehow it didn't feel like he was leaving anything behind.

"Carlos, get your boys to help me take down this Last Chance sign, then I'll be ready to go."

THIRTY-SEVEN

ADDICTED TO LOVE

Apounding on the door pierced through the layers of fog that enveloped Jeffrey Mayeaux's mind, waking him out of a blissful few hours of sleep. He hated the constant interruptions that came with being an "important man." Well, in another year he could forget all that bilgewater.

Mayeaux woke up, smelling the disorienting strangeness of new sheets. Pieces fell into place. Two-story resort apartment in Ocean City, a getaway Weathersee had arranged for him a month ago. And nobody was supposed to know where he was. Pickled crawfish! Weathersee must have blabbed.

The pounding returned from somewhere outside the darkened bedroom . . . the front door. It was too damn early for a person to think. Besides, this was what, Sunday?

He started to roll over and get off the bed when the woman beside him moaned softly in her sleep; her head rested on his arm. Mayeaux could still smell sweat on the sheets. She was in her early twenties, large breasts, small ass, long blond hair. She brayed like a mule when she came, but it had turned him on. Too bad she had the face of a mule, too, but who cared?

As memories of last night came back to him, he felt another erection stirring. Weathersee had arranged for the babe to be waiting for him at the condo. Mayeaux never knew whether his Chief of Staff actually paid for these women, or if he enticed them in some other way. Good old Weathersee.

Mayeaux's wife knew the locations of his "love nests," and she even called him once in a while when she needed his help with one of the houses or some other emergency. But no one was supposed to know about the Ocean City place.

The door would probably splinter soon under the relentless pounding. The sheer monotonous nature told him it was probably some security goons. Anybody with half a brain would have figured out by now that Mayeaux didn't want to talk to anybody. What a great way to wake up and start the day.

Mayeaux somehow managed to slide off the side of the bed and pick up his robe without waking the babe.

He could hear a muffled voice yelling his name as he closed the bedroom door behind him and padded down the stairs. "Hold on, Boog, for gawd's sake," he said.

The seaside apartment smelled of stale wine and ripe cheese. Sunlight streamed across the foyer where he had forgotten to close the curtains the night before. How he wished he could find someplace in the D.C. area that served decent café au lait and beignets for breakfast.

With the spreading panic and the mechanical breakdowns caused by the gasoline plague sweeping across the country, Mayeaux should have realized he couldn't get away for a day. Just one fucking day, and it had been planned for months. Granted, he could recognize the magnitude of the growing crisis—but *he* wasn't in charge. Other people could take care of things for a few hours, couldn't they?

By Friday night only a few outbreaks had been reported in Maryland and a few in Virginia, but the news got more frantic hour after hour. California had closed its borders, far too late to stop the spread of the plague, and information from the West Coast was sporadic.

Vice President Wolani had been stuck in Chicago on a speaking tour when the FAA ordered an immediate shutdown of the entire commercial airline industry in the wake of a dozen major crashes that had been blamed on disintegrating plastic components.

Mayeaux had chuckled upon learning that President Holback was stranded in the Middle East on his widely publicized diplomatic tour to Qatar. When Air Force One itself was found to be infected with the petroplague . . . and now the petroleum-eating microorganisms were ravaging some of the largest Arabian oil fields. He wouldn't want to be in Holback's shoes at the moment.

"Mr. Speaker? Are you in there?" The voice from outside sounded loud and firm enough to pierce the solid door.

Mayeaux peered through the peephole. Two men in dark suits stood on his porch, wires running from their collars to earplugs. He could see three other men standing out in the sand, facing outward. *Secret Service?* Jeez, couldn't they be a bit more subtle? They stood out like a Day-Glo billboard in this beach town.

A chill raced down his back. Damn, what could they want? Was this a sting? His initial fear that he was in trouble left him quickly—someone in authority would be present, an official from Justice, if he had done anything wrong. And Mayeaux had never made any secret of his affairs.

But Secret Service, *here?* If it was so damned important to wake him up on a Sunday morning, Weathersee should have telephoned him. Then he remembered having his calls forwarded to the office; he'd unplugged the phones here since his wife and kids were staying with friends.

The Secret Service man seemed to sense him standing

on the other side of the door. "Mr. Speaker—it's important, sir. We have to speak with you."

Mayeaux peered beyond the man in the peephole. The beach had been cordoned. The place was surrounded by plainclothes officers.

"Yes?" *Oh, shit.* Mayeaux's mind whirled. For the first time in years, he found it difficult to keep his political mask in place.

"It's urgent, sir."

As Mayeaux unbolted the door, the Secret Service man pushed his way in. The other, as big as a professional linebacker, motioned to the rest of the team. Mayeaux smelled the wash of cool, damp air from the ocean.

The first Secret Service officer seemed relieved to see him. "Mr. Speaker, thank God we found you." But he didn't look Mayeaux in the eye as he spoke—instead, his eyes darted around the apartment, checking, verifying. He wasn't sweating, or ruffled in the least from all his pounding on the door.

Mayeaux sputtered. "What are you talking about?"

Another agent pushed into the townhouse. He spoke to the first man. "Satchmo's secure?"

"Right," said the first agent, who relayed the information through a microphone in his sleeve.

Mayeaux drew his bathrobe around him, and suddenly froze. *Satchmo?* The Secret Service used code names for the president, the vice president, and their immediate families. . . .

He'd had enough of this crap. "All right, what's going on? Did Holback send you here to harass me?"

The first agent stopped, his face suddenly screwed into a hard look. His blue eyes continued to flick back and forth. "No, sir. We have to inform you that Vice President Harald Wolani was killed last night in an elevator accident in the Sears Tower in Chicago. The plague has spread there, sir, somewhat more extensively than expected."

"Wolani's dead?" Mayeaux stepped back, bumping

into the pale blue sofa. He automatically started to sit down, but he locked his knees and stood up again.

Mayeaux wanted a Bloody Mary—hell, make it a George Dickel, neat!—but he couldn't get up the nerve to walk to the wet bar.

"We have also lost contact with the president, sir," the first agent said. "There's a great deal of turmoil in Qatar, and the last communication we had from the ambassador was that the Qatar government is refusing to guarantee the president's safety. We have been unable to reestablish communication."

"Jeffrey, what's going on? Should I come down?" A sleepy voice drifted from the bedroom upstairs.

"No!" Mayeaux shouted. He didn't have the slightest idea what the bitch's name was.

An agent ran up the stairs. "I'll check it out."

"You know what this means, sir—" the first agent continued, finally halting his roving gaze and meeting Mayeaux's eyes.

"Of course I know!" he said. Then he finally allowed himself to slump onto the sofa. "I'm acting as president until you can reestablish contact with Holback."

"*If* we can reestablish contact, sir. President Holback is a prime target for retribution."

"You damn well better reestablish contact!" Mayeaux climbed to his feet again, feeling his legs shake. "Get me some coffee." Turning his back on the Secret Service agent, he walked slowly and carefully toward the kitchenette.

The agent continued, as if he had been wound up and needed to finish his routine. "The beach area is secure, sir. We need to get you back to D.C. To swear you in."

Mayeaux drew a breath and felt his head hammer with panic. Everything was happening too fast. He had expected to retire after this term, and settle back in New Orleans. He had arranged everything for a quiet and lucrative lobbying career. Everything had been arranged. Mayeaux flopped out a hand to steady himself.

Strangers shoved into the apartment; loud voices and activity swirled around him. Everything seemed unreal. Outside, the Secret Service people checked the convoy. An army gasoline truck pulled up, ready to follow the limousines. It was only a three-hour drive back to the White House. Even if some of the vehicles broke down en route, at least one would make it all the way.

And Mayeaux would be sworn in.

He stood blinking in surprise.

He didn't want to be president in the middle of what looked like the gravest crisis since World War II. If not worse.

THIRTY-EIGHT

SHOP AROUND

The world around Albuquerque broke into smaller and smaller pieces, and General Bayclock knew survival might depend on the Air Force Base's stockpile of emergency supplies. In the late afternoon, he stepped out of the dim base HQ building and looked around at the streets of Kirtland, appalled at the rapid change.

The silence was deafening, where once the roar of airplanes landing and taking off from the flight line had soothed Bayclock all day long. No flights had come into the airport in two days, now that all air traffic had been frozen.

Relying only on scrambled, broken communications that did more to cause panic than convey information, Bayclock had placed Kirtland Air Force Base on DefCon 3 status, pulling all essential personnel onto the base and increasing guards at each of the gates. Within hours of the first evidence of the plague's effects, he had ordered the commissary and BX on strict rationing.

Now, the once-chaotic streets were empty of traffic. Under Bayclock's orders, the base quickly adapted to the new routine. A few airmen and civilian workers walked down the sidewalk across the street, past a parking lot full of cars, vans, and government vehicles that would probably never start again. One rider puttered down the empty lanes on a moped that ran on alcohol. It wouldn't be long before its plastic components gave out and caused the vehicle to break down like its gas-burning counterparts.

Having dismissed his aide, Bayclock set off on foot toward the base exchange to take care of his own needs. Food. Canned goods. Bottled water. His personal quota should be there waiting for him. He wondered if he needed to place an extra set of armed guards at the BX doors.

He trusted his people, and he knew they would follow orders. They'd had the chain-of-command drilled into them since Basic Training, but Bayclock felt uneasy about his tenuous grip on civilization. He felt out of touch, forced to make decisions with too little information. He was reluctant to risk overreacting in the face of the plague, but now it appeared that the germ was even more voracious than his worst fears. In mere days, Albuquerque had become a shambles.

Bayclock crossed Wyoming Avenue in front of the HQ, habitually looking both ways before stepping into the crosswalk, then headed down the block. He saw no lights on in any of the barracks-style buildings, though some of the base personnel had opened windows to let the breeze in.

As he walked through the eerie, stifled silence, he thought about the death of Vice President Wolani two days earlier. It had shocked him deeply, but even with the President out of the country, Bayclock had solid faith in the chain of command.

The base exchange annex looked too crowded as he approached. Bayclock straightened his cap and walked briskly forward, squinting in the low-slanted sunlight. Hand-painted sandwich-board signs stood propped by the BX gas pumps. CONTAMINATED FUEL.

A handful of people in and out of uniform milled around the BX. A ripple passed through the crowd as a tall captain noticed Bayclock and gave a salute. Bayclock returned the salutes and walked through the open glass doors.

He set about gathering up anything he might need for the next few days, focusing his attention with relentless determination. The shelves looked half empty, well picked over. Up at the cash register, the middle-aged male checker argued with an enlisted man over how many boxes of dried milk he could take. Bayclock felt as if he were in combat again as he took the two remaining cans of soup—tomato and split pea, which he didn't even like—and some bags of Cracklin' Hot pork rinds.

As he picked up the pork rinds, though, his fingers slipped through the plastic package as if it were a half-cooked egg white. The thin film broken, air seeped out of the package, and the bag collapsed into a mucuslike slime. He stared in disgust and shock, then shook his hand to fling away the goop.

Down another aisle, plastic bottles of soda wept droplets of moisture. One bottle of Nehi grape split and collapsed, spurting purple liquid over the floor. From the sticky mess on the floor, he could tell that random bottles had been doing that all day long as different types of plastic succumbed to the microbe.

One of the BX employees, a youngish black woman with her hair trimmed as bristly short as Bayclock's, seesawed with a mop, frantically trying to clean up foul-smelling chlorine bleach that dribbled over the shelves into boxes of other detergents. Bayclock stiffened as he thought of the nearby plastic bottles of ammonia. If all the chemicals spilled together, they might mix to form a cloud of deadly chlorine gas.

"You! Move those bottles of ammonia!" he snapped. The woman jumped, looking at him. She dropped the mop handle. It clacked against the metal shelves as it fell. Bayclock raised his voice, annoyed at her hesitation. "Do it now."

Without watching to see if she followed his order, Bayclock collected his rations and took his place in line at the cash register. The woman in front of him held a plastic gallon container of milk; as Bayclock watched, the handle stretched and snapped off. Milk poured down the woman's leg and gurgled onto the floor. She dropped the container, staring stupidly at it as if her pet dog had just bitten her. Milk splashed on Bayclock's clean trouser leg.

He stepped back, frowning at the mess she had made of his uniform. The floor felt tacky, as if from many spilled substances—but then he noticed that the linoleum itself had begun to soften.

He grabbed his supply of canned food, glanced at it, and tossed a twenty-dollar bill at the middle-aged cashier. "Keep it," he growled. "That's more than enough."

Bayclock left the store at a brisk walk. He wanted to get back to the base Command Post, where he felt in control of things. It was time to establish more stringent control of the whole rationing process. Time to crack down on a lot of things.

THIRTY-NINE

I WILL SURVIVE

Heather Dixon wasn't the only one who had realized the world was going to hell. Not by a long shot.

She fought with the crowds in the camping-supply store, smelling the sweat of other people. It would take little to turn the rest of the shoppers into a mob.

Heather began to panic, moving quickly and breathing hard, afraid she wouldn't get the equipment she needed to survive the coming months. She pushed past a tall, rail-thin woman in dissolving polyester slacks, banged into a half-empty set of metal shelves, and made her way toward the back of the store.

Two truck-driver types—one bearded, one balding—came to blows over nylon sleeping bags; Heather wondered if the nylon would last after the petroplague swept through.

At the front counter, the owner of the store—a dumpy man who looked as if he had never been camping in his life—rang up purchase after purchase with a glazed look in his eyes. He couldn't seem to believe his luck.

Heather made her way down the aisles, clutching a

sweat-wrinkled piece of paper on which she had jotted down her list of essentials. She felt sick when she saw that all of the large aluminum-framed backpacks were gone. Why had she wasted time writing out the damned list? She should have run the half mile to the store to fight for the items she *had* to have. Obtaining the right equipment could mean the difference between life and death, and people—a growing number of them—were just beginning to realize the scope of the breakdown.

She pushed to the backpack section, saw labels and crumpled tissue packing material scattered across the floor—and a single remaining backpack frame on the bottom shelf. One of the aluminum support bars was twisted, as if someone had tripped over it; the neon-pink fabric was garish, but what did that matter? She hoped the fabric wouldn't dissolve, but there wasn't anything she could do about it.

As she hurried to the last pack, a man wearing jeans and a Bugs Bunny T-shirt sprinted for it. Heather hesitated, then decided to race him. She'd had enough of being stepped on, and things were damn well going to change!

Bugs Bunny had tucked three bottles of propane for a gas cooking stove under his arm, which gave him trouble running. Heather grabbed the bent strut of the backpack, and the man pulled on the opposite side.

"I got it—" the man said.

Heather answered by jamming an elbow in his gut. With a surprised "oof!" Bugs dropped his three metal bottles of propane. They clanged and bounced on the floor, and Bugs released his hold to scramble for them.

Heather yanked the neon-pink backpack free and clutched it to her chest. "It isn't your color anyway," she said, then stalked down another aisle. The incident sparked her mood. It was time to stop accepting everybody's leftovers.

Heather stood taller than most of the other women in the store and a good many of the men. She quit excusing herself every time she bumped into another shopper.

They could damned well get out of her way. She recalled the advice given in the self-defense seminars Surety Insurance required their employees to take. "Don't look like a victim." She tried to appear stern, imagining Al Sysco standing in front of her. The thought brought a flash of cold-metal anger, and she could feel her face tighten.

People moved out of the way. She shoved aside the ones who didn't.

She stuffed the backpack with dehydrated food in foil packages. Staring at a tiny gas-burner backpacking stove, she decided that she could cook over a campfire. She opted for a large hunting knife, some fishing equipment, and a mummy sleeping bag rated to twenty below zero.

Heather glared around the store, rejecting most of the items. A tent would be too bulky to carry all the way home. Some compact pots and pans would be nice, but unnecessary—she could adapt her own utensils. She took matches, a snakebite kit, a solar still for purifying water.

Heather felt supercharged. On a normal day, she would have been at the office processing forms, answering telephone calls, gritting her teeth against Sysco's treatment of her. *But not today, honey,* she told herself. *Not anymore.*

Then, realizing that she wouldn't have a car, or even a bicycle unless she could find one without a plastic-based inner tube, Heather remembered the most important piece of her ensemble—sturdy hiking boots, made of leather with genuine rubber soles. She had to avoid anything with plastic stitching, vinyl sides, synthetic rubber soles. Just in case.

Guarding her stuffed neon-pink backpack, she searched through the ransacked boxes of hiking boots. Other people had the same idea, but this caused her less concern. Heather had big feet, and shoes her size wouldn't fit many other women.

Finally, dangling a pair of black hiking boots with sparkly purple laces, she waited in line. She had little cash in her savings, and she no longer had a job—but the man at the cashier counter was accepting credit cards. Credit cards! As if they were going to be worth anything!

Heather smiled smugly. *Unclear on the concept,* she thought. She just hoped she would reach the counter before the plastic cards dissolved in her purse.

The power went out for the second time that day, and Heather had no real expectation it would ever come on again. She sat in her living room with the drapes open and the windows cracked to let in a breeze. While she still had enough light, she wanted to sort her new equipment. From now on, she had to plan with a whole new mind-set.

She lived in the suburbs of Flagstaff in a two-bedroom rental house with a small backyard and a carport instead of a garage. Aluminum awnings thrust out above every window. The place had been built in the fifties, with the stomach-turning decor of the times: yellow siding, olive-green carpeting, speckled Formica countertops. Heather had rented it for four years now, always intending to move to something better, but never able to. She suspected she would be leaving the city soon, though.

Heather tied her hair back in a ponytail, then squatted on the floor to organize the dried food and read the instructions on the camping gear. She had gone back-packing in the Grand Canyon with her last boyfriend, Derek, a fellow employee of Surety Insurance. He had eventually dumped her when he took a promotion at a competitor's company in Tucson. Nothing much about the relationship had been memorable, but she had enjoyed the camping, and she missed the sex. The Grand Canyon was only an hour-and-a-half drive north of Flagstaff, but for some reason Heather had never considered going back there alone.

Why the hell not? she asked herself. *Stop being a puppy dog trying to please everyone but you!*

The phone rang twice, then fell silent before Heather could reach it. She stared at it. The phone lines had been dead four of the five times she had tried to dial out, and the one time she heard a dial tone she hesitated and then hung up again.

Her family would be trying to call her from Phoenix, but she had no interest in contacting them. They would want her to come back home so they could weather the tragedy together. And that was definitely not in Heather Dixon's new agenda.

Her family lived three hours' drive away. She had two sisters and three brothers, with Heather right in the middle, the "undistinguished child." Growing up, she'd had to put up with sisters' boyfriends, brothers' softball games, without finding her own niche.

The university at Flagstaff was far enough away that she could find independence, but her interest faded quickly. She quit school after a year and took a job at Surety Insurance. She never admitted that she had missed her home—but every conversation with her parents made it clear that they knew so. It was time to get away and go someplace safe.

She thought of Al Sysco weaseling into the promotion that should have been hers; she thought of Derek, using her as a springboard for jumping to another insurance company.

Well, what goes around comes around. Sysco was probably still waiting for a phone call from the Boston office, telling him the crisis was over. Heather tried to imagine him fighting to survive, hunting his own food; she started to snicker. Then she realized that Sysco probably couldn't conceive of clunky, unassuming Heather Dixon doing that either. She had not found the nerve to make her escape until the petroplague struck.

Kneeling on the threadbare olive carpet, Heather unfolded her AAA maps of northern Arizona. There were trails, and she had supplies; she saw no reason why she couldn't hike from one end of the Grand Canyon to the other. Where else could she find somewhere as safe to go?

She had just begun taking inventory of her dried food when a knock came at the door, putting her on guard. Once the stores ran out of food, looters would go door to door, breaking in and raiding pantries. But they certainly wouldn't politely knock, would they?

Heather debated not answering, but her drapes were open and she sat in plain view. She couldn't pretend she wasn't home. Taking a deep breath, wishing she had a gun, she strode to the front door. She was tired of turning her back and hiding.

She twisted the deadbolt locks with a sliding click, then yanked open the door with more force than she intended. "What?"

The man waiting on her front porch gaped at her in sudden surprise. He looked flustered. He was in his early thirties, with a large and muscular build; his face was sunburned and framed by lanky blond hair. He looked like an out-of-luck surfer. "Who the hell are you?" he demanded.

Heather started to slam the door in his face; but something new inside her found the man's blustering question amusing. "Well, who the hell are *you?* I'm Heather Dixon. Pleased to meet you. And why are you standing on my front porch?"

The man took a full step backward. "Where are my parents?"

The question threw her. "Who?"

"Jan and Howard Brooks. I'm Connor Brooks, their son. They live here."

Now Heather began to understand, and her initial anger gave way to a little pity. "Sorry, but they moved. I've rented this place for four years now. I used to get junk mail addressed to Brooks, but that was a long time ago."

Standing on the porch, Connor Brooks shook his head in amazement. "They moved? They didn't even tell me!"

Heather stayed quiet; it sounded like a bad joke.

Connor thought it over. "I don't suppose they left a forwarding address?" His eyes were wide and blue and hopeful. Heather sized him up and for some reason liked what she saw.

"Afraid not. The landlord might know, but he lives down in Sedona, and the phones are out. I don't expect you've got a car?"

Connor grasped the porch railing as if to prevent himself from falling. "If I had a car that worked it wouldn't have taken me a week to get here. I can't believe it! After all I've been through—and they moved!" He ran his hands through his hair in apparent anguish, but Heather got the distinct impression it was just an act. He tried to peer inside the house. "Hey, could you spare anything to eat? I'm starved."

She thought for a moment. Did she really want this guy around? Everything he said sounded reasonable. And there were some leftovers in the fridge. Still . . .

She said, "Wait here." She bolted the door after she stepped back inside.

She watched him for a minute from the corner window. He stepped off the porch and looked up and down the street. Jamming his hands in his pockets, he rocked back and forth on his heels, waiting for her to return.

Heather grabbed some stale bread and cheese from the refrigerator; before opening the front door, she returned to the kitchen and took out two beers.

Connor turned when she came outside. "Not much of this looks familiar to me. My parents moved here after I left home, and I . . . I haven't been back to visit too often."

She raised her eyebrows. "No kidding." She handed him the food. "Here."

His eyes widened at the beer. "Thanks!"

As they spoke she could not say why she found him intriguing, but Connor Brooks gave the impression of being a survivor. He had no connection to her old life. She began to calculate whether it might be worthwhile having him around.

He seemed to read her thoughts. "Do you think I could impose a little more? I'd really like a shower. It's been a rough couple of days, and I feel like I've been run over by a truck."

She thought it over; the suggestion sounded so preposterous that it made her pause. Funny what a difference a few hours can make. The old Heather would have been flustered, even terrified—and that was enough to make her change her mind. "You do smell like you could use a bit of freshening up. The water will probably be cold, but I've got a hose out back you can use."

"Out . . . back?"

"Consider yourself lucky," Heather smiled. "Times are changing. Besides, I'll bring you a towel."

FORTY

URBAN COWBOY

Alex Kramer's two horses were excited to be taken out. Todd ran his callused right palm along the hot, soft neck of Ren, the palomino, patting gently; he stepped into the stirrup, hauling his leg over the horse's back.

He reached back to gather the reins from Stimpy's bridle, looping them around the saddle horn. The corral gate stood open, and Todd squeezed Ren with his knees, nudging the horse toward the open road. "Let's head 'em out!" he said.

Todd reveled in the warm redolence of the horses. The thick scent brought back fond memories of his younger days, as did the hollow clatter of hooves on the hard road surface. It had been a long time since he'd taken a horse and slept under the Wyoming stars. Of course, it would be different riding through downtown San Francisco, and a heck of a lot more dangerous. He kept Alex's old Smith & Wesson loaded and at his side.

Whispering to the horses, Todd guided them alongside the paved road. The hills were quiet and still. It was time to move on, to stop waiting for the world to fix itself. Besides, he had to go rescue Iris, whether she wanted it or not. Staying in the city would be plain stupid. If the downtown areas weren't already burning, the mobs would be out of hand before long.

Todd kept his eyes forward, Alex's abandoned house at his back. On the winding road, he passed mailboxes, driveways, but the houses sat quiet, deceptively peaceful. Blue-gray wood smoke curled from one chimney. He came across a man walking his German shepherd, as if it were a normal afternoon; Todd and the man nodded to each other, and the dog barked, but the horses continued down the road.

It seemed unreal to him. Elsewhere in the world, planes were crashing, buildings falling apart, communications severed. The last he had heard, the president was stuck out of the country. The C&W radio station had mentioned something about the vice president being killed in an elevator accident, but they had not been able to confirm the rumors . . . and then the radio station blinked out, replaced by static. Todd couldn't get any other stations on the radio either. When he pried it open, he discovered the plastic circuit board had melted.

Only a week ago he'd been flying in the Oilstar helicopter, spraying the Prometheus microbe. At the time, Todd had considered the *Zoroaster* spill a terrible disaster. Now his entire definition of disaster had changed.

After an hour he reached U.S. Highway 101, which stretched down the Marin peninsula, across the Golden Gate Bridge to San Francisco and then the South Bay. Todd took the two horses at a rapid trot down the middle lane. The hard road would not be good for the horses' hooves, and he moved over to the grassy median whenever he had a chance. He wondered if the asphalt itself would turn soft and spongy once the petroplague got hungry. The microbe's appetite for plastics seemed random and unpredictable.

He felt idiotically out of place on horseback in the

middle of a six-lane highway that should have been filled with vehicles zooming by at seventy miles an hour.

Groups of scavengers moved among the dead cars littering the highway, smashing into locked cars or just pushing windshields through the soft insulation holding the glass in place. One tall man without a shirt tucked a set of hubcaps between his elbow and his ribs, leaving a serrated smudge of grease and dirt along his side. A middle-aged woman in a red canvas jacket carried a paper grocery bag stuffed with loose cables and metal housings of car stereo boxes. A blond-haired teenaged boy slashed out seat belts with a long knife, draping a long tangle of them over one shoulder. Todd couldn't imagine what the kid would want them for. As Todd approached, the boy jerked his head out of a Volvo and flashed a broad grin.

At a fast trot, the horses made good time on the empty highway. Before long, Todd reached the cavernous tunnel that cut through a ridge. The horses trotted into the tunnel, their hooves booming inside the enclosed space.

Cars had stalled there, smashed into a tangled mass. Both lanes had been cut off, and no traffic had been able to pass this way for days. The ceiling lights had gone out, but enough daylight streamed in from both ends to let him ride next to the cold tile wall. The horses moved nervously from the close shadows. The empty metal hulks made ticking sounds. Ren and Stimpy began to trot, startled by the reverberating explosions of sound made by their own hoofbeats.

Finally bursting out to the sunlight, Todd took a deep breath of the cool ocean-tainted breeze and stared ahead at the Golden Gate Bridge, and beyond that at the San Francisco skyline.

Not long ago, Todd had been below on the heaving deck of the *Zoroaster*, trying to off-load as much of the crude as possible before the tanker plunged into the channel. There had been helicopters, news crews, boats, rubberneckers. . . .

Now, as he guided Ren and Stimpy onto the bridge, he

heard only the whistling sounds of the wind. The foghorns no longer sent forlorn tones out to warn ships. The water, far below, made hushing sounds against the support piers. In addition to the sea dampness, the air carried a sulfurous stench. Leaking crude oil from the sunken *Zoroaster* continued oozing to the surface, and Prometheus thrived.

Puffing and red-faced, a sweat-suited jogger ran by, intent on the sidewalk in front of his feet. Todd shook his head—people were crazy! How could anybody go through a daily routine in the middle of a crisis? He seated his cowboy hat more firmly; no matter how much the world changed, he thought, some rituals remained the same.

The bridge cables high overhead thrummed in the breeze. The lowering sun dazzled on the water far out to sea. He saw no navy ships or freighters or fishing trawlers. A shiver went up his spine as he realized just how deeply the plague had separated the world into thousands of tiny pieces of a jigsaw puzzle.

Grim-faced backpackers headed along the walkway, moving briskly in a forced march. A gaunt man with red-rimmed eyes, gray stubble on his face, and a SURF! T-shirt called to Todd, "Hey, you're going the wrong way, man!"

"I know," Todd said.

A young couple with three children—the oldest no more than eight, and crying—carried lumpy packs on their shoulders as they hiked toward the Marin peninsula, in the opposite direction Todd was going. The little four-year-old girl carried a cloth doll with yarn hair; dark indentations marked where plastic button eyes had dissolved.

Within ten minutes the two horses approached the southern end of the bridge. Waves crashed against the rugged shore of Fort Point. The deep-green cypress trees and red-roofed military housing of the Presidio shone with brilliant color, as if someone had twisted up the contrast knob. At the end of the bridge, an unlit sign demanded STOP! PAY TOLL. Todd directed Ren and Stimpy through the empty toll booths. He smiled ironically to himself as they passed through the unused "carpool" lane.

On horseback, he entered San Francisco.

Todd avoided the densest part of the city, planning to ride full tilt through Golden Gate Park, keeping his head low and a firm grip on Stimpy's reins. His horses were among the most valuable possessions in the world right now. He kept the pistol within easy reach and urged Ren and Stimpy to a fast trot.

Reaching the large forested area of the park, the small lakes, and the wide grassy clearings made him forget he was in the middle of a city, for a short while. In the grassy expanse, Ren tried to stop and graze, but Todd wouldn't let him, jabbing with his boot heels to keep up the pace. He saw no kids tossing baseballs or Frisbees, no fun and games.

A cluster of men and women worked by the trees with handsaws and axes taken from downtown hardware stores. Not one of the people looked accustomed to manual labor, and they took frequent rests. With a scurry, they fled to one side as a eucalyptus came crashing down; then they set to work chopping it into smaller pieces. A mound of firewood sat stacked to one side. Teenagers took turns with sledgehammer and wedges to split the chunks. Two older women with new rifles stood guard over their wood.

Todd urged Ren and Stimpy eastward out of the park and into more dangerous crowds, following the Panhandle under large oak trees. Old Victorian houses towered over the boulevards on either side of the narrow strip of park, but Todd kept the horses on the grass as long as he could, until he was finally forced to return to the city streets in Haight-Ashbury. It did not surprise him to see various apocalyptic street preachers hawking recipes for salvation to the wandering crowds. Every time someone looked at Todd too closely, he conspicuously pulled out the pistol.

In front of a row of dark coffee shops, Chinese street vendors had set up food kiosks with sidewalk barbecues, burning sticks of what appeared to be broken crates and pieces of furniture. They cooked on Weber kettle grills and cast-iron woks over open fires. Looking at the exotic food as he rode by, Todd had a sudden craving for a decent steak. He wondered how hard it was going to be to find food from now on.

A lump caught in his throat, claustrophobia from the jammed, breaking-down buildings, the sounds of breaking glass, shouts from the sidewalks; he realized he had lost his way. "Calm down," he said to himself, "calm down." Breathing deeply, trying to quell his panic, he reined the horses to a stop and unfastened his saddlebags to take out a map. He unfolded it and tried to get his bearings, figuring out the best way to return to Highway 101. He felt absurd sitting on horseback in the middle of a deserted intersection, staring at a street map like some lost tourist.

He had just decided which way to turn when a series of popcorn noises came from a rooftop a block away. It took him a moment to identify them as gunshots. Across the street, Todd saw a flash of stone dust and heard the *spang* as a bullet ricocheted from the wall of a building. "Jeez!" he cried, and yanked out the pistol again, waving it in the air. Another gunshot struck nearby. Todd fired off a round in the direction of the sounds, but knew he had no chance of hitting anything.

"Yah!" he shouted at the horses. Both Ren and Stimpy galloped away from the sniper, down Van Ness toward the highway leading out of the city.

With the horses hidden in a cluster of live oaks on the ridge crest, Todd prepared to spend the night in the highlands of the Peninsula, west of the freeway. By nightfall, he had traveled south, through the hills rim-

ming Daly City and San Bruno. He could see San
Francisco International Airport, deserted, like a vast
parking lot.

The gunshots and the turmoil made him want to avoid
contact with people. He followed fire roads up into the
rugged hills, heading in the right general direction.

He kept thinking about Iris, knowing he needed to
hurry, to get her out of a dark, dangerous apartment in
Stanford. Heck, she probably wouldn't wait for him
anyway. But on the slim chance that she would, he had
to get his backside there as soon as he possibly could.

He decided to rest for a few hours, start out again
before dawn, and make a good distance by daylight. He
built a campfire in a clearing and heated a can of
Wolfbrand chili, eating it with a spoon he had taken
from Alex's kitchen. If he had been able to forget about
the rest of the world, he might have enjoyed the evening.

The countryside seemed too quiet, wrongly so. Out in
Wyoming the silence had never bothered him because he
did not *expect* to hear bustling noises. But the San
Francisco peninsula was supposed to be a Christmas-
tree network of lights, moving traffic, busy lives. From
his high vantage point, he could see only a few glimmering signs of life below—bonfires, Coleman lanterns,
battery lamps, flashlights.

Todd fell asleep huddled in two blankets.

Before setting out in the early-morning darkness, Todd
munched dry Frosted Flakes from a single-serving box
he had found in Alex's pantry. The cereal tasted stale.
Todd wondered how long it had been there.

This time he mounted Stimpy. They followed the
ridgeline, then descended to the freeway again in the
stillness of the rising sun. Birds began to sing to
the morning, unaffected by the crumbling of the cities.

The rest of the ride to Stanford seemed like a repeat of
the previous afternoon, as he passed through suburbs
and South Bay carbon-copy cities with different names.
It seemed as if every person had decided to wander the

streets, either defending their homes or looting somebody else's. He found an isolated, tree-shaded park in Palo Alto and studied the map again, then headed toward the Stanford University campus.

In one city block, a loud crashing sound startled the horses. As he rode closer, Todd saw that crude barricades had blocked off a twelve-story office building. Every few minutes, one of the glass windowpanes would pop free of its dissolving plastic housing and tumble to the ground, reflecting the sun like a strobe light until it exploded on the pavement. Students gathered across the street, drinking beer from bottles and applauding each new fall of glass.

Todd shook his head and rode on, close now.

When he finally tracked down Iris's street address, he waited outside her three-story apartment building, having no idea what to do with Ren and Stimpy. He couldn't just padlock the horses to a bike rack, and he didn't want to leave them tied out front. He considered his options outside the complex, baffled, until he finally decided to take the horses in with him. Why the heck not?

Ren and Stimpy dug in their hooves, reluctant to go through the narrow glass door. Finally, he coaxed them into the sparsely furnished lobby, where he tied them to the wrought-iron stair railing; at least they were hidden from outside view. Standing beside a tattered sofa and an old end table, the two horses looked at Todd as if he were crazy. He tipped his cowboy hat at them, then bounded up the stairs, his boots echoing on the hard surface.

After turning down the wrong hall, he followed the numbers to Iris's door. He took off his hat, then rapped on the wood. He waited. His stomach knotted. She probably wasn't home. Iris was a smart lady, and she should have had the good sense to pack up and leave already.

Even if she was home, Todd had no idea what to say to her.

The door finally opened on its flimsy security chain,

and Iris peeped outside. When she saw him, her face lit up in surprise.

"So you made it," she said, regaining her composure. She removed the security chain and opened the door wider. "How was the ride? I'm all packed, so we can get out of here."

Wringing the cowboy hat in his big hands, Todd said his line. "I don't usually have to go to such lengths for a date!"

Iris raised her eyebrows, but he could see amusement behind her eyes. "Oh? Then how come you forgot to bring flowers?"

FORTY-ONE

GOOD VIBRATIONS

A dozen saddled horses grazed on sparse vegetation outside the fence that separated the desert from the White Sands missile range. The baked ground was scabbed with alkali, but showed none of the glittering gypsum sand that made other areas look like a snowfield. To Spencer Lockwood the expedition looked more like a Western cattle drive than a convoy setting out for the microwave-antenna farm.

Spencer tugged on the knots securing the bedrolls, canned food, water, toolboxes, rope, wire, and first-aid kit in the old wagon hitched behind two of the horses. He looked over the ragtag collection of five scientists and three young ranch hands hunched around the back of the wagon. Several of the Alamogordo ranchers worked on the axle.

He wiped dirt from his hands and squatted next to the ranchers. He felt silly wearing a floppy cowboy hat, but even Lance Nedermyer, who had found himself stuck at White Sands with no possible transportation back to his family in Washington, D.C., had doffed his dark suit and now wore jeans and a straw hat. "Is it going to work?" Spencer asked.

"The wheel is sticking, Doc, but it'll get you out to your site," said one of the ranchers, applying a handful of animal fat to the axle. Being called "Doc" made Spencer feel like he was in an old Western movie. "Never thought I'd have to use lard for axle grease!" The rancher spun the wooden wheel.

Spencer and his crew out at the antenna farm had always kept a stockpile of supplies, MREs surplused from closed-down Holloman Air Force Base, and pioneer-style accommodations. After his cross-country drive through Death Valley, he had been back home for less than three days before everything else started going apeshit around White Sands.

Thinking ahead, Spencer had visited some of the small ranches in the lush hills, the ranchers who had bought into his power experiment as a way to get cheap rural power. Their own power had blinked off days before, the first expendable victims of a decaying electrical grid. Spencer gave them a talk with more fervor than he had been able to manage for any of the Sandia scientists, acknowledging the riskiness of his venture, but vowing that he could get power up and running again with his smallsats and his microwave receiving farm. Some of the ranchers had run him off their land. But a few offered to help, donating enough supplies to keep Spencer and his crew working out at the block-house.

Lance Nedermyer looked exhausted. He had been even crabbier than usual from worrying about being out of touch with his wife and daughters. Back east, in the thick metropolitan areas, conditions were bound to be far worse than they were here in the rural, self-sufficient southwest.

Nedermyer scowled at the wagon train. "I still think it's better to forget about your whole microwave site,

Spencer. We've completed the evacuation plan at Alamogordo, and we'll need your horses for the trip up to Cloudcroft."

Spencer sighed. They had argued about it the night before. "You're welcome to go with us and see for yourself, Lance. I'm betting we can switch out and replace most of those components with fiberglass or ceramic in the shops. It's a simple system, and we can't give up without trying our alternatives."

The bureaucrat shook his head, hiding his personal worries behind wire-rimmed sunglasses. "Just be forewarned that if the mayor decides to head everyone up to the mountains, we're not going to wait around for you."

"They can go if they want." An awkward silence fell as they both shuffled their boots in the dust.

Now that the solar-power project was isolated from the rest of the world, political games were a thing of the past, and Spencer knew of no quantitative unit small enough to measure how little he cared. But he tried to remember that Lance Nedermyer had once been a talented researcher. If only Lance could remember that himself, he might provide valuable help.

A bearlike rancher in a red cotton shirt turned to the side and spat chewing tobacco. He nodded at Nedermyer. "If this plague keeps getting worse, Doc Lockwood is the only one offering electricity at all. What've we got to lose?"

Spencer ducked his head to hide a grin in the shadow of his floppy hat. "Even if it works it'll only give you power for a few hours a day."

"Better'n nothing." The rancher still eyed Nedermyer.

Gangly Rita Fellenstein tightened her Australian bush hat and swung up on a sturdy brown-and-white horse. The mount pulled back, but Rita snapped the reins to bring it under control. The stirrups had been adjusted for her long spindly legs. She looked quite at home in her Western gear. "Hey, Spence, it's not gonna get any cooler today. Get your butt in gear."

"That's right!" The bearlike rancher stopped by a speckled gray horse and handed the reins to Spencer. He lowered his voice, speaking seriously. "We all know it'll be a lot easier if we head up to Cloudcroft. They got plenty of water, firewood, and game. But we've lived here too long just to give up and leave. People still remember what it was like when the Air Force pulled out of Alamogordo—damned near shut down the whole town. We didn't abandon it then, and we sure as hell won't now."

Nedermyer scowled, and Spencer felt embarrassed. He swung up onto the horse, feeling off balance. "Ready, Rita?"

Rita leaned over her horse's neck and spoke with two of the cowboys accompanying them. They seemed to be flirting with her. She grinned at Spencer. "You gonna be able to handle that horse, or do you want to ride in the wagon with the supplies?"

"Madam, I am a physicist," he said with mock indignation. "I can handle anything!"

Out at the site without air conditioning, it was over a hundred degrees. Rita brushed sweat away from her high forehead as she tinkered by candlelight in the dim blockhouse, looking like a female scarecrow. Juan Romero, the electronics technician, tugged on his huge black mustache and watched, offering suggestions.

Spencer stood behind them both. He scratched at the beard stubble on his face. He'd given up shaving. "You know, Rita, the real reason I keep you slaving away is so you can get the jukebox working again."

"Take another look, Spence. The forty-fives have already dissolved." She sighed. "Now, will you leave me alone? I'm trying to concentrate."

He remembered the celebration with champagne and reporters as the smallsats beamed down power for the first time. About a million years ago.

Rita held up a thin wire. "All right. Marconi would

have been proud. One shortwave radio, ready to go, built with stone knives and bear skins. Got any more of that dry lubricant?"

"Yeah." Romero scrounged behind him and held open a jar of graphite powder made from finely ground pencil leads. Short and swarthy, Romero had the largest smile and the biggest mustache Spencer had ever seen. Through his ability to Band-Aid together gadgetry from spare parts, the smallsat project had managed to move ahead even on a bare-bones budget.

Rita poked the wire in the jar, stirred it around, then removed it to make a final connection. "Okay, *bwana*. All the plastic in this unit has been replaced by ceramic chunks from the maintenance shop with a little cannibalized fiberglass thrown in."

Spencer crossed his arms over his chest and looked down at Rita. "So let's connect it to the battery and turn it on."

"Roger dodger." She made a contact with one of the batteries originally charged by the orbiting solar satellites. Static erupted from the speaker.

Spencer placed a hand on the back of their communications expert. "Okay, Romero, get on this thing and see who's out there listening. Try to get hold of JPL."

"Okay," Romero said, shaking his long black hair behind him. Rita stood up, arching and rubbing her lower back to work out a cramp; then Romero slid into the chair and began working with the shortwave radio. "You sure anybody at JPL is listening?"

"Won't know unless we try. If there's anybody in the U.S. still broadcasting, those people will be."

The wooden floor creaked as Spencer went to the open aluminum door of the blockhouse. He stood on the steel grid of the porch, trying to enjoy the hot breeze. The air smelled baked and dry.

Spencer narrowed his eyes against the bright sunlight searing off the white gypsum sands. He had to keep his group going, work with them to find a new way out of this mess. Everyone in the country was in the same boat, isolated, focused on survival and local concerns, rather than global decisions made by people a thousand miles away.

Rita stepped outside the dull concrete blockhouse and lounged next to him against the shade wall. She fished a pouch from her pocket and placed a pinch of chaw in her mouth. "Why on Earth are you trying to contact JPL? That's news to me. Why not DOE or some emergency headquarters?"

He ignored her question. "When did you start chewing tobacco?"

"When did you start being my mother?"

Spencer lifted a brow and tried to keep an amused look from crossing his face. Ever since interacting with the local ranchers, Rita had become touchy. But she seemed to be enjoying all the new attention.

"Sorry," she said after a moment. "Tommy, the blond-haired guy, is trying to give it up, and he's got a couple month's supply. So he gave it to me. The ranchers think it's hilarious to see a woman chew." She spat. "It's worth putting up with this awful taste just to see the expressions on their faces." She took another mouthful. "But you do get used to it."

Spencer touched the hot doorjamb and quickly pulled his fingers away. Three others besides Romero and Rita worked in the trailer inspecting the satellite equipment. The rest of the group, as well as their two ranch guides, stayed outside in the shade of useless vehicles or in the maintenance shed, resting through the heat of the day.

Rita wiped her mouth. "We can swap out the less-sophisticated equipment with stuff that isn't oil-based, but do you really think we can replace enough to tap the satellites?"

He pondered before answering. "Seems kind of crazy, doesn't it? Forget the delicate computer diagnostics, the mainframes, the precision switching—that's a lost cause. We'll just keep the beam on all the time. The

Seven Dwarfs are still up there, coming overhead every day, unaffected by what's going on down here. We can probably refit the receiving system. Not much of the other equipment relies on petroleum seals or lubricants anyway. That's the beauty of having very few moving parts."

She grunted, unconvinced. "How long do you think it'll take?"

Spencer met her gaze. "Does it matter? I'd rather be trying to get this damn thing working again than high-tailing it up to the mountains like Nedermyer wants to."

He stood, feeling antsy. Rita's questions brought out his own doubts about getting the microwave farm working. Maybe he should examine the antennas one more time. "I'll be back. Call me if Romero finds anything."

"Going to check out the antenna farm?"

He tried to look surprised. "Naw—just going for a walk."

"Yeah, right."

He returned to the cluster of trailers and buildings two hours later. The sun lowered toward the mountains in the west, diminishing its intensity. Rita stepped out of the doorway, waving her arms for him to hurry.

"Hey, Spence! We've got something."

He jogged the rest of the way, feeling his throat dry and clogged from the dust. Inside the stuffy, dark blockhouse, Romero gestured from the gray-painted metal workbench next to the jury-rigged radio. Spencer leaned close to the hissing speaker. "What you got?" He wiped sweat from his face.

Before Romero could open his mouth, a static-filled voice burst into the room. "—Institute of Technology, radio free Caltech, under operation by the Federal Emergency Management Agency. We can barely hear you."

Spencer pulled a seat next to the cluttered workbench; Romero pushed the microphone to him. "This is Dr.

Spencer Lockwood, calling from White Sands, New Mexico. We need to get in touch with the Jet Propulsion Lab in Pasadena. Can you help us out?"

"If you've just picked us up and have not yet registered, we need to get some information from you." The voice on the radio paused, then sounded indignant. "FEMA guidance is that airwaves are currently for emergencies only and not for personal calls."

Spencer scratched his rough beard and spoke into the mike, excited and annoyed at the same time. "Okay, but right now I need to speak with someone from the solar satellite division at JPL. We are a federal installation and this is important business."

The radio fell silent for several minutes. Spencer hoped the battery wouldn't die before the FEMA people got back to him. He tapped his fingers on the metal bench, waiting, waiting. Romero looked at him and shrugged. Finally, the woman's voice returned. "Hello, White Sands? Part of JPL was hit by the rioting. We should be able to get someone back to you shortly, if you're still on the air. Can we get some information from you for our files?"

Spencer pushed the microphone over to Romero. "Go ahead and help them out," he said.

As Romero grinned and started to answer their questions, Rita raised an eyebrow at Spencer. She cocked back her hat and let her braided hair fall down. "You've got more up your sleeve than just getting this microwave farm back on line."

Spencer tried not to smile as he ducked outside to scan the desert restlessly. "If we can get this receiving station back up again, wouldn't it be nice to increase the amount of power we beam down? Keep us on line for hours at a time. Just think of those twenty satellites sitting at JPL, all finished and waiting to be sent into orbit. If Nedermyer hadn't deep-sixed the acquisition process, they'd be here already . . . or maybe even up there."

Rita spat a wad of tobacco off to the side. She seemed to be aiming at a small lizard, but the glob struck a rock instead. The lizard scurried away.

"Now I know you've flipped a byte," she said. "Say those satellites still work—they've been in a clean room and they're vacuum sealed, away from this petroplague, so I can buy that—and just suppose we could somehow get them a thousand miles from LA to New Mexico. Then what do we do with them? We still need to get them into orbit. Are there some rocket launchers left here at White Sands that I don't know about?"

She trailed off as Spencer looked toward the north, toward Oscura Peak. A long thin housing for the five-mile-long electromagnetic launcher ran up the side of the mountain.

She started laughing as it hit her. "I don't believe it. You're crazy! Absolutely nuts! It's one thing to change parts in a simple AM radio and make it work. It's a thousand times harder to change out every single seal and joint in our microwave farm. But to bring those satellites cross-country and use a launcher that's only worked *once?* They need to finish that thing before it can launch our satellites into a high enough orbit! And how the hell do you think we're going to get those satellites out here—by wagon train?"

Spencer stopped humming to himself. He was disappointed she had guessed it so easily. "How did you know?"

FORTY-TWO

LONG TRAIN RUNNING

Clear blue but smudged with clouds, the Napa Valley sky hung over the tourist train station. But, son of a brick, the tourist trade had sure gone belly-up.

Rex O'Keefe didn't really miss the crowds, the automobiles, or the fat self-styled wine connoisseurs who hopped from one winery to the next, gulping the free samples and rolling the fancy names on their tongues. Rex liked the world better this way. Peaceful, uncomplicated, giving him a chance to kick back and relax. When the food ran out, he'd probably be all uptight again, but he tried not to think about that just yet.

Leaning back on the old wooden bench, Rex took a sip of red table wine—Gamay Beaujolais 1991, liberated from the Sandstone Crest winery, best served at room temperature, which was about all he could get these days, now that refrigeration was out of the question. He rolled the wine on his tongue, swallowed slowly to feel the warm bite, to taste the oak.

In front of him, bright in the morning sunshine, the refurbished old steam locomotive sat on the tracks.

Steam Roller. He admired the train, wishing the day would go on forever. And because of the petroplague, it just might. Nothing much would change around here for a long time.

For the moment at least, Rex had everything he could want—plenty of wine, the run of the tourist train station, and no one to bother him now that the weekend crowds fought for survival in the big cities rather than taking a leisurely ride through wine country on an authentic turn-of-the-century steam train.

He had pulled all the dried food and snacks from the refreshment stand, adding to his own stockpile in the small home behind the station. He figured he'd stashed enough food to get by for half a year. The eating would get dull, imported water crackers and some cheese, canned vegetables to supplement whatever he could scrounge from his garden, bottled mineral water. But there was plenty of wine. He would survive. Boy, would he.

He was forty-five and without a family, and Rex O'Keefe's world extended little beyond the railroad tracks and the train station, even now after the petroplague had caused the old Steam Roller to gasp her last breath, unless he could find some other lubricants and gaskets.

He hadn't cared much for the people when they came around anyway. What was the point being boot-licking and nice to strangers who would never come by again? The locals themselves never bothered to ride Rex's train; they had their own tourist industry to watch over.

Rex was content to be alone with his memories. From the time he'd been old enough to own an electric Lionel until he got his first job at fourteen stoking wood on the refurbished Steam Roller, Rex had lived for the day when he could work on the trains.

But now the damn locomotive just sat there, unable to move, stalled in place.

Rex stood on tired legs and sauntered out to the behemoth that sat frozen on the tracks. Painted a deep black, the Steam Roller burned wood in her furnace, heating water in the boiler to drive one of the last locomotives that had not transferred over to coal or diesel. He could smell the creosote from the railroad ties, the old deteriorating oils on the driving wheels, the caked soot from the furnace.

Even motionless, Steam Roller was a sight too pretty just to look at. Rex pulled a red bandanna out of his blue-and-white railroad overalls—the clichéd outfit the tourists expected him to wear—and began to polish the brass pistons.

He ran his hand along the metal siding, then boosted himself up to the engineer's cab, where he tried to work the controls. For a moment he imagined himself riding the tracks as the train chugged through the valleys, a throbbing rhythmic rattle as the wheels passed over crossings. The lush green vineyards extended on either side of the cab, pale vines stretched out along wires in flickering razor-straight rows that looked like optical illusions extending to the hills.

Blinking his eyes, Rex reached up to grab the steam release, when a low voice came from behind the cab, startling him. "Shame to let a beauty like this rust away."

Rex whirled, opening and closing his mouth as if he expected the right words to fall automatically out. He took a second to focus on the stranger: a bearlike man, built short and stocky, with blotchy dark skin and not a hair on his head. The stranger's scalp had been freshly shaved; even the eyebrows were gone.

Rex felt the sour taste of wine claw up his throat. He said hoarsely, "Yeah, she's my train. What do you want?"

The bald man said nothing, only turned to look over the train, admiring it. Rex wanted to leave, to go back into the station, but he couldn't move, couldn't leave the locomotive unguarded. What if the strange man was a vandal or something? The bad taste in his mouth wouldn't go away.

Rex hadn't had much trouble in the week or so since the plague struck the wine country north of San Francisco. The train station was away from most of the town buildings, and he didn't have anything marauders would want.

Rex waved an arm, shooing the man away. "You shouldn't be here. This place is closed."

The bald man hauled himself up into the engineer's cab beside Rex and ran his hand along the wooden console, the controls. "How long since you fired her up?" His voice was confident, as if accustomed to taking charge of such a vessel.

"Uh?" Rex stopped at the question. "Started the train? Are you crazy? Nothing runs anymore."

"Well, I probably am crazy. But this train was built long before we started using petroleum products for everything. It was designed for other alternatives, no matter what you've been using lately," said the man. "With a few people to help, we could get this train running again."

"*We?* Whose train do you think this is?" Rex cocked his head to one side. "You are a crazy man!"

The squat stranger raised the folds that used to be his eyebrows, wrinkling the shaved skin on his forehead. "You got any other plans for it?"

Two days later, when Rex believed the stranger meant what he said, he persuaded the Gambotti brothers and Frank Haverson and Jerry Miles to leave their vineyards and spend a few hours in the afternoon joining in the effort.

They took apart the Steam Roller's gearbox, the piston shaft, the axle, and the controls. Forced by a long screwdriver and steady pressure, each item reluctantly opened up. Smelly lard and gobs of fat, skimmed off the surface of a boiling pot brought in from the Gambotti vineyards, yielded enough lubricant for the first round.

The bald, dark stranger spoke little, sweating and working harder than two of them combined. Rex tried to keep up. The stranger became obsessed with getting the train working again.

Rex couldn't pinpoint when the stranger took control of the effort, nor did he care. They worked from the first light of dawn until they could no longer see in the dark. The stranger ate his water crackers and vegetables in silence. Given the choice, he drank mineral water instead of wine.

Rex O'Keefe took a long gulp from his cup— Gewürztraminer this time, a bit young but bright and fruity—and watched the swarthy man with the shaved head. The man put down his empty plate, lit a candle, and went back outside to work.

Rex wondered what burden the stranger bore that drove him to work so hard.

FORTY-THREE

BIG SHOT

Armed guards, once discreetly hidden behind banks of high-tech observation equipment, now openly patrolled the White House complex. Barricades cut off foot traffic on Pennsylvania Avenue to the north and E Street to the south. The Old Executive Office Building and the Treasury Building served as heavily fortified buffers to the west and east.

Hunching down, Jeffrey Mayeaux walked in the middle of his team of escorts through the wrought-iron gate. Leather patches on the hinges served as makeshift lubrication for the gates. More sophisticated artificial lubricants could have been shipped in from the Department of Commerce's NIST laboratory in Gaithersburg, Maryland, but those were being stockpiled for emergency use.

Mayeaux thought of the briefing given to him while he was driven back to Washington with a military guard. Four of the convoy trucks had succumbed to the petroplague during the three-hour drive.

As of an hour ago, President Holback was officially declared dead. Shortwave radio transmissions stated that some sort of mob action in Qatar had killed the president and his escorts, then burned the American embassy in retaliation for the petroplague ravaging the Middle East oil fields.

With the breakdown in communications, none of this could be incontrovertibly confirmed, Mayeaux knew. But none of that would let him off the hook. He was going to be sworn in as the actual president, not just the acting commander in chief. No pomp, no ceremony— just an emergency action. The world was turning into one giant dog turd, and it was being plopped right in his lap.

Even under normal conditions, he'd never felt comfortable coming into the White House's snobbery—a Southern boy, he didn't have the right background, attend the right schools, or come up through the political system in the right way. The White House staff had treated him with disdain only a few days ago—now Mayeaux looked forward to putting them in their places. From now on, he was going to have to take his pleasures wherever he could. He wondered how the kitchen would react to a request to serve Creole red beans and rice every Monday, as was traditional.

A maintenance woman unrolled heavy-gauge emergency telephone wire across the top of the West Wing; flanked by MPs, navy personnel lugged baskets of food across West Executive Avenue to the White House mess.

"This way, Mr. Speaker." The Secret Service escort motioned him toward the heavily guarded side door. Any other time, the president-to-be would have been received at the front of the White House like a conquering hero, chauffeured through the yawning gates to where the marine guard stood stiffly at the front. The side entrance was reserved for lowly political appointees. But with the turmoil in the city and rumors of snipers, Mayeaux wanted to make himself as small a target as possible. He didn't need all the fuss. Hell, he didn't even want the job.

A crowd of bureaucrats stood just inside the door. A slight smile came to Mayeaux as he recognized the former president's chief of staff, the science advisor, the budget director. He had seen the others before, but they were too far down the food chain to elicit acknowledgment.

The chief of staff steered him past the Situation Room and up the stairs. "Mr. Speaker, we're required to swear you in before updating you on the status of the current emergency. Things have deteriorated and require some drastic decisions." The chief of staff had too much of a "trust me" tone. Mayeaux would see to it that good old Weathersee took his place, pronto!

"We've already frozen our borders," Mayeaux said. "I was told that the National Security Council is recommending martial law across the entire country, confiscating all untainted oil."

The science advisor nodded grimly. "Yes, but it might get tougher still. This is the moral equivalent of fighting a war. Our nation is on the verge of collapse."

Mayeaux paused and studied their grave expressions. What the hell was he supposed to do with an attitude like that? "Gentlemen, I have absolutely no intention of letting the United States break apart, if it is within my power to stop it." He extended his palm, indicating for them to lead the way and get a move on.

They took Mayeaux through the Roosevelt Room to the Oval Office, past military campaign streamers, polished wood, fine art, and a Nobel Peace Prize on display. A lanky man with long sideburns stood by the Secret Service agent outside the door. He carried a Bible and seemed nervous; he must be one of the lower officials in the Justice Department dug up to administer the oath of office. Figures, they wouldn't get the chief justice for him.

The group moved into the Oval Office, filling the room. A row of bushes blooming with flowers outlined the Rose Garden just outside the window. Mayeaux could see the jogging track that encircled the south lawn; a walkway led to the outdoor swimming pool. It seemed too perfect, too good to be true.

He didn't want to be here.

The lanky man with the Bible cleared his throat. "Please raise your hand and swear on the Bible, Mr. Mayeaux."

"Right."

Jeffrey Mayeaux repeated the man's charge, mouthing the oath as it was said to him. The words meant nothing; they were just another set of guidelines to follow, just as his congressional oath or marriage vows. It wasn't the words that mattered, it was the position, and what he could do with it. He mumbled "So help me God," and felt no different. With the minor scandals dogging him throughout his past two terms, he had never dreamed he would keep his congressional office, let alone fall face-first into the presidency! He wasn't ready for this.

As others in the room shook his hand before leading him to the Situation Room, the science advisor's comment stuck with him. This crisis was like fighting a war.

Well, in war, the commander in chief needed to be obeyed. Mayeaux couldn't afford to have his staff second-guess him. The first thing he would do was fire these throwbacks from Holback's administration and surround himself with people he trusted. Finding a good vice president was high on the list.

"Mr. Speaker—I mean, Mr. President," the chief of staff corrected himself, "we need to get to the Situation Room." He moved to the door.

"In a minute," Mayeaux said. "I have a few things I want to discuss first. A few changes."

FORTY-FOUR

PLEASE, MR. POSTMAN

MEMORANDUM FOR THE PRESIDENT

FROM: ASSISTANT TO THE PRESIDENT
             FOR SCIENCE AND TECHNOLOGY

SUBJECT: PETROPLAGUE-AFFECTED MATERIAL
             ADDENDUM 3, CONTINUED

We have again revised our list to include the following items:

    Toys
    Sixpack beverage can rings
    Photocopy machine bodies
    Tupperware
    Polyethylene food wrap
    Handles/knobs/buttons
    Toothbrushes
    Hair dryers
    Garment buttons
    Hairbrushes
    Coffeemakers

Watch faces
Most clocks
Videotapes
Movie film
Photographs
Floppy diskettes
Adhesives
Faucet gaskets
Electrical switchplates
Laminate films
Orange highway cones
Plastic buckets
Shower curtains
Plastic tarpaulins
Varnish coatings
Marquee lettering
Drivers' licenses, laminated IDs
Petroleum jelly
Credit cards
Lighting fixtures
Athletic balls
Wastebaskets
Disposable diapers
Adhesive tape
Plastic utensils

FORTY-FIVE

SLEEPING BAG

On horseback, Todd led Iris quickly away from Stanford, out of the city of Palo Alto, and across the South Bay flatlands. Although he wasn't certain where he wanted to end up, he knew they had to head east, away from the Bay Area cities.

The mud flats smelled rancid in the low tide, with spoiled garbage and iridescent scum drying under the sunlight. Gnats buzzed around his face, and the horses' tails whisked like scratchy brooms to drive the pests away. When they finally rode north, reaching solid ground, the tall grass whispered and shushed beneath the horses' legs, the only sound except for the wind and a few circling birds over the empty network of highways.

Iris rode beside him, jarring him into conversation. Although he felt confident on the horse, he didn't know what to say—he had spent so much time riding down to Stanford to pick her up, he couldn't for the life of him think up any small talk. He had much bigger things to think about—like their survival. But he was content just to be with her, and she seemed not unwilling to stay with him awhile.

The sun beat down on his cowboy hat and his callused, tanned hands gripping the reins. He could smell the horses and his own sweat, which made him wonder if Iris liked cologne. Probably not.

"So," Iris said, jet-black hair blowing around her face, "you haven't actually agreed yet. Do you think it's a good idea to make our way to the Altamont and the community up there?"

Todd nodded, but he had been avoiding the question. He was still surprised that Iris had come along with him. "Sounds like a good idea, especially if they've got access to food from the Central Valley, even better if they've managed to rig power from the windmills." He tugged his hat down tighter as a Bay breeze gusted past him. "I'm just a little uncomfortable about living with a bunch of hippies."

"What's the problem? They've been living off the land there for years."

Todd was quiet for a moment. "What if they're growing drugs or something?"

Iris laughed at him. "I'm sure they'd let you have some, if you asked nicely."

Todd felt his skin prickle. "That's not what I meant—"

"I know, I know. I'm sure they'll be a lot more concerned now with planting vegetables. Don't worry about it, Tex."

"Stop calling me that," he growled. "I'm from Wyoming."

"Would you rather I called you Wye?"

Todd kept looking ahead, squinting into the sunlight. "I'd rather you just called me Todd." Then he added defensively, "Okay, Professor? Or should I say, Little Miss Rock Star?"

She started to retort, but chuckled instead. "Okay, you made your point."

They left the water behind as they headed between
grassy hills crowned with dark green live oaks. Iris urged
Ren ahead a few steps to parallel Todd. "We should
avoid Hayward, Newark, and Fremont as much as
possible," she said, pointing to the wrinkled, flapping
map spread on the saddle in front of her. "No telling
how bad those cities have gotten. If we keep away from
the interstate, there are plenty of hills, ranches, and
grazing land between here and the Altamont. Think we
can make it there by nightfall?"

Todd laughed. "We didn't leave Stanford until after
lunch. Maybe by tomorrow afternoon."

Iris looked down at the map again. Her dark eyes
flicked back and forth, as if checking directions and
distances. "I can drive it in an hour."

"You really are an academic type, aren't you? Horses
don't go quite as fast as cars. And they're not nearly as
comfortable." Todd finally felt reassured to be talking
about a subject he knew. "Anyway, after about twenty
miles or so, your butt is going to feel sore enough to fall
off. I'd just as soon keep that from happening." Todd
suddenly realized what he had said and he clamped his
lips down hard together. His ears burned.

"Gee, thanks," Iris said. "Are you willing to give me a
massage if I ache too much?"

It was Todd's turn to snort; but inwardly, he wondered
if she really meant it.

That night they sat around a small campfire. The only
thing missing was a pair of wailing coyotes in the hills.
He heard a few distant gunshots after dusk, but that
wasn't quite the same.

Iris removed a can of peaches "in their own natural
juice" she had taken from her pantry and opened it with
a hand can opener. "Too bad we don't have any beans
for dinner," she said, scooping the mess into their
traveling bowls. "Then we could re-create that scene
from *Blazing Saddles*."

Todd laughed. "You think all cowboys are like that?"

"Aren't they?"

"Right. Just like all professors are rock-and-roll addicts." Todd ducked when Iris threw a clod of dirt at him. Afterward, they managed to have a decent conversation over dinner.

Todd finally began to relax with the fact that he was riding alone across country with a beautiful woman who confused and excited him. It had taken him hours, but he could finally start talking to her without being so self-conscious.

Darkness spread across the sky. Iris stood up and went to the pile of saddles and blankets they had removed from the horses. Ren and Stimpy blew and whickered from where they were tied under the trees. Todd poked around, securing the campsite.

Iris returned to the level ground near the dying fire and tossed down both sleeping bags. Todd picked up his bedroll. "You can sleep by the fire. I'll stand watch over here."

"Wait. You want to help me zip these together?" she asked. "You promised me a massage, remember?"

Todd hesitated, not sure what to say. This didn't make sense. He turned away, feeling his face flushing bright red.

Iris giggled at his reaction. "You're cute, Todd." She grabbed his bedroll and started unrolling both bags, searching for the zippers. "I can't tell how much of this Big Lunk routine of yours is an act and how much is real."

"What Big Lunk routine?" he asked, genuinely baffled.

"Oh, shut up and get inside the sleeping bag," Iris said. Her smile seemed to sparkle in the smoky light. "Would it help if I sang country and western?" She crooned in a warbling drawl, "Aaahm so lonesome Aaah could craaah!"

Todd stared doggedly. "You're teasing me, aren't you?"

"Me?" Iris looked shocked. "I'm dead serious about that massage. My butt feels just as sore as you said it would."

Confused, Todd snatched his bedroll away from her. "Either that's the first thing you've said that isn't sarcastic, or I'm missing something. Good night, Professor. We've got a long ride tomorrow." He stomped off without waiting for her reaction.

Minutes later, as he spread his sleeping bag out across the dry grass, he debated going back to her. He couldn't figure Iris out. One minute she'd lash out at him, the next she wanted to jump in the sack. Weird.

He listened for any sound that she might still be up, maybe even waiting for him. But besides the fire crackling and one of the horses snorting, he didn't hear a thing.

FORTY-SIX

SPACE COWBOY

On the equipment table at the microwave farm, Spencer glanced over the components they had outfitted with fiberglass and ceramic: diagnostic sensors, a switching cable, and fiber-optic relays. In the oppressive heat, useless computer monitors stared like lifeless eyes; the hard plastic housings had sloughed aside, leaving heavy glass cathode-ray tubes canted among wires and the debris of circuits.

At the rate they were going, his small team would have the entire microwave farm fully converted within the next two weeks.

"Supply wagon's coming!" Rita Fellenstein shouted from the doorway. She sprinted out into the desert sunlight.

Spencer watched with amusement as Rita hurried to the wagon, her braided hair dangling beneath her Australian hat. By now her infatuation with the pair of ranch hands was common knowledge.

He tugged on his own floppy hat and followed her out

of the blockhouse. He squinted in the glaring brightness of the desert, but without air conditioning inside the building, the temperature differential wasn't much of a shock.

The two young ranch hands guided the horses that pulled the old wooden-bed wagon. From the shortwave radio, Spencer knew that some of the ranches around Alamogordo had donated barrels of water and boxes of MRE rations from storehouses they had looted from mothballed Holloman AFB. Wiry Juan Romero, sweat dripping down his back, started unloading, stashing boxes of dried beef and aluminum containers in the shade beneath the blockhouse.

A small Hispanic man with short salt-and-pepper hair and a narrow chin rode in the back of the supply wagon. Spencer didn't recognize him. "A visitor?" he asked Rita.

Rita flipped her braids over her shoulder and pushed her lips together like a small wad of paper. "Not sure."

Spencer kept his expression neutral as he walked to where the short stranger was getting off the wagon. The man held out a small, narrow hand to him. "Are you Spencer Lockwood?" he said in a way that showed he was accustomed to taking control. "I'm Gilbert Hertoya. Lance Nedermyer insisted that I come see you."

Spencer shook the man's hand, feeling a surprisingly rough and leathery grip, and suppressed a scowl, wishing he could just turn the wagon around and send the man back home. He carried himself with the air of an executive with nothing left to manage. "Yeah, Lance is always looking after our best interests—according to him. How can I help you?"

Hertoya smiled, apparently without malice. "Actually, I think I can help *you*."

"Oh?" He waited for Hertoya to spring the bad news on him. "I need all the help I can get. I hope you came to lend a hand."

"Well, I got tired of sitting on my butt in Alamogordo. I left my family there for now so I could get to work. You know we've got the potential here to—" Hertoya hesitated, then raised his dark eyebrows. "I guess I shouldn't blame you for not recognizing me. I'm from the Sandia Lab in Albuquerque. I head up, or headed up, the electromagnetic launcher up on Oscura Peak." He let that sink in.

"The satellite launcher? Now, that's interesting." Spencer broke into a wide grin. If this guy knew how to run the EM launcher, he might be useful after all.

"Hey, Rita and Juan!" he called. "You guys finish unloading the wagon—we'll need it for a trip to Oscura Peak."

Spencer watched eagerly as Gilbert Hertoya opened the door to the stuffy bowels of the railgun controls. Sunlight pouring through the ceiling windows left pale patches of illumination in the control area. Dust motes settled through the air.

Spencer looked along the railgun corridor. Parallel steel beams extended to a vanishing point in the distance up the slope of Oscura Peak. He lost all sense of perspective. On either side, blue-painted boxes containing high-energy-density capacitors crowded the rails. Their footsteps echoed on the concrete floor.

"The EM launcher was a smaller project even than your antenna farm," Hertoya said. "At least you started out with serious funding—we got zip from DOE, a little from NASA. To keep going we had to beg money from Sandia's in-house research fund, mostly because we had our roots in the weapons community."

"Well, we had to pinch a few pennies ourselves," Spencer said, trying not to sound defensive. With the world irreparably changed around them, he noted with annoyance that he was still falling into old political patterns.

Rita squeezed next to him, looking down the long

rails. "Wow." She coughed in the dusty air, but didn't say another word.

Gilbert ushered them along the corridor. "You can only see the first two miles of the launcher. It extends another three miles up the foothills—for peak performance we need to install another mile and a half of railing. We can launch small payloads to low-Earth orbit with what we have; we need the additional mile and a half to get us up to the higher, useful orbits.

"My team has been steadily putting this together for the past six years. Before the petroplague, that is. We used mostly grad-student labor from New Mexico State—cheap and enthusiastic." He shook his head sadly. "We've got piles of railing and capacitors stored near the top of the peak, more than enough to finish putting it together. If we were funded like other Sandia projects, we could have become a real launch facility years ago."

Hertoya stepped under the twin rails and pointed to the first bank of capacitors. Spencer ran a hand along the rail. The steel felt cold and slick. The wheels in his mind spun furiously, trying to figure how they could get the launcher up and running.

"We place the payload on these rails in a conducting shell called a sabot. We charge the capacitors and fire them off, one after another in a sophisticated timing operation. Each one adds to the total magnetic field that pushes the sabot up the launcher, nudge after nudge after nudge. By the time the payload reaches the end of the rails, it's traveling over ten klicks a second—more than enough to reach low-Earth orbit."

Spencer nodded with continued interest. "The payload weighs what, a couple hundred kilograms, if I remember right?"

"The entire package can weigh a thousand kilograms. Three hundred of that is pure payload. Most of the rest is the guidance system and a small rocket to insert the payload into orbit."

Spencer looked at the blue capacitor boxes, then suddenly felt a sinking at the pit of his stomach. *Well, that's that,* he thought. The entire setup was as worthless as a Detroit auto factory now. They had been so close.

"I shouldn't have gotten my hopes up." Spencer started to turn away. "Capacitors have oil dielectrics. They're useless."

"Oil?" Gilbert made a dismissive gesture. "No, we decided against an oil dielectric in favor of some new insulating technology. These just use distilled water."

Spencer froze. "Water-based capacitors?"

Rita laughed. "Where you been, Spence, on Mars?"

"If we could use this launcher to get the rest of our satellite constellation in orbit, we'd have practically a continuous ring of smallsats. It would be easy to add other antenna farms on the ground."

"Spencer, we have to figure out how to survive the winter!" Rita interrupted. "Aren't you getting a little ahead of yourself? It needs another one and a half *miles* of railing. It's taken them six years to get this far." Rita smiled apologetically at Gilbert. "Spencer gets this way sometimes."

"There are plenty of people back in Alamogordo who'd break their backs to get this thing working, because it's one of the only chances we have for the future," Spencer insisted, "even if it does take several years."

As he spoke, he grew more passionate. "They've got nothing to do, and they want to help get the world back on its feet. You saw the response we got from the ranchers."

"That was for horses and food, Spence, not for . . . for working on the railroad!" Rita said, exasperated.

Spencer slung an arm over Hertoya's shoulder. "Rita can handle the supply details if you oversee finishing the railgun project. The microwave farm doesn't need any more people for the conversion process—"

He grew more animated with every step. "We could

have limitless energy from the satellites. White Sands can be a new Atlantis, the only place left with the comforts of twentieth-century life!"

As they stepped into the sunshine, Rita shook her head. "Sometimes I think his brain is just going to explode."

FORTY-SEVEN

WELCOME TO MY NIGHTMARE

The Sandia Mountains east of Albuquerque turned a deep pinkish red as light from the setting sun struck them. Desert sunsets were stark and pure, filled with a silent *rawness* that always reminded General Bayclock of his days in Gulf combat.

And *that* reminded him of the thirty thousand lives under his charge at Kirtland Air Force Base. *Thirty thousand souls,* he thought. All in his hands, at this time of crisis.

The first directive from newly sworn President Jeffrey Mayeaux had come down like a hammer on an anvil. All military commanders were to bring cities under strict martial law. They were to enforce curfews, stockpile supplies for orderly distribution among the populace, and enforce a rule of order at all costs. Via shortwave radio the president had ordered local commanders to call up nearby contingents of the National Guard.

With the radical changes forced by the petroleum plague, society would be like a wild horse trying to throw

the reins of law and civilization. Bayclock had to ride
hard and not let his determination falter for an instant.

When he had visited Kirtland AFB, Mayeaux had told
Bayclock they could work well together, whatever might
come up—and now Mayeaux was his commander in
chief. In the petroplague crisis, Mayeaux was shoulder-
ing a burden vastly more difficult than Bayclock's own,
and Bayclock vowed to give the new president his fullest
support.

He breathed deeply, scanning the Sandia peaks before
turning back to Mayor David Reinski. A squad of fifteen
security policemen, all beefy young men over six feet
tall, protected them against the anarchistic elements that
had already caused so much damage. The MPs faced
outward, holding their automatic weapons loosely, ready
to snatch them in a second. Bayclock had refused the
protection of the few civil police officers still on duty.

They stood in the center of City Plaza, an island of
enforced sanity amidst the turmoil. Shattering glass and
sporadic screams peppered the dusk; fires burned from
several buildings. Hiding behind a dark window, someone shouted taunts across the plaza.

In front of the adobe Spanish mission, Bayclock's
horses were tied together and guarded by another group.
The scene could have been part of a Mexican showdown
in an old Western movie. The citizens would writhe at
the enforced discipline—at least at first—but they
would get used to it. And one day they would thank him
for saving them all.

Mayor Reinski fidgeted; he looked from side to side, as
if uncertain that Bayclock's MPs could offer sufficient
protection. Bayclock let the mayor squirm for a moment
before speaking. "Seen enough? Tell me how you could
possibly handle this yourself."

"I—I don't know how much longer we'll be safe out
here."

Bayclock snorted. "You think we're safe now? Look up
there." He nodded to the building behind them. "The

only reason we haven't been attacked is because of my snipers stationed on the rooftop. They've already shot two would-be assassins."

Reinski looked around. "Okay, you've proved your point."

"I don't think I have. Not sufficiently." Bayclock turned to the security police squad leader. "Lanarelli!"

"Yes, sir."

"Neutralize the mayor."

"Yes, sir." It took the gaunt sergeant only a second to react. Lanarelli stepped forward and cocked his weapon, pointing the M-16 muzzle at the mayor's head. "Get on the ground, sir."

Reinski turned pale. "What?" He looked to Bayclock, who only stared back blandly.

Lanarelli growled, "Move it—now."

Reinski slowly lowered himself to the concrete. Lanarelli pressed his weapon at the mayor's head while Bayclock crouched next to the man. He spoke softly.

"There will be no 'shared responsibility,' Mr. Mayor, do you understand? I am following the direct orders of the president of the United States, and they don't require me to ask permission from any local mayors."

He stepped back. "This is just my way of showing you how ridiculously vulnerable you are. Where is your police escort that's sworn to uphold the peace? Tell me, where's the man at the bullhorn right now who's supposed to be ordering me to leave his mayor the hell alone? We're not in Mr. Rogers' Neighborhood!"

Reinski answered only by moving his head back and forth.

Bayclock crouched on one knee and lowered his voice. "I'll tell you where they are. Most of the people sworn to guard you are at home with their families, protecting *them* against the lawlessness all around us. Duty obviously doesn't mean a hell of a lot to them. If they were under my command, I'd court-martial them as traitors and deserters."

Reinski squirmed on the ground. Bayclock motioned

for Lanarelli to let him lift his head. "You don't see my men running away, do you? Even if we didn't have access to synthetic lubricants for our weapons at the base, you'd still see my people here. They would use night-sticks, or swords, or their bare fists to protect me and any other officer. That's their duty."

Bayclock stood, brushing the knees of his uniform. "That's the difference between civilians and military— we're sworn to follow orders, no matter what else happens. You might manage to keep the water running, Mr. Mayor. You might keep the sewage under control. But anyone could step over the city line and tell you to go to hell."

Bayclock disliked making his point in such a dramatic matter, but Reinski was still naively convinced this whole thing was going to blow over after a few days, that something miraculous would happen, that he could somehow compromise the orders issued from the president himself.

Bayclock reached down and grabbed the mayor by the arm, easing him back to his feet. "Thank you, Lanarelli. Return to your post."

"Yes, sir." The weapon disappeared as the sergeant stepped back in one fluid motion. Once more Bayclock and Reinski were left alone, surrounded by an unbroken ring of men. Reinski's eyes were open wide, red and brimming with tears of shock and outrage.

Bayclock said gently, "The President instructed all military commanders to take whatever measures are necessary to enforce his order." He paused. "I'm already responsible for the lives of thirty thousand people on Kirtland, Mr. Mayor. By Presidential directive, the city of Albuquerque also falls under my purview.

"You're just not cut out for something this crucial. I *am*. It's a responsibility that runs very deep, and I'm going to need the trust of your people to pull this off. If I have your support, it's going to be a lot easier."

Reinski nodded. He didn't seem to have his voice back yet.

"My people are sworn to obey me," Bayclock continued. "Don't make me take the next step to demonstrate this to the people of Albuquerque." He narrowed his eyes and watched Reinski closely.

Reinski finally spoke. His voice shook as he tried to keep his voice from cracking. "What—what are you asking me to do?"

Bayclock allowed himself to relax imperceptibly. "Publicly throw your support behind me when I announce martial law."

"When will that be?"

"Immediately."

"Do I have a choice?"

Bayclock shook his head. "No, *we* don't."

FORTY-EIGHT

IF I FELL

The Visitors Center was closed, leaving only two abandoned cars in the parking lot. Heather tried to lead Connor to the spectacular overlook on the rim of the Grand Canyon, but he picked up a rust-colored rock and smashed a window of the deserted museum building. "We didn't come all this way not to look at the exhibits," he said.

No alarms rang, no park rangers came running. Heather didn't think Connor had any real interest in the museum; he just seemed to enjoy breaking in. That was just like him. She shrugged and let him have his fun. What did it matter, anyway? Satisfied, Connor followed her to the overlook.

It had taken them a week on foot to reach the South Rim of the Grand Canyon. When Heather had come here before with her old boyfriend Derek, they drove up, stayed in one of the lodges, and paid little attention to the surrounding scenery. Hiking in with Connor, though, gave her a greater appreciation as anticipation built mile after mile. Now she had time to inspect outcroppings, time to absorb the vastness of the landscape.

The Grand Canyon looked so spectacular that she couldn't comprehend the vastness. Her mind swelled with details—jagged mesas, bands of color ranging from ocher, tan, vermilion, and scarlet. Shadows carried orange tinges deep in the crevasses. The wind whipping up and over the rim enhanced the isolation.

Coming in, they had walked along the rim trail, stopping at every viewpoint, relaxing, taking their time. They had no agenda, no reservations, no jobs to get back to. Heather felt invigorated, a new person.

They heard no screaming children, no yelling parents, no arguing tourists, no sightseeing planes buzzing along the rim. The sky was as deep blue as a Christmas-tree ornament. In front of her, the canyon dropped a mile like the gulf between the old ways and the new world that would eventually emerge in the aftermath of the petroplague. Heather Dixon was on the right side of that chasm.

After standing there for a moment, Connor grabbed her from behind, pulling her against him as he wrapped his arms around her waist. When he nuzzled his chin against her shoulder, Heather squirmed from his scratchy beard stubble, then giggled.

He fluttered his fingers against her pants pockets, then crept slowly down her hips and across her abdomen. A sudden, startling shiver traveled like a ricochet up her spine, and she wiggled her buttocks back against the hardness in his groin.

Connor rubbed his hand against her crotch, pushing his fingers against the denim. His touch sent a warm glow through her. He ran his fingernail in a quick *tik-tik-tik* up the length of her zipper, teasing her.

Heather squirmed away, blinking in the bright sun and looking at the guardrails in front of her. "If you get any hornier, we'll fall off the edge."

Connor shrugged, grinning at her with his disarming

"good old boy" expression. "It's a long fall. We'd still have time for a quickie before we hit bottom."

"I'd rather find a place in the shade."

"Good idea."

The day Connor appeared on her doorstep, turmoil had seethed inside her. She knew what the stronger part of her wanted, but she was also afraid of being rejected, afraid of what might happen with this total stranger. Maybe that's why she had banished him to the backyard.

He had his shirt off when she appeared at the door; water sprayed from the hose, soaking the ground. He held his shirt balled in one hand.

She motioned him in, trying to sound upset. "You're wasting water. Turn that off and come inside."

With the electricity out, Connor had no light in the bathroom. He left the door ajar as he shucked his pants. Heather went into the kitchen, but soon she found herself drawn back to the partially open bathroom door.

The gap looked wider, as if Connor had opened it a bit more. She could see only dim shapes, then a flash of bare skin as he slipped into the shower. He turned and seemed to look directly at her before ducking behind the cloth shower curtain.

Heather was sick and tired of being afraid. She had already begun working the buttons on her blouse. She undid her bra. She stepped out of her jeans, listening to him splashing water and gasping in the cold. She would never have done anything like this before—and that was exactly why she insisted on doing it now.

Heather stood naked in the doorway. She knew she had a good figure, and she probably looked best without any clothes on, since she had found no fashion that didn't make her look cumbersome. Connor watched her through a gap in the shower curtain. He didn't say anything.

Moving slowly, she left the door open behind her and walked to the shower, peeled the shower curtain back, and stared at him. She smiled. He looked lean and well-muscled—and erect.

She stepped into the tub. Goose bumps crawled over her skin. She wrapped her arms around herself, trying to block the cold water. Connor twisted the shower head to deflect the spray against the tiled wall, leaving only a misty splash in the air. "You'll get used to it in a minute. If you stay in long enough, that is." He was staring at her. "I think you will."

"You don't seem surprised."

Connor shrugged. He still hadn't moved to touch her. "I thought you might do something like this. I could see it in your eyes."

Heather looked up at him, trying not to shiver. "Is that why you asked for a shower?"

Connor shook his head. Water droplets fell from his shaggy blond hair. "No, but I can roll with the changes and think on my feet."

The cornball line came out of her mouth before she could stop herself. "But can you think in *bed?*" Heather tried to make her voice sultry, but the cold water dripping off the tip of her nose ruined the effect.

"I won't be too concerned about thinking when I get you in bed." Before she could say anything, Connor bent down and took one of her nipples in his mouth and sucked hard. She gasped, partly in surprise and partly in pleasure, then moaned as he slid his fingers between her legs.

The shower water sprayed off the wall, splattering down their bodies, but Heather stopped noticing the temperature. . . .

Now, standing on the South Rim of the Grand Canyon, Heather turned and looked at the small village that had once lived off the tourist trade. The place was a ghost town. Most of the employees had probably tried to get back to "civilization." None of them would want to be stranded with no way back to the cities.

Connor stroked her from behind. "Let's forget about finding a spot in the shade," he said. "I'm tired of sleeping on the ground. Let's get a room instead." He gestured to the imposing, posh Bright Angel Lodge farther up the rim trail. "We can get one of the penthouses!"

Heather had never done that before. Never anything nice. It always seemed too extravagant. "Yeah, they might have a room or two available." She grinned at him. "All right, we'll get something special."

"About time, if you ask me." Connor's face became self-righteous. "All my life I've been watching everybody else get the things I deserve. I'm sick of it."

Heather loaded the pistol at her hip. Connor shifted the long rifle on his back. "Let's go," he said.

Hand in hand, they walked toward the Bright Angel Lodge.

FORTY-NINE

RUN FOR THE JUNGLE

Air Force security policemen spread up and down the street in a show of force. On horseback, an officer shouted orders like a cavalry commander. Uniformed men and women fanned out, securing the intersection. Two elite MPs used the butts of their rifles to knock in the glass door of an office building, then climbed three stories to position themselves on the roof. They sprawled out, covering the area with their rifles.

Forced into the streets by military teams pounding on doors, civilians gathered in the intersection. Some rubbed their eyes out in the open for the first time in days; some protested as they were herded to the center of the street. The crowd remained quiet except for a few small children crying and three teenagers protesting about being treated like animals. It took only fifteen minutes, but over five hundred people filled the intersection.

Down the street, General Bayclock watched the assembly from atop his own horse. Five security policemen surrounded him, guarding against malcontents and assassination attempts. It was the fourth such gathering he had witnessed, and the twentieth conducted since the orders declaring martial law throughout the greater Albuquerque area.

In the center of the crowd a master sergeant stood on several overturned crates stenciled with the words HATCH GREEN CHILES. According to the schedule, down on Central Avenue another enlisted man would be making similar pronouncements.

The sergeant raised his arms for quiet, then recited the familiar speech. "Under martial law, absolutely no breach of security will be tolerated. Without radio or TV, we don't have the means to broadcast this order to the public, so everyone needs to make darn sure their neighbors get the word. At the moment we are unable to print this information for wide distribution.

"Until such time as that becomes feasible, every day at—" The sergeant looked down at a sheet of paper listing intersections and times. "—Thirteen-thirty, that's one-thirty in the afternoon, we will hold announcements right here in this intersection. We will also distribute food, water, and medical supplies for those in need. But listen carefully—because of the large number of people under our protection, we will have only one hour to accomplish these tasks."

A low rumble ran through the crowd. The sergeant held up a hand. "Just a minute—I'm not finished!"

When the crowd did not immediately fall silent, one of the security officers fired his rifle up in the air. The sergeant looked around, then continued.

"Several new laws have been established. The most important is that a curfew will be in place from sundown to sunup. Because we have no electrical power in the city, it is difficult to provide protection for everyone at night. By order of President Mayeaux, Brigadier General Bayclock, the base commander of

Kirtland, has assumed command during this interim period of martial law. Mayor Reinski fully endorses these measures and strongly encourages all citizens to cooperate."

The master sergeant looked over the crowd. "We're here to help you. Until things return to working order, we're all in this together, and we have to do the best we can."

Satisfied that the exchange was under control, General Bayclock pulled back on the reins of his horse. The gelding backed up a few paces, then wheeled around.

Bayclock faced Mayor Reinski, who quietly watched the exchange. "The next few days are going to be critical—we've got to use an iron hand."

The young mayor seemed to have lost weight; his eyes were red, encircled by dark rings. Reinski did not respond.

Bayclock snorted, half inclined to ignore the mayor, but he realized the importance of appearances, even during times of martial law. "I'm heading back to the base, moving my headquarters to the more secure Manzano Mountain complex, and I advise you to come with me. Not everyone agrees with what we're doing, and I won't be able to protect you unless you're under my charge. I have doubled security at the base."

Reinski spoke in a low voice. "Aren't you going a bit overboard, General?"

Anger flashed through Bayclock's body like a snapped rubber band. "Maybe you don't remember your history, Mr. Mayor, but the most effective military bastions live as a symbol of threat, especially in times like these. Remember the Bastille."

Reinski merely pressed his lips together. The sounds of the uneasy crowd caused Bayclock to twist around in his saddle. When the security policemen shoved several people to the ground, loud shouts erupted. One man reached up, flailing to protect himself. Above the shouting, the master sergeant waved his arms and tried to bring the crowd under control. Slowly the people at the edge of the crowd started to disperse, defusing a potential riot.

Bayclock turned back to Reinski. "This is going to have to continue until we make an example of someone. These people have to get it through their heads just how serious we are."

FIFTY

BURNING DOWN THE HOUSE

Still filled with hellfire-and-damnation from the previous night's rally and the march up the abandoned freeway, Jake Torgens and the mob arrived at the Oilstar refinery demanding vengeance—but the guards had already abandoned the front gate of the refinery complex.

Jake glared through the dusty glass of the empty guard shack. One of the windows had fallen in, and only a metal-springed skeleton of a chair waited to greet them. Jake was disappointed to meet no resistance.

Many times in the past, the Oilstar security officers had calmly met them at the fences, while Jake and his protesters engaged in "nonviolent civil disobedience"—all perfectly mannered, like a high tea.

But they had vowed not to stop at mere passive resistance this time. Civilized protests were for civilized times—not when the country was falling apart. From now on there would be no armbands signaling which demonstrators wanted to be arrested, no waving placards in front of TV cameras. This wasn't a show; it was survival.

"Inside!" Jake waved his arm forward like a commander ordering his troops. "This place is ours now!" He clutched the chain-link fence as others flowed past carrying sticks and crowbars. He had pulled most of the crowd from angry people on the streets, the ones who wanted to strike out because they had already lost their future. It would solve nothing, but at least the symbol of evil would be removed.

Jake raised his fist in the air. The gesture rippled through the crowd, a mark of solidarity. Jake Torgens could have stopped the entire petroplague disaster from happening if he had taken extreme measures in the first place. It was his greatest failure.

He had been at the Oilstar town meeting, one of the loudest voices opposed to the spraying of Prometheus. He had managed to get a temporary restraining order from Judge Steinberg—and with his network Jake could have filed appeal after appeal to stall the cursed spraying forever. He had held the court order in his own hands while his people stormed the Oilstar pier, waving it and demanding that the helicopter land and obey the law. The *Law!* But the helicopter had sprayed the deadly microbe anyway.

Now the whole planet was paying for it.

Curses erupted around him. Jake drew in a monumental breath and shouted, "Burn Oilstar to the ground!"

The refinery complex was an Escher nightmare of fractionating towers, piping, valves, ladders, and catwalks. Small white Cushman carts sat abandoned next to enormous metal contraptions. The admin building and research facilities stood in the center of the complex, like an oasis surrounded by the industrial no-man's-land.

Huge natural gas, crude oil, and gasoline storage tanks rested on the sides of the hills, great metal reservoirs closed off by metal caps. No doubt some of them still held viable fuel—it would have been a precious commodity if the petroplague continued to devour only octane, but with other long-chain polymers falling to pieces, no engine could still function even if it did have uncontaminated fuel.

But the gas could still burn. *Oh yes,* Jake thought, *it will still burn.*

Inside the bioremediation wing of the Oilstar complex, Mitch Stone stared helplessly at the scrawled notes in front of him. He had used a metal bar to break open the locked drawers of Alex Kramer's desk, ransacking the original lab books and notes the microbiologist had left behind. The official data and quarterly reports had already been copied and sent to the plague research centers around the country, but there had to be more. Mitch went straight to the source. There had to be more!

"Dammit, Alex! Are you doing this to me on purpose?"

Mitch stared at the handwritten comments. Kramer's computer—nothing but warped circuit boards, wires, and glass CRT—sat on the desk. The diskettes lay dissolved in unrecognizable piles. But Mitch knew that the old-timer kept actual logbooks. Mitch had teased Alex about it before, but now he blessed the old man for his prehistoric ways.

As he flipped through the pages and stared at the data, despair poured through him. He held the lined paper up to the light from the window. The other pane in Alex's office had fallen out, dropping three stories to shatter on the ground below. Wind whistled into the room.

Emma Branson paced in front of the desk, waiting for him to answer her. "Stone, are you even more incompetent than I thought? We've got to give them something! You were involved in this from the beginning, don't you remember anything?"

Helpless, Mitch wanted to shrug and make some excuse, but Branson looked ready to claw his eyes out. She would see right through any patronizing explanations. "I was involved with it, but . . . but I worked mainly on the management end. I attended the meetings and took care of public relations. Alex was the one doing the work!" He swallowed, realizing how stupid he sounded. He ran a hand through his itchy hair; he hadn't had a trim in over a month.

"That's not the way you made it appear in your reports," Branson said with ice in her voice.

Mitch averted his eyes and looked again at the scrawled data. It took a while, but once he recognized the pattern, he felt too sick and embarrassed even to point it out to Emma Branson.

"Well, what is it?" she demanded.

"Uh, it appears that Dr. Kramer faked his data. He wrote incorrect results in his notebooks."

"Are you sure?" she said.

Mitch jabbed his finger at the columns of numbers. She could see it for herself. The figures were simply placeholders, taking up space; Kramer had jotted down the square root of two, pi, and others. Branson's eyes widened, and Mitch wondered if she was going to fly into a rage or break down and cry.

Before she could react, the sound of an exploding natural-gas tank shook the room. The *thwump* came first, loud enough to rattle the other window in Kramer's office. Booms echoed around the refinery complex.

Branson dropped the notebook and pushed toward the window. "What the hell is going on out there?" she said.

Outside, a towering ball of blue-orange flames roiled to the sky. Flaming, molten shards of metal clattered to the ground. One of the fractionating towers buckled from the explosion.

A crowd roared below. Tiny forms, people, scrambled on the gasoline reservoirs and the crude-oil storage tanks. Were they going to burn those, too?

"Son of a bitch! Peasants bearing torches, can you believe it?" Branson said. "Come on, we've got to get back to the admin building. I've still got my private guards there."

Flustered, Mitch said, "Yes, ma'am."

He followed, leaving Alex's doors open. Gunshots rang out as Branson's guards responded to the assault, but their guns fired only a few times before the weapons seized up. The shouts grew louder.

Before he and Branson made it down the three flights of stairs, they heard breaking glass below. "Oh, shit!" Mitch's voice wavered.

Branson looked ready to dive into the fray herself and start tearing the saboteurs limb from limb. "Up the stairwell. We'll go to the second floor and down the back. Maybe we can get out the emergency exit."

Mitch ran after her, pursued by the sounds of smashing and yelling. When they reached the other stairwell and hurried down, the bottom door burst open. Four people charged in.

Mitch froze, hoping the intruders wouldn't look up. But his luck didn't hold. One of the women glanced up the stairs, spotting both of them. Her face ignited with glee. "There they are! Two of them!"

Mitch spun around and scrambled up the stairs, leaving Branson behind. The old woman came panting after him.

Mitch's mind whirled. He had seen plenty of those stupid suspense movies where the victims continued to run up the stairs while being chased. But what other choice did they have? The people were below, swarming up.

"Floor four," he said. "There's the vault! I think it's open—I cracked it this morning to get at Alex's records. If we get in there, they'll never be able to reach us."

Branson stumbled beside him. Below, the attackers had reached the second-floor landing.

By the time he got to the fourth floor, Mitch had gained a good lead on Branson. He ran down the corridors, ducked through an open typing-pool complex of dissolving cubicles, toward the document vault in back. The heavy steel door stood partway open.

He glanced behind him and saw Branson turning the

corner, her arms outstretched, gasping. Her hair had come undone, and she had flung off both shoes as she stuttered forward. Fewer than ten steps behind her came the roaring mob.

Mitch ducked into the vault; a dim, battery-powered emergency lamp flickered from the ceiling. If he waited for Branson, he would never get the heavy steel door closed before the others wrenched it out of his hands. He couldn't hesitate. He tugged at the handle and hauled the door closed, digging his feet into the floor.

Emma Branson reached the vault just as it shut. She screamed at him through the tiny gap before the pursuers grabbed her shoulders. Mitch jerked the vault door closed with the last of his strength. The combination would reset itself automatically, and none of these people would ever get inside. He heard muffled screaming, but he could make out no words.

He didn't want to know what was happening to Emma Branson.

Mitch slid down the back wall and sat in the corner, spilling confidential documents marked PROMETHEUS around him as he shivered uncontrollably. Finally, he began to laugh as he realized that he was safe. He had found the papers.

Jake Torgens's face stung. His eyebrows and much of his hair had been singed in the monstrous natural-gas explosion. At least fifteen people had died, their flaming ragdoll bodies flying through the air, spraying droplets of smoking blood.

But the strike force would do what had to be done, regardless of casualties. This fire was going to be an environmental catastrophe of its own, but at the moment Jake considered that concern secondary. Some of the environmentalists had even cheered the petroplague as a final solution to the worldwide problems of industrial pollution. Jake figured they might eventually be right, but for the moment they had their heads up their asses.

Several protesters came to Jake with metal buckets and glass bottles of contaminated gasoline they had poured out of the sealed storage tanks. They had opened the valves and let the trapped fuel spill down the hill. Once his people got clear, Jake would order the whole thing blown sky high.

Polly ran up to him. A fat woman who described herself as "pleasantly plump," Polly had a mild manner; but when her anger got stoked, she was ready to kill. Grime streaked her face, and her eyes were bright.

"We found two of them inside the research building there. One locked himself inside a vault upstairs, and we can't get to him, but we caught the old witch, Branson. She's still alive. In a lot of pain. Should we bring her down?"

"No," Jake said. "Leave her upstairs, and make sure she stays there. Tie her to the vault door and get everyone else out of the building." He raised his eyebrows at Polly. "You know what to do with witches, don't you?"

Polly grinned. She took one of the buckets of gasoline and ran toward the building.

Black smoke poured in through the air vents of the vault. Mitch Stone coughed, then scrambled across the floor. The carpet itself was smoldering. The pages turned brown on the documents lining the metal shelves.

The whole building would burn to the ground. Mitch would be trapped inside this vault like a roast in an oven. He had to get out. The thick smoke burned his eyes. He couldn't breathe.

When he grabbed the release bar, the metal was so hot it sizzled the flesh on his palms. He shrieked. Mitch fumbled with a roll of papers to shield his skin and pushed down on the release bar again. He forced the door open.

And the blackened clawlike arm of Emma Branson fell inside. The skin on her skeletal body was charred to paperlike ash. Her mouth still open, she slumped into the gap.

Mitch staggered backward. The documents in the vault ignited with a flash all around him. The furnace flames blasted inside.

FIFTY-ONE

HANG 'EM HIGH

When Lieutenant Bobby Carron's eyes opened, he was fully awake but completely disoriented. Nothing familiar, just a big blank spot where he thought he should remember things. No longer in his Bachelor Officers' Quarters at China Lake, he lay in bed in a strange, dim room. In pain.

Bobby saw stark featureless walls, smelled antiseptic-clean bedding, felt a cottony mass in his mouth as his tongue ran over his teeth. Bad, flat, rancid-tasting mouth. The window blinds were drawn, and the little sunshine that diffused through looked as if it had been washed and sterilized. *Where the hell am I?* Somewhere outside the room came a muted chanting, like the throbbing of machinery. He couldn't figure out what it was.

His arms ached as he tried to move. He'd been taking a cross-country flight with Barfman Petronfi, on his way to the beach where he could bask in the sun and forget about the navy. He'd climbed aboard his jet, taken off for Corpus Christi—

Bobby tried to raise his head. He felt bandages, constraints. And then it came rushing back to him: losing power, electrical systems crapping out, watching Barfman's plane break apart and drop away into a bright explosion. His own aircraft failing, straining to reach the Albuquerque airport. He had ejected, watching his own F/A-18 plummet into the desert, as the rocky ground rushed up at him like a giant slapping hand. . . .

He had survived, but how badly was he hurt? His body shivered in waves of pain and numbness. Was he paralyzed? Where was Barfman? Where were the nurses? Why weren't they watching him? How long had it been?

He struggled to raise himself on an elbow. They didn't even have a monitor on him! If this was a real hospital, then they should have diagnostics, air conditioning, not this damned silence. He grabbed the call button by his bed, but found only bare wires.

Bobby drew in several deep breaths. In all his years in the navy, he'd never even been in a hospital except for the "turn your head and cough" routine. He forced himself to relax back on the pillow. Listening, Bobby couldn't hear a cart creaking down a hallway or even a nurse going to check on a patient; he heard only muted crowd sounds outside the closed window.

His mind raced through the options. If he was in a hospital, something was definitely wrong. He should hear *something*.

Bobby pushed back the sheets. Moving as if he were in a room covered with broken glass, he lowered himself to the floor. He discovered several sore muscles and bruises that he hadn't had before. His right leg was wrapped with a cloth bandage, but he could put weight on it. Both ankles felt swollen. His head throbbed with the fuzziness of painkillers and sedatives, and a ringing sound echoed in his ears.

His body struggled to remember how to walk. How many days had he been out? He grunted, trying to keep the pain away.

Bobby shuffled toward the window, one step at a time

across the cold tile floor. A minute later he stood at the window, staring down at the crowd gathered below.

Outside, thousands of milling people filled a plaza, chanting: "String 'im up, string 'im up, string the bastard up!"

The crowd clustered around a platform like an angry river against an upthrust rock. Timbers had been erected in a crude gallows. Bobby blinked in shock. What the hell?

Five men dressed in sand-colored camouflage uniforms stepped onstage. A lanky boy, no older than sixteen, staggered up from the ground, fighting against the ropes on his legs. Thrusting arms helped him along.

The boy was roughly led to the gallows at center stage, where a burly man in uniform met him. Some of the people continued to chant, others seemed oddly subdued.

The uniformed man held his hands above his head, and silence fell like a blanket on the plaza. The boy kept struggling, shouting in terror. The uniformed man gave another signal, and one of the guards stuffed a gag in the prisoner's mouth.

Bobby leaned forward to hear the man's shouted words. He rested his numb fingers on the grille of the window. Had the world gone crazy? Was he hallucinating?

"—a chain that depends on the strength of one link. And whenever a bad link threatens the good of the whole, it must be removed! I don't like what circumstances have forced me to do, but now more than any other time in our history as a nation, we must adhere to the law without question. The president has given us explicit instructions. The rules are just. Our future depends on strict obedience." The man looked grim as he surveyed the crowd. No one cried out; murmurs ran through the periphery.

One of the men in camouflage threw a long rope over the gallows arm. Another quickly stepped up and secured the noose over the neck of the young boy, who whipped his head back and forth in panic; his hands were tied behind his back. The burly officer stepped back as the airman tested the noose.

"My sworn duty is to protect the people of this city. The odds are stacked against us, but I will not allow looters to make things worse. Any person who refuses to work with us is a threat to everyone." He jerked a thumb behind him.

Immediately, three men stepped forward and grasped the rope. On the count of "Ready, ready, now!" they pulled the rope, jerking the young man off his feet.

The boy dangled in the air, kicking his feet and swaying back and forth as he struggled. His body arched, his elbows spread out to strain against the ropes binding his wrists. His chin jerked from side to side as he twisted his head. Within minutes, his face swelled into a dark, bruised purple. A wet stain spread from his crotch.

Bobby stumbled from the window. He felt his stomach tighten as he tried to vomit on the floor, but he heaved only sour saliva.

He shook his head to clear it. The entire scene seemed like a morality play in hell. He eased himself back onto the edge of the bed, stunned. With this brutal frontier-style justice, he must be in some Third World banana republic!

The door of his room swung open, and a grim-faced staff nurse stared at him. She raised her eyebrows. "You're awake, Lieutenant. You had a terrible concussion, and we didn't have our usual facilities to treat you. I hope you're feeling better?"

"I—don't know." Bobby blinked his eyes in shock.

The nurse glanced at the window and strode over to close the blinds. "You'd think the damn kids would know by now that the curfew's serious. Makes you wonder how many more times they have to set an example before it finally sinks in." She came over and inspected the wrapping on Bobby's legs. "It's good you're moving around. I need to contact the military liaison."

"And he just happens to set up his gallows right outside the hospital?" Bobby couldn't believe what he was hearing. "Why here?"

The nurse shook her head, scowling toward the window. "No, he's got several stations all around the city. If the general's going to make a good example of it, he has to make his punishments visible to a lot of people, and these days communication is very difficult. Can't just pick up a newspaper or turn on CNN anymore, you know. Getting word out about the curfew was tough enough."

Things were moving too fast. Bobby swallowed, still tasting sour dryness in his throat. "But why is there a curfew at all? And why hang anybody who breaks it?"

"The general's enforcing martial law against looters and rioters. No one likes it, but without those drastic measures, the VA hospital would of been taken apart for drugs and equipment. We have guards stationed at every entrance."

"But why is there martial law? What's happened?"

She smiled and patted his shoulder. "You got a lot to catch up on, don't you? You're lucky the general wants to meet you."

PART THREE

AFTERMATH

FIFTY-TWO

HAIL TO THE CHIEF

The Cabinet Room in the White House was filled for the morning staff meeting in a desperate attempt to pretend at normalcy, but few of those present actually held cabinet rank. It was far too difficult to assemble the remaining high-level officials every morning. Instead, the White House staff served as conduits for the rest of the Executive Branch, relaying information to and from President Jeffrey Mayeaux by any means available—wireless, messengers, handwritten instructions. In an effort to ensure continuity, the new vice president and his staff were being heavily guarded at his residence in the Naval Observatory.

In the Oval Office, Mayeaux stared out the window at the motionless tanks and armored personnel carriers on the Ellipse, south of the White House lawn. A military show of force. The reinforced vehicles served more as a Maginot Line than as a practical mechanism to stop the rioting around Washington, D.C. After the petroplague had swept across the capital city, the tanks stood frozen in place. They could not move, could not operate the turrets, nor swing their heavy gun barrels around. But Mayeaux still thought they looked damned impressive.

Mayeaux sipped a cup of weak chicory coffee, a completely inept attempt at café au lait. White House coffee had always been extravagant and rich, made with dark-roast gourmet beans. Now the best the kitchen could manage was a muddy, boiled brew that tasted bitter no matter how much sugar he added. Mayeaux stirred it, staring down at the swirling tan liquid.

He hated getting up so damned early in the morning, but there just wasn't time for enough rest. He had heavier responsibilities now that he held the Chief Executive job. His own plans for a bright future had swirled right down the toilet, gurgling loudly as they went. A million people supposedly dreamed about becoming president of the United States—how did he get to be so damned lucky? It was like reaching into a new box of Cracker Jacks and pulling out a brand-new, shiny bear trap as his prize!

Stuck inside the White House compound, Mayeaux had no opportunities to blow off steam. He knew about Kennedy sneaking in the babes . . . but JFK only had the Bay of Pigs, the Commies, and the Cuban Missile Crisis to worry about. Under the Mayeaux administration, the petroplague had messed up every little detail of daily life. He couldn't even slip off to Camp David for a break from this damned place. He was being asked to cope with a turn-of-the-twenty-first-century world, but given only the technology available to Thomas Jefferson!

"Mr. President, everybody's here." Franklin Weathersee stood at the door to the Oval Office. He seemed to be rubbing it in every time he said the words "Mr. President"—he wouldn't put up with that attitude from anyone else, but Weathersee . . . well, he owed Weathersee a few favors. More than he could remember.

Mayeaux set down his cup. "So what's on the agenda today, Frank? Visiting dignitaries? Trips to Acapulco? Business as usual?"

Weathersee answered bluntly without looking at the handwritten agenda. He never seemed to have any sense of humor. "The Joint Chiefs have an update on martial law enforcement. They're being pretty tight-lipped until you get in there."

Mayeaux turned from the view of the south lawn. "Let's get this over with. These guys make my skin crawl, and if they aren't going to support me, we'll get someone in there who will."

The halls were dim, lit by sunlight trickling through office windows. Metal sculptures, given as presents from foreign governments, sat on tables lining the hallway. Most of the carpet had deteriorated down to the bare wood floors, leaving only stains of residue.

Weathersee lowered his voice as they approached the Cabinet Room. "It's not so easy to replace them, Mr. President—"

Mayeaux stopped outside the door and snorted. "What the hell are you talking about, Frank? I didn't ask for this job—I should be back in New Orleans fishing right now. If I'm going to be anything more than a placeholder, I've got to have a team that works with me."

Weathersee held Mayeaux back. Several people had already noticed them and stood. Two Secret Service agents waited at the end of the hall, studiously watching nothing.

"These people are military types, Mr. President— they're not political hacks. They aren't yes-men. They don't have an agenda. Their allegiance is to the U.S. Constitution."

Mayeaux scowled. "Don't kid yourself, Frank. *Everybody's* got an agenda, including these tin pots. They just have different buttons to push. They still serve at my pleasure, don't they?"

"Yes, sir."

"Then they'll support me—or find another job, petroplague or not. I have enough to worry about."

He stepped through the door, smiling his best media

smile as the others stood to greet him. Mayeaux headed for his high-backed chair. He dispensed with shaking hands. "So, what do we have?" he asked. "Give me the slicked-down version."

The four military officers sat directly across the table, next to the secretary of defense. Brass plates on the backs of the chairs identified each cabinet member. The chairs were arranged around the table in the order the office had been elevated to cabinet level.

General Wacon, chairman of the Joint Chiefs, a graying man who looked like an airline pilot in his air force uniform, pushed a briefing packet across the table. The papers were handwritten—the few rebuilt computers working in secured vaults were reserved for more important tasks than preparing briefing charts.

"We have managed to establish communications with seventy percent of the military bases, Mr. President. We don't know why we've lost contact with the remaining thirty percent, but we don't believe it's because of a technical breakdown."

"Tell me what that means." Mayeaux shoved the papers back at the chairman. "I don't have time to read all this."

"There's enough redundancy in our emergency communications that we should still be in direct contact with every installation commander. The petroplague did not disable backup wireless communications."

"So what the hell is the significance of that?" Mayeaux looked around the table. "I asked a simple question, now give me a simple answer. No double-talk, no techno-jargon."

The general continued smoothly, not quite managing to cover a frown. "Widespread riots, sir. The out-of-contact bases are located next to cities with large populations—Los Angeles, New York, Philadelphia. With so many people in the neighboring communities, we suspect the civilians are not cooperating with the military's enforcement of martial law."

"So the people are disobeying emergency orders from the president of the United States? And the military commanders can't back up our demands? Maybe we should all go hide in the closet and cry."

"We don't know for sure, Mr. President. The military bases still in contact report increasing unrest among the civilian populace. Every commander has lost personnel to mobs, even in Southern states where the military is traditionally viewed with more respect."

Mayeaux's jaw clenched and relaxed as General Wacon spoke. He couldn't get his military commanders to enforce a straightforward directive in a crisis situation. Against civilians, yet! Being the "most powerful man in the world" wasn't all it was cracked up to be.

Even with the communications breakdowns, the people would listen to a strong leader, not some limp dick too frightened to back up his own threats. Mayeaux knew that much. It was just like raising kids—you set the rules, and whenever the kid stepped over the line: *wham!* Behavior modification.

It worked in Louisiana, rewarding the parishes that toed the line, and it worked in Congress when he had been Speaker of the House. The congressmen who didn't fall in line when Mayeaux made it clear he was calling in a personal favor found themselves suddenly without any federal projects for their districts. As far as the American people were concerned, they didn't know how far they could push Jeffrey Mayeaux.

Not very damn far.

The chairmen of their respective services sat back in their seats and waited for the president to speak his words of wisdom. Mayeaux felt like a preacher under a revival tent. What the hell did they want from him?

"What's the status of the rest of the military? What other national defense matters aren't we ready for, gentlemen?"

The question seemed to throw the officers. They looked at each other. "Each stateside installation is utilizing its resources to enforce martial law, Mr. President. They are relying on the National Guard as well as local law-enforcement groups. None of our forces is poised to prevent an attack from an external threat, but frankly I don't see how such an attack could be feasible without any fuel—"

Mayeaux dismissed the observation with a wave. "Not an attack from outside, from *within.* If civilian disobedience is affecting every installation, we've got to get those commanders firmly in control. We've got to let the people know we won't take any crap. These are not normal times."

The five officers remained stone-faced, keeping their thoughts to themselves. What a bunch of nippleheads! Mayeaux pushed back from the conference table, feeling his control slipping away. *Didn't anybody take this seriously?* Well, if they weren't going to come up with a solution, then he sure as hell would. He had the entire country to look after, whether he wanted to or not.

Mayeaux stood and started for the door of the Cabinet Room. "Gentlemen, get me a complete review of your forces—personnel, capabilities, whatever you've got. I want you all to be ready to answer questions whenever I need you. Camp out in the Old Executive Office Building. Get that information to me in one week. If things haven't gotten better by then, I'll make some decisions for you." Franklin Weathersee followed Mayeaux out as he strode from the room.

In silence, everyone stood in the President's wake.

FIFTY-THREE

NO BLADE OF GRASS

White gypsum sand glittered like an ocean of bone-dry sparkle dust. With nothing more than a small spade, Spencer Lockwood dug only a few feet before he reached moisture.

The water table around White Sands had always been near the surface, though it had steadily fallen for the past half century, drained by massive pumping stations along the Rio Grande corridor. But not any longer, not after the petroplague. The aquifer was exceptionally pure from natural filtration—and it was available, rapidly replenishing itself.

Adjusting his floppy hat, Spencer applied a handful of soft lard on either side of the ceramic washer and tightened the cap to the water pump. A long strand of cloth-wrapped electrical wire ran from the pump to a telephone pole, then to the power substation. Transformer parts lay strewn around the substation, prominent against the bright sand: open coils of copper windings, ceramic insulators, iron cores. The new substation looked like a Rube Goldberg collection of giant Tinkertoys. A hundred yards away, three ranch hands stood around a pile of scrub wood, waiting for the order to light the signal fire.

Beside him, Rita Fellenstein tipped back her Australian hat and spat to the side, adding another blot to the scattered tobacco stains on the snowy gypsum. "You really think this is going to work, Spence?"

He used the fine sand to scrub smelly animal fat from his hands, then wiped the grit on his frayed pants. "If we can't carry power from the microwave farm to the pump station, it'll be impossible to get it to the outlying ranches."

"That's not what I asked you."

Heat shimmered from the ground like blurred fingers reaching to the sky. Spencer could see for miles all around. "There's no reason why it shouldn't work. Basically, it's a no-brainer. We hook it up and it starts pumping water."

Rita worked up a mouthful of saliva and spat again. She seemed to enjoy the disgusted frown on his face. "If you say so. You weren't the one trying to figure out how to fix it."

Spencer grinned, keeping his doubts to himself. "That's what engineers are for."

Rita strode back to the ranch hands. Her gangly legs put a rolling swing into each step. Good-natured catcalls greeted her, but Rita told the men to shut up and light the signal fire.

Spencer took one last look at the pump—he always became obsessive before starting an experiment. Everything appeared ready, but he never believed it. The transmission line ran to the substation, all the pump parts had been inspected a dozen times.

He remembered how paranoid he had been about his antenna farm on the day of the first test. Now he'd be even more excited if he could just get a simple water pump working out in the desert.

One of the ranch hands squatted by the pile of wood,

striking a flint and a piece of metal together. They still
had some matches among their supplies, but those might
be the last ones they would ever have. Fine steel wool
brought in from the microwave farm caught the spark
and started smoking. Pieces of shaving, then larger
pieces of mesquite began to burn, crackling and sending
rich-smelling smoke into the air.

Rita stood back, shielding her face as one of the ranch
hands tossed a handful of green piñon needles onto the
growing fire. The smoke thickened and billowed. Rita
said, "All we need now is a blanket to send smoke
signals!"

"We don't want to have a conversation with them,"
Spencer said. "We just want them to turn on the juice."
He knew the radio man Juan Romero would be back at
the microwave farm, waiting to see the smoke.

Spencer watched the water pump, not sure what to
expect. Once Romero switched on the electricity from
the farm, a motor would move a series of gears—what
could be so tough about that? The substation would
transform the oscillating voltage collected from the
microwave antennas to power the pump. If this worked,
it would be the first step to reestablishing a power grid
for the area, electricity that did not rely on petroleum or
plastic components for distribution.

By erecting similar antenna farms, simple metal wires
spread out on flat ground under the orbital path of the
smallsats, and launching the remaining satellites in
storage at JPL, Spencer could return electrical power to
a broad band of the country—even the world. He liked
crazy, optimistic plans, and hey, it gave them something
to work toward.

A high-pitched popping, sizzling noise jarred him out
of his daydream. Acrid smoke spewed from the nearby
utility pole. Spencer caught the sudden smell of creosote
burning. "The substation's going up!" he yelled.

The ranchers grabbed shovels and started throwing
gypsum sand on the equipment to smother the fire.

White sparks danced around the transformer units, accompanied by loud snaps and cracks. The signal fire continued to blaze, sending streamers of smoke into the windless air.

"Great!" Spencer ran to the bonfire. "Help me get this thing out!" He knew Romero would keep the juice flowing until the smoke signal stopped.

The dry mesquite burned hot and bright. He picked up a bucket of sand and threw it onto the blaze; the sand simmered on the coals. Smoke continued to boil into the air. Finally, a blanket thrown over the fire extinguished the flames.

Spencer stood back and waited as the smoke leaking from the blanket turned from black to gray-white. The substation continued to crackle like an electric heater dropped into a bathtub. As the smoke trailed away, the inferno at the substation subsided. Romero had shut down. The electrical equipment looked scorched.

A real no-brainer, Spencer had called the exercise. Right!

Rita wiped a hand over her sooty face. "So, we fix it up and try again?"

"Must be an engineering problem," he said, scowling at the substation components.

Before the petroplague, the station had been a crossroads for power generated by the Public Service Company of New Mexico and the Rural Electric Network. Now nothing remained but a smoldering pile of resistors, coiled windings, and insulators. At least the electric company wouldn't come after him for damages.

"Let's find out what went wrong," he said. "That's the only way we'll learn anything. I want to get back to the microwave farm by sundown for the JPL contact."

"You don't seem too upset after just blowing the hell out of that substation," Rita said.

"Job security," Spencer said, and faked a shocked expression to mask his disappointment. "You've been hanging around Nedermyer too much."

*   *   *

Romero tugged on his drooping black mustache. "Caltech's on the wireless, Spence. They're ready for you."

"Thanks." Spencer took a seat. Now that the sun was down, their shortwave radio could eavesdrop on the world.

The blockhouse was illuminated by beeswax candles. They had a few battery-powered lights, but they tried not to use them much. Shadows cast by the flickering light danced on the trailer walls.

Static came from the radio speaker like ocean surf, distorting the voice that relayed news across the country for local dissemination. Romero repeated the news back to the emergency broadcast channel, verifying that he had correctly copied the contents.

Rita whispered, "You're not going to tell them the test failed, are you? JPL might not send the satellites if they find out you can't even get the power lines to work."

"The experiment didn't fail," Spencer said. "It just pointed out some deficiencies in our assumptions."

"*Now* who's been talking to Nedermyer too much?" she snorted.

Romero handed him the makeshift microphone. "All set. You've got five minutes."

Spencer fingered the button, clicking it twice. "Hello? This is Spencer Lockwood from White Sands."

A moment passed. Nothing but static came over the speaker. He frowned and started to repeat himself when a voice broke through. "Dr. Lockwood?"

Spencer leaned forward. "Yes, that's me."

"Stand by, one. We've got someone here for you."

The microphone rustled as it was handed over. "Spencer? Is this the same Dr. Lockwood I taught at Caltech?"

Spencer stopped. The voice sounded familiar, but it had been so many years. . . . "Seth—Seth Mansfield? Is that you?"

Coughing. "Spencer, are you still playing with those smallsats? Dr. Soo at JPL tells me you've been pestering her to ship the remaining satellites cross-country to you. What's this nonsense? Last time I checked, you were a physicist, not a rocket scientist. At least that's what I wrote on your diploma."

Spencer rolled his eyes. It was nice to hear from his gruff mentor again. "Seth, what are you doing there? I thought you retired years ago."

The Nobel laureate's voice came back strong for a seventy-four-year-old man. "Did you expect me to roll over and play dead? I returned here after the plague hit. The least I could do is wash bottles while the microbiologists try to figure this damn thing out."

Romero leaned over and whispered, "You've only got four minutes, Spence." Spencer waved him away.

"Seth, I'd love to talk, but I just don't have the time."

"Oh, all right! I hear you were going to transmit electricity today to power some damned water pump."

"Well, Seth, it—"

"Good thinking, Spencer. You'll need the infrastructure up and working before the smallsats can do any good. Doesn't matter if you have all the microwave energy in the world if you don't have any way to get it to people. How did you do? Did it work?"

Rita leaned over and scowled. Spencer saw his precious time slip away. The Caltech emergency network operators adhered to a ruthless reputation when it came to partitioning radio time. He sighed; it was a lost cause to argue with his old professor.

"Uh, it didn't go exactly as planned, Seth. There are more problems than I suspected with the transformers. But it's just an engineering problem." Romero clapped a hand to his forehead and snickered; Spencer turned back to the radio. "We'll fix it. I've already got a team working on design changes, using what we learned from the test."

"Engineering problems! Those are the best kind," Mansfield said. "You think your idea will still work?"

"Of course it'll work! Look, we transmitted the power at least twenty miles, and that's a lot farther than we thought would be possible with these primitive lines. It blew out a transformer at the substation, so we know the electricity got that far."

Spencer threw a glance at Rita. She mouthed, *Less than one minute.* Spencer thought he heard the hint of a laugh over the static-filled channel. "Plenty of people here at JPL thought you were just pipedreaming, son. There's starvation and rioting going on out here, in case you haven't heard."

"We have the same reports coming out of El Paso and Albuquerque," said Spencer. "All the more reason to give people some shining example of hope, something to show that we can get back on our feet again."

"Okay, Spencer. The JPL folks wanted assurance of two things: that you weren't lying, and their efforts wouldn't be wasted. I think I've convinced the JPL acting director that you haven't gone loony tunes. Of course, I don't know how the hell you expect to get twenty three-hundred-pound satellites from Caltech to White Sands. By a wheelbarrow? A refurbished Conestoga wagon?"

Spencer didn't know what to say. "Uh, that's the next question, but it's really just another engineering problem. We can solve those."

The old man laughed. "If you manage this one, Spencer, you deserve a Nobel Prize of your own!"

FIFTY-FOUR

HOME ON THE RANGE

Todd Severyn cocked back his cowboy hat and scanned the rolling vista of the Altamont range. His chocolate quarter horse snorted at the dry, unpalatable grass on the ridge. The sky above was as blue and smooth as a robin's egg, cloudless; he didn't expect to hear a discouraging word . . . at least not until he rode back to those weirdos at the commune.

Todd urged Stimpy down the slope, following a cattle trail toward the glistening aqueduct that directed fresh water from the mountains. Moving again, Stimpy crashed through the grass with an energetic gait that showed Todd how much the mare was enjoying her regular long-distance rides.

Gleaming white windmills, spinning in rampant breezes that gusted over the range, lined the crests of the rounded hills. Many of the wind turbines had burned-out rotors with gummed lubricants; Jackson Harris and his group of washed-up hippies spent much of their days trying to repair them.

Far below to his left Todd could see the empty interstate freeway dotted with wrecked and abandoned cars. With the traffic gone and the people scattered from the corpses of the cities, he found the world more palatable in a way. Like his beloved Wyoming, everything had slowed down, gone back to the ways of a century before, when communities worked together to survive, and each small town was its own little world.

That was how Jackson Harris and the Altamont commune managed to succeed, but Todd didn't fit in. Philosophically, they were poles apart, yet he did enjoy belonging to their settlement. As long as he didn't have to sing along with their campfire concerts of old rock & roll songs. And Iris Shikozu certainly seemed comfortable with the arrangement, even if he wasn't. . . .

When he reached the aqueduct between the hills, Todd directed the horse to follow the concrete embankment. Two men and a teenager dangled their feet in the languid canal, fishing with bamboo poles and cotton fish line. As Todd pulled the horse to a stop, Stimpy stuck her nose in the water, blowing out her nostrils and drinking deeply. "Any fish in there?" Todd asked.

A man in a battered straw hat shrugged. "Carp."

"Are they good eating?" Todd noticed a chain-link basket slung low in the water.

"Depends how hungry you are," the teenager said.

When the fishermen didn't offer to continue the conversation, Todd rode off along the Altamont Pass Road and back over the crest of the hills. He dreamed of eventually making his way across country, riding back to his parents' ranch, maybe even with Iris. But not for a while yet, not until things were a bit more settled.

Jackson and Daphne Harris, Doog, and the rest of the wacked-out commune had welcomed him and Iris in, giving them an old trailer to stay in. Todd was still embarrassed to be living with Iris without being married, but neither Iris nor the hippies seemed to care; it just didn't fit in with the other women Todd himself had known, who either jumped from bed to bed or were dying to get married. But he stuck to his guns, insisting he would move out as soon as another place became available. He'd promised to take her away from Stanford, which he'd done, but he had not demanded to sleep with her as some kind of reward.

Iris accepted his companionship at face value, and from the other bed in the trailer she talked to him far into the night when he just wanted to go to sleep. During the day, when he didn't think she was looking, he admired her petite figure, her dark almond eyes, and her jet-black hair. Iris seemed to have the energy of two people coiled inside her wiry body. He'd learned not to underestimate her. He felt his attachment running deeper, so deep that it frightened him.

But he didn't want to just stay here and settle down. Todd found himself growing restless, wanting to do something more than mundane chores. He still felt responsible for the whole mess they were in—if he hadn't been so eager to spray Alex's darned bugs, the petroplague would never have happened. To soothe his own restlessness, he took long rides on the horses, ranging far from the commune when the goofballs drove him crazy.

He had appointed himself liaison between the Altamont colony and the remnants of the Livermore Lab on the other side of the range, where the once-large government research laboratories still had a few programs cobbled together with scraps of barely functional equipment. Following the road, Todd reached the crest of the hills and headed west toward the city of Livermore to see if the labs had come up with anything new.

Thanks to her small and agile body, Iris Shikozu got the assignment of climbing the windmill masts to replace rotors as they burned out. With her toolbox stuffed in a canvas backpack between her shoulders, Iris clambered up the metal rungs to reach the top, where the three-bladed aluminum wind turbine hung frozen, rattling in the breezes.

The windmill rows looked like a giant field of metal

cornstalks on the hills. The wind gusted, making the mast rattle. Iris had to hook her arm through the rung to steady herself.

"Hang tight up there," Jackson Harris called from below. Iris glanced down to see him cup his hands around his mouth. He said something else, but the wind snatched away his words.

It didn't matter; she knew what she was doing. Reaching the top, she secured herself and unslung the backpack to find a screwdriver so she could unfasten the metal housing covering the wind turbine's rotors. She had done this a dozen times before.

On the hills below, Doog and a couple of the refugee city kids amused themselves by tossing rocks into a gully. Doog always seemed to find simple things to keep himself preoccupied. Work usually wasn't one of them.

Iris succeeded in removing the bolts from the housing and lifted up the protective metal. The lightweight aluminum blades were shaped to catch the wind from any quarter; a vane at the rear helped to align them in the proper direction. The blades spun, turning a rotor that generated electricity. But without petroleum lubricants, the rotors burned out; and Iris had to keep replacing them. Back at the commune, Daphne Harris and some of the Oakland kids spent hours tediously rewrapping copper wire along the rotors.

As Iris removed the repaired rotor from her backpack to exchange the burnt-out one, she paused a moment. She was engrossed in her work, finding happiness in the aftermath of the petroplague, content in a way she had never experienced before. She felt at home.

It was very different from the life her parents had pushed her to pursue—to be the front-runner in the rat race, to work sixty hours a week, to focus her goals on being the *best*, on getting ahead. Iris was normally high-strung, always on the move—but she was learning that it was okay to be different. She liked these simple comforts.

And she liked being with Todd.

She caught Todd looking at her many times when he thought she wouldn't notice. Even when they were together he still seemed to long for her like some unreachable object. He was so clean-cut and straightforward; it calmed her to believe he had no private agenda, that he wasn't after her for any reason other than herself. In his puppy-dog way, Todd couldn't hide anything; subtlety was not his strong point, but she found it kind of sweet.

"Hey, you gonna daydream up there all afternoon?" Jackson Harris shouted up at her.

Iris quickly stripped out the old rotor and placed it in her backpack, then installed the new one. Clambering down the metal rungs, she overheard Harris and Doog talking.

"I sure wish we had some music during all this. That's what I miss the most. Who'd have thought the Grateful Dead would finally die?" Harris kicked a stone into the gully.

As she stepped down the last rungs from the windmill mast, Iris remembered all the CDs she'd loved to play. The hardest things to live without were coffee and rock & roll. She dropped to the gravel pad around the mast and turned to Harris and Doog.

"I miss the music too," she said. "So what are we going to do about it?"

Todd Severyn rode his horse through the gates of the Livermore branch of Sandia National Laboratory. Spirals of razor wire crowned the tall fences, but the guard station sat empty. Nobody bothered to impose security anymore. Most of the lab facilities were broken down and unoccupied, but some of the researchers still came in to work, while others camped out in RV trailers in the parking lots.

For a month or so the teams had banded together, frantically trying to find some way to eradicate the petroplague; but as equipment broke down, computers malfunctioned, and the entire complex collapsed, most of them had given up hope. A few still continued plugging away to come up with innovative solutions.

Todd tied Stimpy up front to the bicycle rack and went inside the administration building. The lobby area for welcoming visitors had been turned into a command center. The bright and cheery PR posters for America's national labs had been replaced by a large map of the United States studded with colored pushpins.

One of the administrators, Moira Tibbett, stared at the map with a sheet of paper in hand. She wore a dressy cotton outfit. Tibbett glanced at a list of locations on the paper, fingering a pushpin. She squinted at the map like an entomologist about to spear a specimen, then jabbed in the pushpin.

"More stuff for the Atlantis Network?" Todd asked. He poured himself a glass of warm sun tea; it tasted good.

"Yeah. Three more stations came on-line this week. For a political dumping ground, FEMA is doing a pretty good job tracking these enclaves and linking us together." She thrust another pushpin into a different location.

Todd lifted his eyebrows; her former disdain for the Federal Emergency Management Agency had come around a hundred and eighty degrees. "So what's new this morning? Give me some news I can take back to the colony."

"Well, locally the usual stuff is happening," Tibbett said. "The Livermore city engineers are trying to make sure people have access to enough water. We have a whole lot of problems with just our sewage system. The fire patrols are more organized, but we've been lucky so far. And it's same-old same-old on the food story."

Todd nodded. At fifty-thousand people and somewhat isolated, the city of Livermore was probably the right size to weather the petroplague: not so big that it had no way of getting its own supplies, yet large enough to have an infrastructure with some chance of functioning.

"What's new on the big board?" Todd asked, gesturing with his chin toward the wall map. Tibbett withdrew a pushpin and stabbed another set of coordinates, this one in Missouri.

"Kind of ironic actually. Spencer Lockwood at the solar antenna farm in White Sands knows that the remaining smallsats he was supposed to put into orbit are sealed in launch canisters at the Jet Propulsion Lab in Pasadena. He's rigged a way to launch the satellites in New Mexico, but he can't get his hands on them."

Todd scratched his head where the cowboy hat had pushed his brown hair into strange twists. He didn't know whether to be skeptical or amazed. "We can't even get our sewer systems running, and this guy wants to put a satellite into orbit?"

Tibbett's face looked carved out of stone. "Twenty satellites, actually. But if Lockwood says he can do it, believe him. I gave him a tour here not long ago. He's a real hotshot."

Todd looked at the map, saw pushpins in New Mexico at the White Sands missile range, another one near Los Angeles in Pasadena. He began to imagine grand schemes, a great expedition across the Southwest hauling the satellites from Pasadena across Arizona into New Mexico. A regular wagon train to the stars!

But it would never come to pass. He said goodbye to Moira Tibbett and headed home to Iris.

FIFTY-FIVE

DOWN THE HIGHWAY

Outside of Albuquerque, concrete buildings and bunkers were set into the side of the hills—"Bayclock's Empire," as Navy Lieutenant Bobby Carron had come to think of it. Encircled by four metal fences, the thousand-acre Manzano complex had once served as a storage facility for nuclear weapons; now Bayclock used the fortresslike bunkers as his headquarters.

The guards outside the chain-link gate popped to attention and threw Bobby a salute as they waved him into the facility. He felt strange wearing an Air Force uniform.

Accompanied by escorts, Bobby hobbled up a series of stairs and entered a fortified building. Bobby gritted his teeth. His still-healing wounds sent tremors of pain through his body.

Concrete walls two feet thick, barred windows, and piles of useless electronic gear made the place seem like a twisted version of a medieval castle. Finally, he passed two more guards standing like moat dragons outside Bayclock's office.

"Stand at ease, Captain."

At first Bobby didn't realize that Bayclock was speaking to him. In the sprawling office the general had commandeered, once-plush carpet edged up to dark wood paneling that had blistered as the glossy coatings had dissolved; military awards, lithographs of fighter aircraft, and school diplomas covered the wall.

"Please come in, Captain. Are you fully recovered from your injuries?" Bayclock waved Bobby into the secure office, then slumped in an overstuffed leather chair behind his desk. Narrow window slits barely lit the room.

Bobby stepped forward, stiff and formal as he remembered from his training at the Naval Academy. The memory of the curfew-breaking teenager dangling on the gallows still burned clear in his mind. "It's lieutenant, sir. Not captain. You didn't have any navy uniforms I could wear."

Bayclock narrowed his eyes, then laughed. "That's right, Lieutenant. Calling you a captain is like promoting you three ranks! Never figured out why the military couldn't standardize the whole damn rank structure." He motioned toward one of the chairs. "Go ahead, have a seat."

"Yes, sir."

Bobby had expected Bayclock to be some sort of ogre, hunched over his desk and ready to snap necks with his thumbs. Instead, the general had bright eyes, regulation-cropped dark hair, and an easy grace as he folded his hands in front of him. Bayclock held himself poised, continuously taking in his surroundings. It was obvious to Bobby that Bayclock had himself been a fighter pilot; but Bobby felt no rapport with the general. Bayclock inspected him closely. Bobby wondered how he would measure up.

Bayclock pulled a paper from the stack on his desk. He scanned it in the dim light and spoke without looking up. "I've kept up with your recovery, glad to see you're doing better. You've been briefed on the situation here—martial law and all that, by the president's order?"

"Yes, sir." How could he *not* notice? After seeing how the general dealt with unrest in the city, Bobby felt extremely uneasy just to be in the same room with Bayclock.

"Some people are savages and want to steal everything in sight. My troops are stretched to the limit, Lieutenant. Every able-bodied person I have is trying to keep the peace in the city. I'm using military finance clerks as squad leaders, aircraft mechanics as forward observers. They serve according to their abilities, and they're doing a super job, but I can't ask them anything else."

"Yes, sir." Bobby sat straight in his chair, watching the general. *So what's the point? This isn't a social call.*

Bayclock continued. "In addition to upholding the law, I've got to care for these people, keep the place going in the long run. That means coordinating food expeditions, fixing waterlines, staying in contact with the president in case orders change."

"So, are communication lines open?" Bobby must have sounded incredulous, because Bayclock snorted.

"The plague didn't affect the electromagnetic spectrum, Lieutenant, just oil!" Bayclock rocked forward and pushed the paper to Bobby. Bobby caught it as the sheet spun off the edge of the metal surplus desk. "In fact, we've intercepted some messages from White Sands coming across the FEMA emergency network."

Intercepted? thought Bobby, keeping a stone-straight face. That was the most important thing he had learned in all his military training—how to smother his reactions. This guy sounded as if he was at war!

"Somehow they've reestablished full electrical power down there, using it to run their water pumps. Water pumps! Do you have any idea how many of my people it takes to pump water up from this damned aquifer we're sitting on top of? That's a major part of that manpower drain I was talking about. People are getting away with murder because good military personnel are pumping water instead of patrolling the city.

"Now, White Sands is technically under my jurisdiction, and the president has reconfirmed it. We're all in this mess together, and if those wizards have managed to get back on their feet by producing electricity, then I need it."

Bobby Carron sat in his chair like a statue, ignoring the pain in his leg and ribs. Shadows in the room highlighted the intensity in Bayclock's face. He had seen a few squirrelly commanders before, but Bayclock seemed to think he was Napoleon of the Apocalypse.

"I can't trust any of the damned civilians to head up this expedition—the scientists at Sandia Albuquerque turned tail and deserted their labs at the first sign of a riot; my Phillips Lab troops aren't much better. I haven't been able to reach the enclave of researchers up at Los Alamos, and I've never trusted those bomb designers anyway. But down in White Sands they've made a little Atlantis for themselves."

The general cracked his knuckles one at a time. It sounded like someone snapping twigs—or neck bones.

"I need someone I can trust, Lieutenant Carron—an *operator* who's used to working alone and can function when things get tough. In short, I need a fighter pilot." Bayclock drew himself up, setting his mouth. "When I took this command, I saw it as an opportunity to instill some of the esprit that pilots have . . . you know, the sense of duty that comes from being in an operational fighter unit. These scientists and nonrated pukes have a warped sense of duty, more allegiance to their profession than to the overall mission."

Bayclock looked suddenly tired, as if the effects of his orders wore at him. "I don't know if it's a coincidence or not, Lieutenant. I just met you, but I know you wouldn't be flying fighters unless you had the right stuff, even if you did join the navy instead of the air force." He smiled wearily.

"A colleague of mine once said, 'There's two types of people in this world: fighter pilots and weenies.' Well, I'm surrounded by weenies. What I need is a fighter pilot to head up an expedition to White Sands, then return here with a report."

Bobby tried to keep the astonishment off his face. The events of the past few weeks swam through his mind—waking up in the ravaged hospital, the execution of looters, seeing the full effects of the petroplague. . . . The general probably thought Bobby would be apprehensive about leaving the "security" of a city under martial law.

Bobby saw it as an opportunity to get away from this insanity, but he knew it would be the worst thing in the world for him to show his eagerness. He stood and reached across Bayclock's desk, extending his hand. "General, you've got your man. Where do I sign up?"

The horses kept to the side of Interstate 40 east out of Albuquerque, paralleling old Route 66 in the pass between the Sandia and Manzano mountains. The spongy asphalt highway was too soft to bear any weight, and the horses clopped along on the shoulder. The riders carried several dozen liters of water along with their food rations.

Beside Bobby at the front of the five-person expedition, his assigned escort—a stout, gruff sergeant named Caitlyn Morris—had not spoken in an hour. Three scientists trailed behind—two from Sandia's Albuquerque Labs and one from the Air Force's Phillips Lab—who would study the White Sands power generators and take back whatever components the general might need in Albuquerque.

The horses walked through the pass. Boulders littered the sides of the barren hill, sloping up on either side like a giant brown funnel that had been cut in half and laid on its side. Although he had lived at barren China Lake for the past two years, Bobby still missed the thick trees in Virginia where he had grown up, the ocean, and humidity. This seemed like an alien landscape.

Bobby turned to the taciturn woman sergeant beside him. Caitlyn Morris was a helicopter mechanic who had flown many times along the corridor to White Sands. Her blond hair was clipped short, accenting her stout frame and full hips. She stood no taller than five feet, but she rode high in the saddle, confident.

"Seems like we're making good time," Bobby said. "How long do you think it'll take to get to White Sands?"

Sergeant Morris didn't look at him as she answered; she kept scanning the road in front of them. "Depends."

"On what?"

"Lots of things."

Bobby felt a flash of annoyance. "Look, Sergeant, I don't want to play Twenty Questions—"

She interrupted him by holding up a hand. "Wait up." She slowed her horse and placed a hand against her revolver. It glistened from her cleaning, polishing, and refurbishing.

Bobby pulled back on the reins. He started to speak, then glimpsed several figures scrambling down the sides of the hill. They were dressed in dusty jeans, threadbare shirts; some of them tried to take advantage of the brush cover, while others didn't care if they were seen. They all carried sticks, crowbars, or unwieldy knives. It took them only a minute to spread out in a line, blocking the highway fifty yards ahead. Bobby counted fifteen men. Half were teenagers.

"Hey, what's going on?" said Arnie, one of the scientists behind them. "What do they think they're doing?"

Sergeant Morris turned in the saddle. "It's your game, Lieutenant Carron. The rest of you keep quiet."

"Thanks," muttered Bobby. He left his rifle in the holster at the back of the saddle, not ready to pull it out yet.

One of the men stepped toward them. Bearded and

balding, his patchy skin peeled from sunburn. The man
stopped twenty yards away. He held a long iron bar like
a swagger stick in his left hand. "Where you folks
headed?"

Bobby wondered if the man was going to ask for a toll
to use the road. He turned at the crunch of gravel and
saw five more people come up behind them, blocking
their return.

"White Sands. I'm Lieutenant Carron, representing
General Bayclock at Kirtland." Maybe the general's
bloodthirsty tactics would scare these people off.

"You're going the wrong way. White Sands is due
south."

"So is Laguna Pueblo. We're respecting Native American land. There's been some trouble down there."

The man grinned. "Good for you, Lieutenant. Still, a
long way to carry your own food and water. I don't think
you're going to make it. Your horses would fare better
here, I'm sure."

"We'll resupply at Clines Corners before turning
south. The general authorized us to exchange some
supply chits, redeemable at Kirtland."

"Redeemable at Kirtland?" The man roared as the
rest of the group broke out in chuckles. "So Generalissi-
mo Bayclock is going to let people walk into Albuquerque and pick up food? Well, then. You won't mind
donating some chits to make sure you get through the
pass? For protection, you understand."

Bobby drew himself up. This was weirdly medieval.
"The chits aren't for passage. We're an official military
expedition, operating under martial law. I'll ask you
gentlemen to allow us to pass, or face the consequences."

The men laughed among themselves. The bearded
man stepped closer. "Maybe you didn't hear me, Lieutenant. I was asking for a donation. If you can include a
couple of these horses, and some of your supplies along
with the chits, we'll help you along." He spoke softly and
stared at Bobby.

As he approached, he seemed to notice Sergeant Morris for the first time. His eyes widened. "So what are you, missie, his protection? You're probably worth more than a horse, aren't you?"

Sergeant Morris pulled out her revolver. The man grinned. "You military types haven't used those guns for a while, have you?" He puffed up as he walked, changing his path from Bobby to Caitlyn. "What makes you so sure they'll work?"

Bobby raised his voice. "This is your final warning."

The man ignored him. He was within five yards when Sergeant Morris calmly brought the revolver up. She aimed at his crotch and glanced at Bobby; Bobby nodded, and she clicked off a round. The explosion of the gun echoed off the bare boulders.

The man grabbed at his groin and fell, screaming. The others in the mob stood in shock, uncertain what to do.

Bobby yanked out his rifle and moved it from side to side. The men took a hurried step back. Bobby raised his voice over the man's screaming. "Anyone else?" He flipped off the safety.

The men murmured and made an opening for them. Bobby pointed his rifle at a teenage boy nearest the road. "Help your friend—Kirtland hospital will do what they can. The rest of you listen up! What goes on up here is your business, but down in the city, you're under martial law. That law extends to any military personnel traveling through this pass." He held up his rifle. "Our weapons still work just fine. Remember that next time."

Bobby motioned with his head for Sergeant Morris and the three wide-eyed scientists to follow. "Move it."

They rode the horses at a fast trot through the opening made by the bandits. Behind them, the scavengers muttered in indecision; the wounded man screamed on the ground. Bobby and Sergeant Morris kept their weapons leveled.

They didn't speak until they left the group far behind. Soon, the rustling of their horses moving along the dusty roadside was the only sound. After another ten minutes, they rounded a curve to where the steep mountain pass opened up to show the eastern valley spreading out in front of them. Bobby could see mountains on the horizon, eighty miles away. Below them, the skeletal interstate highway wound through foothills. He saw a small town off in the distance.

Sergeant Morris turned and spoke her first unsolicited words to him. "You handled that nicely, Lieutenant."

Bobby felt his shoulders sag with the release of tension. He gulped, feeling a sour taste claw his throat. "Nice shot yourself." He yanked back on the reins, pulling the horse to a stop. Leaning over, he vomited.

Sergeant Morris came around. "You all right, sir?"

Bobby heaved once more, then wiped his mouth with the back of his hand. He struggled to sit upright in the saddle. "Now I am. Just getting prepped for the exciting part of this trip."

FIFTY-SIX

GIMME SHELTER

The ranch house sat alone at the far end of a winding dirt driveway. Penned in by a barbed-wire fence, sheep grazed among the scrub around the house. Beside the house, a nineteenth-century windmill stood motionless, waiting for a breeze so it could pump water from deep beneath the high desert.

Heather Dixon shifted the neon-pink backpack on her shoulders. She brushed a hand across her forehead to wipe sweat and road dust away. The sun pounded down on them as she and Connor trudged up the long drive, leaving imprints from their hiking boots in the dirt.

Connor insisted that Heather take her own turn carrying the pack. He kept time on his watch, making sure that he didn't do a minute more work than she did. *Equality at its best,* he called it. Heather wanted to carry her own weight, but he didn't have to be so nitpicky about it. Instead of the pack, Connor carried the shotgun and the big hunting knife.

"We can get some water up there," she said, "maybe some food."

Connor's face had been sunburned, but it didn't seem to bother him. The ruddy change in his skin gave him a rugged appearance. He hadn't shaved, but his beard was pale like his blond hair, making him look like a California beach bum. "I could use a shower too." Connor winked at her. "Like to join me? I had fun the last time we took one."

Heather answered him with a forced laugh, and turned away. Over the hard days of walking she had rapidly grown tired of Connor Brooks. She began to regret going with him at all, wandering on this aimless trek across the southwest, moving eastward with no destination in mind.

The sex had been good, one of the better parts of the whole experience. Lying under the stars, camping wherever they felt like, and totally free for the first time in her life—without a job to go back to, not caring about the social conventions that had tangled up her life. But lately even making love with Connor had become unpleasant, as if it was now *expected* of her, instead of being spontaneous.

Connor called them the "Bonnie and Clyde of the apocalypse," and his goofy routine grated on her. The look in his eyes and the hidden focus of his thoughts scared her. She realized just how alone she was with him day after day.

Long before they reached the ranch house, Heather heard a dog start barking. She could see the big black mutt tied to the windmill frame by a long rope. The dog was shaggy, mostly sheepdog but with a dash of Labrador and German shepherd. The dog barked and barked, but Heather detected no growling menace. After the petroplague, it probably saw few strangers.

Connor walked beside her carrying the shotgun as if he thought it made him invincible.

The front door opened, and a woman emerged; her openmouthed smile was like a flower unfolding. She was in her late thirties with her hair tied in an unflattering ponytail. Her clothes had the worn broad-strokes appearance of homemade garments. The woman's face lit up like a full moon, making her eyes seem small but bright. "Hello! Can we help you?"

Connor, playing his part of tough guy and asshole, stepped forward. He lowered his voice intentionally, like some kind of vigilante. "We came to take food and water."

Heather shifted her pink backpack. She smiled at the woman. "Can you spare some?"

A second woman stepped out, looking wary. She had hovered just behind the other in the darkness of the house, watching and listening. This woman, perhaps a year or two older, wore similar clothes. Her face was gaunt, as if someone had nipped and tucked and tightened her expression over the years. She gave both Connor and Heather a wary look. "We've got a little."

Connor craned his head, squinting to look through the shadows of the doorway. "So where's the man of the house?"

The good-natured woman piped up, "He's returning from temple in Salt Lake City."

The gaunt woman answered simultaneously, "He's out back."

Connor snorted, ignoring the obvious lie. Turning to the good-natured woman, he said, "In Utah?" He pronounced it "U-*taw*." "At temple? What are you, Aztecs or something?"

Heather glared at him and muttered, "They're Mormons, stupid."

"Mormons?" Connor straightened up and let out a guffaw. "So, these must be the guy's two wives." He laughed again.

The gaunt woman snapped, "Shelda's my sister."

"Hey," Connor said looking to Heather with an expression of concentration on his face, "aren't Mormons supposed to keep a year's supply of everything? In case of emergencies. They must have plenty to share."

The gaunt woman eased back toward the house,

vanishing into the shadows. Heather knew she was going to go for a hidden weapon. Connor jerked up the shotgun in a frightening, smooth movement and pointed it toward the doorway.

The dog, its protective instincts suddenly ignited, went wild, barking and straining to the edge of its rope.

Connor pointed the shotgun at the animal as if extending a finger at a recalcitrant child and squeezed the trigger. The explosion echoed around the ranch yard and the dog flew backward into the air, its side ripped open by the scatter blast of the shotgun pellets. It tangled two legs into the rope as it somersaulted and lay in a bloodied heap in the dusty yard.

A smothering silence fell. Everyone stood transfixed. The old windmill, finally stirred by a breeze, creaked and turned twice, then fell still.

Heather stared at Connor, not knowing what to say. The gun was so loud. This was the first time he had actually fired it, for all the threatening and blustering he had done over the past few days. It smelled foul and sulfurous.

Connor's face took on a pinched, calculating look. "Maybe we should just stay, Heather. This place has everything we need, and I'm sick of hiking everywhere." He laughed. "Go on, ladies, get your tennis shoes on. You've got a lot of walking to do."

Heather put her hands on her hips, refusing to let him see her fear. "Connor, cut it out!" She grabbed at the shotgun, but he snatched it away, glaring at her.

The moon-faced woman fell to her knees on the porch. She kept staring at the motionless dog bleeding into the dust.

The gaunt woman reappeared, her eyes as wide as coins. She gripped the doorframe but she didn't move a muscle.

Connor spoke to Heather while keeping the shotgun trained on the women. "What's your problem? We've been trudging around this state like scavengers, and these bitches are sitting fat and cushy on a year's worth of food. It's our turn! We deserve a bit of convenience for a change. I thought you wanted to get back at the people who stepped all over you your whole life."

Heather's words came out quieter than she intended. "These people never did anything to me."

"Well then let's get that Al Sysco you keep complaining about." He dropped the barrel of the shotgun and pointed toward the ladies' feet. "I can make him dance like in an old cowboy movie. Pow, pow, pow!"

"Right, I want to hike all the way back to Flagstaff just so I can make a pathetic little man squirm. Cool it, Connor, we've got better things to do." She turned to the gaunt woman, the only one capable of doing anything at the moment. "Would you get us some water and some packaged food?" She hesitated. "Please?"

Connor pointed the shotgun at her moon-faced sister. "And don't try anything!" Heather didn't like the predatory look in Connor's eyes. More and more of his real personality was unfolding before her eyes. With a chill she wondered what he might have done to the women if she wasn't there.

Connor snorted at Heather. "Man, what made you turn boring all of a sudden?"

Minutes later the gaunt woman returned with the supplies. Heather's heart raced and she tried to slow her breathing. She was afraid the woman might have gone for a rifle of her own, and then things would have gotten messy. But she carried only water and some boxed food. "Here . . . now please, leave us alone."

Connor was about to retort, but Heather grabbed his arm and forced him to turn around. "Let's go," she said, and they set off back down the dirt driveway.

As they departed, Heather glanced back. The gaunt woman took her sister's hand and pulled her to her feet. The two of them moved slowly forward to stand in shock over their dead dog.

FIFTY-SEVEN

HELLO, GOODBYE

"Hey, Spence—visitors!" The words echoed in the still air around the electromagnetic launcher on the slopes of Oscura Peak.

"Who is it?" Spencer asked with a sigh. Even with the isolation of the post-plague world, people still found ways to interrupt his work a dozen times a day. He swore that *he* would never be the person to bring back the telephone.

Gilbert Hertoya shrugged, his small, compact body silhouetted against the door of the tin-roofed accelerator. "Don't know, but they're riding down from the north."

Spencer put down his wrench and wiped sweat from his forehead. His new beard itched like crazy in the stuffy heat. Pinholes of light punched through the metal siding, but no breeze came at all. Spencer could only stand to work inside the enclosure for half an hour at a time.

He left a jumble of wiring on the concrete floor. For

the past few days it was the only work he could do that wouldn't bring a squawk from his experimentalists. They kidded him and told him to keep away from the delicate refurbished equipment after the water-pump fiasco. Short on unskilled labor, Gilbert Hertoya had cheerfully put him to work laying down relay switches on the EM launcher facility. "If liberal-arts students can handle it during the summer, I think you can manage," Gilbert said.

Spencer emerged from the dim building into the brilliant desert sun; he held up a hand against the glare as he stared down the mountain slope. Gilbert stood on a pile of metal siding to get higher, pointing toward the north. "Looks like five of them."

Spencer squinted. "All on horseback?"

"Yeah. And they're not from Alamogordo unless they got lost coming back from Cloudcroft."

"Too far south. Besides, they'd stick to the mountains if they were lost." Spencer thought for a moment. "You know, Romero's been getting some disturbing reports—martial law in Albuquerque, riots in El Paso, a lot of the Indian pueblos killing anyone who comes on their land. We've been lucky up here."

Gilbert gingerly stepped down from the pile of rattling metal. "What should we do?"

"Send out the welcome wagon, what else?"

In the concrete blockhouse at the base of the railgun launcher, Spencer and Gilbert waited in the shade. The travelers arrowed straight for the facility—the five-mile launcher could be seen for miles around.

Spencer pushed back the drooping brim of his hat, arms folded as he watched the riders approach. The two in front wore air force uniforms, and he could see rifles packed behind their saddles. He had a sudden vision of the cavalry riding into town.

"What are they up to?" he muttered. Gilbert shaded his eyes and kept staring.

The broad-shouldered man in uniform looked young

and big enough to be a football player. He called out when they were fifty yards away. "Yo! I'm Lieutenant Bobby Carron, looking for Dr. Lockwood. Can you tell me where to find him?"

Spencer squinted at the young man; the voice sounded familiar, but he couldn't quite place it. Had they met before?

One of the three men in back leaned to the side and shouted, "Hey, Gilbert! That you, you old sand rat?"

Gilbert Hertoya broke into a grin. "Arnie!" He turned to Spencer and dropped his voice. "I used to work with him at Sandia. He's okay."

Arnie spread his arms. "They made me an offer I couldn't refuse. Come on, let's talk." As the visitors kept approaching, Spencer saw a troubled look cross Arnie's face. "You're lucky you were down here when the plague hit, Gilbert. A lot of people died."

Lieutenant Carron swung off his horse; Spencer racked his brain, trying to recall where he'd seen the man before. And then he remembered: the drive back from Livermore, the rental car breaking down out in the California desert. Spencer grinned and held out a hand. "I knew you looked familiar, Lieutenant. I'm Spencer Lockwood—you rescued me, just about two months ago, when I ran out of gas near Death Valley."

Bobby held on to the horse's reins and squinted at Spencer. A smile grew across his face. "You're right. You know, I'd forgotten your name—and you didn't have a beard then, did you?"

"No need to waste razors."

Bobby laughed. "It didn't occur to me that you'd be the same person I was supposed to find." He introduced his group. Everyone seemed pleased except sour-faced Sergeant Morris. She stiffly shook Spencer's hand without a trace of warmth.

Spencer said, "What can I do for you, now that you've come across half the state looking for me?"

"We heard you've been generating electricity down here," Bobby said. "We came to get the full details."

Spencer rolled his eyes. "Oh, boy. I was afraid this might happen."

Bobby fumbled with the button on his uniform shirt. He pulled out a folded sheet of paper, smoothed it, then handed it to Spencer. He looked embarrassed. "We're actually on an official mission, for what it's worth. I'm representing General Bayclock from Kirtland."

Spencer held on to the paper, but kept looking at Bobby. "I thought you said you were assigned to China Lake. What's a navy man doing in the middle of the desert?"

"That's a long story. Here, this explains part of it."

Spencer started to read the paper. The words ATTENTION TO ORDERS were stamped across the top. He lifted an eyebrow. "Bayclock is the head guy up at the base, isn't he?"

"Base commander . . . and, uh, marshal of Albuquerque, I guess, with the martial law and all that."

"Marshal, huh. Like Matt Dillon?" Spencer scanned the dense paragraphs, growing more uneasy. "So this general thinks that, since he was technically responsible for our logistics before the petroplague, we're under his martial-law authority now?" Spencer looked up. "He never once visited our facility, never so much as called me on the phone—and now we're supposed to develop a plan to provide Albuquerque with electricity, just because he says so?" It might have been funny under other circumstances. "Do you know how ridiculous that sounds?"

Bobby shrugged.

"The general is not kidding, Dr. Lockwood," Sergeant Morris said stiffly.

Spencer folded the paper, resisting the impulse to rip it to shreds and scatter the pieces across the desert. He ignored Sergeant Morris. "So what do you think of this, Lieutenant?"

Bobby held up his hands. "Hey, I'm only the messenger. . . ."

"Don't worry, you saved my life once, and I won't

shoot you for bringing bad news. In fact, I don't even have a gun."

Spencer turned to the rest of the visitors. Gilbert Hertoya and Arnie stepped up beside them. Squat Sergeant Morris remained on her horse like a statue of an old war hero that belonged in some small-town square.

Spencer said, "Okay, so what's going on? What do the rest of you know about this?"

Bobby Carron said slowly, "Can we get out of the sun?" He took Spencer's arm. Stepping away from Sergeant Morris, he whispered, "I've got stuff to tell you about Bayclock that you won't believe!"

Spencer, Bobby Carron, and Sergeant Morris sat on their mounts outside the fenced-off antenna farm. Rita Fellenstein and the three visiting scientists stood on the other side of Spencer. The expanse of whiplike microwave antennas spread out before them, like a field of gleaming silver stalks.

Spencer leaned on the saddle as Bobby spoke. The young officer seemed to have trouble verbalizing his thoughts.

"I'm not a scientist or anything like that," said Bobby, "but I had enough engineering back at Annapolis to know the difference between what's possible and what's likely. I'd sure hate to go back and tell the general that although it might be possible to generate electricity this way, it isn't likely to happen on the scale he envisions. This is really just a test bed! There's not enough power for everyone in Albuquerque. So what should we do? Tell him it was a waste of our time?"

Spencer shifted his weight in his saddle. "I don't think I'd want to supply Bayclock with electricity even if I could. And if I can believe what you told me, they should oust him!"

"Believe him, Dr. Lockwood," Arnie broke in harshly. "My wife and children would still be alive if it wasn't for Bayclock's crackdowns."

Spencer scratched his beard. "Helping Bayclock amounts to validating his position, agreeing with the atrocities he's committed." He shook his head. "I'm sorry, Lieutenant, but I can't help you. We've got a fragile enough toehold out here, and taking on anything else right now would push us over the brink. Between you and me, if the general were running a different sort of operation, we might be able to take on some extra people, try and help him in the long term. I don't want to seem like a jerk, but . . ." He shrugged.

Bobby's horse lifted its head and snorted, as if to agree with what Spencer said. Bobby pulled back on the reins. "I can't blame you." He smiled weakly. "I'm not looking forward to going back and delivering the bad news."

Rita Fellenstein pulled her horse over to join them. Her long legs dangled down to the horse's knees, even in her stirrups. She spat a wad of chewing tobacco at the ground. "So why go back, Bobby? We could use some help getting the launcher running. A big guy like you would come in handy with the launcher."

Bobby looked out across the desert. Spencer guessed he had been thinking the same thing himself.

"If nobody goes back, how's the general going to know that something didn't happen to you?" Rita continued. "He knows about the gangs outside the city, and he probably doesn't have a clue what other crazies are out here. It took five of you two weeks to get here. So what's he going to do, force an army to march down to rescue you? Sounds like he's got enough trouble in his own backyard."

Arnie placed a hand on Gilbert Hertoya's shoulder. "No way am I going back there. I'm staying here." The two other scientists quickly voiced their agreement.

Bobby stared out at the antenna farm. A warm breeze whipped around them, driving a miniature dust storm.

"The lieutenant and I are not deserting," Sergeant Morris said. "You can talk about him all you like, but General Bayclock *does* have the proper authority—and you are all obligated to follow his orders."

Spencer turned his horse around, putting his back to the wind. Through the rising heat he caught a glimpse of the supply wagon from Alamogordo coming toward the blockhouse in the distance. "Let's get out of this wind. We'll unload the supply wagon and talk about this later."

By the time the group reached the command trailers, the supplies were mostly unloaded. Spencer was surprised to see Lance Nedermyer standing on the flat back of the cart, helping roll a fifty-gallon aluminum container of water off the side. Spencer pushed back his hat. "Hi, Lance. Need help?"

"Sure."

With the extra people, it took little time to unload the ten drums of water. Rita went to check the supplies stored under the trailer, taking the three new scientists with her. Nedermyer leaned back against the wagon and wiped his face with the back of his hand; his mirrored sunglasses had fallen apart more than a month ago, casualties of the petroplague.

"So what brings you out here, Lance?"

The Washington bureaucrat took a long drink of tepid water before answering. Like the others, he had not shaved in nearly a month. His beard had shifted from looking scraggly to the verge of bushiness. Lance looked as if he missed his suits even more than his wife and daughters back in the D.C. area.

He sounded bitter. "They've changed their minds about heading up to Cloudcroft. You've got them excited about bringing electricity on-line, and they don't want to think about wintering in the mountains. I guess too many people remember the old ways, and you're giving them false hope to hang on."

"How do you know it's a false hope?"

A bemused smile came over Lance's face. "You really don't know, do you, Spence?"

"What are you talking about? We need all the hope we can get."

Lance shook his head. "They're barely hanging on down there. It's *tough*, Spencer, not a game. The majority of people might not make it through the first year."

Spencer looked incredulous. "All the more reason to get things going here! What good does it do to herd them into the mountains?"

"There's game, firewood . . . and water, for God's sake! At least they've got the basics to keep them alive. Down here, all you have is desert—and your damned microwave farm that can't even transmit power more than twenty miles. Hell, we'd be better off in Albuquerque—at least General Bayclock is doing the sensible thing, feeding the people, keeping the law. He's a hell of a lot more realistic than anyone around here."

Spencer bristled at the criticism. He really didn't need this; maybe it was time to do what a leader was supposed to do, and toss the bugger out! He'd put up with Lance for too long, hoping he'd change his ways.

"We ought to feel pretty lucky, Lance. From what Lieutenant Carron here has been telling us, things are ten times as bad in Albuquerque. I can't buy any of this 'Jeremiah Johnson' survival talk. I think it's about time we all start pulling together."

Spencer nodded to the three scientists who had accompanied Bobby Carron and Sergeant Morris down from Albuquerque. "Ask those three what it means to have hope, where somebody's actually trying to make things better."

Lance stared at Spencer. "What are you saying?"

Spencer felt light-headed—in the past he had tried to avoid direct confrontation, but these were new times, new ways. "This job is tough enough without being second-guessed on everything I do, Lance. It's time for you to either pitch in or get out."

"Second-guessed? What, are you afraid to get a little valid criticism? Come on, Spencer—every science project in the book debates the issues."

"That's just it—this *isn't* a science project anymore. It's survival. We've debated things long enough. Either throw your hat in the ring or get out." Spencer breathed heavily, his face flushed.

The smile on Lance's face tightened. "So it's put up or shut up? I didn't think you had it in you, Spencer."

"If you're going to Cloudcroft, I want you on the wagon when it heads back. You can have your pick of supplies before you go and a horse." Spencer paused. "Lieutenant Carron's heading back to Albuquerque if you'd rather go there. It's your choice."

Lance's mouth twisted up. He turned to Bobby Carron. "When are you heading back, Lieutenant? Mind if I come with you?"

Bobby turned away; his massive hand opened and closed.

Sergeant Morris looked to Bobby, but when he still didn't answer, she said, "I'd like to get back as soon as possible, sir. The general was quite explicit in his orders."

Bobby kept staring out in the distance. Lance turned to him. "Lieutenant? Is it okay if I ride along?"

"Do what you want." It took Bobby an effort to speak. "I'm staying here." He looked to Spencer. "That is, if Dr. Lockwood needs another hand getting this microwave farm to work."

Spencer blinked. "Sure, uh, we can always use someone who wants to help. Same for you, Sergeant Morris." He hesitated. "And that goes for you, too, Lance, if you change your mind."

Lance Nedermyer shook his head; his entire gaunt body moved with the movement. "I've made up my mind. Sergeant . . . ?"

The woman's mouth was drawn tight; she looked at Bobby as if he had become the lowest form of slime. Her deep voice sounded harsh. "The lieutenant is old enough to know what he's doing . . . and knows the conse-

quences for disobeying an order, deserting during martial law. They hang people for less than that."

Bobby nodded, still looking at the horizon. His hand
continued to open and close. "Yeah," he said. "I've seen
Bayclock do it."

FIFTY-EIGHT

CANNONBALL

With pillars of steam and dark smoke, the train announced its presence in the morning calm. The whistle, thin and tinny in the distance, was loud enough that the people in the Altamont commune dropped their work and ran to hilltops to see what was coming down the Central Valley.

"It's a train," Todd Severyn said in disbelief, shielding his eyes with the palm of his hand and craning forward. "It's a friggin' train! Can you believe it?"

Jackson Harris stood next to him, his dark skin glistening with sweat. His beard and hair stuck out in all directions, as if he had wrestled with a hurricane. "An old steam train," Harris said. "How did they ever get it running?"

"How do they *keep* it running!"

The distant locomotive hauled four cars behind it, a passenger car, dining car, and two boxcars, as well as a car filled with wood mounded high behind the engineer's cab.

"This is great news," Todd said. "I'll check it out. Looks like he's heading toward the town of Tracy."

When Todd whistled, both horses trotted over, eager for a ride. He patted Stimpy on the neck. "Next time, girl. It's Ren's turn."

Todd saddled Ren and made ready to swing himself up, then ran back toward the small house trailer. Though Todd got up at dawn, Iris was never an early riser. And although they shared the trailer for convenience, Todd was careful to respect her privacy. He banged on the side. "Hey, Iris—come on out!"

She stepped out the swinging door, bleary-eyed and blinking at the commotion.

"It's a train, Iris! I'm going to check it out. I'll be back as soon as I have some information."

"A *train?* Impossible." She folded her arms. "How does is it work? They couldn't have found a way to neutralize the petroplague."

"Do you want come with me?"

She ran a hand through her unkempt black hair and seemed to think about it. "No, go on. Just let me know what you find out."

Todd had already turned for Ren, too excited to reply.

The locomotive sat ticking and hissing, at a standstill in the Tracy railyards. Sleek like a giant black caterpillar, its wheels and cowcatcher were blazoned in bright scarlet. The ornate handrail running along the boiler, the hinges, the bell, and the steam whistle all shone bright gold. The sooty smokestack flared out in a wide black cone, and all its rivets glittered like brass buttons. In gold-painted letters under the two windows in the engineer's cab was the name STEAM ROLLER.

Todd led his horse in among the people crowding the tracks. Iris was right—what was the catch? *If this one train works, then where are the rest of them?*

Other people arrived, walking along the railroad tracks, stepping between the ties. They had seen the locomotive approaching for miles, and they had walked from their homes and their work out in the produce fields. Todd sensed a childish excitement, as if Santa Claus had appeared to them long after they had stopped believing in him.

The locomotive steam whistle blew with a screech that set them all jumping. Todd grabbed Ren's bridle to keep the horse from rearing in panic. The crowd fell silent as someone stirred in the locomotive's engine cab and stepped out, squinting in the bright sunlight and looking at his audience. Three other men stayed inside the cab, watching the crowd and allowing their spokesman to meet the spectators alone.

The man wasn't tall, but his build was massive and bearlike. He had broad shoulders and a muscular chest stuffed inside a cotton engineer's coveralls. His dark and splotchy complexion hinted at a mixed race; his skin glistened with sweat.

But the most striking feature was that his completely hairless head sat on his shoulders like a bowling ball: no beard, no mustache—even his eyebrows had been shaved away. As the bald man gripped the doorframe with one hand, Todd noticed dark hair sprouting from his knuckles. *What would make a man want to shave his entire head like that?*

The engineer bellowed at them in a voice that seemed used to giving orders and shouting long distances. "Civilization isn't dead if you don't *let* it die! We can't give up! With human perseverance, we can bring it all back."

The man's words seemed rehearsed, as if he had shouted the same thing at every stop along the track. Still, the speech reflected Todd's own thoughts. "As more and more of us pitch in, we can make a miracle happen."

The people standing on each side of the train murmured, as if they didn't believe him. But at least they listened to the man—he had impressed them just by arriving in his train.

"What's your name?" Todd shouted.

The dark man looked at him. "Call me . . . Casey Jones."

Some of the people snickered, others didn't get the joke. "Listen to me," said the man claiming to be Casey Jones. "We got this train running again. Wood-burning locomotives were used long before we became dependent on plastics and fossil fuels. We had to refit some parts, but it was nothing that a little know-how and persistence couldn't do.

"We're traveling through central California to collect your extra food, the stuff that'll decay in your fields. We intend to take this train down to Los Angeles and bring relief to the starving people there."

"Boo!" someone shouted. "What about ourselves, man? L.A. deserves what they got—polluting the air, squandering water! And what about San Francisco?"

Casey Jones glared at the audience from his high position on the Steam Roller's steps and began to speak with the fervor of a revivalist preacher. "They're cut off down there! They need the supplies. They're starving. *Starving.* You've got too much here. You can't use everything in your fields, and you know it." He held his hands out, pleading, as if he needed this mission to succeed more than the people in Los Angeles did.

"Give me your surplus. We'll take it down to feed the people. It's the least we can do. Consider it the first step to reconnecting the United States. How can you argue against that?"

"Screw the U.S.! What have they done for us?"

"What will they give in exchange?" the mayor of Tracy asked.

"Who knows?" Casey Jones said, as if angry at the suggestion. "What's important is we'll be *helping* them. On my trip back up, we can haul industrial supplies, things they can't use. We'll try to barter as best as we can. How would you like new pieces of sheet glass, or metal, clothes, ceramic parts?"

"How do we know you'll bring anything back?" the mayor said.

"You don't! You're missing the whole point."

"I'll give you some," a tall, thin man said. Todd recognized him as Marvin Esteban, one of the local farmers. "I've got cabbages. I'm already sick of cabbages. We're going to be eating sauerkraut all winter." People chuckled.

As a few others chimed in with offers to donate bushels of almonds or tomatoes or fruit, Todd found his mind wandering. This train was making a beeline down the Central Valley toward Los Angeles . . . toward Pasadena and the Jet Propulsion Laboratory.

And the solar satellites.

Todd leaned over to pat Ren's neck, his face burning with excitement. This just might be a chance to do something worthwhile, something that could really make a difference—besides acting as a technical liaison for Doog's commune. He didn't know if that crackpot solar-power scheme would work, but just having the chance made it worth the trip. And the fact that it seemed so impossible made it all the more desirable to do. Anything was better than sitting around and growing sprouts.

He grinned and yanked on Ren's bridle as the horse began to sniff the ground. Todd wondered what he would have to do to talk Iris into going with him.

Back at the Altamont commune, Todd and Iris's trailer sat on four wheel rims, leveled with concrete blocks. Todd had meant to move out as soon as he found another place, but he never seemed to get around to it.

The trailer had once been hauled around the country by a retired couple from Alexandria, Louisiana. Abandoned in the Altamont and scavenged by Doog, the trailer had begun falling apart long before the petroplague hit. Its sides were white aluminum, bent in places, stained with green traces of moss.

After Todd and Iris had patched the cracks and stuffed rags into the holes left by dissolving insulation, the trailer remained cozy even in the evening chill. Remembering that first night together by the campfire, Todd had suggested they sleep in separate beds. Iris had shrugged, not pushing the issue—and Todd kicked himself, too embarrassed to raise the issue again.

Now, snug inside their trailer with the door closed and the windows shut, Todd and Iris argued far into the night.

Iris talked, her words growing sharper. "Todd, you're just excited. You're like a little kid in a toy store and you're going off half cocked. You can't save the world by yourself. And all you'd be doing is running away when we need you here."

"But we're not *doing* anything here," he said in exasperation. "We're like a bunch of old soldiers who never saw battle, sitting around talking about the war. You worked so hard at Stanford, trying to stop the spread of the petroplague. And now that the world has changed, you just want to roll over and play dead. There's still a lot more things we can do, and this is one of them! Casey Jones and his train are proof that it's not as hopeless as we thought. Let's at least try it." He hesitated, and said almost as in afterthought, "We can always come back here if it doesn't work."

Iris rolled her eyes. "Casey Jones!" She sat forward on the edge of the small bed. Anger vibrated from her. "Get a *grip,* Todd. Look at a map for once. We don't have any real transportation. We can't just think of ourselves as the jet-setting crowd like before. You don't leave San Francisco, jaunt down to Los Angeles, pick up some satellites, hoof it over to New Mexico, and then trot back here if it doesn't work."

"Don't you feel any responsibility for what happened? Remember spraying Prometheus? Well, I do."

"But there are so many important things we can do here. I agree that the world is going to have to pick itself up, but it has to be a grass-roots movement, in small places like this Low Tech. We have to build from the bottom up, not the top down. We don't have a foundation anymore, that's what we have to work on."

Todd thought of the days he spent aimlessly riding around the hills, just talking to people, shooting the breeze, carrying news and gossip from one group to another. What point did that serve? He tried to keep from snorting. "Like what?"

"Like fine-tuning trade between the communities surrounding us. Like working on getting those electrical lines laid from the windmills out to Tracy, or back down into Livermore. You said yourself the lab people there have come up with ways to refurbish substations and bring back limited electricity. Think of what that would mean in rebuilding the world."

Todd didn't see how that was different from using the solar-power satellites. Besides, once the smallsats were functioning they could serve a much wider area than just a limited island up in the hills. But that wasn't the main reason he wanted to go.

"Everything that we do here sets an example. It has an impact, Todd. Just stick with it and you'll see."

"Yeah, like your music concert. Tell me how that's more important than getting an entire solar-power farm working. Explain to me how finding a way to play rock and roll is going to help a lot of people."

Iris looked stung. "You've got to have a dream, Todd."

"Sounds more like a nightmare to me," Todd muttered, his own anger growing . . . he couldn't rein it in anymore. "Bringing back drugs and noise and juvenile delinquents—that's one thing I'd rather leave behind with the old society. Iron Zeppelin and Visual Purple and Neon Kumquats or whatever those bands are called. You can keep them."

Appalled, Iris actually giggled. "Todd, you're so stupid sometimes."

Todd knocked the wooden chair backward as he stood

up. The chair would have tipped over, but the trailer was so cramped it merely bumped against the wall and righted itself again.

"Fine, Iris," he said. "If trying to make the world a better place makes me stupid, I'll just go on being an idiot. But at least I'll be helping a heck of a lot more people than these wackos we're living with." He opened the door.

"Todd—where are you going?" Iris's dark eyes widened.

"Out. Away from . . . from *this.*"

"Todd!"

"Don't worry, I'll be back. That's a promise," he growled, and stomped outside.

The door slammed by itself, and he heard Iris calling, "Wait!" But her words were cut off by the smack of the door, which sounded like a gunshot in the darkness. Todd stamped off. He considered taking one of the horses to Tracy, where Casey Jones and his steam train waited. But he knew the commune would need Ren and Stimpy—and they'd be safe here, just like Alex Kramer would have wanted. He went off on foot into the moonlit night.

Inside the refurbished dining car of the steam train, Captain Miles Uma, formerly of the *Oilstar Zoroaster,* relaxed and pondered the night. Used for storage, the dining car now carried crates of ripening fruits and vegetables, nuts, and other produce. The odors mingled in the tight space.

Rex O'Keefe and the Gambotti brothers kept to themselves in the passenger car; Uma didn't mind. Once Uma had gained their confidence, they did what they were told, as if they were happy that someone had finally stepped up and taken charge, accepted some responsibility. Like any good captain, Uma treated them with respect—and now that they had order back in their lives, they didn't mind the work.

Uma cracked open two of the narrow windows to let

the night breeze in. Outside, the sleeping city of Tracy was dark, save for the fires of a few late-night people; everyone else bedded down with the fall of darkness.

By the flickering light of a stubby beeswax candle, Uma dipped his fingers in a bowl of tepid water, took a bar of soap and lathered his face and head. He removed a long, sharp straight-razor, propped a small mirror up against the inner wall of the train where he could see his reflection, then began to shave by candlelight. First, to hone his attention, he shaved his eyebrows; then he worked at his beard stubble, and finally scraped his head, shaving the back by feel alone.

It made him feel clean, and renewed and different. He wished he could slice away the pounding guilt as easily.

Guiding a train along the abandoned tracks was very different from captaining an enormous supertanker like the *Zoroaster*. But it kept him moving and gave him some way to stop the clamoring depression; Rex O'Keefe and the others were swept along with his dream. Uma found that by focusing on a task, he could stop thinking about the wreck against the Golden Gate Bridge. . . .

As everything fell apart, Uma had wandered north from San Francisco, changing his name, fearing that someone might recognize him. Uma had been doing a good job of blaming himself. He worked odd jobs, trying to run from himself and watching with a growing anguish as things grew worse. Until he stumbled across the train station in Napa Valley.

Uma finished shaving and blew out the candle, feeling his way to an empty, comfortable seat in the refurbished dining car. He was exhausted, not from the work that he did to keep the wood piled in the furnace, but from being sociable tonight.

He didn't enjoy social occasions, but the people had prepared a meal for them, wanting to talk for hours, until Uma and the others had finally gone back to the train. He had tried to answer most of their questions, but it got tiresome after a while.

In the morning, at dawn, just as he was struggling to

awaken from his cramped sleeping space on the dining-car bench, Uma snapped his eyes open when he heard a rapping on one of the half-open windows.

"Hey, Casey Jones, you in there?" Uma wrenched his stocky body into a sitting position and blinked out at a tall cowboy. "I want to join your group," the cowboy said. "I think you need another person."

Uma went stiffly to the window of the dining car, not welcoming the man inside. The cowboy walked over with a large nervous grin on his face and stuck his hand through the open window.

"I'm Todd Severyn, pleased to meet you." Uma shook his hand warily. The cowboy looked strong, but troubled circles surrounded his red-rimmed eyes. Grass stains splotched his pants. "I walked all night long just to get here."

"We could maybe use some help," Uma said, "but it's a backbreaking job. You sure it's worth it to you?"

"It depends on your priorities." Todd's gruff answer seemed to speak to more than just the question Uma had asked. "I got my reasons."

Uma stepped aside just enough to let the cowboy onto the train. "Don't we all?"

FIFTY-NINE

A MATTER OF TRUST

Five miles south of General Bayclock's Manzano Mountain headquarters, a field of mirrors spread across three acres. Though gaps separated the three-foot mirrors, the reflected glare gave the impression of a seamless plain of molten silver.

The suggestion to use Sandia Albuquerque's abandoned solar test project to generate electricity sounded like a good idea, but Bayclock wanted to see the apparatus himself.

The computer-controlled mirrors were designed to rotate, follow the sun and focus the blinding rays on a three-story concrete tower. The intense illumination heated a special vessel to generate steam that would turn turbines and produce power. Now the mirrors stood frozen in place, useless without hourly brute-force manual adjustment. It would take years to polish the mothballed mirrors back to the accuracy needed for optimal focus.

The scientific pinheads didn't have the common sense

to engineer anything practical, Bayclock thought as he scowled at the useless apparatus. *No allowance for contingencies.* They reveled in the nifty toys they built and patted each other on the back. The general held little hope that refurbishing this system would be anything more than a futile effort. He had seen enough. He strode through the field of mirrors, back to where his horse waited with the armed escort.

The woman who headed up Sandia's energy research program—Bayclock had already forgotten her name—trailed after him. She looked as overbearing as the number of programs she had once managed. At just over six feet tall and weighing close to two hundred pounds, she rivaled Bayclock in size; her big butt and flabby arms implied a contempt for her own physical health. Her ragtag group of scientists followed as she kept up with Bayclock, step by step.

"You want the electricity, we'll deliver. It's a simple matter of granting us access to the dry lubricants. I guarantee we can have part of the mirror field up and running at minimal levels within a week. Replacing the seals comes next. And after that, eighteen months to optimize the mirrors. No problem."

Bayclock reached the edge of the mirror maze. His executive officer and three armed guards waited on their own horses. Bayclock said, "You told me this field was computer controlled. How are you going to synchronize the mirrors' movements to the sun without computers?"

The woman waved her hands while she talked, as if pointing at an equation-strewn whiteboard. "We'd need less than a hundred people, each physically positioning ten mirrors apiece."

Bayclock snorted. "A hundred people out in the sun everyday? While you're polishing mirrors? That's an awful lot of work to get a hundred kilowatts of power. Intelligence reports that's ten times less than the White Sands group can deliver!"

The Sandia woman put her hands on her hips. "That's a hundred kilowatts more than you have right now! And it's a lot fewer people than you use to chase kids after curfew. What's more important?"

Bayclock walked away, ignoring her. She grabbed him by the elbow. "Look, General, you wanted a way to generate electricity. We can do it. It's not much, but it's a start."

Bayclock shook his arm free. One of the guards unshouldered his firearm, but the exec put out an arm to stop him. The exec called, "Messenger approaching, General."

Bayclock spotted a lone horseman traveling across the desert. He had left orders not to be bothered—unless it was important. He turned back to the scientists. "There's not enough dry lubricant to go around. We need it for refurbishing our weapons, so you'll have to come up with another way. In case you haven't noticed, there's a slight problem obtaining supplies right now."

"But without the lubricant, the mirrors won't turn," the woman said.

"Figure out a way! Your minimal electricity should be enough to power the Manzano complex. I want it before the end of the week. The rest of the city will have to wait."

Dismissing the Sandia woman, Bayclock turned as the approaching horseman reached the field of mirrors. Wearing desert camouflage, the rider dismounted and popped to attention, snapping off a salute. "The White Sands expedition has returned, General."

Bayclock said, "Thank God for that navy pilot." He swung up on his horse, leaving the scientists in the middle of a thousand reflected suns. The exec motioned for the guards to follow.

The Sandia woman raised her voice. "General, you're asking the impossible!"

Bayclock dug his heels in the black gelding's flank, turning the mount around. "Do you think you're playing in some R and D sandbox? Just do it! You also better be ready to interface with White Sands. I've had it with people questioning my authority."

As the general rode off with his escort, he felt a grim satisfaction that at least Lieutenant Carron had come through. Two types of people—*fighter pilots and weenies*. He knew who he could trust.

Bayclock took the point at a fast trot as his party rode through the high chain-link gates of the Manzano complex. Armed guards stood at attention in the shade, giving their commander a salute as he rode past.

Four razor-wire fences surrounded the complex, twenty feet apart with bare dirt in between, making the area look like a giant racetrack draped over the rugged hills. Several two-story buildings, made of wood and covered with chipped white paint, formed the central part of the installation. Dozens of concrete bunkers dotted the four hills.

Bayclock rode directly up to the largest bunker behind the old wooden buildings. Only two horses stood outside tied to a NO PARKING sign, nuzzling the dusty ground for something to eat.

Bayclock turned to his exec. "Get Mayor Reinski out here ASAP. Tell him Lieutenant Carron is back from White Sands. His luck just changed."

Reaching his office, Bayclock found Sergeant Caitlyn Morris and a gaunt bearded man he did not recognize. They both stood when the general entered. Covered with trail dust, the stocky blond sergeant looked as if she hadn't had a shower in weeks.

"Afternoon, General."

"Sergeant." He nodded at the stranger, looking around for the navy pilot. "Welcome back. Where's Lieutenant Carron? I expect him to give me a full debriefing."

Sergeant Morris drew her mouth tight. "Well, sir—"

The bearded man stepped forward and held out a dirty hand. "I'm Dr. Lance Nedermyer, General. We met a few months ago at a ceremony to turn over the adaptive optics facility to the University of New Mexico. Jeffrey Mayeaux was with us."

Bayclock returned the handshake and squinted at Nedermyer's face. He remembered the stranger as a heavier man with mirrored sunglasses and a brusque manner. Nedermyer looked as if he had lost thirty pounds; the beard offset the thinness of his face. Bayclock did not approve of beards. The Washington bureaucrat looked more like an old prospector than a DOE official.

"Okay, what the hell is going on?" Bayclock asked, looking at Sergeant Morris. "And what are you doing here, Nedermyer?"

Sergeant Morris stiffened as Nedermyer spoke quickly. "I was stuck down at White Sands when the petroplague hit. I tried to help the people of Alamogordo move to safety in the mountains, but they elected to throw their hats in with Spencer Lockwood. He's a loose cannon, General, does whatever he damned well feels like, without regard to the consequences.

"He's got them convinced he can save the world with his solar satellites. Instead of trying to make themselves self-sufficient with the resources on hand, he's got them working on a railgun launcher, running electrical wires out to substations in the middle of the desert."

Bayclock sat behind his desk. "Does the solar farm work?"

"That depends." Nedermyer fidgeted. "But—"

Bayclock raised his voice. He'd been doing that a lot lately. "I asked a simple question, Nedermyer. Does it work?"

"Well, yes sir, it does."

"So, Lieutenant Carron and the Sandia scientists I sent down there are finalizing plans to bring the microwave technology up to Albuquerque? How soon can we get it working here?"

Nedermyer looked annoyed. "You don't understand, General. Lockwood's dangerous. He's got his priorities all wrong. He's having trouble even transmitting the power over twenty miles—"

Bayclock interrupted, tired of being nickel-and-dimed

to death. "Do you damned scientists have to find a caveat in every argument? The microwave farm works, does it or doesn't it?"

"Well, yes it does, but—"

"Then I don't care if they transmit the power into the New Mexico utility grid or if they build us another microwave farm up here. It works—that's all that matters. The orbiting satellites are immune to the petroplague, and it's a resource we should use. I've got two laboratories full of people that can work out the details. Got it?"

Nedermyer opened his mouth to speak, but quickly closed it, frustrated. Sergeant Morris stepped forward. "General, I'm afraid you're not going to get any support from White Sands."

"What?" Bayclock looked up. "That's ludicrous. The White Sands facility is under my command. Did Lieutenant Carron stay down there to iron out the details?"

Sergeant Morris looked hopelessly to Nedermyer, who shook his head. Nedermyer said, "Your boys have jumped ship, General. Not only is White Sands refusing to help you, but the scientists you sent and your navy lieutenant have elected to work for Lockwood. They're not coming back."

"They deserted," Sergeant Morris said, as if it was her fault.

A storm gathered inside Bayclock's head. "Impossible! Carron wouldn't even think of desertion. He's a fighter pilot! He *can't*."

"I'm afraid it's true, General," said Sergeant Morris. Her voice sounded strained, as if each word might carry her over the edge of a cliff. "I . . . I warned him about what he was doing. He fully understands the consequences."

Bayclock felt his face flush with anger and disbelief. He looked at his lithographs of fighter aircraft, his awards, his diplomas. Survival in the post-petroleum world was built on a foundation of eggshells, and cornerstones could not be allowed to crumble. He'd trusted the navy lieutenant—fighter pilots were a special breed, too tightly taught, too highly focused and motivated to make frivolous decisions. Dammit, there had to be a mistake, some other reason why Carron would appear to bug out.

Bayclock looked narrowly at Nedermyer. "Could this Lockwood character have coerced Lieutenant Carron into staying, forced him in some way?"

Nedermyer shook his head. "No, General. It was pretty clear the lieutenant chose to stay. Dr. Lockwood vowed never to help you and practically dared you to come take over his site . . ."

Bayclock's breathing quickened. "Sergeant? Is that your assessment as well?"

Sergeant Morris held Bayclock's gaze. This time her voice was firm. "That's pretty much it, sir. Dr. Lockwood also said that the people of Albuquerque should revolt and oust you."

The general simmered. When he was in a fighter plane and lost control, Bayclock relied on his training: keep a cool head, run through the procedures. Losing control of himself as well as the machine he commanded would kill him for sure. The same thing was happening now on a larger scale. He focused his anger into a small, laser-bright pinpoint.

He knew his priorities. Returning electrical power to Albuquerque was the next crucial step in pulling the city out of this mess. He intended his operation to be a model for President Mayeaux's monumental efforts to keep the country together. The U.S. needed reliable electricity to bring access to water, food, transportation, communication.

And they needed law and order. With half a million people relying on Bayclock's effort, he knew what he had to do.

His exec stepped through the office door. He tucked his blue cap under his arm and wiped a sheen of perspiration from his sunburned forehead. "Sir, Mayor Reinski is on his way over and will be here within the hour. Do you still want to see him?"

"Later." Bayclock dismissed his exec with a wave. His jaw tightened. "Nedermyer, what do you know about Lockwood's operation at White Sands?"

Nedermyer looked puzzled. "Most everything, I suppose. I approved all his designs back at DOE headquarters."

"Could you get it fully functional?"

"Why?"

"I didn't ask you that, Doctor. Are you as good as Lockwood?"

Nedermyer lifted his chin. "If I'm given the authority and the manpower, I can do it."

"All right. I want you to shave off that beard and make yourself presentable." He turned to Sergeant Morris. "It took you a week to get down there?"

"Yes, sir."

On horseback, thought Bayclock. That meant about three weeks on a forced march. Could he afford it? With superior weaponry and training, an armed expedition to White Sands would require relatively few men, and the payoff would be enormous, both in the technology they would liberate and in reinforcing the general's authority.

He spoke to his executive officer with a heavy voice. "Get Colonels David and Nachimya in here. White Sands doesn't seem to appreciate the fact that they're still under martial law."

He cracked his knuckles again. "They're about to have their assets confiscated."

SIXTY

LOCOMOTION

The train journey gave purpose to Todd's life again.

Once the locomotive got up its full head of steam, Todd helped the Gambotti brothers and Rex O'Keefe toss split wood into the furnace. Dax and Roberto Gambotti hoarsely sang old songs while Rex sat behind them, supervising the stoking. Waving smoke from his eyes and sipping on a coffee cup filled with Chardonnay, Rex expounded on the virtues of the wine they carried with them: Merlot, Cabernet, Riesling. Todd had never been much of a wine drinker himself.

The big coffee-colored man who called himself Casey Jones didn't move from the engineer's cab, as if he had sworn to keep vigil over their journey. Covered with soot and sweating from both the work and the heat, Todd exhilarated in the constant physical effort, helping the Steam Roller chug ahead.

The tracks unreeled in front of them across California's brown Central Valley. To their left, a low line of hills grew larger hour after hour as the valley widened, and the tracks swung east to flank the foothills of the

Sierra Nevada. Every ten or twenty miles they had to stop to clear debris from the track; they pushed wood, cars, and once the carcass of a Piper Cub aircraft off the metal rails. Even out in the unpopulated areas, people came running after the train. Once they heard gunshots. Casey Jones wanted to make it the rest of the way to Los Angeles, though, and pushed on without further delays.

The locomotive's top speed was only thirty miles per hour. The monotonous landscape crawled along, but they made progress. It felt good to be moving. Todd stripped off his shirt and tied it to a post by the locomotive's open window. Gusts of summer air felt cool on his skin.

He preferred to work with Casey Jones, as the others were too quick to make light of their situation. It was as though they used their wit to deny what had happened to the world around them.

On the first night, Todd and Casey labored in silence, trying to outdo each other in their prowess for manual labor. Todd had to chuckle as he thought of how Iris would react to their posturing: "Figures," she would have said with scorn, "the fall of civilization, and you macho men are still competing against each other!" Sometimes he imagined her standing next to him; in his daydream they journeyed across the world, trying to make up for the devastation they had helped to unleash upon it.

He felt a pang from missing her, and he felt guilty as he tried to ignore it . . . because he was enjoying himself.

His companion was reticent, preoccupied to the point of gloominess. He seemed to wear a shroud of his own guilt. Todd tried to draw him into conversation as they stood side by side in the crowded engineer cab.

"Who are you?" Todd said. He had to shout over the roar of the furnace and the clatter of the train.

"I already told you."

"Right. What's your real name?"

"None of your damn business!"

Todd brought more wood.

The train chugged along, hour after hour. Todd and Casey changed to working in shifts with the Gambotti brothers and Rex O'Keefe. As he rested, Casey Jones refused to engage in conversation. Todd sat in the dining car munching tomatoes and peeling the outer leaves of cabbages. *Damn rabbit food,* he thought. He longed for a thick cut of juicy steak, or even a McDonald's hamburger, but he didn't have much choice.

The train tracks led to Fresno and then Bakersfield, cities surrounded by sufficient agriculture that the population could feed themselves, though they had no great amounts of food to spare. Casey stopped the train only briefly to exchange news with the gathered crowds. Todd stood back and watched as they flocked to see the Steam Roller puff into the city, a black-and-scarlet icon of lost technology.

On the second day, a spur of the Southern Pacific Railroad hooked west from Bakersfield, taking them toward the Los Angeles metropolis. Casey slowed, allowing Todd and Roberto Gambotti to drop to the ground and run ahead to strain at the lever that switched the track. At first Todd was afraid the switch was frozen, but after laying into the mechanism, the two men slowly muscled the track section about.

Though the boxcars were piled high with fruits and vegetables, Todd didn't know what that amount of food would do for LA. How many millions of people lived in the huge dying city? But Casey insisted they continue, fixated. Todd didn't try to talk him out of it. He just wanted to get to JPL.

The men rotated duty during the night. The train moved through the darkness with a hypnotic, monotonous clacking. Twice they hit something on the track, but both times it was too small even to slow their pace.

In darkness, Todd stood by the closed door of the roaring boiler. He could feel waves of heat mixed with counterpoints of cool air gusting through the windows. The moon hung overhead, shining down like a milky spotlight illuminating the silvery tracks ahead.

Exhausted from the day's labor, Todd wrapped his knuckles around the open window. He stared into the oncoming night, and thought of Iris.

Steam Roller chugged westward, belching steam as it approached the hills around Los Angeles.

From a distance, the city looked frozen into a snapshot. The clusters of buildings grew thicker on the sharp hillsides. Squinting through the locomotive's soot-smeared front windows, Todd could see crowds emerging from houses to stand in the streets. They squinted toward the railroad tracks as the steam engine puffed clouds into the sky. Some people ran up to the tracks and threw rocks at them; others tried to follow.

Casey Jones, standing at the engineer's station, reveled in their reception. He hung his dark, meaty arm out the window and waved. Some waved back; many just stared. A few stones ricocheted off the metal casing. Rex O'Keefe raised his wine-filled mug in a toast at the crowd.

Uncertainty gnawed at Todd. They had barely reached the fringes of the sprawling city, yet already they saw vastly more people than had arrived to greet the train in Bakersfield. What if the mob surrounded them and rocked the train off its rails?

The dining car was stuffed with crates of food and produce, but even that much wouldn't last a day here. It wouldn't feed a fraction of these people, and every face held a ghost of hunger behind the eyes. Did Casey really think they could just stop the train, distribute the food in an orderly manner, and wait for the grateful men and women to bring them items for trade?

"Okay, Casey Jones," Todd shouted into the din of the pumping locomotive, "what's your plan?"

But the engineer just grinned at him and continued

looking out at the people. Rex O'Keefe and the Gambotti brothers sat on top of the passenger car and watched as they drank their wine.

In the stillness of a city without traffic, the sound of Steam Roller carried for miles. People lined up on the embankment to watch the train roll by, but Casey continued, pushing ahead until the outlying residential areas dwindled again, and they approached a dirtier industrial section of the city. Going still slower, the train pushed aside debris and wrecks of old cars piled up on the tracks.

Todd looked up. The sky was crystal blue and clear. He could see for miles. "I'll bet the air of Los Angeles hasn't been this clean in over a century!" he said. "I guess the petroplague can't be all that bad."

Near Pasadena they passed ugly abandoned gravel quarries with mounds of crushed rock and dirt eroding away. Tall metal chutes and rock conveyors stood like pieces from a giant Erector set beside hulking dump trucks. The San Gabriel Mountains rose sharp and monolithic behind them, grayish with summer.

Steam Roller approached a cluster of warehouses, sheet-metal factories, and industrial-park buildings about the size of airplane hangars—many of which stood black and gutted from recent fires. Delivery spurs split from the main railway line like spiderwebs between the large buildings.

Casey slowed the locomotive as they started into the warehouse complex. Todd saw tongues of brownish black smoke curling into the air ahead. It made him uneasy; things seemed too quiet. . . .

They rounded a curve and saw three wrecked cars on the railroad tracks. Beneath the hulks blazed a bonfire of scrap wood.

"Whoa boy!" Todd screamed. He reached to pull the emergency brake but grabbed the pull cord for the steam whistle instead, which let out a shriek loud enough to rattle the empty buildings.

Casey Jones bellowed and hauled back on the emergency-brake lever. The driving wheels of the locomotive locked. Sparks flew from the metal rails as the Steam Roller tried to swallow its momentum in only a few feet. Rex O'Keefe yelped from the rear.

Todd lost his balance and slammed into the hot front plate of the boiler. He felt his skin sizzle, and he scrambled backward, wincing with pain.

Casey squeezed his eyes shut as if in silent prayer as he threw his weight behind the brake. The wheels made a groaning sound. The boxcars behind the train crunched as they tried to stop, but the locomotive slammed like a cannonball into the wrecked automobiles.

One of the hulks, a red Volvo, was tossed into the air and fell back on its roof. The other two cars tangled in the Steam Roller's cowcatcher. One rode up to smash the front window of the engineer's cab. Chunks of burning wood scattered in all directions like embers caught in a draft.

The boiler hissed as Casey Jones swung down from the engineer's cab and worked his way through the wreckage to see what damage the automobiles had done.

Todd's palm throbbed from where he had burned it on the furnace door. He shook his hand, then sucked on the dirty ball of his left thumb where the burn was worst.

The large industrial park was silent, even more so than the rest of the world. A few seagulls spiraled over two of the largest warehouses—

An arrow clattered against the window of the engineer's compartment right next to Todd's head.

"What?" He turned and saw four men dressed in dark jackets and torn jeans. They emerged from the abandoned boxcars scattered around the railyard. One clambered to the top of a old Soo Line boxcar to get a better shot.

They fired with makeshift bows using steel-tipped arrows. Another arrow struck the side of the locomotive. For an instant Todd was too confused to move, unable to believe he was standing in a nineteenth-century steam train being shot at by arrows . . . in downtown L.A.!

Casey Jones seemed unaware of the danger as he strode toward the train. Todd shouted "Casey!" as one of the arrows struck Casey in the back, sticking into his shoulder blade. Casey reached behind him to swat the arrow away. The sharp tip had sliced his skin, but it didn't sink deep. Blood began to flow down his back.

Other gang members sprinted from the warehouses on their left, all charging toward the trapped train. Todd looked at the controls. The steam was still up, simmering in the boiler.

In the engineer cab, Todd pulled back on the gearshift lever, heaving with both arms to shift the locomotive into full reverse, his hands afire with pain. The four driving wheels spun as the connecting rod rammed back and forth to build momentum in the stopped four-car train.

The locomotive shuddered. Steam poured out of the stack, mixed with black smoke. The train jerked as it fell back a few inches along the tracks. The two auto hulks tangled in the cowcatcher groaned and scraped. Roberto Gambotti yelped as he fell from the train.

Roberto's brother yelled angrily to Todd. "Hey, you asshole! See what you did?" He jumped out to help.

The gang members ran closer. The Steam Roller's driving wheels spun slowly, laboriously. The train inched backward. Todd could see other attackers with knives, metal pipes, spears. He ignored his burned hand and yelled, "Casey, get your butt in here!"

The big man clambered back into the engineer's compartment, but they could both see that the locomotive would never gain speed fast enough to take them to safety. "Quick—in the back."

Todd gingerly opened the back of the engineer's cab and slid through to the dining car. Gang members reached the train and began swarming over it, smashing windows with their clubs. Up front, others scrambled onto the moving locomotive. The gang members reached the rear cars.

Todd opened a window on the opposite side of the dining car. He looked at the bleeding wound on Casey's back. "Is it bad?"

"I'm okay," said Casey, but the words seemed to require an effort.

"Go!" said Todd. He pushed Casey toward the window. "We're sitting ducks here."

Casey crawled out and fell to his knees from the moving train; Todd landed beside him, but kept his balance. He spotted Rex O'Keefe running back along the tracks, coffee cup still dangling from his fingers. They started to follow Rex, but were cut off as three gang members jumped from the train.

Todd looked around and made a split-second decision. "Here, this way." Todd and Casey turned and ran toward the nearest warehouse.

The warehouse stood like a barge made out of aluminum siding, scrawled with unintelligible graffiti. Todd reached the nearest door. It was locked, but rattled loosely in the frame. Todd hit it with his shoulder. Casey Jones joined him for a second blow, and the frame bent enough for the door to pop open. Casey left a splattered red smear of blood on the metal door.

They ducked inside. Todd shoved the door shut, looking around in the dimness for something to barricade it. They stood in a forest of metal shelves, crates of car parts, and pieces of equipment under scraps of canvas. Catwalks hung overhead, connecting the tops of the towering shelves. Three automobile engine blocks hung on chains suspended from high pulleys.

Near the door, Casey Jones found several round oil drums. "Here—help me out." Some were filled with scummy water, others with a caked sludge. Casey wrestled one of the heavy drums in front of the door. Todd grimaced as he helped him move a second. Shaking his still-smarting hand, he heard the first gang member strike the barricaded door. The metal smacked into the oil drum, and he heard an "oomph!" from the other side.

Todd spun around to grab another barrel. The drum was lighter than he expected, and it toppled over, spilling its contents on the concrete floor with a sound like hard plastic cups. Todd gingerly picked one up, then dropped it.

It was a human skull. The barrel was full of them.

The next drum was stuffed with bones; all the meat had been sliced off.

"I don't think the food on the train is going to distract them very long," Todd said, forcing his words through a dry throat. "It doesn't look like they're vegetarians."

Todd and Casey ran into the prisonlike labyrinth of the warehouse. Light slid through the broken panes of skylights above, shining down in blunted spears. Dust drifted in tiny glowing speckles through the light.

A shaft of sunlight poured in as the gang members forced open the door. The attackers split up and stalked through the warehouse. They banged their steel pipes on the metal shelves. One laughed in the shadows.

"This doesn't give me a good feeling," Todd muttered.

Casey Jones looked around and grabbed one of the heavy engine blocks dangling from the chains. "Over here," he whispered.

Todd joined him. They grasped the engine block and pulled backward, one step at a time, as they lifted it up on its arc. They could hear one of the gang members approach as he rhythmically struck the metal shelves.

"Come out, you motherfuckers!" the gang member yelled. The banging got louder. He stepped around the corner of the metal shelves.

Todd and Casey shoved the engine block in unison.

The block crashed into the man, driving him back against the shelves. Crates fell off the upper levels and tumbled around him like an avalanche. He cried out, and the other attackers stopped their taunting and came running. The bank of shelves tipped over just enough to smash into the next line of shelves.

Todd and Casey ran. At the back corner of the warehouse they saw stairs leading to the network of catwalks overhead. They couldn't see how many gang members had followed them inside.

"Go on," Casey said, then pushed Todd up the stairs. The steps creaked, rattling as they bumped against supports on the wall. The gang members heard them and came running.

Todd reached the catwalk and started across the open space. The catwalk throbbed with other footsteps. Halfway across, Todd turned as a lean opponent strode across the metal grille toward them, holding a long switchblade. "Casey—behind you!"

Casey turned and waded toward the oncoming gang member as if he meant to take part in a barroom brawl. The attacker grinned and slashed with the switchblade.

With remarkable speed for his burly frame, Casey Jones grabbed the man's forearm and slammed it onto the rail. Thin wrist bones snapped like balsa wood.

Even as the gang member screeched in pain, Casey grabbed him by the seat of the pants and lifted him over the edge, tossing him headfirst to the concrete floor. The attacker didn't even cry out as he fell. The only sound he made was like a melon struck with a baseball bat when he hit the floor.

Todd reached the roof door before another gang member managed to get to the top of the stairs. Sunlight spilled in as he opened the door; Todd and Casey ran out onto the roof.

Another warehouse butted up against this one with only a six-foot gap between the two rooftops. Todd cleared the distance easily, jumping across and landing with an explosion of noise as his cowboy boots crashed into the corrugated metal roof. Casey Jones landed beside him, falling to his knees. He panted.

Todd looked behind them. "Once we get ahead of them, we can disappear into the city."

Casey Jones didn't answer. Instead, he turned to stare

at his train, which had reached the far end of the industrial park before someone stopped its backward acceleration. The Steam Roller's furnace burst. The entire engine compartment spat flames out the windows, curling up to lick the smokestack. He could see people swarming on the train, grabbing crates of food from the dining car, tearing the neat black-and-red sides to pieces.

"My train," Casey Jones said dully. "My train."

Todd gripped his arm. Blood still flowed from the wound on Casey's shoulder; Todd's own hands felt raw. "Come on, we can't do anything to help it."

"What are we going to do now?" Casey asked. "Where do we go?"

Todd secured the cowboy hat on his head as they started to run. "We make our way to Pasadena. Let's find the Jet Propulsion Laboratory. We've got a job to do there."

SIXTY-ONE

ROCK & ROLL FANTASY

The curled paper sign said ALTAMONT SPEEDWAY with a black-and-white checkered racing stripe along the bottom. Someone had tacked it up at eye level on a creosote-stained utility pole, but it had not survived the weather well.

As they tramped across the grassy hills, Iris wondered how long it had been since the speedway had actually hosted public races. The enclosed area was surrounded by loose, rusty barbed wire with occasional signs declaring, POSTED NO TRESPASSING.

Iris, Jackson Harris, and Doog stopped against the fence, looking down at the oval racetrack, the stacked bleachers on either side, the gray wood and peeling white paint of the announcer's stand. Harley, the teenaged street kid from Oakland, clambered between the barbed wire; one of the prongs snagged his T-shirt, and he cursed.

The silent emptiness was disturbed only by the wind blowing across the dry grass. "This place is spooky," Harley said.

"A racetrack isn't much good after the petroplague," Doog said in his slow voice.

At first Iris had thought Doog was just plain ponderous, or maybe even slow in the head, but his mannerisms came from a completely unhurried personality—not lazy, just not willing to rush. He chose his words before he spoke them, and then said exactly what he intended to say. Jackson's wife Daphne kept insisting he was worthless, but Iris didn't think so. Iris watched, and Doog did as much work as the rest of them. He just moved at his own speed.

Doog had a full beard streaked with premature gray, making it look like tufts of raw wool poking out from his chin. His face was saturnine, with crinkles around the eyelids; he wore full-moon spectacles like John Lennon. He took his glasses off and wiped them on his dirty shirt.

"Well, the racetrack is good for something now," Jackson Harris said. "Let's check it out, see how some music might sound." He pulled the barbed-wire strands apart for Iris and Doog, then he swung his own legs over.

Harley sprinted ahead through the summer-dry grass over the rise to the edge of the stands. A couple of the heavy wooden bleachers had collapsed from age.

Iris pointed to them. "We'll need to repair the seating."

"Yeah." Harris nodded. "But we'll have time. It'll take a while to get everybody here. It would have been nice to hold the concert on the Fourth of July, but's that's next week. Let's be more realistic and shoot for Labor Day."

"Good idea, man," Doog said.

"Yeah," Iris agreed. "That'll give us time to bring in some musicians and try to patch together some instruments."

Harley called from the top of the rickety bleachers. "Do you think there's any stuff left in the refreshment stand?"

"Go ahead and look," Harris called.

Harley delighted in smashing open the boarded-up windows. Around them, the sun pounded down on the speedway. Within view up in the hills they could see the empty lanes of the interstate highway, pointing aimlessly in the direction of L.A.

Iris tried to picture what a concert would be like in this place. In the next couple of months she would throw herself entirely into the project . . . if only to keep her mind off Todd.

After walking out in anger, he still hadn't come back after four days. She knew deep down that he had gone south with the steam train. Now, in a world with only harrowing alternatives for long-distance travel, she wondered if he might never come back.

Doog and Harris were both calling this event "the Last Great Rock & Roll Concert." Iris had tried, but there was nothing inside Todd Severyn that would make him understand how the concert was just as important to the *heart* of the people as laying electrical power lines or a heroic quest to deliver satellites that would probably never make it to space.

Todd didn't care about her type of music. He didn't *dislike* it, but rock & roll just didn't affect him the way it touched her and Harris and so many others. She supposed she would feel the same if Todd had an obsession to hold the last great Country & Western concert. But there was just something depressing about music that glorified faithful dogs, cheating wives, and pickup trucks. . . .

"We can probably use the speedway's PA system," Harris said, pointing to the metal horn speakers mounted on poles around the track. "Maybe we can get some of the closet geniuses at Livermore to rig up some amps. Then we'll get power running out here from the windmills and pipe it through those big speakers."

"It's gonna sound like shit," Doog said.

Harris slowly shook his head. "Man, it's been so long since I've heard loud music, right now even Barry Manilow would sound good!"

Doog sat down roughly on one of the bleacher seats,

which creaked beneath him. "Man, then it is the end of the world."

Iris stifled a laugh and watched the two men.

Harris sat down next to Doog. They waited in silence for a few moments. Below them, Harley rummaged around inside the refreshment stand. He didn't seem to be finding anything, but it sounded like he was having fun.

Harris finally shook his head and set his scruffy chin in his hands. "It feels so right to be having this here. Kind of like redemption, you know. To make up for the last concert."

They both stared at the opposite bank of bleachers as if watching crowds screaming and cheering for the band.

"Yeah. Remember? The Stones didn't play until nightfall," Doog said. "The show opened up at ten in the morning. Santana, I think, then it was Jefferson Airplane, the Flying Burrito Brothers, and Creedence Clearwater Revival."

"No way!" Harris interrupted. "Creedence never played the Altamont! It was Crosby, Stills, Nash, and Young, then the Stones."

"I thought the Dead were there."

Harris put his head in his hands as if he could not believe the stupidity of his friend. "Jeez, you're all mixed up! The Grateful Dead suggested to the Stones that they hire the Hell's Angels for security. They didn't come here themselves."

Iris watched them, amazed. This appeared to be some sort of ritual. "Were you guys actually there?" she said. "At the Altamont concert?"

"Doog was," Harris said.

"No I wasn't."

"You always talked like you were!"

Doog just shrugged. "I don't know. Maybe I was."

Iris looked out at the empty stadium, trying to imagine how it must have been, listening to ghostly echoes of music and cheers and screams of pain echoing through the hills. That had been ten years before her time.

Doog said, "They paid the Hell's Angels five hundred dollars' worth of beer to work security, so the Angels went around bashing peoples' heads in with sawed-off pool cue sticks." Doog looked at Iris with an ironic grin. "Mick Jagger got punched by some fan as the Stones tried to make it to the stage."

Harris said, "You should have seen how he whipped up the crowd singing 'Satisfaction.' They all wanted to go out and just rip people's arms and legs off. Then when he was playing 'Sympathy for the Devil,' some kid pulled out a gun and waved it at the stage—"

"It wasn't 'Sympathy for the Devil'!" Doog interrupted. "That's an urban legend. It was 'Under My Thumb.'"

"That's not how I remember it," Harris said, glaring at his friend.

"What happened to the guy with the gun?" Iris said. "Was he the one who got killed?"

"Yeah," Harris answered. "Guy pulled out his gun, and before you know it the Hell's Angels stabbed him and stomped him to death. Great security, huh?"

Doog shook his head. "Man, the Altamont concert was probably the darkest hour of the sixties. So much for all the love and peace and harmony crap the hippies kept talking about. Gave us all a bad image."

Iris stood up from the bleachers and brushed off her backside. She felt her knees crack. "Well, then let's make sure it doesn't happen again at the *second* great Altamont concert."

Harley returned from the refreshment stand. Dirt streaked his clothes, and some splinters stuck in his nappy hair. "Found some," he said excitedly. "Two cans of Budweiser and an Orange Crush. I get one of the beers."

"No you don't," said Harris, "hand them over."

"I found them!"

"You're still too young."

Grudgingly, Harley handed the warm cans over.

They had sent out notices with their runners to the people in Tracy and the other towns in the Central Valley, as well as to the enclave around Livermore. They would broadcast it across the Atlantis network to anyone listening in on the shortwave radio. Word would spread, summoning the audience and the musicians for the Last Great Rock & Roll Concert.

They sat in silence sipping their warm beer and passing the two cans back and forth. By Labor Day the unnatural quiet would at last be replaced by human sounds, music rising to the sky.

SIXTY-TWO

WAGON TRAIN TO THE STARS

The woman at the Jet Propulsion Laboratory blinked. "You've *got* to be kidding."

Todd and Casey Jones looked at each other and both shrugged. Todd removed his cowboy hat. "No, ma'am, we're serious. We've come to take those solar power satellites and haul them off to New Mexico."

The woman gestured them inside the concrete research building, still looking at them with a mixture of amazement and disbelief. "Come and get washed up, you two. I think you're suffering from heat stroke."

She was a tough Asian woman, about fifty, with wide hips and heavy arms. She looked like the type who'd move heavy equipment by herself just because she didn't have the patience to wait for help. She pinned her gray-white hair back with elaborate pins. Her name, she said, was Henrietta Soo.

The dim facility looked like a 1960s version of a "high tech" building, an eight-story-tall cube with dark windows and light cement. The aluminum miniblinds had been taken down to allow the maximum amount of light to pour through the windows. Inside, the petroplague had dissolved most of the carpets and linoleum, leaving only concrete and plywood baseboards.

Henrietta Soo took Todd and Casey past empty offices and a conference room where a half a dozen people stood brainstorming, scribbling things on a pad of paper propped on an easel.

In a kitchen area, Henrietta twisted on a faucet. Water trickled out with low pressure, but it was enough for them to drink and wash. Droplets sprayed from side to side in the gasketless faucet nozzle. She disappeared, leaving them to take turns at the sink, splashing their faces and pulling brown paper towels to wipe themselves off.

"Boy, this feels good!" Todd said as water dripped from the stubble on his chin. Casey Jones doused his bald head, kneading his dark skin with his fingertips.

After the train wreck, they had hiked for two days northwest of Pasadena. They passed through the sprawling, confused metropolis of Burbank and Glendale, asking directions from people on the street. They must have painted an absurd picture: both of them streaked with grime, the back of Casey's shirt stiffened with drying blood, asking for somebody to point the way to the Jet Propulsion Laboratory.

In Pasadena, the Rose Bowl sat empty, but a flea market had sprung up by itself, though the vendors sold a new selection of post-plague items. The lush and well-manicured country club golf course was ragged and overgrown.

By now Todd and Casey were hungry and exhausted, but they had reached their destination. The bright flowers and arching willows made JPL look like a campus, 175 acres jammed up against the sheer green-brown mountains. Once they passed into the JPL complex, they tracked down the headquarters of the satellite division. The Jet Propulsion Lab normally held over five thousand workers, but now the site was quiet and lethargic.

Henrietta Soo returned with a metal first-aid kit and opened it up, poking around to find cloth bandages. "Let me look at your back," she said to Casey, and he dutifully removed his shirt. With a cotton swab, she dabbed and poked at the infected arrow wound. In her other hand she held a brown bottle. "I got a glass bottle of alcohol from one of the labs. All of our plastic tubes of first-aid cream are . . . no longer with us. I've got a few antibiotics, but we're saving them." She smiled apologetically, then said to Todd, "How about you?"

Todd flexed his hands; he was lucky they hadn't formed any large blisters from the burn. "I'm okay."

Casey Jones stared at the wall as she prodded crusted blood, cleaned the wound, and bandaged his shoulder. Finished, Henrietta clicked the first-aid kit shut and turned to face them.

"Now then. I've got some of Dr. Lockwood's smallsats sealed up and ready for launch, but there's no way you'll be able to take all of them. When he asked for help getting them shipped to his railgun launching system, I never thought anyone would take the challenge. The satellites have been sitting in one of our clean rooms for months—but what I want to know is just how you two propose to get them to White Sands?"

She waited. Todd looked down at his dirty boots and shuffled his feet. Casey didn't offer any ideas.

Todd refused to meet Henrietta Soo's eyes. "Um, I was hoping you might have a suggestion, ma'am."

Todd sat in front of JPL's shortwave radio, looking befuddled. He stared at the microphone. "Is everything ready?"

"Yes," Henrietta said, leaning over his shoulder. "Go ahead."

Todd touched the microphone again. "You're sure it's at the right frequency and everything?"

"Yes!" Henrietta said again, a bit more impatiently.

"And I just hold down the microphone button?"

Henrietta scowled. "You're new at this, aren't you?

We're all connected to the Atlantis Network. We've cleared our own node here and knocked off the Feds so we can get some decent radio time. FEMA is pissed off at us, but they'll pick up the signal on this frequency and reroute it up to the Livermore receiving station. It'll probably also be picked up by other substations and broadcast around the country."

Todd felt a knot in his throat at the thought of thousands of people listening in on his personal message, but before he could lose his nerve he gripped the microphone.

"This is Todd Severyn calling for Moira Tibbett at the Sandia National Laboratory in Livermore, California." He hoped Tibbett was there listening. From what he could tell, she never went home, she never left her map with its colored pushpins marking the growing number of stations on the emergency shortwave network.

"Sandia, can you read me?" he repeated. "This is Todd Severyn transmitting from the Jet Propulsion Laboratory in Pasadena."

Tibbett's gruff voice came out of the shortwave speaker. "Todd, we read you! I take it you made it down to Los Angeles? Over." A squeaky background hum accompanied her transmission.

"I arrived just fine. Our locomotive was destroyed by a gang down here, but Casey Jones and I are safe and unharmed."

"That's good news, Todd," Tibbett replied. "Over."

"Could you . . ." Todd said, then paused. "Uh, could you make sure that message gets passed along to Iris Shikozu at the Altamont settlement?"

"We'll send it with the next courier that comes down. Over."

"And tell her . . ." The words clogged in Todd's throat. He made a silent excuse to himself that he just had stage fright, but deep inside he knew that wasn't really what stopped him. "Just tell her I'm OK. We'll be taking the satellites and setting out for New Mexico. Wish us luck."

"Good luck, Todd," Tibbett answered. "We'll all be keeping our fingers crossed for you. Over."

"Over and out." He signed off.

Henrietta Soo stood behind him with arms crossed over her chest like a stern grandmother. "Sounds like you should have rehearsed your words a bit, Mr. Severyn." She smiled. "Come on. Let me show you the smallsats. Maybe that'll give you an idea how to transport them, if your friend doesn't find anything today."

Casey Jones had gone out by himself that morning to see if he could find any solution to hauling the satellites. The wide-faced man had used the water trickle and a little bit of soap to shave his entire head so clean that it glistened even after he toweled it dry. Obsessed again, Casey set out to see what he could find in the chaos of Pasadena.

Todd could not talk openly with his partner, though they had come hundreds of miles together and narrowly escaped death. The man who called himself Casey Jones had some sort of parasite of guilt inside him, chewing away.

Casey had been all right when he was moving, bringing supplies down to Los Angeles, taking direct action to alleviate his conscience. The moment they stopped and ran up against a problem, though, he became restless as a lion in a cage. Todd guessed he would have done the same thing. In some ways, he and Casey were a lot alike.

Henrietta Soo led Todd deeper into the laboratory complex, away from the offices and conference rooms. The partially dissolved linoleum on the floor left hard cheeselike remains in strange patterns on top of the plywood underfloor.

At the end of the corridor an emergency exit sign marked a red-painted door. Banks of gunmetal gray lockers lined the left side of the hall, like a high-school corridor. On the other side, dark windows gazed in on a warehouse-sized clean room.

"This is where we assembled the smallsats," Soo said. "It's a Class One Thousand clean room. The air inside was filtered and refiltered so that it had a thousand times fewer particles than outside air. Even that couldn't stop the spread of the petroplague, of course, but twenty of the solar smallsats were already finished, packaged and sealed, ready for launch. The original plan called for constructing nearly a hundred of them, but Lockwood's project was on a shoestring budget, and we had to go one step at a time. We probably have the components and spare parts to complete another twenty smallsats, though. In addition to these."

Through the glowing lights of luminous power sources inside the clean room, Todd could make out the hulks of the twenty packaged solar satellites like meter-long pods on the tables.

"Have you spoken to Dr. Seth Mansfield?" Henrietta asked. "He got interested in this work after speaking with Spencer Lockwood over the wireless—Seth has a lot of admiration for that young man. Seth still comes in here, helps us brainstorm last-ditch solutions. Did he put you up to this?"

Todd shook his head. "No, ma'am. I just heard on the radio that the White Sands folks needed someone to transport these sats and that it could be a big payoff to the country's recovery. I was tired of sitting on my butt." He refrained from saying anything about his part in the Prometheus spraying.

Henrietta leaned closer to the glass, jabbing her stubby fingers at something Todd couldn't see.

"Each smallsat is about the size of a large scuba tank, weighing nearly a hundred kilograms. It uses solar-electric propulsion for attitude control and has a super-computer brain the size of a deck of cards. It's got a microthin array of solar-power panels accordioned into a layer a few centimeters thick, but once extended the panels cover several hundred square meters of collection area."

Todd put the edge of his hand against the glass and tried to peer inside, but he saw no further details. "Sounds delicate," he said. "Are we going to ruin these things by carrying them a thousand miles cross-country?"

She shook her head. "Everything's been hardened to withstand over ten thousand gees of acceleration during launch, standard stuff for this type of equipment. If Dr. Lockwood hadn't specified using silicon sealants, the petroplague would have done them in."

As they walked back toward Henrietta's office, he looked around; the other rooms were empty. "We saw a big meeting yesterday when we came in. Where is everybody? How many people still work at JPL?"

Henrietta Soo shrugged. "Quite a few, actually, but most of our people have thrown themselves into practical problems, trying to develop technological Band-Aids for crucial city services. The big one is the Emergency Broadcast Network. It's linking more and more as people build shortwave radios."

As she stepped into her dim office, Henrietta flicked the light switch out of habit. She frowned at herself when nothing happened. "It's really not as bad out there as we thought at first. PVC seems to be unaffected, the hard plastic pipe that most of our underground conduits are made out of. Same with natural rubber, though synthetic rubber gets all spongy and doesn't function well. Bakelite, that old amber-colored plastic you find in antique stores, resists the petroplague. It's brittle, but it still holds up pretty well. Some nylon even managed to survive."

He knew that was good news, but he could not get too excited about it. "Yeah, but if we don't have the industry to keep making this stuff . . ." Todd let his voice trail off.

"Ah, but that means we *can* find substitutions—given time—but it's going to be hell to survive the transition."

Later, when Henrietta convinced Todd that he should contact the group at White Sands, he grabbed the microphone with much less trepidation and waited for Spencer Lockwood to acknowledge his transmission.

"Lockwood here," said the man's voice. "Who am I talking to?"

"You're talking to the guy who's going to deliver your solar-power satellites from JPL."

"What!" Spencer's voice was suddenly high-pitched with childish excitement. "Hot damn!" Then he dropped off again. "I hope we're still ready to receive them when you get here. We might be having a few minor problems with the military. Some big bully wants to take all our toys. We hope we can hold out."

"We'll get there as soon as we can," Todd said.

"Good luck. We'll be waiting," Spencer said.

After they exchanged a few more details, Todd signed off. He felt the sense of urgency bubble through him again. They had made it all the way to Pasadena, but practical matters had brought them to a screeching halt.

Todd was still pacing the floor when Casey Jones returned from his day's search. The grin on the burly man's face made Todd stop in his tracks. "You find something?" he asked.

"Maybe," Casey answered. He held out a battered old book. "I got a map of all the main lines and spurs of railroad tracks in the southwestern United States. From here, we can hook onto the Atchison, Topeka and Santa Fe line, which will take us east to Barstow, Flagstaff, and straight to Albuquerque. From there, another spur heads south, right into White Sands."

"Rail lines?" Todd said. "Where did you get that book?"

"At the library." Casey set the book down and dropped himself heavily into a folding metal chair. "It was a zoo down there! You should have seen the people. They were grabbing all sorts of books on do-it-yourself stuff. How to make your own clothes, build your own furniture, gardening books, that sort of thing. The library is kind of messed up, but I got the book I needed. Can you believe a lady even asked me if I had a library card?"

"That's a sign some parts of civilization are still

working," Todd said; then he scowled. "But what do you want with railway maps? Your train is wrecked!"

"Ah, but I've come up with something else," he said. "In an old railyard I found two handcars. They're rusty, but nothing a little lard and sandpaper won't fix; and we can link them together, ride the rails, pump ourselves across country. I figure we can get a wheelbarrow to haul the smallsats down to the rail line. From there, we'll . . . just head off. Simple." He grinned with deep satisfaction.

Todd looked skeptical. "You realize there's twenty satellites here? These things are *heavy*."

"So we only take half of them. After we prove we can do it, we can come back for the rest of them. Or somebody else can."

"That's ridiculous!"

"I know." Casey shrugged, but he kept smiling.

They left at dusk, hauling the ten packed smallsats in wheelbarrows as well as all the bottled water and food supplies they could carry, and three metallized survival blankets to shield them from the desert heat and night cold. Even with help from some of the other JPL workers, it still took five trips to get everything to the hidden handcars.

Henrietta Soo surprised them both by insisting on coming along on the rigorous journey. "The smallsats are my babies," she said. "How do I know I can trust you two? I have to watch them." She stood firm.

Todd argued with her, but Casey Jones just wanted to leave. Finally, as Henrietta trudged along hauling a loaded wheelbarrow of her own and keeping pace, Todd believed her when she said she could do her share of the work. It reminded him of Iris—she insisted on pulling her own weight.

According to Casey's railroad map, they had about a thousand miles of track to cover. He guessed they could make ten to fifteen miles per hour pumping the handcar, once they got it going. With three of them, they could take shifts and keep going maybe ten hours a day. By traveling at night, they hoped to avoid gangs like the one that had blown up Casey's locomotive. If they started at dusk, and pumped straight through the night, they could be far from Los Angeles by dawn.

Casey linked the two handcars with a pin and slid them along the track to show how easily the old vehicles moved. "We could be there in a week," he said.

"Is that an optimistic estimate?" Henrietta asked.

"It's just the one I'm counting on," Casey answered.

They loaded up the handcars, tying down the carefully wrapped smallsats and their supplies for the trip. Once everything was secure, they climbed onboard the lead car.

"This really is crazy," Todd said again. "Dr. Soo said we're carrying a metric ton of satellites!"

"So what?" Casey said. "Let's shove off before somebody sees us." He stood with his back to the wind, facing east. He gripped the metal push bar. "How are your hands?"

Todd faced him, taking the opposite end of the seesaw bar. "Don't worry about it. How's your back?"

"Are we going to talk or go?"

Todd grasped the bar. "On three: one . . . two . . . three!" Together, they began to push.

Up and down, slowly at first as the linked cars moved forward, picking up speed. Up . . . down . . . up . . . down . . . Finally, as they gained momentum, they could feel the movement, see the rails slide by beneath them.

"We're heading out," Casey shouted.

Todd said, "I've got this sudden urge to sing 'I've Been Working on the Railroad.' "

Simultaneously, Henrietta Soo and Casey Jones shushed him. Todd threw his back into the pumping.

The two handcars moved on into the night bearing the solar smallsats and three passengers. Todd could hear only the sound of the steel wheels humming along the track.

SIXTY-THREE

WOODEN SHIPS

"The NSA team is here, Mr. President," Franklin Weathersee said, rapping on the door to the oppressive, lonely room.

Jeffrey Mayeaux grumbled to himself as he sipped then put down his drink. *Let's pass a good time!* Two shots of old bourbon, neat. His wife would be sleeping by herself in a different suite down the hall, so at least Mayeaux had that much peace. Now that her social life had fallen to pieces, she had started wanting to spend time with him again, and he didn't like the change of pace. One more mess to cope with. He'd just gotten undressed, ready for bed, when Weathersee came in to announce the meeting. What good did it do to be in charge of the fucking country if he had to cater to everyone else's schedules?

Weathersee's face was outlined with deep shadows thrown from the single low-wattage bulb hanging from the ceiling. Mayeaux could see two Secret Service agents standing just outside the bedroom door.

"Thanks, Frank. I was getting sick of relaxing after a

whole five minutes or so. You wouldn't want to spoil me."

"No, I wouldn't, sir," Weathersee said without so much as cracking a smile.

Before communications had been disrupted with the military bases, Mayeaux would have postponed the meeting until morning. Teach them all some respect. Lordy, he hated working by the dim light almost as much as he hated getting up early in the morning. But he grabbed his bathrobe and headed for the door. If they expected him to show up in a formal suit, they had their heads up their asses.

The staff engineers had wired the elevators to work—but after what happened to that idiot Vice President in Chicago, Mayeaux never wanted to use an elevator again. He headed down the long two flights of stairs from the third-floor living quarters to the Oval Office.

Because of the enormous effort required to generate electricity with the old steam-engine equipment hauled out of the Smithsonian, there weren't many functional lights in the White House. Over three thousand military troops were devoted to collecting wood, stoking the fires, and running the converted steam generators around the capital city. Generously, Mayeaux signed an executive order directing most of the electricity to go to local hospitals, but the marginal remaining supply kept the main communication lines open.

Mayeaux almost tripped on a rug in the dark. He cursed; if things got any worse, he'd have to cut a hole in the floors and install a fireman's pole so he could whiz down to important meetings. Now, wouldn't that look presidential?

The team from the National Security Agency met him outside the Oval Office. He noticed two women in the group, but was not impressed; they both looked hardened to their duties, not the least bit attractive. *The job must be getting to me,* Mayeaux thought bitterly. He ushered them into the office and got right to business.

"I called you here to give me another perspective, *cher.*

I'm not sure I can trust the bullshit my Joint Chiefs are feeding me. Don't mince words—tell me what's going on out there."

The team leader, a middle-aged woman who wore no makeup at all and let her hair fall loose to her shoulders, pushed a large sheet of cardboard across his desk. She had fastened white sheets of paper to the stiff backing, drawings of the downtown Washington area. The woman pointed at the Mall extending two miles from the Washington Monument to the Capitol building.

"We've finished installing the underground Extreme Low Frequency antennas, Mr. President. In addition, there are five shortwave antennas around the White House." She pointed to various locations on the drawing.

One of her aides handed her a sheaf of papers. "The ELF antenna has already raised communication with six Trident-class submarines, still underwater and still unaffected by the plague, as far as we know. That leaves ten subs unaccounted for, and three confirmed missing after the plague. We assume they have been destroyed, probably because their watertight seals were breached, but it's not a foregone conclusion."

"Destroyed?"

"Yes, sir. They either surfaced and the petroplague infiltrated their systems, or they were so close to the mix layer, the petroplague got to them that way."

Mayeaux glanced over the material. Page after page of handwritten code appeared on the pages, with elaborate decoding inked in by hand after each line. Even the decoded material seemed a jumble of nonsense.

"So, can we still communicate with the surviving nuclear submarines? Can I issue them new orders?"

She nodded. "That's right, sir. At least to a fair fraction of them. We're still attempting to raise those assigned to ocean areas in electromagnetic voids, but we should have confirmation in a week."

Mayeaux pushed the papers back. "What does the navy think about this?"

The team chief spoke slowly. "We haven't seen their complete analysis, Mr. President. Our instructions were only to collect unbiased communications traffic."

Mayeaux thought it over for a moment. So far none of this new information conflicted with what his military chiefs had told him, but he still wasn't convinced he had the whole story. He made a mental note to have Weathersee scare up a new list of advisors he could trust. "Okay—next topic. What's the status of those out-of-touch military bases? Are you doing any better than the Joint Chiefs in raising them?"

The NSA staff exchanged glances. The team chief cleared her throat. "No, sir, we have not. We're working closely with our military counterparts out in the field, and we have not yet been able to reestablish communication."

Mayeaux shook his head. He knew he should have gulped down the rest of that damned drink before coming downstairs. "What about the communities outside the bases? Are they responding at all?"

"Well, sir, about the only thing we have are reports of looting and out-of-control fires in the larger cities: Philadelphia, Chicago, Dallas, and Denver."

Mayeaux looked up from his desk. "What happened to L.A.? That was a hot spot before."

"That's a problem, sir." She shuffled through her papers again, but he could tell she was just avoiding his gaze. "We think perhaps another organization should handle this—"

"I'm sick of doubletalk," Mayeaux growled, flicking his glance to skewer every person in the room. "I asked a question—give me the fucking answer!"

The NSA team chief continued. "Los Angeles refused to establish martial law, sir. We have word from the city's mayor that they are considering seceding from the nation. They do not want to participate in conscription activities or food taxation. The mayor has ordered breaking open all military stockpiles of food to the populace at large. From what we can tell, the military in the Los Angeles area is cooperating with this action, directly countermanding your orders."

She stacked her papers neatly. "The last we heard was a call for action to help some sort of expedition going to New Mexico from the Jet Propulsion Laboratory. It wasn't clear what was going on, but the New Mexico connection may be a symptom of breakdown in martial law across the country. JPL has commandeered Caltech's Emergency Network radio node and they also refuse to cooperate with FEMA or any other emergency agencies. They are apparently behind this expedition."

Deep resentment ran through Mayeaux. He had to push with a crowbar to get anyone to tell him bad news. Did they really fear him that much, or were they crawfishin' around the issue?

"Mais, let me tell you something. This crap has gone too far. It's going to stop, right now. I didn't ask for this damned responsibility, but I will not be remembered as the man who allowed the United States to fall apart." He turned to Frank Weathersee. "Pull the Joint Chiefs in here, right now. I want more information, and if they give you any grief in return, throw their asses out. Period."

Weathersee stiffened. "Very well, Mr. President."

Mayeaux was on a roll now. Sometimes it felt damned good to kick some butt. He hunched over the table, talking rapidly. On reflection, he thought he sounded very presidential. "That expedition to New Mexico. Are they spreading this call for secession? Did they instigate this damned mess in L.A.? Who was that general I met at Kirtland a few months ago, on my way to Acapulco—" He snapped his fingers, trying to remember.

"Bayclock, sir."

"That's right. Have the Chiefs warn General Bayclock there's some sort of traitor movement heading his way. He seemed like a down-to-earth man. Make sure the general understands that everyone must support him, nip this thing in the bud, all that rah-rah stuff. This might be the test for keeping anarchy in check."

Weathersee looked unconvinced. "Yes, sir, traitor movement. Any other items the Joint Chiefs should work on?"

"So far we're nothing but a voice over a radio to these people. We don't have any way to back up our threats." He set his mouth. "Make sure the Vice President has this information at the Naval Observatory. And have the Chiefs draw up a plan to make an example of . . . something—if L.A. is going to try to secede, maybe they need a knock on the head to set them right."

He steepled his fingers. "Take a lesson from history. Abraham Lincoln took that step. He threw most of the Baltimore businessmen and newspaper editors in jail when they wouldn't support him. Sure taught them a lesson!"

"What do you propose, Mr. President?" Weathersee said.

He glared at his chief of staff. "Hell, I don't know. Maybe take out Catalina Island with a nuke. We're in touch with the subs again, after all."

Weathersee stood tall, his arms at his sides, as he looked at Mayeaux. "If you're going to take a lesson from history, sir, perhaps you should remember what happened to President Lincoln. I just thought I should remind you of that."

SIXTY-FOUR

UP, UP AND AWAY

"Hey, Lieutenant," Spencer asked, "what do you know about military intelligence?"

"Military intelligence? That's how I remember the definition of the word 'oxymoron.'" Bobby Carron looked up from untying the tentlike sunscreen at the blockhouse corner. The sun had set over the Organ Mountains, and already the high desert air took on a chill. "Me, I just flew fighters—you know, grapefruit and peas."

"Grapefruit and peas?" Spencer made a disgusted grimace. "Is that what they feed you guys?"

Bobby laughed. "No, sir. It's just what they say about us fighter pilots. Balls the size of grapefruits, brains the size of peas."

"I see." Spencer chuckled. "Come on inside the trailer. You're the only military type around here. You might be able to figure this out."

"Right." Bobby left the cords dangling from the sprawling sunscreen tent made of parachute silk. To keep the bunkers cooler during the hottest part of the day,

Spencer's group had obtained some surplus fabric in Alamogordo. Stenciled on the parachutes were the words HOLLOMAN AIR FORCE BASE, taken from the closing of the base a few years earlier. After high evening winds had torn away the last sunscreen, taking down the parachute had become Bobby's nightly ritual.

Bobby followed Spencer inside the trailer, where Juan Romero listened to the voices coming over the static-filled speaker, pursing his lips in a confused frown that made his black mustache stick out at the sides. Electronic equipment lay on the tabletops, cannibalized for parts used in the makeshift radio. Romero rolled his eyes at the signal. "Everything's encrypted."

". . . Niner niner rog. Turtle mound advised of bandit watch." Other nonsensical phrases jabbered over the channel.

Spencer watched Bobby Carron as the navy pilot digested the cryptic information. "Any idea what they're saying, Lieutenant?"

"I recognize some code words," Bobby said, frowning as he concentrated. "Maybe they can't get their regular encryption gear working." He stared at the makeshift equipment as if in a trance. Spencer said nothing.

Three electric lanterns lit the control room against the darkness outside; they used electricity from solar power, stored in batteries during the day's transit of the smallsat cluster. A cool breeze swept through the door, bringing a sweet hint of yucca.

Romero glanced at Bobby. "How can he understand what they're saying when the static is this bad? Must be sunspots."

"Ever heard a pilot talk on the radio?" Spencer said. "You can't understand a thing they're saying until you do it yourself."

Bobby held up a hand. He spoke as if he were reciting a passage: "They're saying something like: Events have gotten out of hand. Take all actions necessary to ensure the continuity of—" He hesitated, then shook his head.

"Damn," he muttered, "some of the stuff just doesn't make any sense."

"Go on," said Spencer. He motioned for Romero to sit back down. Rita Fellenstein joined them from the back room. She had been making eyes at Bobby ever since he had arrived, much to the dismay of the other ranch hands.

Three minutes passed before the mixed-up transmission stopped. Bobby scribbled in pencil on a small notepad. His forehead held a sheen of sweat.

"As far as I can tell, General Bayclock has been ordered to occupy your installation at White Sands. He's to show an iron hand. All assets of something—the California expedition?—are to be confiscated and turned over to the United States."

Spencer exchanged glances with Rita. "I hope that doesn't mean the mission from JPL."

Bobby continued, "The general is authorized to use whatever force necessary to preserve the integrity of the United States."

"What the hell does that mean?" muttered Rita.

"It means we've been declared open game, and this Bayclock clown can come and blow us away, man!" Romero stood up, knocking back his chair and flinging his long black hair out of his eyes like a dangerous bandit.

"He's crazy enough to do it, too," Bobby said. "Your wagon train carrying the smallsats got out of the Los Angeles area just in time. The mayor of L.A. has taken over the National Guard and is declaring Southern California a free state. Bayclock wants to stop the JPL people from getting to you."

Spencer shook his head. "This is ridiculous. Does he think the expedition from JPL is some kind of armed force? How paranoid can he get?"

Bobby said, "I know the general has been monitoring radio transmissions from White Sands—that's how he discovered you have a working power station."

"Yeah, for all of twenty minutes a day," said Spencer, "and a bunch of leftover battery power."

"That was enough for him to send me down here after you." Bobby's face tightened. "He's serious about enforcing his martial law, and he must have gone nonlinear when you guys didn't roll over and cooperate. He probably thinks the group from JPL is part of a conspiracy to subvert his authority. With the White House backing him, I bet he's decided to make an example of us."

Romero laughed, but Bobby spoke in a level tone. "In Albuquerque, he was hanging teenagers for stealing cans of tuna or staying out after dark."

The trailer fell quiet. Bobby looked from person to person. Spencer placed a hand on his shoulder. "Look, why don't you finish taking down the sunscreens outside. I'll have Romero run through the FEMA frequencies and see if we can find any other information that confirms what we've heard."

Bobby stopped at the door. "You know, I'd feel a lot better if we could just see what that bastard Bayclock is going to do. I'd hate to have a few thousand fanatics sneak up on us without warning. No telling when he'll make his move."

Spencer pictured the state of New Mexico in his head. "It'll take him at least a week to get down here, even if he started today. I'll notify Alamogordo. Maybe some of the ranchers can help us out. Give us quarter, if nothing else. We can get away."

"But that means abandoning the antenna farm, man!" Romero cried. "Spencer, you can't do that!"

"Maybe we can station lookouts on Oscura Peak, use smoke signals to warn us like we did for the substation test," Rita suggested.

"It would be more effective to have lookouts nearby," said Bobby. "What would happen if the peak got socked in with clouds? Or if Bayclock decided to attack at night? What you need is a thousand-foot-high tower, or an airplane." He grinned halfheartedly, his mind obviously elsewhere, as if knowing he would never fly again. "Never mind. I've got to finish packing the parachutes."

Spencer had a sudden thought. "That's not such a crazy idea."

"What?" Bobby turned around.

"The parachutes," said Spencer. "I bet if we sewed some of them together, we could make a hot-air balloon, just like something out of a Jules Verne novel. Fill it with hot air, and up it goes."

"The fuel, Spence," Rita reminded him with an elbow to the side. "In case you haven't noticed, there's no propane around for the central heater."

"The Montgolfier brothers didn't have propane," Spencer said, "but they did have wood, and even better, we can make charcoal. Hot air is hot air, right? You take along some charcoal and burn it in a big metal hibachi—presto!" He put a finger to his lips and started muttering. "In fact, we can loft a series of balloons, even equip them with weapons. . . ."

Rita sighed and got a faraway look in her eyes. "I can just see it now—the first Aeroballoon Squadron of the White Sands Regiment. Risking their lives, tethered a thousand feet up, keeping watch over the advancing barbarian hordes." She motioned for Bobby to stand back. "Better stand back, Lieutenant."

Bobby looked from Spencer to Rita. "What? What's the matter?"

"He's thinking so hard you might get splattered when his brain explodes."

Gilbert Hertoya rode in from the electromagnetic launcher, looking even smaller on the back of a big horse. The group frequently got together to coordinate technical directions, but this time they had more serious matters to discuss.

"Okay," said Spencer, "the first question is if we should even try and fight these guys."

Bobby Carron snorted. He folded his arms and looked

around. "If we don't do something against Bayclock, he'll institute the same type of bloody martial law down here."

Spencer looked around, but no one spoke. "I think we all agree about that, so we don't surrender. But what's the consensus? Fight or run?"

"Bobby's right. If we run, we'll never get this facility back," said Rita. "No telling what Bayclock would do here."

"That's the crazy part," said Bobby. "What *is* he going to do when he gets here? I mean, I'm a one-each, navy-issue, real-live aviator and even *I* know you can't just pack this place up and take it back to Albuquerque!"

"But how do we stop him?" asked Romero. "Our guns will only fire a few times, if they haven't seized up already."

"The ranch hands will help," said Rita. "They aren't going to let the general waltz down here and take this place."

"Romero's got a point," said Spencer. He looked around the group. "Even with the ranchers helping, we'll be fighting *military* troops, not a bunch of scientists. Anyone here besides Bobby know anything about the military? I mean, we aren't even weapons scientists."

Gilbert Hertoya cleared his throat. "That's not entirely true." The small man ran his fingers through his salt-and-pepper hair. "I haven't been working on the EM launcher all my career, you know. Sandia Lab is a pretty big place, and I've been involved in a lot of different areas, including weapons."

"Do you have any ideas? Will they enable us to win?"

Gilbert grinned and shrugged. "Sure, I've got ideas. But ask me in three weeks if they'll help us *win*."

"Okay, let's hear what you got."

"Well, first idea. It won't take much to build a homopolar generator—"

"A what?" said Bobby.

"Homopolar generator," said Rita, batting her eyes mischievously. "Don't you know nuthin'?"

"We can cannibalize some rails, capacitors, and batteries at the launch site and build a railgun," Gilbert said.

"Railguns haven't been too successful even under normal circumstances, have they?" said Spencer.

Gilbert looked hurt and slouched down in the chair. "We were able to build our satellite launcher, based on the same principle. We won't try to get orbital velocities this time, though, just enough to make a crude weapon."

"Okay," said Spencer. "That's one then. Anything else?"

"Well, we can produce explosives, or at least gunpowder. You know the old formula: one part charcoal, two parts saltpeter, and four parts sulfur."

"Where are we going to find *that?*" said Rita.

"Muck, piss, and beer," recited Bobby. "They used to feed saltpeter to us all the time at Annapolis. Dampens the sex drive."

"Great." Rita sounded disappointed.

"I agree that might be a bit problematic," Gilbert said, "but we don't have any other explosives. Seems that in World War II they ground up citrus fruit rinds and extracted the oil for explosives." His eyes widened at the skeptical looks he was getting. "No kidding! It's actually pretty easy to make: one gallon of orange-rind oil to a hundred pounds of ammonium nitrate, kind of a distant cousin to the explosive ANFO, used all the time."

"Ammonium nitrate? Where do we get that?"

"Simple," Gilbert said with a grin. "Otherwise known as fertilizer. Southern New Mexico has plenty of orange and lemon groves. It won't take much to extract what oil we need. And I know there's plenty of fertilizer around. All we have to do is use a little TNT to detonate the stuff, and *kablooie!*, we've got homemade bombs."

Bobby shook his head and groaned, "Maybe we should reconsider fighting the general."

Rita stood up, looking like a lamppost next to Bobby's massive frame. "You trusted the scientists who designed your fighter, didn't you?"

Bobby snorted. "I don't fly fruit crates."

"But you will fly balloons burning charcoal?" said Gilbert.

Romero cleared his throat. "As long as we're trying out crazy ideas, does anyone mind if I set up a telegraph link between the microwave farm and the EM launcher?"

Gilbert frowned. "The wireless is working just fine, Juan."

"Ah, but Bayclock could never monitor a dedicated telegraph line. And there's plenty of telephone wire I'm sure Southwest Bell won't miss anymore."

Bobby chuckled. "Maybe we should hang a wire from the balloon, too."

Gilbert said slowly, "You're not going to believe this, but I remember reading that somebody did that during the Civil War."

Bobby groaned. Spencer stood. "Okay—three weeks. Let's give it a go. All of it."

"Hold it right there. Steady, steady—now keep it open!" Spencer pushed the rolled cylinder of aluminum siding into the roaring fire. Smoke spewed from the top into the stitched-together parachutes.

"Ouch! Hurry up, Spence. Not so much smoke!" Rita shouted.

"One more minute!" Spencer held the cylinder with gloved hands, but he could still feel the heat burning through the insulation. Bobby Carron waved at the fire, directing more hot air into the two-foot-thick cylinder. Like water pushing up through a straw, the hot air raced down the aluminum tube and spilled into the deflated balloon sack on the ground.

Parachute material billowed out as Romero raced around the periphery, keeping the silk from catching. Gilbert Hertoya directed a squad of ranch hands to hold lines tied to the top of the inflating balloon.

Slowly, ponderously, the khaki-colored sack swelled as hot air and smoke tumbled inside the cavity. The balloon pushed against the sand, unfolding dozens of yards of fabric as it struggled to rise. Within another minute, Spencer pushed the aluminum piping upright into the fire and secured it in the middle of the gondola; the balloon groaned as it weaved back and forth, flexing to all three stories of its height.

"Don't let it get off the ground yet!" yelled Gilbert. His eyes were wide and soot covered his face; sweat gushed off his forehead. The ranch hands held their ground, hauling on the long lines anchoring the balloon in place.

The hot-air balloon looked like a crazy quilt of psychedelic material: multicolored patching of parachutes sewn together, a gondola made of an aluminum shell, at the bottom of which stood an oversized Weber grill burning a pile of charcoal.

Bobby joined Spencer. Both men were covered in black grime and dust. Bobby rubbed at his red eyes, looking up. "How much of a daredevil do you think I am? This thing could blaze up in a second if the fire gets out of control. I'd rather be flying experimental aircraft out at China Lake."

"Once you're up, you won't need to keep a big flame going. Just keep feeding the fire to maintain the hot air in the cavity."

"How long can I stay aloft?" Bobby stared upward. The balloon strained against the ropes. Part of him longed to be up in the air again.

"Probably an hour with the load of charcoal you're taking," Spencer said. "That's enough for a good look around."

It had taken nearly ten people from the microwave farm to ready the single balloon for flight. "I hope this is worth the effort. It doesn't seem too efficient to keep using this many people just to mount a lookout."

"You should provide us with at least a day's notice of Bayclock's army, so it's well worth the trouble. Besides, once we get this up in the air the first time, the rest is easy. We'll just bring it down, add more charcoal, and send it back up again. As long as we keep it tethered, we can send it up every morning."

"And pray for no wind," said Bobby.

"We've sent word down to Alamogordo and Cloud-croft, and they should be mobilizing to help us," Spencer said. "They think of us as their friends, and they don't want any Napoleon taking over their chance at having electricity again."

"Okay, Doc. Let's hope this plan of yours works."

"My plan?" said Spencer, astonished. "You're the one with the grapefruits and peas, remember?"

Spencer craned his neck and held a hand to his forehead to cut the glare. Bobby's balloon was no more than thirty feet off the ground on its third flight, and it looked like it would tip over at any minute.

Romero and the technicians were back attempting to optimize the antenna-farm power conversion; Gilbert had returned to the EM launch facility up on the peak. Within the next few days, the ranchers from Alamogordo would start arriving to set up defenses.

Bobby Carron kept the piñon charcoal in the big hibachi to a minimum. The ranch hands released their guide ropes, letting the strands dangle from the top of the balloon. A tether, tied to a massive concrete anchor, ran down from the bottom of the gondola. Bobby had borrowed Rita's old bush hat. He stood at the side of the gondola peering into the distance, but he raised no alarm.

Spencer doubted Bayclock could muster his troops within the next few days; if he didn't have enough horses for his men, it might take weeks before anyone showed up.

But Bobby insisted they get "operational testing time" for the balloon. That way, when the general finally did appear, the lookout procedure would be second nature. And they could concentrate on the hardest part— stopping Bayclock's army.

SIXTY-FIVE

LUCIFER'S HAMMER

By the fifth day of the forced march, Lance Nedermyer wasn't sure he liked the idea of taking over the White Sands solar facility—even if General Bayclock had promised to put him in charge.

The cross-country expedition consisted of 100 soldiers, all armed and walking in a loose formation, plus supply carriers, followers, and message-runners. The soldiers wore leather combat boots and desert camouflage, led by a vanguard of ten horses—all that Bayclock would spare from his Albuquerque forces. The general himself rode at the point on his black gelding from the Kirtland stables, flanked by Colonel David from the Phillips Lab and Colonel Nichimya, the Personnel Group commander; the general's elite security police guard rode directly behind them.

The expedition force had set out eastward, following the shoulders of Interstate 40, next to the old Route 66 that had once sparked America's wanderlust. When they reached the town of Moriarty, they hooked south, passing through the tiny settlement of Estancia, where a few people came out to stare at the military contingent. On his impressive black horse, Bayclock kept his chin up as if he were heading a proud cavalry outfit.

Lance stumbled along with the foot soldiers, trying to keep in formation, but frequently falling out of line, stopping to gasp for breath. He hadn't gone through the training the rest of the air force troops had; in fact, he had never exercised much in his life. Some of the other officers, and occasionally Bayclock himself, admonished him to keep up. Lance couldn't understand why walking in formation was so important out in the middle of the desert, but he didn't argue with the general.

Sergeant Caitlyn Morris led the group, once again making the trek to the bottom of the state. No expression marred her stonelike face. *Haughty little bitch.* She hadn't even talked to him during the return trip from White Sands.

In the late-morning heat Lance was already sweaty and exhausted. His clothes dragged on him. Back at the Air Force Base, they had outfitted him with a uniform the right size, void of rank insignia. The uniform fit well at first, but now it felt as if every thread and every seam found a way to chafe his skin. He was thirsty, he was hungry, and he was afraid to complain.

Lance fell into a routine of just walking. Every fifty-five minutes the call would come down the ranks to "Take Five!" and Lance would slump against his backpack. He tried to conserve energy, but how could he recharge an hour's worth of walking in only five minutes? It reminded him of the time he had tried to hike Old Ragtop Mountain in the Appalachians, not far from Washington, D.C. He had been forced to turn back after only an hour. But there was no turning back, here.

Sergeant Morris came back and chided him. "Keep standing during your break. Otherwise you'll tighten up." He ignored her advice and sat panting.

Distances were deceptive out in the desert. The troops seemed to hike forever, yet they made no progress. Mountains on the horizon shimmered like a milestone to reach by nightfall, yet after a day of hiking the haze-blue mounds looked no closer. Lance tried setting near-term goals instead, looking at a scraggly mesquite or a cluster of rocks not too far away.

On the first hard day, Lance again made the mistake of thinking about his wife and two daughters, stranded back East. In his job at the Department of Energy, Lance had always spent too much time traveling. He rarely spent more than two weeks a month with his family, and he hadn't thought anything when he left home to visit Lockwood's smallsat demonstration or to attend the tech-transfer ceremony at Kirtland.

He hadn't seen his wife or daughters since. In fact, with the phone lines breaking down early in the crisis, he had only managed to speak to them twice. And all they had talked about were how bad things were getting . . . little Lisa had cried, and it made things even worse.

Since that time, Bayclock had carved himself a position as military dictator in New Mexico; Jeffrey Mayeaux was acting president of the United States. And Lance was in the middle of an endless trek across a godforsaken parched wilderness.

He smiled with cracked lips; he couldn't wait to get the White Sands antenna farm up and running under his control—so they could start restoring modern conveniences, like a humidifier.

By afternoon on the sixth day, they approached a small Native American pueblo. A cluster of rickety house trailers, cabins, and a general store stood like a careless pile of refuse at the intersection of a narrow potholed road and a winding gravel path that led into the mountains.

General Bayclock raised his hand for attention and swiveled around on his gelding so he could shout back at his troops. "We'll reprovision here," he said. "It'll count as a rest break. Take no more than half an hour."

The pueblo seemed to have more buildings than inhabitants. Behind each cluttered shack, children and old women came from small gardens of beans, chiles, and corn to watch the soldiers. Lance saw no adult men. Were they out hunting? Chickens clucked by, pecking at weeds and insects. A dog barked and scattered the chickens.

Two small black-haired children, naked and covered with dust, played in the street. Even before the petroplague, this place must have seen little traffic. Pickup trucks and gutted cars were scattered randomly between house trailers. Lance had no idea if these vehicles were also victims of the plague, or if they had fallen into decay long before.

Everyone in the pueblo stood motionless as the contingent approached. A stocky, matronly woman stepped out of the general store and held on to one of the support beams on the wooden porch.

Bayclock rode directly up to her. "We need food and water, ma'am. Enough for a hundred men."

The woman stared at the general. She looked hard and weathered, like a schoolteacher Lance once had. Even in the summer heat she wore a red flannel shirt and didn't seem to be sweating at all. "You're welcome to water at the well," she said, gesturing to a community pump near one of the empty house trailers. "But we have no food to spare."

Bayclock's face darkened, as if a sudden winter storm had crossed his features. "Nevertheless, you'll provide what we need."

Other people from the pueblo began approaching. The woman crossed her arms over her chest. "And if we refuse?"

Bayclock scowled down at her from his tall black horse. He shifted as if in a conscious effort to make his general's stars glitter in the sun. "I'm invoking eminent domain, requisitioning supplies. My authority comes directly from the President of the United States. It's against the law to refuse."

The woman raised her eyebrows. She stepped off the porch of the general store into the full sunlight. "Is there a United States anymore?"

Lance cringed. Bayclock glared. The general gestured to the front row of foot soldiers. "You men, take sufficient supplies to carry on our march. Do it now."

Several pueblo women left their gardens and stepped onto the porch of the general store. A young teenaged boy with his left arm wrapped in a filthy cast joined them. They stood in front of the door, blocking the way.

The general's men hesitated. "You people clear a path," Bayclock said, watching from astride his gelding. "Or we'll have to use force."

The men unshouldered their weapons, looking uncomfortably at each other. Some faced forward, entirely focused on their targets.

The storekeeper looked at them without blinking, facing down the rifle barrels. She jutted her prominent chin forward. "Are you sure those weapons work? Our own shotguns fired once or twice, and then they're no good. You going to risk a backfire that'll kill your own men?"

Bayclock's voice was grim. "I assure you these weapons will work."

"So what are you going to do?" she continued. "Shoot women and children?" She looked to the others standing on either side of her. Most of them did not look nearly as confident as she did.

Bayclock said, "Clear a path. This is your final warning." In that moment, Lance could see that Bayclock believed his own threat.

The stern woman must have believed it herself. Her shoulders slumped as she stepped to one side. "I suppose that doesn't surprise me." With a nod, she signaled the others to stand down.

Bayclock did not gloat. "We'll take only what we need."

The woman shook her head. "You're taking what *we* need."

Later, as the troops moved out, the horsemen took the point, riding ahead as the foot soldiers marched behind them. Lance could not stop himself from looking back at the angry, betrayed glares of the people in the pueblo.

The expedition made another five miles before stopping for the evening. The troops built fires, while camp personnel set up tents and prepared a meal with fresh supplies from the pueblo.

Lance wanted to collapse. His muscles felt like tangled piano wires; his body was a mass of aching blisters, dried sweat, and stinging sunburn. But he was deeply troubled by the events of the afternoon, and he went to speak with Bayclock—partly as an excuse to avoid doing more backbreaking setup work, but also because he wanted answers.

"General, why did we have to bully those people at the pueblo? It could have escalated into a hostile situation, and we already had enough rations to last us for the whole journey."

Bayclock looked at Lance as if he were an interesting but minor specimen in an insect collection. "You're missing the point, Dr. Nedermyer. Missing it entirely. The supplies are an irrelevant detail in all of this."

He folded his hands over his hard stomach and stood beside the command tent, watching the preparation of the campfires. "This expedition isn't merely to go to White Sands and occupy the solar-power farm. It's also a unifying tactic, a demonstration of how we must hold together. Without our lines of communication, the United States is unraveling. People must not be allowed to think they can just laugh at the law."

Bayclock narrowed his eyes as he stared into the deepening dusk. "I'm one of the men charged with that responsibility. Often I don't like it, and it's a great burden to protect humanity from its own tendencies toward anarchy." He turned to Lance. "But just because I don't *like* the job, doesn't mean I can shrug my shoulders and ignore it. I have a responsibility to this nation, to the people.

"I am like a great hammer and these people are the anvil. Between us, we can forge the nation again—but it won't happen spontaneously. Only through effort, strenuous effort." Bayclock said softly, "Now do you understand, Dr. Nedermyer? Is that clear enough for you?"

Lance swallowed. "Yes, sir." He was afraid he understood the general . . . all too well.

Lance awoke to the sound of gunshots breaking through the darkness.

As the troops scrambled out of their blankets, he sat up on the hard ground, wincing in pain from his stiff back and looking around. He grabbed his glasses and tried to make out details in the blurred shadows. He heard horses, but they sounded scattered, growing more distant.

Climbing to his feet, Lance stepped on a sharp rock and hobbled backward. More small popping sounds came from off to his left. Other men scrambled in that direction. They shot their weapons into the darkness, but those shots sounded different—clearer and more contained.

They were being attacked by people from the pueblo! But how could the Indians have working rifles? Lance took a deep breath. The attackers could still use shells and gunpowder to make small explosives, tiny bombs that would shatter the night.

The horses ran in the other direction, on the opposite side of the camp from the explosions. A diversion? He heard the general bellowing, but the men were panicked, and even Bayclock could not keep the situation under control.

One of the airmen finally shot a flare into the sky; it burst into an incandescent white spotlight surrounded by glowing smoke streamers. Under the sudden glare splashing across the landscape, they spotted horses running off in all directions.

Two young men rode a pair of stolen horses, galloping off into the night. Bayclock yelled for the riflemen to shoot, but they missed. The young riders vanished into the dark distance. Waving his arms, Bayclock sent his troops out to round up the horses and to search for the attackers.

Lance hurriedly pulled on his hiking boots and went to help, but he knew it was a lost cause.

SIXTY-SIX

THE DOGS OF WAR

With somber tears burning his eyes, Spencer stood at the electromagnetic launcher. Although he knew in his heart it was necessary, the beautiful dream he had chased for so long was being torn apart piece by piece to build a defense against "barbarians." He felt sick at what they were doing to the launcher, possibly destroying his hope for the solar-power satellites—it wasn't fair, especially now that an expedition from JPL was on its way!

Rita Fellenstein supervised connecting the power-transmission line from the microwave farm to the launcher's battery facility. He was thankful they didn't need a transformer to boost the voltage, like the one that had failed at the water pump. Spencer's other techs were still working on *that* problem.

Gilbert Hertoya grunted as he helped Arnie, his refugee scientist friend from Sandia, pry open an aluminum side wall of the launcher housing. Spencer glimpsed the two gleaming parallel rails lined with capacitor banks and batteries.

Gilbert's workers had unbolted and lifted a ten-meter-long section of the launcher, mounting it on a swivel so the railings could turn through a forty-five-degree arc, horizontal as well as vertical. The launcher looked like a giant tuning fork jutting from the dismantled building, anchored by black cables running to the capacitors. He called to Spencer. "What do you think?"

"This thing is going to save us from Bayclock, huh?" Spencer stepped over the cables, careful not to trip. He sighed, trying not to show his brooding despair.

Gilbert proudly swept an arm along the length of the device. "The hardest part was mounting the rails on the swivel." He motioned. "Get behind the base."

Stepping around blue capacitor boxes, Spencer could see the equipment he himself had worked on just a few days ago. Now, timing cables, rail-gap switches, induction lines, and wire from the battery array littered the floor. Gilbert had cleared the area by the base to where they could lift five-pound metal-coated sabots onto the railgun.

Gilbert pointed out the switching mechanism. "The homopolar generator is over here. The rail is short, but we should still be able to launch the projectiles at a couple of kilometers a second. That'll pack a real punch."

"I hope so," sighed Spencer. "But is it worth it?"

"If it works it will be."

"Does it work?"

Gilbert shrugged. "Let's see."

They left Arnie to continue his work and met Rita outside by the transmission line. She pushed back the bush hat she had reclaimed from Lieutenant Carron. "This should do it. I need to get back and help Bobby extract the citrus oil for the explosives." She nodded toward the electrical wiring. "Gilbert only needs a ninety-second cycle time to recharge his capacitors. With the current we can draw from batteries, he can probably get nine, maybe ten shots before we're depleted."

Spencer looked worried. "I'd hate to dismantle our

precious satellite launcher for something that might not be decisive against Bayclock."

Gilbert rolled his dark eyes. "That's the physicist in you. Listen to an engineer for once. These projectiles are four to five times faster than a bullet—"

"So the energy is *sixteen to twenty-five times greater*," finished Spencer. "But still, what if you miss the target?"

"Wide-area munitions," Rita said. "Gil's got us filling sabots with shrapnel, so when we launch it'll be like a super shotgun." She turned to the short engineer. "Bobby wants to push the trigger himself when you go after Bayclock. If he's not flying his balloon, that is."

Spencer scowled at her eager smile. "Rita, this is going to be messy. We busted our butts to cobble this antenna farm together, but I never thought I'd have to *kill* anybody for it."

Rita whirled. "Spence, a lot of people have died since the petroplague. This is a war here! Civilization against the cannibals. The golden age against the dark ages."

Her voice became quieter. "When I was a kid, I took a lot of shit from gorillas who wanted to pick on a beanpole, eggheaded girl—but now I am not going to let a bully come down here and take away our dreams. Not when I can still fight."

"Incoming!"

Bobby Carron looked up just in time to be hit on the side of the head with a soft orange. Already leaning forward, he lost his balance and tripped into the tank half-filled with ripe citrus rinds. He sputtered and gasped at the bright, acidic stink. He climbed back out of the knee-deep vat, picking clots of spoiled lemons and oranges from his hair.

Rita grinned as she tossed another orange into the air and caught it. "Gotta keep those reflexes tuned up, flyboy. Hate to have a killer orange take out your balloon."

Bobby brushed himself off in disgust. "What did you do that for? I was checking the acidity."

"Awww, the big sensitive football player got his feelings hurt? You were too good a target to miss. You're lucky it wasn't the batch of saltpeter!"

He held his hands in mock apology as he stepped toward Rita.

"Hold it right there, you uncouth, smelly excuse for a pilot," said Rita. She cocked back her arm. "One more step and you're dead, zoombag."

Bobby sprang forward and grabbed her by the wrist, yanking her to the edge of the vat. "Okay, beanpole!" He picked her up and heaved her headfirst into the fruity mixture. "Now who's calling a navy aviator a 'pilot'?"

Spencer's body ached from riding back and forth: railgun launcher, microwave farm, and the encampment for the crowd of Alamogordo ranchers and townspeople. Too many things still needed to be done, and General Bayclock could arrive within a week—if he was coming at all.

The Alamogordo city council had assigned nearly fifty people to prepare a site where the coalition of ranchers, businessmen, and city workers would establish their defenses. Spencer had insisted that the encampment be far enough away from the circular expanse of whiplike microwave antennas to avoid danger from the smallsat power beaming every day at noon.

Now he sat beside a small cookfire outside the command trailers. Rita joined Bobby and Gilbert as they formulated plans for the next day; she made an extra effort to sit by Bobby, Spencer noticed, who seemed too accommodating when she motioned for him to scoot over to give her more room.

Rita turned to the side and spat some of her last tobacco. "If Bayclock has a couple hundred soldiers, there's only one direction he can come—north. I rode out west today, and the Organ Mountains are too damned rough for an army to negotiate."

"Could he approach on the other side of the mountains and circle up from the south?" said Gilbert.

Bobby shook his head. "Bayclock isn't going to be interested in surprise. I'll bet he doesn't expect much resistance from a few wimpy scientists. He plans to strut in here, puff out his chest, and ask us to hand over the keys."

Spencer grunted. "Then he's in for a shock." The others gave a nervous chuckle. "How are the other defenses coming?"

"Railgun test in three days," said Gilbert. "We'll try to calibrate the range. And the big catapults are almost complete. They can throw a hundred pounds of rocks half a mile. That'll add to Bayclock's misery."

"Good," said Spencer. "Any luck with the citrus explosives?"

Bobby rocked back on his heels and tossed a small stick into the fire. "Last week we located a couple hundred crates of oranges and lemons decaying at the depot in Holloman Air Force Base. One of the local businessmen remembered delivering a batch right before the base closed down; a wagonload more is due in from the surrounding groves. Rita's, uh, *coordinating* the extraction and it looks like we can start mixing the stuff by day after tomorrow. If Romero can get the catapults ready, we can try the first test after Gilbert's calibrated the railgun."

"Good. What about the gunpowder?"

Bobby shook his head. "The piss detail—er, I mean the 'saltpeter resource group'—has already done their part, and we've made plenty of charcoal. But we're having trouble finding enough sulfur to make it worthwhile. It would take a month to ride over to Silver City and back, where they've mined gobs of the stuff. We're lucky to have any gunpowder at all for the rifles."

"Everybody keep thinking," said Spencer. "I hate these one-point solutions. We're just begging for something to go wrong at a bottleneck." He felt a cramp in his leg as he stood. "Let's get back to work. Sleep in shifts. We're running out of time."

As he bent to massage his calf, he watched Rita and Bobby head out side by side. He didn't know why, but he felt a pang of loneliness. He remembered Sandy, the dark-haired girl who had rescued him from a life of nerddom back in high school; as he turned back to work, he wasn't sure she had entirely succeeded.

Juan Romero surveyed the crowd of old farts by the catapult and suppressed a sigh. It wasn't much of a fighting force, but all the men and women who could shoot or ride were training with Bobby Carron, learning details of guerrilla warfare. The few aviation-trained volunteers took turns in the lookout balloon; others had evacuated to Cloudcroft in the mountains.

That left Romero's catapult group. *Forty-two members of "the gang that couldn't shoot straight,"* he thought. *Why do I feel like this isn't such a good idea?*

Seventeen of the group must be eighty years old, and the rest looked like they would be more at home in a library, squinting through Coke-bottle glasses. *Well,* Romero thought, running his palms over his face to slick down his long mustache, *if life gives you limes, it's time to make margaritas.* He chuckled at that. He really enjoyed playing Pancho to Spencer's Cisco Kid, overdoing the stereotyped Mexican much the same way a cartoon Frenchman wore a beret and slapped his forehead with a *"Sacre Bleu!"*

He stepped up to the ten-meter-long bar cannibalized from the scraps of the railgun launcher. Ropes dangled from the bottom of an oversized bucket bolted to one end; a set of heavy-duty springs from disassembled truck shock absorbers hung on a rotating base anchored to the other end, weighted down with concrete blocks. Buckets of rusting scrap iron made indentations in the white sand.

Romero clapped his hands to get their attention. "All right, listen up!" He pointed to three old men standing in front. "Grab onto the rope and cock back the lever.

The rest of you, stand back. Remember, there's only one of these catapults, so if you get in the way and splatter yourself all over the workings, we'll lose our heavy defense."

No one laughed at the joke. If he didn't explain, the safety lesson would be lost. "You three—be careful no one's in your line of fire. The rest of you got that?"

The three old men strained against the ropes as they dug their heels into the loose sand. The metal arm of the catapult came back, groaning at the limit of its flexibility, until it lay quivering, parallel with the ground.

He held up a hand. "*Do not* let go of that rope!" Romero scrambled beneath the catapult arm. Reaching up to the base, he connected a hook around the lower part of the arm to secure it. "Okay, keep the rope taut, just in case, while I load the bucket."

Romero and three helpers struggled with scraps of iron, dumping them into the oversized bucket. Satisfied, he stepped back and nodded to the boys. "Okay, release the lines—slowly!"

Shooing them away from the coiled weapon, Romero gathered the gang around him. Perspiration ran down his face. "That's all it takes, ladies and gentlemen. Remember, don't let go of the ropes until the safety hook is on."

A feisty-looking woman with white hair sticking from under a ten-gallon hat held up her hand. "Son, how do we shoot this thing?"

"Rotate the base to aim the throw. Unfortunately, the distance varies with the weight of the projectile, so our range is always going to be a rough guess. When the catapult is in position, the trigger is that line that runs from the hook."

"Can I try it?"

Romero said, "Satisfy your curiosity now, rather than waste time in battle." Ducking under the catapult arm, he picked up the trigger line, then walked back to the elderly woman.

"Now, if you're frightened, I can help you. All it takes

is a quick pull—" He hadn't finished his sentence before the woman viscously yanked back the line.

The catapult slammed forward and banged against the restraining bar in front. Seventy pounds of rusty bolts, twisted nails, sharp-cutting pieces of metal flew in a low arc like a cloud of bees. The team watched the metal disperse until they lost sight of it; seconds later, it rained down in a cloud of dust a football field wide, kicking up debris as though an invisible warplane had strafed the desert floor.

The old woman cackled. She clenched both fists above her head in triumph. "Ha! Just let those bastards try and get through that!"

"Bank's going hot," Gilbert Hertoya said at the railgun controls. "Charging capacitors!"

"Notify Bobby—we're ready for ranging."

Spencer put a finger in each ear to muffle the sound in case one of the capacitors prefired and caused a catastrophic failure. It was another weak point in the defense—they were using *research* apparatus for weapons, and no one seemed concerned but him. Even though this was a full dress rehearsal, things still hadn't come together. His stomach was sour with worry.

Gilbert jerked a thumb at Rita by the control blockhouse twenty yards away. She knelt next to Romero, who was relieved to be back from his hours with the catapult team. The two busily worked a makeshift telegraph connected to a severed telephone line. Wires, a small speaker, a battery, and a couple of resistors with a switch completed the apparatus.

Two days ago, the dead telephone line had run along Route 57, as useless as a magic wand in a science lab. Rita had supervised tearing the wires down from the utility poles, and now one end was connected to Romero's telegraph machine; the other ran to Bobby Carron's observation balloon a thousand feet in the air.

The short scientist dug an elbow in Spencer's side. "Think she's worried about Bobby up there?"

"The way they've been acting, you'd think the petroplague removed their libido inhibitors. No wonder the other ranch hands are sulking around and not getting their work done."

Gilbert threw Spencer an exaggerated glance. "You aren't jealous, are you?"

Spencer dropped his hands, totally shocked. "What, jealous about *Rita?*" He had never even looked at Rita that way. After years of working together, she was just "one of the crew" to him.

"Whatever," Gilbert said, "but personally, I think 'the lady doth protest too much.'"

Spencer snorted and looked away. "I'm not even remotely jealous."

"Right."

"I'm not!"

Gilbert raised an eyebrow.

Spencer started to speak, but stood quiet for a long minute. "It's just that Rita is the last person I'd expect to see getting dopey over someone. I guess I was starting to feel lonely myself." He smiled wearily. "Looking for that girl with the sunburned nose, I guess. Too many Beach Boys songs."

Gilbert smiled. "No problem, old man. I miss my own family, and they're just in Alamogordo."

Arnie yelled from the blockhouse. "Charging complete. Five seconds!" They put fingers in their ears, anticipating the sound.

A loud *crack* sizzled through the confined chamber. Spencer tried to follow the five-pound sabot as the railgun accelerated it down the tracks in a blurred streak. He smelled metallic ozone from where the plasma armature ionized the air.

"There it hits!" Gilbert pointed downrange. Spencer had to squint to see the dust kicked up where the wide-area munition pummeled the desert.

Rita waved from where she and Romero squatted by the telegraph. She slapped the radio man on the back and straightened, then pointed up in the air to Bobby's balloon. "From Bobby's guesstimate the projectile hit five miles away and spread out in an elliptical area fifty by twenty yards. If the metal bearings separated like we think, everything in that area should be shredded like mozzarella cheese on a pizza."

Spencer brightened. "Get the results analyzed by tonight's tech meeting." He shook his head as Rita threw him a snappy salute. *She's totally lost it,* he thought.

But Gilbert looked dismayed when Spencer returned to the railgun. The small engineer had a foot up on the base of the gun, reaching up to run a hand along the railing. Scorch marks marred the surface of the once-gleaming metal.

Spencer frowned. "What's the matter?"

Gilbert shook his head. "We shorted out some capacitors. Unless we get this whole rail replaced, we'll be up a creek."

"But you've got miles of railing to work with."

"That's not the problem," said Gilbert. "Yeah, we can replace the railing, but we have to take the whole friggin' railgun apart to do it—and *that* will take nearly five days."

Spencer tried to sound upbeat. "You can do it—"

Gilbert interrupted irritably, "Don't you understand? Even if we get the railgun fixed, that doesn't mean it'll work again. What's to prevent the same thing from happening?" Gilbert turned to the blockhouse. "I can't believe I wasted the last three weeks and damaged our satellite launcher for one shot!"

Spencer started after the man, but stopped. It *had* been three weeks, and what did they have to show for it? The railgun worked, but it might have fired its last projectile. The citrus explosives were still not finished; and their only defense besides the Alamogordo towns-people was a medieval catapult!

It chilled him. Maybe Bayclock would laugh at them after all.

SIXTY-SEVEN

THE SHOW MUST GO ON

The pregnant girl from Oakland gave birth to a baby boy in the middle of the afternoon. The young father hovered beside her in a panic throughout the ordeal, in deeper shock than the mother herself. He chewed the ends of his fingers and kept asking, "How long is this going to take? How long is it going to be?" The commune's three self-proclaimed midwives tended the girl.

When they finally brought forth the baby, everyone began cheering and singing in a way that embarrassed Iris Shikozu. One woman ran out and hammered on the iron triangle that served as their dinner bell, raising such a celebratory alarm that several men came running in from the wind turbines.

While this baby was certainly not the first to be born in the Altamont settlement, it was the first since the petroplague. The midwives used cool, dampened rags to wipe clean the mother and baby. The fifteen-year-old girl lay trembling and exhausted, holding the baby against her as the father stroked her forehead.

Iris sat down outside the small house and was glad no one had even asked her to boil water. She knew nothing about the birthing process.

Daphne Harris came up and extended a hand to pull Iris to her feet. "Come on, get off your butt! There's work to do!"

"Gee, thanks for cheering me up," Iris said, and brushed dry grass from her pants.

Daphne looked so healthy and full of restless energy that she practically glowed. Upon first arriving at the commune, Iris had liked Jackson Harris's wife immediately. Daphne appeared driven, consumed by an ongoing battle inside her; now that she had settled down, she seemed more at peace . . . but she still required some way to burn her restless energy.

"We need to clear some spots down by that cluster of live oak, then you can help me set up a few new tents. We got some more people showing up for the concert, even though it's still a month away."

Iris raised her eyebrows. "Musicians this time, or just spectators?"

Daphne shrugged. "I didn't interview them, girl! Some of both, I guess."

Once the announcement had gone out about their windmill-powered Labor Day rock & roll concert, people started trickling into the Altamont settlement. Jackson Harris let them stay, as long as they were willing to feed themselves and do work.

And Todd had been gone only a week.

Harris and Doog and a large group of the commune dwellers worked out at the Altamont Speedway, repairing bleachers, rigging wires, fixing the metal loudspeakers. Another group set about laying cloth-wrapped cable from the windmill substations to the sound system at the racetrack.

Daphne handed Iris a shovel, then took a long rake for herself. "The new folks will think it's romantic for about two nights to sleep out under the stars, then they'll want a tent. We'll need to dig a few more privies, too, but *I'm* not doing that. We got plenty of hands around here to help out."

Under the live oaks at the far end of the trailers, huts, and reinforced tents, Daphne began attacking the underbrush. She yanked twigs and tore loose grass to clear a firepit and to make flat foundations for new tents. Iris set to work with her shovel, chopping out heavy roots and removing stones.

"So, do you miss him?" Daphne said after a few moments.

Iris's instinctive reaction was to say "Who?"—but she knew that would be ridiculous. "A little," she admitted, trying to keep her voice flat and guarded.

"You gonna wait for him? Do you think he'll come back?"

Iris shrugged. She gripped her shovel and looked the other direction. She didn't want to meet Daphne's eyes.

Daphne said, "If you ever think that cowboy of yours ain't coming back, just let me know. We'll set you up with somebody. You notice all the other guys staring at you?"

Iris nodded. "Yes, I've noticed—and I don't think I'll need your help setting me up. Thanks, anyway."

Daphne was silent for a moment, then giggled. "Oh, I almost forgot! I got a message for you. Todd radioed from down in Pasadena. He got on the emergency shortwave network and talked to the lab in Livermore."

Iris turned quickly, trying to hide her reaction, but she was too late. "What did he say?"

Daphne spoke with agonizing slowness. "Well, he sent a special message to inform you that he made it to L.A. just fine. They had some trouble with the train, but they're at the JPL now, making plans to head out with the satellites. He's gone that far—and personally, I'm surprised."

"Was there more?" Iris asked. "Did he say anything else?"

Daphne shrugged. "Probably, but it was an unspoken

hint. He was talking to that Moira Tibbett, you know.
That woman wouldn't know an emotion if it slapped her
in the face!"

Feeling dizzy, her thoughts in turmoil, Iris plunged
back into her work with the shovel.

The musicians making their way to the Altamont commune were a mishmash of drummers, singers, guitarists.
Each one had cobbled together musical instruments
from pieces that survived the ravages of the petroplague.
Many carried wooden flutes, harmonicas, metal auto-
harps, and expensive classical guitars with ivory instead
of plastic tuning pegs and expensive gut strings instead
of nylon.

Several engineers in Livermore had taken the challenge to build functional amplifiers and pickups. Two of
them even hoped to build a working electric guitar to
really shatter the silence.

After dark, the musicians sat around the evening fire
and jammed. The crowds grew bigger and bigger as the
days went by, and people rode in from the surrounding
towns just to hear the evening practice sessions.

Ironically, before the petroplague, most of these people would never have gone to the same bars or the same
concerts. Divided into their own little cultural sub-
groups, cliques had used fine divisions of music to
separate themselves: classic rock, folk music, heavy
metal, technopop, easy listening, country. Now though,
with everything else falling apart, the music itself—
regardless of brand or flavor—brought them together
and they listened without the scorn they would have
shown before.

Satisfied, Iris sat on her lumpy cushion under the
stars, sipping strong herb tea from a metal cup. They had
stuffed themselves with a delicious stew made in a big
pot: vegetables from Tracy, herbs from the gardens
planted around the commune, and beef from the local
ranchers.

Iris lounged back and looked at the people, thinking how strange a mix they seemed—Jackson Harris's inner-city refugees, throwback hippies, herself a Stanford microbiologist, and redneck ranchers, cowboys, and migrant workers.

Doog started off the singing himself, accompanied by a quiet, unobtrusive harmonica. He had a rich, mellow voice, and he closed his eyes as the words came from his lips. The firelight reflected from the circles of his John Lennon glasses. He seemed to be pulling the music out of his soul as he sang.

It didn't really matter that Doog's own taste in music was radically different from what hers had been. Now, as she listened to his voice and thought of her own driving obsession to make the Altamont concert a reality, her need to bring not just music, but rock & roll, back to the world.

Then she thought of Todd's need to help start the world on the long journey back to civilization—even if it meant a fool's errand of carrying solar-power satellites across the country.

What right did she have to step on his dreams?

Long before the music ended for the night, Iris went off to bed, alone.

SIXTY-EIGHT

WHEN WORLDS COLLIDE

Todd Severyn rode high on the buckboard of their commandeered wagon and stared across the landscape of the American Southwest.

Beside him, holding the reins of the three horses pulling the wagon, burly Casey Jones sat hypnotized by the desert terrain. He fixed his big dark eyes on the horizon as if willing it to come closer. Casey pushed at the old shirt wrapped like a turban around his bald head to protect him from sunstroke.

He and Todd rode together in the comfortable silence of two men who had already spent too much time together and had used up their conversation. In the wagon bed behind them, Henrietta Soo snoozed in the afternoon heat. Lying against the ten smallsats they had hauled from Pasadena, she sweated under the reflective blankets that tried to keep the heat away.

Todd slouched his cowboy hat over his eyes as the horses plodded along. His arms still ached from days of pumping the railroad handcar across Southern Califor-

nia and part of Arizona—but overall he was amazed at
how uneventful the journey had been.

Todd kept tattered old maps in a sack under the
buckboard, marking his best guess of where they were on
their trek. Once they had abandoned the handcar and
taken to the roads, Casey's railroad chart hadn't been
much help. By Todd's reckoning, they had crossed
Arizona into New Mexico, then veered south toward
Alamogordo and White Sands. Pushing hard, they might
reach Spencer Lockwood's solar-power farm within the
next two days.

Early that morning, the last settlement they encountered was a Native American village and old trading
post. They had refilled their water containers and traded
gossip and news for a delicious breakfast of fresh eggs
and tortillas. The desert road stretched arrow-straight
ahead of them. The three horses trotted along the easy
path with a distance-eating gait.

"People up ahead," Casey Jones said. His deep voice
was gruff and startling in the sleepy afternoon stillness.

Todd cocked his hat back and squinted at two people
walking down the road out in the middle of nowhere.
Both were tall, a man and a woman; the woman carried a
brilliant neon pink backpack.

As the wagon approached, the two hikers stepped off
to the side of the road and stood, hands on hips, and
waited. The man, tall and broad-shouldered with a mane
of straw-colored hair and a devil-may-care grin, stuck
out his hand in a classic hitchhiker's pose. He carried a
shotgun over one shoulder and a broad hunting knife at
his belt.

Beside him, the woman looked tired. She was well
proportioned and stood like an Amazon. She had au-
burn hair and a strikingly pretty, strong face—nothing
dainty about it. She probably hadn't been much to look
at competing in a world of fashion models and heavily
applied makeup; but now she was quite memorable.

Casey reined in the horses, and the wagon came to a

stop. In the back, Henrietta Soo sat up blinking; she crinkled the reflective blanket away from her.

"Hey, can you give us a lift?" the big blond man said.

The woman smiled at Casey, then flashed a broader grin at Todd, as if she had just seen saviors coming to rescue her. "We'd really appreciate it," she said. "I'm Heather Dixon."

She stretched out her hand, and Todd didn't know if she meant for him to shake it or just give her a hand up into the wagon. She turned to her companion. "And this is—"

He cut her off with an almost savage grin. "Clyde," he said, "you can just call me Clyde."

By now, Miles Uma had grown accustomed to the assumed name "Casey Jones." After months by himself, hiding from anyone who might recognize him, Uma had successfully walled himself off from his former existence as the captain of an oil supertanker. He had never told his real name to Rex O'Keefe and the Gambotti brothers, now lost somewhere in L.A., alive or dead. He had never told Todd.

The parched scenery around him with its palette of tan, mauve, and rust seemed a million miles from the ocean and the knotted gray clouds he had seen every day on the bridge of the *Zoroaster*. Uma drove the team of horses, trying not to recall the times he had captained the enormous steel ship.

He had spent his life on the sea: working on tugs up in Alaska, spending six months on a barge, then working his way up to the supertankers owned by Oilstar. He had served in the merchant marine, spent a few years in the navy when he was younger, and learned everything he needed to know about oceangoing vessels. The sea was his family, his lover. Ever-changing, the sea was always there.

But now the air around him smelled of sage and yucca. He couldn't recall how the ocean smelled—

though he could never forget the stench of spilled crude oil.

Uma extinguished most of those stray thoughts from his mind. He found it easier to forget by latching on to a task, pouring his entire being into accomplishing it. Whether it was fixing up the locomotive Steam Roller, gathering food to bring to the starving masses in Los Angeles, or carrying satellites off to New Mexico.

He still had nightmares about seeing the towering Golden Gate Bridge in the darkness, breaking through the control-room door locked by Connor Brooks. He still felt the millions of barrels of oil gushing out from his fragile tanker, saw the TV footage of the spill crawling across the San Francisco Bay.

Uma remembered the brutal finality of the swift board of inquiry that had stripped him of his captain's rank. Oilstar had fired him, of course, and Uma couldn't argue with their decision. He was the captain of the *Zoroaster*, he was responsible for the actions of his crew. Anything else was just an excuse . . . and Miles Uma did not believe in excuses.

It didn't matter that Connor Brooks had actually caused the crash of the oil tanker. It didn't matter that one of Oilstar's microbiologists had actually spread the Prometheus organism that devoured gasoline and petroleum plastics. It didn't matter that everyone else had found some way to pass the buck.

Uma vowed to spend the rest of his days atoning, to make amends in any way possible, one task after another, from now until the end of his life.

When he and Todd Severyn and Henrietta Soo had left the Jet Propulsion Laboratory, they worked the handcar to propel them along the tracks away from the city, through the San Gabriel Mountains, and into the great southern basin that was one of the least populated areas in the entire United States. He took twice as many shifts as Todd or Henrietta, refusing to rest, enjoying the pain in his arms because that seared

away distractions. Rolling along the rails, they got up an
even greater speed than he had estimated, moving along
at near twenty-five miles per hour on the long straight
stretches across the desert.

The distance from Barstow to Needles was murder,
some of the bleakest, hottest wasteland he had ever
imagined. Even though they worked through the night, it
took them three days to cross the distance and to ascend
the near-impossible slopes of the mountain range that
stood like battlements across their path. But they made
up for the time descending the east side of the slopes,
across the California border, into the more hospitable
terrain beyond the Colorado River.

In eastern Arizona they passed an abandoned ranch
with horses running loose in a large pen out back;
wagons rested in a supply yard by the barn. The ranch
house stood silent, and as they rolled the handcar into
the dawn light, ready to stop for the day, Todd kept
staring at the horses. Uma knew what was on his mind.

With a wagon and team of horses, they could make
better time without killing themselves from the effort.
By now, Uma himself felt ready to drop from aching
muscles, and Todd and Henrietta were worse off. Their
pace had decreased over the last two days.

They stopped and went to the ranch house, hoping to
replenish their supplies and at least have a good rest
inside a real house on real mattresses, possibly even
wash. Todd called out as they walked around the ranch
yard. He saw no one moving, only the horses in the back
meadows. Uma went to the ranch house, finding it
unlocked. No one answered their shouts, and all three
entered the darkened home.

The air smelled heavy and musty, as if no one had
moved there for months. Everything was reasonably
neat, unmolested by scavengers. Underlying it all hung a
sour, rancid stench that was oppressive in the thick heat
of the house.

They went into the kitchen, where morning light

spilled through a broad window onto ceramic tiles and countertops. Uma opened the sealed refrigerator, and a strong gust of rotten meat drifted out. He did find some cans of soda and beer, which they took with them.

"Look at this," Henrietta said. She reached to one of the door shelves and pulled out a cardboard box that contained five glass bottles. Prescription labels marked it as insulin. In another package, glistening needles lay surrounded by globs of translucent mucus—the remains of plastic hypodermic syringes.

In the big reading room and study, they found the corpse.

The man had been there for probably two months. The dry desert had preserved him somewhat, but not enough. He lay blackened and swollen in a big, over-stuffed leather chair. His eyes were closed. His hair and fingernails had continued to grow.

Todd stumbled and sat down heavily in a chair, hanging his head in his hands. "Just like I found Alex," he said. Uma didn't know what he was talking about.

The study had tall French windows, covered with sheer curtains. Books lined the oak shelves along two walls, and a large fireplace sat black and cold, mounded with white ashes. . . .

That afternoon, they buried the man out back.

They spent the rest of the evening gathering supplies. The isolated ranch apparently held many months of stores. All the meat in the freezer had turned rotten, but a large cache of canned goods, as well as dried and smoked meats, remained.

Todd seemed to enjoy rounding up three of the horses and hitching the wagon. Together, they strained to load the ten solar satellites into the bed of the wagon. Uma, Todd, and Henrietta washed with tepid water from the emergency tank by the barn; Uma took the time to shave his entire head with the straight razor. They stayed the night, getting a good rest on comfortable beds, then set out the following morning.

Uma drove the horses as they turned away from the railroad tracks and headed toward New Mexico. They made good time, and Uma began to feel a numbed contentment at seeing the landscape roll by beneath them. *Doing something.* He did not think about his past.

While he doubted he would ever be happy again, for the first time in many months Uma did not feel miserable. He thought of himself as Casey Jones. . . .

And now, in an incredible, vengeful coincidence, they encountered Connor Brooks, like a great kick in the crotch.

Uma hunched down and kept silent under his rag turban while guiding the horses. Perhaps Brooks just wasn't bright enough to recognize him, but Uma could never forget the face of the maniac that had caused the wreck of the *Oilstar Zoroaster.*

Throughout the day, Brooks rode in the back of the wagon, acting charming and talking with Henrietta Soo. She extolled the importance of the solar satellites, talked about where they were going, and how their mission could bring about a renaissance of civilization.

The young woman, Heather Dixon, latched on to Todd. She sat beside him in front asking questions about himself, appearing demure but not sure if she was going about it the right way. Todd was overwhelmed by the attention. He avoided Heather's eyes but glanced at her whenever he thought she wasn't looking.

On the other hand, Heather and Connor Brooks seemed to resent each other a great deal. Uma saw it all.

As the miles passed, he just sat on the buckboard guiding the horses. A storm raged within him, and he didn't know what to do.

Todd looked up from his conversation with Heather when Casey Jones stopped the wagon. By sunset, they had reached the wooded foothills of a low line of mountains. It amazed him how fast the afternoon had gone by.

Heather chuckled. High thin shreds of cloud started to turn amber in the slanting light. Just a short walk away, Todd could see a slash of green through the hills that marked a small stream. Casey Jones jumped down from the buckboard and unhitched the horses, hobbling them so they could graze on the thick scrub.

The big dark man had been unusually reticent since noon, but Todd was preoccupied talking with Heather. Her companion, Clyde, climbed out of the back of the wagon and helped Henrietta down, smiling graciously at her.

"I noticed you had decent supplies in there," Clyde said. "It would be great to have a nice dinner for a change."

Todd kept looking at the green line of the stream. At the abandoned ranch in Arizona he had taken a couple of bamboo fishing poles and lures, hoping to find a chance to use them. "I think I'd rather try for some fresh food," he said, pointing toward the stream. "Why don't you fix up what meal you want. I'm going to try my hand at catching some trout over there."

"If you've got two poles, I'll come along and help," Heather said, startling Todd. As soon as she spoke, he realized that was exactly what he hoped she would say.

In his former life, working around oil fields and dirty rigs, he never considered himself an expert in the social graces. Heather seemed a bit too eager to go off alone with him, and he felt a stab of guilt thinking about Iris—who was now about fifteen hundred miles away.

Todd remembered his awkward courtship of Iris, a few telephone calls, the long horseback ride from Alex Kramer's home down to Stanford to pick her up, and the enjoyable times they'd spent in the Altamont commune. But he never understood why a woman like Iris Shikozu would be remotely attracted to an old cowboy like himself. Was it just a relationship of convenience? Someone to team up with during the crisis of the spreading petroplague?

Todd's head hurt. He wasn't used to thinking like this. Things happened or they didn't, and bumbling with psychological explanations, trying to second-guess what had occurred or what might have been—all that kind of garbage was for people who didn't have anything else to do with their lives . . . people who wanted a ready excuse for anything.

He recalled the last thing Iris had said to him before he left. She had called him stupid and laughed at his quest to deliver the satellites. Despite all the time he had spent missing Iris, her callousness rekindled his anger. She could stay there in the Altamont and play her rock music for all he cared.

"Sure," Todd said to Heather. "I've got two fishing poles."

The tough blond guy looked at them with a barely concealed sneer as Todd and Heather took the fishing gear and headed off.

The stream had cut itself a deep channel through the loose soil. Water ran shallow but fast over boulders covered with streamers of algae. Todd scrambled down to the bank, slipping with his cowboy boots but trying not to look too clumsy. He helped Heather down, but she seemed perfectly capable of taking care of herself. Her jeans were worn and dirty, but her legs were long and slim. He watched the way she moved down the hillside. Squatting on a rock by the water, she flicked her reddish hair over her shoulder and smiled at him before she dipped her hands in the stream and splashed water on her face.

In the colorful light of sunset, the glittering droplets of water on her skin as she rubbed her cheeks made her look more beautiful than any amount of makeup ever could. Todd caught himself looking at her and turned away.

He tied a small spinner on one of the fish lines. He had spent plenty of time out in Wyoming, catching trout and fixing his own dinner before sleeping under the stars,

with only a blanket and his horse for company. Todd
handed Heather the first pole, then tied another lure for
himself.

"Watch you don't get it snagged in the rocks," he said.
"If there's trout in here, they'll be hiding down under the
shadows."

Heather sat on a rock beside him, dangling her lure in
the water and flicking it back and forth. Todd showed
her how to improve her technique, but Heather seemed
distracted, as if she needed to talk about something but
was afraid to broach the subject. Todd felt his stomach
knotting. He wasn't sure he wanted to hear what was on
her mind.

"We need to get away," she finally said. Her voice was
husky, but frightened. "I've been with Connor for over a
month. We've been wandering eastward, going nowhere—but he's getting more and more unstable."

"Connor?"

"That's his real name. He said 'Clyde' because he
thinks the two of us are Bonnie and Clyde. He's sick, and
he's dangerous. I watched him shoot somebody's dog
just so he could frighten them."

"So . . . what do you want to do?"

"I want to leave. We can start walking now. Follow this
stream up into the mountains. Keep moving! I've been
living off the land for a month. It's not so difficult."

"But—" Todd said, then his mind blanked on him. "I
came all this way with the solar satellites. I can't just
stop now. Casey Jones and Dr. Soo are counting on me
to go with them. Do you think they're in danger just
being with this guy? Maybe we should tell him to be on
his way."

"Of course they're in danger!" Heather said. "But not
unless we go back and spill his story. What's more
important?" Her eyes were big and pleading. "We could
make a go of it, couldn't we?"

"I—" he said; then his fishhook snagged on a rock.
Thankful for the distraction, Todd turned back to the

stream and began yanking on the pole to dislodge the lure. He could feel himself sweating with anxiety. His head was in a turmoil. He had left Iris in the Altamont because he needed to accomplish this journey. He couldn't just run off now.

He finally got the fishhook free and yanked it out of the water. Turning to face Heather again, he froze stock-still.

She had unbuttoned her plaid flannel shirt and yanked it open, untucking it from the waistband of her pants and exposing her large breasts. Her nipples stood out like strawberries on her pale skin. Todd stared dumb-struck.

Silvery reflective blankets and wadded padding covered the solar satellites in the back of the wagon. Connor Brooks poked around, catching a glimpse of the metal-clad smallsats. They didn't look like much, but the lady doctor had been babbling all day about how fucking valuable they were, how they would bring back high-tech civilization.

When he thought no one else was looking, he snooped around, wondering what he could do with the satellites. Maybe he could hold them for ransom or sell them off to somebody. The cowboy and that slut Heather had gone off fishing together, and they were probably banging away in the bushes at this very moment. Connor didn't give a damn. She had grown boring enough in the last week.

He could smell the food the old lady doctor was heating at a small campfire, and it made his mouth water. The dark Quasimodo guy who drove the horses had been skulking around the campsite, but Connor couldn't see him now. The man had some real problems, didn't speak a word to anybody. He looked like a chocolate cue ball when he took off the turban on his head. Weird shit.

Ten satellites lay in the wagon bed. The horses were

unhitched, and he figured it would take him maybe five minutes to hook them up again. After everyone bedded down, he could sneak back here and do it quietly, then ride off before anybody woke up fast enough to stop him.

He heard a soft footstep behind him and turned just in time to see the stocky black man lunge toward him, smashing his ribs against the side of the wagon. Connor let out a startled cry and gasped as the breath was halfway knocked out of him. The big creep grabbed his arm and twisted it behind his back.

"Good to see you again, Brooks! Asshole." The man's voice sounded like a nail file dragged over a jagged edge of glass.

"Hey!" Connor gasped, struggling. "What the hell are you doing?" The man tried to twist him around, but Connor squirmed out of his grip. Dancing back and on his guard, Connor whirled. "Who the hell do you think you are?"

The dark bald man glared at him. His skin had a strange mottled coloration, and his face was wide and flattened in some sort of weird half-breed mixup. "Come on, Brooks!" the man taunted. "You've been in my nightmares for months. You don't recognize your captain?"

Suddenly the pieces snapped into place, and Connor's eyes widened. Impossible! But the eyes, the slash of a lip, the flat nose and high cheekbones were indeed familiar. The last he remembered of the Butthead had been of Uma running from the bridge of the *Oilstar Zoroaster* to answer the false fire alarm Connor himself had set. The man had been a regular ape, full of black bristly hair from his knuckles to his eyebrows. But, the same man was somehow here in the middle of the desert, months after the petroplague—and their paths had collided again.

"You . . . you *fuck!*" Connor shouted.

He ducked his head and launched himself like a bullet to charge into Uma, but the burly captain was prepared. In fact, he seemed eager for the fight.

Uma took the attack in his rock-hard stomach; he pounded down with his fist on the back of Connor's head. Then he wrapped a huge forearm around Connor's neck.

Connor hammered upward into Uma's crotch, making the dark man gasp with pain and release his hold just enough for Connor to struggle free. But Uma didn't appear weakened. He stood with his fists bunched, ready to come pounding again.

"I am going to beat the living *shit* out of you, Brooks, and then maybe I'll stake you out on the desert and let the ants finish you off!"

Connor took a step back toward the wagon. He couldn't run. No way would he get far enough to escape, not that he really wished to. Right now more than anything Connor wanted to put Captain Butthead's head up on a pole for the vultures to eat.

"What are you two doing?" Henrietta Soo came up from the campfire holding a big wooden spoon in her hand like a mother about to chastise two brawling children.

"This man caused the *Zoroaster* spill," Uma said in his low, broken-glass voice.

Connor used the distraction to scramble around the back of the wagon, where he snatched up the shotgun he had carried across two states, the gun he had used to shoot the Mormon lady's dog.

He took one more step toward Uma and raised the barrel. He had shells in both chambers; he cocked back the hammer. "You were the captain of the tanker, Butthead. *You* were responsible. Don't go dumping that crap on me!"

Henrietta Soo looked from one to the other as if she couldn't believe what she was hearing. Uma didn't seem the least bit afraid of Connor's shotgun, and he stepped toward him.

"We're not in front of an inquiry board here, Brooks. You can't get away on technicalities. I may be responsible, since I should have had you confined to your quarters, but you *caused* the wreck. It's your fault, and you'll burn in hell for it."

Connor held the shotgun steady as Uma continued to stride closer. He had no second thoughts about pulling the trigger. He had almost forgotten how much he hated this man. "My fault? None of it's my fault, Butthead!" He laughed and raised the shotgun.

Heather stared back at Todd, alluring but somehow looking just as frightened as he felt. She unsnapped her jeans and pulled the zipper slowly open. "I don't *need* you to come along with me, Todd. I can handle this by myself—but I *want* you there. I made a major bad choice with Connor, but I think you're different. Let's go make our own lives. Let's get out of here!"

Todd's heart hammered in his chest, and his throat became drier than the desert hardpan. "Heather, I . . ."

He kept seeing flashes of Iris. There were plenty of other men at the Altamont commune, and Iris was a person with a short temper and quick passions. She had wanted to move much faster in their relationship than Todd ever would have. He doubted that she would wait for him, and he had never promised to wait for her . . . just to come back someday.

But he shook his head, knowing that, as difficult as it was, his true feelings lay with Iris. He averted his eyes and started to speak, but before any words could form themselves, the cracking echo of a gunshot split the dusk.

"What the heck?" Todd said.

"The shotgun!" Heather said. "It's Connor!" She scrambled to button her shirt again and fasten her jeans. The two of them climbed up the embankment and raced desperately toward the camp.

Connor squeezed the shotgun's triggers, firing both barrels. The bang nearly deafened them.

—but instead of turning Uma's chest into a pulp, the

shotgun itself blew up in a backfire. Shards of the gun barrel and the stock flew in all directions. Black smoke burst out in a cloud. Connor fell backward, screaming as the hot explosion shredded the left side of his face.

With an animal howl Uma was upon him, ripping the twisted remains of the shotgun out of his hand and bringing it down like a club. Connor managed to roll and took the full force of the blow on his shoulder.

Trying to think clearly through the pain in his head and the rage pulsing through him, Connor yanked out his hunting knife. He couldn't see anything out of his eye, and blood blazed like fire across his cheeks and temple. He slashed blindly, hoping to slice Uma's jugular or put out his eye. Instead, the tip of the knife ripped across the dark man's shirt. Uma stumbled back just long enough for Connor to scramble to his knees and grip the knife handle with both hands.

Uma swung again with the ruined shotgun, but Connor ducked low, then came up with all the strength in both of his arms and plunged the knife to the hilt in Uma's abdomen.

Connor yanked the knife away, and blood came with it. Uma didn't even seem to notice. The big bald man dropped the shotgun and came in again with his bare hands. He locked his grip around Connor's throat, and Connor slashed his forearm—but Uma didn't care. He was a vengeful machine, his only thought to kill Connor.

Connor's larynx crumpled like an aluminum beer can. He stabbed Uma again, feeling the blade slip between his ribs and into his side. Foamy red blood came out of Uma's mouth, but the Butthead continued to squeeze.

Connor's eyes bulged; he didn't know how much longer he could hold out. He stabbed again and again. Uma was drenched with his own blood.

Connor began to pass out, when slowly Uma's eyes froze ahead. His grip on Connor's throat eased. He toppled like a great redwood trunk, falling to the dirt at the side of the wagon.

Connor tore himself free, retching and gasping for air. He stepped back, staring down at the wide-eyed corpse of the tanker captain. "You fuck!" He coughed and slammed his hiking boot viciously into Butthead's kidneys. He kicked Uma again and again, feeling ribs crack and his side cave in. Connor couldn't release his grip on the big hunting knife, even though the blood made his hands slick.

Suddenly, he remembered Henrietta Soo. She stood by the campfire still holding her flimsy wooden spoon and staring at him in horror.

A slow grin twisted Connor's mangled face, and he set off after her with the knife.

Todd reached the clearing before Heather. He scrambled down the rocks as he spotted Connor sitting on the buckboard of the wagon, cracking the reins. Todd nearly tripped, but kept his balance and yelled, "Hey—*Connor!* Stop!"

Connor twisted in his seat as if stunned to hear his name. He looked hideous—blood running down the side of his face, a dark splotch where his eye had been. He was covered in dirt, soot, and blood. Connor yelled at the horses. The wagon lurched forward in a cloud of dust and stones.

Todd heard the horses whinny as he smelled an overpowering smell of burning meat. Reaching the bottom of the rocky slope, Todd clunked forward in his cowboy boots. He tried to get up as much speed as he had when he and Casey Jones had leapt across the space between the buildings.

The wagon moved faster as Todd put on a final burst of speed. Reaching out, he grabbed onto the side of the wagon.

Splinters from the rough siding scraped his hands. He stumbled and tried to grab on with his other hand, but the wagon hit a bump and jerked away from him. Todd crashed into the ground, rolling, trying to keep away from the rear wagon wheel.

The wagon clattered past, and Todd heard a mishmash of horses' hoofs and snorting, and then the sound of Connor shouting something unintelligible as he charged away. Todd waited for a moment before pushing himself up.

He heard Heather run up beside him as he inspected his splintered hands. "Oh, Todd—" He ignored her, ticked off that he had let Connor get away.

A cloud of fading dust marked the horses' progress. Todd turned to view the campsite.

Heather brushed back the hair from her eyes. "What now?"

Todd headed for the camp. "Let's check it out."

The campfire still burned, and Henrietta Soo lay sprawled face-first on the ground beside it. Her arm had fallen into the embers of the fire. Her shirt smoldered, and the skin of her forearm blistered a sickly black.

Todd bent down on watery knees and rolled her over. Connor had slit her throat in a long ragged gash. It looked as if she had bled gallons into the dry dirt.

The deepening dusk blurred all the sharp details and the bright colors, but it took Heather only a moment to find the body of Casey Jones. He was much worse. Connor had butchered him.

Before Todd squeezed his eyes shut, he saw at least half a dozen stab wounds in Casey's chest and abdomen.

Todd staggered away and vomited into the scrub brush, then fell back. He sat on the rough dirt and stared at nothing. He had never experienced anything like this before. Connor Brooks couldn't be a human being and do this!

Heather squatted next to him and put her hand lightly on his shoulder. She squeezed it, but Todd barely felt the pressure of her fingers.

"I know I warned you," she said, "but even I didn't think he was capable of this. I thought he might take our supplies and steal the wagon but . . . all the blood!" She shuddered violently, then gasped to herself in disbelief. "I slept with him! I was alone with him for a month.

What if I had said the wrong thing? What if he had done that to me?"

Todd's voice was bitter. "This is what you wanted, isn't it? Now he's gone and we're alone together."

Heather stiffened and drew away from him. "This is not what I wanted!" Then she staggered to be by herself. Any thought of a relationship between them would now be forever stained with murder and violence.

After a few moments apart, Todd made his way to Heather. "We'll never catch him. He's got three horses. Where do you think he'll go?"

Heather took a while to respond. "Anywhere he thinks he can use the satellites to his advantage. But that won't help us."

"We'll bury these two," Todd said, "and then you and I will make our way to White Sands. I've come this far, and I'll be damned if I'm going to turn back, even if I don't have the satellites."

Riding high in his tethered hot-air balloon, Lieutenant Bobby Carron stared across the desert, dozing. The first day he had exhilarated in being up in the air, but this was vastly different from flying a fighter jet: standing in an aluminum basket while a blazing fire scorched his back, bobbing at the end of a thousand-foot-long rope coupled with a telegraph wire.

For the past week Bobby had surveyed the surrounding area, staring at every rock and shrub. He checked the horizon with the metal spyglass Dr. Lockwood's optics workshop had rigged up. He knew the area well enough now to spot anything unusual.

Movement triggered his subconscious. Without thinking, he floated up one level of awareness, letting his mind integrate the area around him. He detected another movement, another . . . and then *scores* of them like an army of ants making its way across the valley—right where Rita had predicted it would come.

He felt his pulse race as he made out a column of

soldiers appearing in the shimmering heat mirage. By rough count, he guessed General Bayclock had brought a hundred troops, plus support personnel. A few rode horses, but the rest marched in ranks.

Then, far in the west, he saw two other figures, two people alone walking across the flat dizzying desert, headed toward the White Sands facility. Bobby turned his spyglass to them and could barely make out a man and a woman striding along.

Bobby grabbed the portable telegraph unit. He tapped the international signal to *drop everything!*, attempting to get Juan Romero's attention: "XVW, XVW, XVW . . ."

SIXTY-NINE

STORM FRONT

In the west wing of the White House, the Situation Room had once been the showpiece of America's military-industrial investment in high technology. At one time, media pundits forecast with uncanny accuracy the level of U.S. response to an international incident by counting the number of pizzas delivered to the Situation Room on any particular night. In the most important city in the nation, at the most important residence, this was without a doubt the most important room.

But now there were no pizzas, no media watchdogs, no technological wizardry. High-definition computer work-stations gave way to blackboards, messages scrawled on scraps of paper, and flickering electric light powered by steam-engine generators on the Mall.

Staffers hurried about, but their focus had shifted from world events to the demands upon the national government made by several unofficial domestic "city-states," which were the new centers of power scattered around the crumbling country.

President Jeffrey Mayeaux sat in a high-backed chair, digging his fingernails into the leather. He tried to digest the information being fed to him in contradictory scraps with confusing lack of detail. *What the hell is going on out there?* The lack of verified information appalled him—it was like trying to make sense out of a TV show on a channel filled with multicolored static.

At his right, along a long wooden table, sat his military advisors, the Joint Chiefs of Staff. The five men looked weary—as they damn well should, since he hadn't let them leave the White House complex in over a week! Their uniforms were wrinkled, stained, but they held themselves up with caffeine-fed dignity. Mayeaux scowled at them, then looked back to the notepapers. Those guys didn't know what pressure was!

At Mayeaux's left sat representatives from his cabinet, the National Security Agency, and his private staff. Three Secret Service agents stood quietly in the background; the agents were usually absent from such closed discussions, and their presence now did not go unnoticed. Mayeaux had started taking such precautions when his military advisors began grumbling more and more loudly about Mayeaux's way of coping with the petroplague situation.

Well, fuck them! No other president had to deal with the whole country falling apart—not even Lincoln! The Civil War had been rational and understandable, a disagreement in politics.

Mayeaux pushed Appendix J-7, the latest list of petroplague-destroyed items, across the desk. He was getting sick of seeing addenda to the original memo. Didn't the compilers get tired of jotting things down? Toothpaste caps? Disposable diapers and condoms? For God's sake, who cared?

Mayeaux scowled and closely watched the reactions of the Joint Chiefs. "The list is not getting smaller, gentlemen. I understand the Dallas/Fort Worth Metroplex has also broken off communication with the central government, and they strung up three of our agents trying to enforce martial law. I've got conflicting reports of some severe problems in San Diego. Are we going to be able to get the country back on its feet? What do we have to offer people as far as restoring the old way of life? How about making some *progress* for a change!"

Mayeaux's science advisor said, "We still hope to someday use methane and propane, but that's impossible until we can develop reliable seals for airtight containers. Eventually, we could extract and refine oil in a closed, sterile environment, but of course that would enormously increase the cost of petroleum products. There may even be certain additives to plastics that will discourage decomposition by the microorganism. The scientists at NIST, NRL, and the CDC are working around the clock—"

"Dammit, I'm not interested in 'eventually'! Our house is in flames and you're talking about inventing a telephone to call the fire department!" Mayeaux slammed his fist on the arm of the chair. "We've got to get the situation under control, and then ease back so we can introduce improvements and gradual solutions."

He studied the Joint Chiefs. "*Mais,* let me tell you somethin'. Since we can't tap anything other than firewood or maybe coal for energy, we are in for one hell of a winter. We don't have any industry left. States and big cities are declaring their independence right and left, and the national government is nothing more than a figurehead.

"We cannot back up our authority or make orders stick—not to mention martial laws, executive decrees, and everything else! What are we going to do about the larger cities defying my emergency orders? Do I just ignore Dallas and Los Angeles and Miami and San Diego? See how they fend for themselves as independent countries? Screw that! Give me an effective strategy I can use *right now* in this situation." Mayeaux turned to General Wacom, the chairman of the Joint Chiefs, a thin, gray-haired air force man in an unassuming blue uniform.

Wacom stared back. "You've said it all yourself, sir. The military is disjointed and relegated to the status of either observers or local police forces maintaining order under the authority of local governments. It may be our most effective tactic to let the country calm down and keep order on a local level until we get the infrastructure back in place. I don't think these states really intend to become permanently independent—once the populace starts to see regular news from Washington again, once they hear the President address them directly, they'll come around. I don't suggest we do anything drastic."

Mayeaux worked his jaw, feeling helpless as he watched the authority of the presidency crumble beneath him.

"That's just great, General. So what you're saying is that I should just sit here and let everything take care of itself? History would really love me for that. I'm sure they'd erect a Mayeaux Monument right there on the Mall, with the three monkeys of Hear No Evil, See No Evil, Speak No Evil! What the hell are you trying to pull on me? Because I talk with an accent, do you think I'm an idiot?"

His military advisors stared blandly back, not offering any solution. As he simmered, Mayeaux got the distinct feeling that they were waiting for him to slip up, to make a wrong move, and then they would crawfish in to accomplish their own agenda.

Were they going to initiate impeachment hearings? He drew in a breath, suddenly panicked. *Or would it be a military coup?*

He glanced at the Secret Service agents standing at the corner of the room for reassurance; it was getting hard to trust anyone nowadays, and he couldn't feel secure in his dealings even with his own staff. Where the hell was Weathersee?

Mayeaux pushed his chair back from the table and strode from the room, accompanied by his Secret Service entourage. Not one person in the Situation Room stood as the chief executive exited.

SEVENTY

FORTY THOUSAND HEADMEN

From his lookout position in the rugged Organ Mountains, General Bayclock searched the sprawling White Sands valley. Behind him on a volcanic outcrop, his two colonels and Sergeant Caitlyn Morris waited for him to decide their next move.

At the base of the mountain, he had directed his troops to rest and inspect their weapons for the final march across the valley. Five miles to the north, they had left the group of noncombatants, cooks, water carriers, supply haulers, food handlers, tent carriers. Bayclock had needed the additional personnel to get this far, but now that he was within sight of the enemy, he insisted on having only the frontline troops present.

Sergeant Morris scrambled up the rocky slope. "See anything, sir?" The two colonels huffed after her, pulling at lone clumps of grass for support.

"Let me have the binoculars," Bayclock said.

Sergeant Morris rummaged in her pack and pulled out a reconditioned olive-green pair of binoculars. She pointed to a thin line running up the tallest peak on the other side of the valley. "That's the electromagnetic satellite launcher, sir. Five miles south is the microwave antenna farm. Lockwood's group has holed up in those few support buildings there. No major defenses, no perimeter fortifications."

Not listening, Bayclock adjusted the binocular sights; the knob squeaked. "I'll be damned!"

"What is it, sir?" Colonel David inched up on his hands and knees. Colonel Nachimya, commander of the Base Personnel Group, joined him. Neither man was a true soldier in Bayclock's opinion—neither were flyers, and neither had ever held a *real* command, but had merely commanded labs or administrative offices all of their careers. Bayclock didn't have many choices.

He wished he had paid more attention to the lectures at the National War College. He had blown off theoretical discussions on ground attacks, interested only in the methodology of air superiority. In his blood Bayclock was a *fighter pilot*. But right now he'd trade almost anything for a copy of von Clausewitz.

"Sir?" said Sergeant Morris. "Is anything the matter?"

Bayclock handed the binoculars to Colonel David. "A *balloon*—can you believe it? What the hell are they doing with a hot-air balloon?"

The colonel searched the sky. "Dr. Nedermyer insists that Lockwood's people are completely focused on that solar-power project. At the Phillips Lab I've worked around scientists like that for years. My bet is they're using the balloon to gather information about the weather."

Bayclock turned to the other colonel. "And what do you think, Tony?"

Colonel Nachimya stared across the valley, but he made no move to take the binoculars. "Observation post maybe? You could see our troops approaching from a long way off, sir."

"That was my own thought. If that's so, they already know we're here." Bayclock studied the area around the distant, glittering antenna farm, unable to see people from this range.

He struggled to his feet and handed the binoculars back to Sergeant Morris. "Assemble the troops. We'll get this over with in a hurry, attack under cover of darkness. I don't trust any of those bastards we're up against."

As the sun set behind the broken mountains, shadows extended across the valley like fingers of death toward the rebellious scientists. By this time tomorrow, Bayclock's troops would have engulfed Lockwood's group and reestablished order, at last.

In the radio trailer, Juan Romero concentrated on a circuit diagram he had sketched himself; he hoped it would improve the microwave satellite switching algorithm. Before the petroplague, intricate new designs had been constructed on workstations optimized for specific configurations. But the overrated software annoyed Romero—why spend so much time studying electrical engineering if you were just going to be a computer jock? He felt a rush of pride to see that he could still do a circuit diagram the old way, with a brain and a pencil.

Static clicks from the telegraph interrupted his thoughts. He grumbled about Bobby Carron picking the worst time to run a test from his observation balloon. Romero listened to the first few lines of code, and then his face tightened. "Hey, Spence!" His own hoarse voice surprised him.

Gilbert Hertoya trotted out of the blockhouse, ducking around an array of cables. "What you got?"

Romero glanced up, but continued relaying Bobby's message to the microwave facility five miles to the south. "It's Bayclock. He's here already! Where's Spencer?"

The short engineer blinked. "Oh, crackerjacks! He and Rita headed off for the microwave facility before dark. They should get there within an hour."

"Bobby's got Bayclock's troops pegged at ten miles out. No solid count on the number, but there's at least a hundred." Romero felt panic clogging his voice. He tugged on his drooping mustache. "What are we going to do?"

"Do you think they'll attack after dark? Can Bobby estimate how fast they're moving?"

"Just a minute." Romero tapped furiously on the switch. The telegraph line from the balloon came back to life. "They're still coming down from the foothills. He estimates they're traveling under three miles an hour."

"Okay." Gilbert set his mouth. "Keep relaying everything to the farm, and let me know when Spencer gets there. I'll set the railgun up for a preemptive strike."

Romero looked up at the other man. "You mean, go on the offense? Shouldn't we give them a warning or something?"

"Ask *them* to surrender? Ha!" Gilbert's face was grim and looked very old. "We're not playing by parlor rules. Bayclock is the aggressor. Time to scare the hell out of him."

The memory of the capacitor banks prefiring on the first railgun test nearly smothered Gilbert's optimism. Now that Bayclock's army was breathing down their necks, he knew it could easily happen again. Or something even worse.

Gilbert refused to wait for Bayclock's army to start shooting at them. The general was on the move, marching closer. As far as Gilbert was concerned, there was no point in negotiating—they hadn't asked for the invasion force, had done nothing to incite the attack. But Bayclock had come strutting in, uninvited.

If some tin-pot Napoleon thought he could march down here with an army, Gilbert intended to send him back home with his tail between his legs. If the White Sands group lost their advantage of surprise, Bayclock could move his troops to safety and come at them from a different direction.

A cloud of metal shrapnel flying at five times the velocity of a bullet would surely demoralize Bayclock's troops—especially coming from a bunch of supposedly defenseless scientists. If nothing else, the railgun would make the army wonder what *else* Spencer's hotshots might come up with.

Arnie poked his head out from the launcher command post. "Ready for the bank to go hot, Gilbert."

"Has the projectile been checked?"

Arnie sighed. "Twice by you and three times by us. We loaded Rita's special shrapnel mix of chopped-up razor blades, nails, and broken glass. If we pop it now, it should spread out to hit their camp. It won't be pretty."

"It's not supposed to be pretty." Gilbert looked around for Romero. "Heard from Spencer yet?"

The radio man shook his head. "The farm says they'll contact us when he gets there."

Gilbert thought fast. He had to go with it. Command decision. Spencer and his crew had been anticipating this moment ever since Bobby Carron had deserted and stayed behind.

Years earlier, Gilbert had been yanked from his work at the Sandia National Lab, sent over to the Middle East as a military consultant during the first Gulf conflict. He had left Cynthia and the kids behind in Albuquerque, unable to tell them what he was doing—much the same way he had left them in Alamogordo during the past few weeks. He hadn't protested then because he believed in his work. And now he had never felt stronger about anything in his life. Spencer's solar-power farm must not fall into the hands of a military dictator.

He drew in a deep breath. "Okay, charge the banks. Launch on my count." He twisted his head. "Romero! Get an updated range from Bobby."

"Right."

Gilbert scrambled over a thigh-thick cluster of cables to position himself at the railgun's crude rangefinder— optics from a high-powered rifle juxtaposed with a protractor and a plumb line. Within seconds Romero relayed elevation and landmark information.

Grunting, Gilbert reached up to rotate the unwieldy device with the hand crank. When the starlit peak across

the valley was in sight on the crosshairs, he elevated the
long metal railings until the plumb line registered the
correct position. "Talk about spit and chewing gum,"
he muttered.

"Bank's hot, Gil. Your call."

Gilbert eyed the crosshairs one more time, then gently
moved away from the device. He slapped Romero on the
back. "Get some cover." He nodded at the tech in the
control room. "Light it!"

"Roger!" Arnie yelled into the blockhouse. "Hit it!"

Fifty feet away from the railgun, Gilbert turned to
watch. He saw a weirdly ionized ball shoot the length of
the rails, sparking across the gaps as the heavy shrapnel
projectile accelerated upward. He had never seen a
nighttime launch, and it looked beautiful.

Then a blinding flash erupted from the capacitor
building. The sounds of the railgun and the capacitor
exploding hit him at the same time.

Gilbert felt the pop of the shock wave as the dynamic
overpressure hit. He started running toward the railgun,
not knowing what had happened. A secondary explosion
came from the capacitor building. "No, dammit!"

He barely saw the fragment of metal spinning toward
him as it hit him in the knees. He fell, trying to pummel
the ground with his fists as he passed out.

General Bayclock rode at the front of the army advancing toward the microwave farm, accompanied by
Sergeant Morris and Dr. Nedermyer. Five security policemen on horseback surrounded him. Behind him and
spreading out like a wedge rode his two colonels and
their respective groups of soldiers.

The troops marched on foot, weary but excited to be
finally reaching their destination. They had lost five
horses early in the trek during the raid from the pueblo
dwellers, but the general had commandeered other
mounts from ranches on the way.

Bayclock still thought of himself as a wing commander, and his two groups made up the remainder of his

military command. The lines of communication were short, and he had no doubt they would easily take the solar-power facility.

But Bayclock remembered from National War College that overconfident troops were easiest to overcome; he did not want his troops to fail because Lockwood's people put up an unexpected fight. Yet it was hard to take the group of scientists seriously. He had not yet decided how lenient he would be with them when it was all over.

Bayclock turned to Sergeant Caitlyn Morris, intending to call the troops to a halt when he first heard the sound—like a million angry insects suddenly buzzing, filling his head.

Sharp, startled screams broke the air. His people dropped, horses bellowed then whinnied in pain. All around him, the peaceful desert seemed suddenly to spew forth a plague of locusts, hard projectiles pattering the ground and whizzing through the air. The screaming buzz seemed to go on and on.

Bayclock pulled his horse around—two security policemen behind him fell on the ground; one writhed, the other lay motionless. Beside them, a horse struggled, trying to get back to its feet and leaving splashes of blood on the white gypsum sands.

Just as suddenly as it started, the deadly rain stopped. The night sky continued to fill with yells of terror.

Bayclock yanked his rifle from its holster. "Sergeant, get my staff up here!"

"Yes, sir!" Sergeant Morris pulled her horse around and galloped back into the starlit night. Bayclock turned in his saddle and yelled at the security policemen. "You, man—help your buddy! You others post a guard in a semicircle. Speed out!"

Chaos overwhelmed the night as the sounds of panicked troops scrambling to follow orders mixed with moans of pain. Bayclock held his rifle on his knee, trying to drive a wedge through the darkness with the sheer force of his anger. *What in the living hell just happened?*

He heard horses come up behind him, and he made out the forms of Sergeant Morris and Colonel David. The colonel held his injured left arm against his side.

"Report!" snapped Bayclock. "What have you got?"

Colonel David shook his head, coughing. "Nothing definite, sir. I don't know how many people I've lost. We've got a shitload of injuries, everything from impact wounds to shatter fractures. I haven't seen anything like this since the fragmentation weapons used in the Gulf."

"Those daisy-cutters were dropped by B-52s, Colonel—have you heard any planes around here lately?"

The colonel shook his head; Sergeant Morris suggested tentatively, "Maybe the scientists have mortars, sir."

Bayclock glared. "Daisy-cutters are five-hundred-pound bombs, Sergeant! I've brought them on my own missions. Now shut the hell up while I speak with my staff."

Sergeant Morris grew tight-lipped. "Yes, sir."

Bayclock turned back to the colonel. "Where's Nachimya?"

"He bought it, General. He was twenty yards away from me when he died. Large wound through the trachea."

"Who's his second-in-command?"

Colonel David shook his head. "Major Zencon took off after some of the troops, sir. It was clear they were deserting."

"Why didn't he shoot the bastards? He has standing orders to shoot deserters!" Colonel David remained silent and closed his eyes. "Answer me, Colonel!"

Sergeant Morris answered quietly, "Major Zencon apparently deserted as well, sir. Colonel David couldn't shoot them because of his own injury. We've probably lost a quarter of our troops already."

The general yanked the bridle on his black gelding. The horse reared up, but Bayclock wrested back control. "Sergeant Morris, round up my security guard. Anyone who isn't injured is to bring the highest-ranking officers to me, ASAP! Their orders remain unchanged—deserters will be shot. We will fall back and regroup until we learn more about the surprise defenses the scientists have set up for us."

"Yes, sir." Sergeant Morris turned her horse and stopped. "General, look!"

Bayclock muttered an oath. In the distance a fire blazed at the base of the electromagnetic launcher. It looked as though a bomb had devoured the entire facility, and fingers of flame licked the sky.

"Halt, who goes there!"

After the long, relaxing ride to the microwave facility, Spencer's first thought was that someone must be playing a joke. Upon seeing the glint of two rifle barrels, his second thought was to answer as quickly as he could. "It's Spencer—don't shoot!"

"Rita Fellenstein," said Rita beside him, just as quickly.

The gun barrel wavered, then dropped as a twangy voice said, "Yeah, it's Spence. Darn—I thought we'd get to shoot our first live ones."

Spencer kept his hands up, still unsure of what was going on. "Uh, can you tell me—" And then it hit him. "My God, Bayclock is here already!"

The voice in the darkness turned grim. "Things are going crazy back at the EM launch site. You'd better hurry into the microwave trailer for a report, pronto."

Spencer didn't reply. He kicked his mount with his heels, urging the horse to a gallop. Rita charged along beside him, her Australian hat flopping back against her neck.

When they reached the blockhouses, Spencer listened without a word as he was brought up to date. The technician at the telegraph unit spread her hands. "Romero managed to keep us updated in real time, up until the railgun fired."

"Are you sure the railgun blew up?"

The tech shrugged. "Who knows? That's what it looked like."

Rita leaned forward. "What about Bobby?"

"I don't know. We can't see the balloon, but that doesn't mean anything. He could be down to refuel."

Spencer clenched his jaw, furious with himself. If only he had waited another hour at the launcher before returning! He tried to calm down; he needed to think clearly. Except for Rita, his closest advisors had been at the ill-fated railgun site.

"So what do we do?" said Rita. "Have we lost our long-range strike capability?"

"That pretty much goes without saying," said the technician.

"Then we're up a creek," said Rita. "Bayclock's boys can be here in three hours if they want!"

"If that's the case," said Spencer, "there's nothing more we can do." *Come on,* he thought. What happened to the whiz kid? The going got tough, and now he was supposed to deliver.

Rita turned toward the blockhouse door with a determined look on her face. "I'll take a couple of ranch hands and scout out Bayclock's position. We can take along some of those citrus-oil explosives and lob the army a couple of nasty presents. Psych warfare. If we leave now, we can get there and back before dawn. We'll stop by the launch site to check things out on the way, and send somebody back if the telegraph isn't up when we get there."

Spencer felt as if he had been hit over the head with a bagful of Higg's bosons. He shook his head. "I don't know—"

"I wasn't asking permission, Spence," said Rita. "Why don't you just go do something you do best—like double the output power from those microwave satellites? Keep yourself busy and out of the way."

Half an hour later, Spencer stood grim-faced as Rita swung a long leg over her horse. Her saddlebags were packed with explosives, pyrotechnics, and ammunition. Two ranch hands accompanied her, both grinning nervously as she leaned over to spit a tiny wad of chewing tobacco before setting out.

"See you in a couple of hours." She leaned over and pecked Spencer on the cheek. "If you get ahold of Bobby, tell him I'm on my way."

"He'll be happy to know that." Spencer slapped her horse on the flank. "Get going—you've got a job to do."

"Make sure the catapult operators are ready for the morning light," Rita called. "They might look like they're over the hill, but they know what they're doing. Just ask Romero."

Spencer watched as Rita and her two companions rode off into the darkness. He stared until they faded from sight. He sighed, then turned back to the microwave trailer when he heard a voice calling him.

"Quick! We captured two people coming in from the west."

A chill ran down Spencer's back. *Oh, great,* he thought. *Nobody around here has any military savvy, and we've just* captured *our first prisoners of war?*

He jogged down the dusty path, nearly stumbling over ruts in the darkness. On the old road to the microwave farm, Spencer met a guard walking behind two people— both quite tall, a man and a woman, their hands behind their backs. Even in the starlight Spencer could see that the man wore a cowboy hat, and the woman tied her long hair in a ponytail. They didn't look like what he expected of Baylock's troops.

The guard said, "Hey, Spencer, come see what we've got here."

The prisoner's voice had a strong cowboy twang. "Are you Dr. Lockwood? Am I glad to see you!"

"I bet you are. Who are you?"

The cowboy pushed himself forward, ahead of the guard. "I talked to you on the shortwave. I'm Todd Severyn. From the Jet Propulsion Lab in Pasadena."

SEVENTY-ONE

GO TO EXTREMES

Rita Fellenstein stood in the stirrups, craning her neck to spot the glow of Bayclock's campfires. For once she was thankful for the petroplague, since the general had no access to infrared goggles or other high-tech night-time defenses. At least she didn't think so.

Even better, his troops were not familiar with the landscape.

Rita intended to use her advantage to the max.

The two ranch hands started to whisper, but Rita put out a hand for silence. So far, she had spotted no roving patrols, but she didn't put it past Bayclock to send out random point squads.

Still without word from the damaged railgun site, Rita rode with the ranch hands and looped south, coming in from behind the camp. Bobby Carron had told her about the "check six" jargon of fighter pilots to guard their rear at all times, but he thought the general might not apply that on the ground.

She really liked Bobby. It was good to finally have a

guy stand up and spar with her instead of awkwardly shuffling his feet like the ranch hands did. But Bobby had nothing to do with her raid now. She pushed thoughts of him out of her mind.

Out of the corner of her eye, Rita caught a glimpse of a man on horseback in the encampment; beyond, she saw the glow of several fires masked by low dirt berms dug by the weary soldiers.

Rita patted her saddle and withdrew three cans of Bobby's citrus-based explosive. She secured her rifle at the back of the saddle and whispered back at the other ranch hands. "Don't get too close or stay too long. We just want to goose 'em. Ka-boom!" Rita flicked the reins and clucked. "Let's go!"

Their mounts stormed toward Bayclock's encampment. Rita bent low on her horse. With the heels of her boots, she urged her horse to a gallop.

Bayclock's troops had bivouacked in a circular cluster a hundred yards across. Rita and the others split off, riding around the camp. Her breath quickened as horse hooves made a thumping sound in the desert night.

The troops lay on the ground, using their packs as pillows; three men tended the fires. Someone in the camp struggled to his feet. His silhouette looked wildly around as he started shouting.

Rita released the spring-wound timing mechanism on her first grenade and hurled it, rapidly followed by two other canisters. By the time the first explosion erupted, gunfire peppered the air. Bayclock's troops shot their weapons blindly into the night. Rita could hear the *zing* of bullets ricocheting off the ground. Another *boom* rolled over them with a flash of light as they turned and galloped back toward the microwave farm.

Only four of the canned explosives went off. Although the small bombs probably caused little damage, Rita could tell by the shouting and gunfire behind them that they had thoroughly stirred up Bayclock's troops.

*   *   *

"Until we spotted your complex from Las Cruces Pass, we didn't know if we'd ever find you," Todd Severyn said, squatting on the ground from sheer exhaustion. "It was pretty touch-and-go there for a while."

Beside him, Heather Dixon agreed. She looked ready to drop. Spencer felt sorry for them, and yelled for someone to bring a full canteen of water.

Heather sat next to the fire, hugging her knees. Her face smudged with dirt, she stared mesmerized into the flames as Todd continued his tale. She looked lost, as though life had let her down once too often. It took an effort for Spencer not to stare at her. He wondered if she and Todd were somehow . . . involved. They sat apart, but after such a difficult journey, that wasn't surprising.

Lately Spencer found himself thinking about being alone, wondering if he might ever find that girl with the sunburned nose. But no time for that now—he had work to do.

He nodded at Todd's description of the journey after Connor Brooks had killed their companions and stolen the satellites. The Wyoming man unballed his fist and rubbed his dusty jeans, as if to crush the memory of the disastrous trip.

Spencer felt sick to hear about the loss of the smallsats. They had come so close! He tried to find some hope that the lost satellites might somehow find their way to the microwave farm. With the Seven Dwarfs still working overhead, it was a shame they couldn't use the low-orbiting satellites as part of their high-tech defense against Bayclock.

But with the new set of satellites gone and the railgun apparently destroyed, not to mention the general's troops massed in the foothills, he found it difficult to be optimistic. What did it matter anymore? Why were they fighting at all? Why the hell had *Bayclock* bothered to come here?

Spencer wondered if his group should just abandon the microwave farm before the army slaughtered them all. They could hide in the mountains, send out guerrilla teams to harass the occupied area, until one day they managed to drive away the military barbarians. Fat chance! His one small consolation was that another ten smallsats remained safe at JPL.

Todd said, "So what's the next step, Dr. Lockwood? You might as well put us to work helping you. No use moping around—not with the general here. Time to fight!"

"We already fired the first shot," Spencer said, "but that seems to have put our railgun out of business and damaged the whole launcher facility. That was really our best chance."

"Is there anything else you can fight with?" Todd asked.

"We had an extensive war council before the troops got here," said Spencer. "Gilbert Hertoya had experience fielding high-risk weapons in the Persian Gulf, and we did just about everything he suggested. We've still got the ranchers and people from the town lying in ambush, and of course there's always the catapult squad. Right now we've got a team tossing some homemade grenades into the general's camp. But every one of these is a last-ditch effort, nothing that can cause any sustained damage. I don't have any more rabbits to pull out of my hat."

He hesitated, then dropped his voice. "I hope to God that everyone's all right up at the launcher site."

Heather continued to stare at the flames, but she spoke in a low, deep voice. "What about your microwave antennas? If they provide so much electricity, why can't you fry people?"

Spencer had to pull himself out of Heather's wide eyes before he answered. He glanced at Todd, but the oil man gave a tired smile, as if amused at Spencer's preoccupation. "Uh, it takes too much power to harm anyone with microwaves—the atmosphere would break down long before the power levels got high enough to harm human beings." He continued to think it through. "Relatively low powers *can* do nasty things to metals or electronics, but after the petroplague there's not much of that stuff in use anymore."

Heather said, "The general's rifles are made of metal."

Spencer opened his mouth to respond, but stopped as her words sank in. "You've got a point. I've been thinking about using microwaves to attack the wrong target!"

Todd looked puzzled. "What do you mean?"

"We're beaming energy from space at relatively low power levels, about a hundred times less than the sunlight that strikes the Earth—that won't hurt anyone if they stand in it all day long. Remember the cellular telephone scare? Cellular phones were monsters compared to this."

He spoke faster as he started to get excited. "But Bayclock's troops *are* carrying all kinds of metal. Guns, knives, bayonets—and that stuff heats up like crazy when exposed even to the microwave power levels we're beaming down right now!"

Todd grinned. "It would give them one hell of a hot-foot!"

Spencer chewed on his lip. "If we can boost the energy by a factor of four and irradiate his troops for twenty minutes, things might get hot enough even to set off explosives. At the very least the troops might drop their weapons and head for the hills!"

Todd looked down at his big hands and flexed them. "So what do we do?"

Spencer thought for a moment. As far as he could tell, it was sometime after midnight by now. He hadn't heard the sentry warn of Bayclock's approach, and that would give them at least an hour's warning. Perhaps Gilbert's preemptive railgun strike *had* set Bayclock back, or maybe the general had sent his vengeful troops up to take over the launcher facility instead.

Spencer said, "The Seven Dwarfs come overhead every day at noon, over eleven hours from now. If we can hold Bayclock off until then, I might be able to re-program the solar satellites to irradiate his troops. It won't be as destructive as the railgun, but it might be enough to keep them at bay."

"Seven dwarfs?" said Todd. "What are you talking about?" He looked to Heather. "What dwarfs?"

"You've got computers here?" Heather sounded in-credulous.

Spencer shrugged, looking at her and ignoring Todd's question. "Mostly what we've scavenged from the work-stations, a few big analog circuit boards that run on the batteries recharged every day at noon when the satellites fly over."

Todd frowned. "I don't know squat about satellites *or* computers . . . or dwarfs for that matter."

Heather looked suddenly awake. "I'd like to stay here and help, if that's what you need."

"Sounds better than rolling over and playing dead," said Todd. "If the soldiers are so riled up they can't get here by noon, a blast of your microwaves might just push them over the edge to retreat." He stood up, ready for action. "Count me in."

Spencer squinted in the direction of the EM launcher. They would have to send Bobby Carron up in the balloon again early in the morning to get a bird's-eye view of the battlefield before they planned their detailed strategy—if Bobby was all right.

Todd repeated himself. "Is there anything I could do? I can ride and I can shoot."

"Help keep a lookout for a sneak attack. When Rita returns, we'll decide how best to keep tabs on Bayclock's troops."

Heather brushed dirt from her jeans. "Just point me to the bathroom and some wash water, then I'll be ready to work." She wrinkled her nose and scratched. "I don't suppose you have anything to treat a sunburn?"

Spencer stopped, stunned. *Sunburned nose?* He man-aged to shake his head. No matter how bad things looked, he had a feeling that the sun was going to shine extra bright tomorrow morning.

"Halt! Who the hell are you?" a woman's voice growled.

Todd Severyn stood his ground, but he could see little in the dark. "Yeah, who the heck are *you?*"

He heard the sound of a rifle brought to bear. "You've got five seconds, cowboy, or you'll be dancing without any toes. Identify yourself!"

His arms waved in the air. "I'm Todd Severyn—I'm waiting for Rita to show up. Spencer Lockwood sent me."

"How do I know you're telling the truth? Bayclock could have sent a point squad."

Why oh why do I always meet women who'd rather wrestle rattlesnakes than bake cookies? "Are you going to ask me who won the World Series in nineteen-sixty-four, for Chrissakes!" He tried to remember the right words even if he didn't understand them. "I'm supposed to say something about a plan to zap Bayclock with the Seven Dwarfs."

He saw the rifle being lowered, then heard a chuckle. The woman spat tobacco to one side. "Okay, Tex, you can tell Spencer that Rita's back. Let's get moving."

Todd sourly brought down his hands, wishing that *someone* would recognize his Wyoming accent and not call him Tex.

Spencer sat next to Heather in the enclosed trailer as dawn broke, working on three crude workstations at once. Even with the nonvolatile memory and low-energy cathode-ray tubes, the energy drain was substantial, and they could only refine their simulations for another hour or so without running down the batteries.

Soft battery light reflected off of Heather's face. She had tied her damp hair back after scrubbing up, and Spencer could see a pinkish cast of sunburn on her nose and cheeks.

Juan Romero's circuit board took up most of the table, and naked wires lay in labyrinthine paths. Heather pushed knife-switch buttons down laboriously, inputting code from Spencer—one letter at a time. She stared at the phosphors on the glass screen of the canted cathode-ray tube. "Okay, I've keyed in the equation you gave me. You'll have to take over from here."

"Thanks." He slid into the seat next to her as he waited for the code to compile. Inside the trailer, the heat pouring from the primitive circuit board felt stifling, and he prayed he could stave off a meltdown for a little while longer.

Just having Heather present to type in the long-winded perturbations to the orbital equations freed him to calculate the necessary solid-viewing angles by hand with pencil and paper. If everything worked, they might be able to nudge the Seven Dwarfs to redirect their microwave transmissions away from the antenna farm and onto Bayclock's encampment. Temporarily increasing the power output by a factor of four was trivial compared to this, requiring much less code.

"Spencer?" Rita's voice came from the trailer entrance. She sounded weary. He turned and saw Todd standing with her just outside the door.

"Rita! How did the raid go?"

"The grenades worked well enough. Got some dozing soldiers to wet their beds, but once they realize we didn't cause much damage, they'll just be pissed off instead. The cowboy here tells me you need another scouting party." She looked at Heather. "Oh, hello."

Heather brushed back a strand of hair. "Hi."

Todd worked his way into the trailer. Rita pulled out a chair by the workstation and ran a hand through her hair. Her long legs pushed up against the table. "The telegraph's up. Romero made his way back from the launcher—he apparently ran all the way here, while the others tried to put out the fire and barricade themselves in the facility."

Spencer sat up, ignoring the satellite calculations. "Romero's back! What's the report?"

"Gilbert is badly injured—both his legs, I think. One tech is dead, and the railgun *ist kaput*. Arnie stayed behind to watch everything, but if Bayclock sent some point men up, he doesn't have much chance to hold them off by himself."

"Great," Spencer said. He wanted to pound on something. "Now what do we do?"

Rita wiped her forehead. "Bobby's going up in the balloon again at first light to get a good look. He thinks Bayclock will probably hold off attacking for another day. So far we've zapped him with one salvo from the railgun and tossed a bunch of grenades into his camp—he thought we were a bunch of unarmed wimps, but now he's not going to take any chances. I say we keep giving the general a healthy respect for our abilities." She glanced at Heather, then at Spencer, and raised an eyebrow. A grin slowly grew on her face.

Spencer stood, more to dismiss any comment from Rita than anything else. "Okay, let's hit them with the catapult first thing in the morning. After that, we call in the townspeople."

Exhausted, sore, and bleary-eyed from lack of sleep, Juan Romero stood next to his gang-that-couldn't-shoot-straight catapult operators. Morning light spilled over the gypsum plains in a whiter shade of pale; the shadows of the mountains retreated across the white sands.

Below, Bayclock's army began forming up and making ready to relocate. Romero's people took longer than expected to move to the highlands where the hidden catapult waited to hurl projectiles. From what they could tell, the single shot with Gilbert Hertoya's railgun had dealt a shocking and devastating psychological blow—but Romero had little hope that his shorter-range medieval weapon would do the same.

Lieutenant Bobby Carron had built a fire in the metal

gondola of his bright survey balloon and rose aloft on the tether cable, sending telegraphed messages back to another listener in the blockhouse at the antenna farm. Romero wished he could be down there instead of up here, watching his team make all the mistakes he expected of them.

The old retirees argued with each other about who would turn the crank, who would aim the shot, who would release the hook. Then they started arguing about which of the barrels of scrap metal would make the best first load.

Bayclock's army began to spread out, breaking camp and marching in several prongs—one headed toward the burned-out railgun facility, another toward the microwave farm. A small group of riders mounted up, ready for a charge. A large part of the troops remained in camp, preparing a second-wave assault.

"Come on, people!" Romero shouted. "If we don't use the catapult soon, we'll lose the most concentrated target."

"We're just about ready!" one of the old men snapped.

"We won't hit anything, so it doesn't really matter," someone else grumbled.

"Now, there's optimism!" an old woman scolded. "One more word like that and you'll be in the bucket for the first shot! Now give me that range finder!"

Finally, they cranked down the arm and cocked the weapon. It took three people to work the pulley and hoist the barrel of rusty scrap iron into the cradle. Fully loaded, the catapult seemed to vibrate with tension, ready to spring.

Romero took the trigger cord himself. In his mind flashed a ridiculous scene from a Road Runner cartoon, when Wile E. Coyote had used a similar catapult against the brainless bird—no matter where he stood, the seige machine somehow managed to dump its boulder on top of him.

Romero held his breath and yanked the wire.

The catapult smashed forward with the sound of an explosion, slamming against the front barricade and hurling its payload in an arc toward the encampment.

Oblivious below, Bayclock's assault team followed some sort of signal and trotted out on horseback, bringing rifles to bear. They rode toward the base installation where Bobby's balloon was tethered. The bastards were going to shoot down the balloon!

On the far side of the camp, the great mass of loose metal crashed into the ground, splattering outward. Through a spyglass, Romero could see that the catapult shot had taken out two small tents and a supply wagon, belching a cloud of dust and sand into the air. People scrambled around like stirred-up hornets.

"Good shot!" Romero cried. "Let's try to step up the ranging just a bit and hit them in the center of camp. We've got only a couple more shots. Once they figure out where we are, they'll come after us, and we'll have to abandon ship."

As the gang that couldn't shoot straight worked at cranking down the catapult again—this time with much more enthusiasm and cooperation—Romero heard a volley of sharp, distant rifle shots. The group of riders approached the observation balloon and fired repeatedly at the gondola, the balloon itself, and the tether cable. The tiny form of Bobby Carron ducked down to the protection of the flat aluminum gondola.

"Ready!" one of the old men shouted. "Look out, Mr. Romero!"

The catapult slammed forward again, sending another payload of iron pieces toward the scrambling expedition force, but this time the debris pummeled the desert a hundred feet short of camp.

Below, General Bayclock's soldiers began to figure out where the catapult shots were originating.

Bobby's balloon had obviously been hit by dozens of direct shots and began to drift wildly on its tether rope. The hand-sewn seams of the parachute material, never meant to take such stress, began to split apart. The colorful sack sagged as it deflated. After another round of rifle shots, one of the marksmen was either extremely skilled or extremely lucky. The tether rope snapped, and the balloon began to move.

The third catapult shot also missed. A group of Bayclock's soldiers pointed toward Romero's position and spread out into the foothills toward the location of the medieval weapon.

"Here they come. We've got to get to safety!" Romero shouted. "Time to retreat!"

As they fled into the tangled foothills, he looked down at the great basin to see Bobby Carron's balloon drifting free and falling toward the ground as the general's men each dropped to one knee and fired their rifles.

Spencer hunched over the tangled circuit board, breathing on it, fanning it with a sheaf of papers, and trying to use his own panic to speed the calculations. Some of the soldered connections had begun smoking, and the batteries were nearly drained. "Come on!" he muttered.

Heather stood behind him and rubbed his shoulders, but she said nothing. It had taken several hours longer than he had expected, and now morning light shone into the blockhouse. Bayclock's troops were already on the move.

He and Heather had needed to recompile half an hour's worth of work when Spencer discovered a sign error he had made with his pencil-and-paper calculations. The bandaged circuit board seemed to be struggling to hold on just long enough to complete the binary instructions before it overheated and dumped everything.

"It'll work," Heather whispered. "It will."

As if to spite her, the homemade circuit board showered sparks in a massive breakdown. Smoke billowed from a dozen different connections.

Spencer tried to think of a way to douse the fire, but it

made no difference. All the calculations were already lost into the ether. The cathode-ray tube displaying the trudging progress of the calculations went dark.

Spencer slumped in his chair and refused to scream. They had already uplinked the instructions to increase the transmitted microwave power by a factor of four; but without the targeting information, the extra radiation would fall uselessly on the microwave antenna farm again, not on Bayclock's new position. Spencer could never get the circuit board up and running again in less than two days.

Bayclock would have taken over the entire facility long before then.

His hopes for the satellites, the solar-power farm, and the future itself had just gone up in smoke.

SEVENTY-TWO

SWAN SONG

The hot-air balloon plummeted toward the rugged ground. Bobby Carron gripped the sides of the aluminum gondola and held on for his life.

Air gushed from rips in the colorful parachute sacks, holes torn open by rifle shots and split seams. Several of the bullets had made craterlike dents in the basket, and Bobby was lucky he hadn't been hit. That relief was only temporary, though, because he was going to crash any second.

The severed anchor rope dangled on the ground as the balloon drifted across the landscape, heading straight toward Bayclock's troops running to intercept him. A few more gunshots broke the air, and Bobby ducked. He saw another bullet punch into the deflating sack of the balloon, but he heard other shouts, people yelling at the riflemen to hold their fire.

The loose metal gondola lurched as the balloon tipped and continued falling. The hibachi full of glowing coals spilled over, dumping hot charcoal that skittered and smoked along the floor. One ember burned Bobby's leg;

he swatted at it, almost losing his grip. The smoking coals spilled over the side.

He ducked as the bottom of the gondola smashed into an outcropping of rock, knocking him hard into the side of the aluminum basket. He hit his head. Blood streamed down his cheek. He blinked to bring vision back into focus, ready to get up and sprint for safety.

The gondola struck the ground again, dragged along as the last remnants of hot air tugged the deflated balloon sack. The gondola tipped over, scooping up loose sand and dirt, until the balloon snagged on a thicket of scrub brush.

Bobby scrambled to keep his balance, but the gondola spilled him into a tangle of guide ropes, parachute fabric, and hot embers. The metal basket tumbled to a halt next to him.

Bobby coughed and tried to get to his knees. He sensed no spears of pain from broken bones, but his entire body throbbed. He clawed at the gondola ropes, trying to pull the parachute fabric away from his face.

As soon as he stood up and pulled himself free, blinking in the bright light, he saw two of Bayclock's horsemen pull up on either side of him. Three riflemen on foot came running after. Bobby looked around for a place to hide, to make a stand—but he had no weapons. He had no choice but to hold up his hands.

Puffing with exertion, Sergeant Caitlyn Morris ran up to him with a rifle in hand; she smiled smugly when she saw him. Two other soldiers pointed their rifles at Bobby. The horsemen stood on either side to make sure he couldn't escape.

Sergeant Morris's face was flushed and streaked with dust. Her short blond hair was tangled with sweat. "Welcome home, Lieutenant. General Bayclock will be very pleased to see you."

Under the morning sun, Connor Brooks drove the three horses and the wagon full of solar-power satellites toward the military settlement. He had watched Bayclock's troops from his small camp for the past two days, until at last he figured out why they were there. He decided that Bayclock must want the stolen smallsats very badly right around now, and he should be willing to pay.

Connor had not built a fire for fear that his camp would be spotted, but he slept comfortably, wrapped in Henrietta Soo's silvery reflective blankets. He had washed the blood from his hands and changed clothes. He ate well from the stolen supplies in the wagon bed.

But his injured face ached like a son of a bitch.

He could see only blurry red fuzz out of his left eye, and his torn cheek and forehead throbbed like a disco rhythm made with ice picks. He had managed to wash his injuries from the shotgun backfire in a stream, but he knew they might get infected, and he didn't relish the thought of the pain increasing. God, what he wouldn't do right now for a handful of aspirin! Extra-strength.

As he drove the horses toward the camp, a handful of armed guards came out to meet him. "Freeze, toadface!" one said, leveling his rifle. "Who are you?"

Connor raised a hand in a wave or a salute, or perhaps just a gesture to show that he was unarmed. He pulled the horses to a stop near the tents, sleeping bags, and supply stations.

"I need to see whoever's in charge," he said hoarsely. His words clawed through a larynx bruised when Butthead Uma tried to strangle him. He gestured back toward the wagon. "Tell him I've got something those solar-power people want very badly."

"Wait here," said the guard.

Connor stood with his hands above his head. The three horses nickered, sniffing other horses with Bayclock's troops. Connor wanted a cold drink, but the two guards watched his every move in sour silence. Even though he had come with a nice offer, they seemed to regard him as some kind of vermin caught in a rat trap. Typical, he thought.

Finally, flanked on either side by an armed escort, a

burly, tough-looking man stumped across the camp toward Connor. He had bristly dark hair and a gimme-no-shit expression.

"I'm General Bayclock," he said, "commander of these troops. What have you brought for me?" Unspoken but visible on his expression was a threat. *If you're wasting my time, I'll strip you naked and make you run through a cactus field.*

Connor tried to turn on the charm that had always served him so well, though he didn't know how much charm he had left with a mangled face and a bruised voice box. "Good to meet you, General," he said. "My name is Connor Brooks—"

"I don't give a damn who you are and I'm sure the hell not happy to meet you. Now, cut the bullshit—what do you want?"

"Uh, yes, sir." Connor wet his lips with a thick tongue and spoke fast. "I got my hands on a bunch of technical equipment on its way to the solar-power farm you have under siege. I thought it might be worth something to you." He raised his eyebrows, knowing he must look hideous with his scabbed and gashed face.

"What kind of high-tech equipment?" Bayclock said, suddenly interested but still challenging him. "Where did it come from?"

"Well, I have ten satellites back here in the wagon. They were made at the Jet Propulsion Lab and they were being brought cross-country to White Sands."

The general's dark eyes lit up. "Are you part of this Pasadena expedition?" He seemed ready to pounce.

"I, uh . . . acquired it from them," Connor said. "The expedition was trying to slip these satellites in past your troops. So I brought them here."

"Satellites? The JPL expedition just carried a bunch of satellites out here?" Bayclock looked at him, incredulous.

"That's all."

An officer standing next to Bayclock asked, "How many were there in the party?"

Connor shrugged. "Two, three maybe."

A murmur ran through his staff. Bayclock looked unconvinced—and pissed off. "Show me."

A minute later, Bayclock ran his hands over the nearest sealed canister. His officers poked around the devices, rapping on the metal cases. They all seemed astonished by the discovery.

Connor positioned himself next to the general. "I thought you might be willing to make a decent trade, sir. These are exceedingly valuable satellites, as I'm sure you know. Priceless, in fact. I'd like a few of your revamped weapons—say, six rifles—and some supplies." He touched the stinging injuries on his face. "And some minor medical attention. As you can see, getting these satellites wasn't all that easy."

Bayclock's expression was hard. He spoke in a low tone, but it looked like it took an effort to keep his voice under control. "I represent the United States of America, and we do not barter while under a declaration of hostilities. Under direct presidential order, I am authorized to simply take what I need. By delivering these satellites to me, you've done service to your country. You should feel proud about that."

Outrage boiled in Connor at the attitude of this butthead general. "That isn't exactly what I had in mind." His stomach knotted. "If that's your attitude, General, then I'll just take my satellites and go, thank you."

He stomped off to the wagon, hauling himself up on the buckboard. *Fucking asshole!* He yanked the reins to turn the three horses around. Connor was amazed at the speed with which five rifles were suddenly pointed at him. "What the hell is this?" he sputtered.

"This is martial law, Mr. Brooks," Bayclock said. "We'll see that you get medical attention, as you requested, and a position in the supply corps. We need every person we can get in our fight against the solar-power station."

Connor felt betrayed and appalled. Worse yet, he felt like an idiot.

A tall thin man came up to Bayclock, obviously a civilian, with wire-rimmed glasses, a weak chin, and a large Adam's apple.

Bayclock spoke bitterly, as if unhappy about the satellites. "Dr. Nedermyer, this man has brought us ten solar-power satellites from JPL. They are now in our possession, and we don't need to worry about Dr. Lockwood getting his hands on them."

Nedermyer came forward to peer over the side of the wagon. "I thought there was some kind of large expedition carrying them."

"This is it," said Bayclock. "And that's all they carried. I want you to draft up a notice to be sent by courier to Lockwood and his little rebels. Tell them that unless they surrender immediately, starting tomorrow morning we will take one of these satellites and smash it to pieces in their full view. We'll destroy one every two hours until they surrender. If this technology means so much to them, let's just see how much of it they'll let go to waste."

Nedermyer looked incredulous. "But General, you can't do that! These satellites can't be replaced. We don't have the facilities to fabricate any more. These are precious items—and if you destroy them, you defeat the entire purpose of our expedition!"

Bayclock's face turned the color of clotted blood, and he turned slowly toward Nedermyer. "The purpose of this expedition, Doctor, is to quash an insurrection. These satellites are toys, conveniences. We can survive without them. We *cannot* survive without order and a rule by law. If a few metal containers must be dented to accomplish that, then so be it."

The butthead general turned back to Connor and pointed for him to get back down off the wagon. Two of the guards took hold of the horses. "Sergeant, take the wagon and animals to the logistics group. You, Brooks, will help the supply personnel for tomorrow's assault. You've just joined the army."

His hands tied behind him with rough rope, Bobby Carron stumbled across the uneven desert. Two horsemen rode on either side, two walking guards behind him and one in front. He had to push himself to keep the pace set by Sergeant Morris.

He tried to remember the time he had spent in survival training, escaping from a mock prisoner-of-war camp. The training had been held in a jungle, and it wasn't meant to be used against his own military. Before they had come within a half of a mile of Bayclock's camp, Bobby realized he was completely out of ideas to escape. He had nothing up his sleeve, no tricks to pull. He saw no way out.

And Bayclock considered him a traitor. But even under combat conditions, Bobby knew the general wouldn't put a service pistol to Bobby's head and pull the trigger himself, without the drawn-out niceties of a court-martial. Bobby was sure he wouldn't. . . .

Bobby was satisfied with how much he had helped Dr. Lockwood and the others at the solar-power farm. He recalled his days as a navy fighter pilot stationed at China Lake. He remembered that last cross-country flight with Barfman Petronfi. Just trying to reach a nice, long R&R in Corpus Cristi, where they would sit on the beach, eating shrimp and looking at bikinis. . . .

The outskirts of the military camp were a bustling confusion of campfires, tents staked out against the day's heat and the night's chill, supply wagons next to unloaded crates. Refurbished rifles stood racked and stacked where soldiers could grab them in a moment's notice.

The troops watched the prisoner arrive. Bobby looked around, trying to make eye contact, trying to recognize anyone from Kirtland Air Force Base—but that wouldn't help. He really only knew Sergeant Caitlyn Morris, and she gave him nothing but scorn.

Sergeant Morris led them directly to the general's command tent. Someone must have warned Bayclock, because the general stepped outside to watch them approach. He recognized Bobby immediately.

Bayclock's face was frigid, and his eyes held a firestorm of anger. "Well, if it isn't our turncoat lieutenant." He nodded to Morris. "Good work, Sergeant."

"He was manning their balloon, sir," she said. "We shot it down and took him prisoner."

"The balloon?" Bayclock said, raising his eyebrows. "Of course, that's a good job for a fighter pilot, isn't it?"

Bobby said nothing.

"You're still on active duty, Lieutenant—or have you forgotten the code of military conduct?"

Bobby maintained his silence, watching the general play the waiting game. No one spoke, but Bobby could feel the tension rising, the general becoming impatient.

Bayclock said, "But then you're no longer a *real* fighter pilot. A traitor and a deserter is not the type of man any flyer would want on his wing. No wonder your aircraft crashed, Lieutenant. Is that why your wingman died— did he crash while you were trying to save your own butt?"

Bobby clenched his jaw, aching to retort, but he kept quiet.

Bayclock startled Bobby by stepping forward and slapping him across the face. "You're not fit to be a pilot, much less an officer."

Bobby's eyes blazed. He remembered Bayclock's office, all the diplomas and lithographs of aircraft. He knew he had found exactly the right button to push.

"You're still fighting the last war, General. The system has changed," he said in a low voice. "Before the plague hit I was flying fighters for my country—while you were flying a *desk*."

Bayclock looked ready to explode, but somehow he contained himself. His hands clenched, as if trying to grasp a cutting reply, but he turned and glared at the other soldiers. "Bind the prisoner and send a general notice to all troops. This traitor and deserter will be executed at dawn. We'll hang him from a utility pole."

Connor sulked. The camp medic had dabbed stinging antiseptic on his facial wounds and bandaged them up, but the medic couldn't say whether Connor would lose his eye. His sight would be permanently damaged for certain.

They fed him a meager meal of crappy food. He would have been better off eating his own supplies, but that butthead Bayclock had callously commandeered Connor's stuff for his own people. *That's my food,* Connor thought. *I came into camp with open hands offering a deal—and they ripped me off!*

But then, why was he surprised? Connor had gotten the short end of the stick all his life. Sometimes he wondered if he had a sign painted on his back that said SCREW ME—I DON'T MIND.

He sat cross-legged on the hard ground, looking at the air force robots wandering around doing busywork. His face burned, his new clothes were uncomfortable. And he had lost everything!

Oilstar had jerked him around. On the supertanker, Captain Uma had done the same. Connor remembered the crummy old station wagon he had borrowed at the gas station in Southern California; even that Stanford preppy moron who had paid him to drive a broken-down AMC Gremlin to Atlanta; or the two Mormon bitches with their year's worth of supplies refusing to give Connor and Heather a few measly scraps.

He seethed, digging his fingers into the dirt. The whole world was out to get him, and none of it was his fault. How about Heather herself souring on him, refusing to put out anymore after only a few weeks? Some relationship that had turned out to be.

Even the damn shotgun had blown up in his face!

Now, after all that bullshit, when he finally deserved some kind of reward, when he finally took the solar-power satellites and delivered them to the army, did he get any thanks? No. Did he get any reward? No! That butthead general wouldn't even give Connor a rifle.

To make things worse, Bayclock had taken all of his supplies, the wagon, the horses—and held him prisoner in camp.

Connor found a rock, gripped it, and threw it as hard as he could. A short distance away, it struck the shoulder of an airman digging a new latrine. The airman turned and shouted in anger, but he couldn't see who had thrown the rock.

Any other time Connor would have snickered at the joke, but now he hauled himself to his feet. He wasn't going to take this crap anymore!

He strode across the camp, fixing the gaze of his good eye on the command tent. Inside the open flaps Connor could see the bearlike general sitting across a small folding table from Sergeant Morris and two colonels, debriefing her. An airman stood in front of the tent, but Connor brushed the guard aside.

"General, I'm leaving," Connor announced.

"What did you say?" Bayclock rose to his feet.

"You can't hold me, General. I came here of my own free will to offer you a deal—which you refused. I'm a United States citizen, and you can't hold me prisoner. I'm going to take my horses and my wagon and my satellites and I'll be on my way."

Connor turned before the general could say anything, glancing quickly at where his wagon had been impounded. He took one step before Bayclock said in a loud growling tone, "Sergeant Morris, I've had enough of this. Take Mr. Brooks into custody. If he resists, shoot him as a deserter."

Connor whirled. His face burned with livid anger; he felt the scab from his slashed cheek break open. "Deserter! I'm not part of your damned army! You're not my commanding officer."

Bayclock gripped the tent flap as if he wanted to rip it

to shreds. "You have been *conscripted,* Brooks. This is martial law, and we don't have time to quibble in a war zone. That is all. Sergeant Morris!"

"Yes, sir."

"Guard him. Don't let him out of your sight. This insubordination makes me want to puke. And if it doesn't stop, there's going to be a bloodbath." He fixed his gaze on Connor. "And we'll start with him."

Late that night, after feigning sleep for forty-five minutes, Connor Brooks opened his one good eye.

The camp was dark and still, with outlying campfires glowing behind dirt berms; extra guards stood on alert because of the previous night's attack by Lockwood's people. Connor didn't move, but kept staring, taking in details. He could feel the ropes against his arms, his legs.

Near him, beside the fire, Sergeant Morris lay curled on top of her blanket. She even slept in an uncomfortable position that gave the impression of readiness, as if she would snap awake and leap into action at a moment's notice. She still wore her uniform—not that he expected the thick-lipped blonde to slip into a sexy nightie!

The sergeant had stuck to him like a leech the whole afternoon. She even stood outside the latrine door when he had to take a crap! She seemed to be on full-time PMS, and Connor was amazed at how fast he began to hate her.

But finally the sergeant slept, as did most of the people around the camp. She had led him away from the main troops, as if afraid Connor might contaminate them. The following morning they planned to take over the EM launcher facility, and they needed their rest.

Connor flexed his arms, minutely loosening the rope that bound his arms and legs. He relaxed his body as much as he could, and was surprised at the play in the rope.

Lucky the bitch tied me up, he thought. She could have gotten one of the security police to help, someone who

knew what he was doing. Connor had drawn in a full
chestful of air and tried to keep his muscles as tight as he
could when she used the rope. Now he had plenty of
slack, and time to escape.

It took longer than he expected, and impatience made
him wrestle unproductively until he scraped his wrists
raw. Finally, the rope popped off the ball of his thumb.

Connor slowly sat up, an inch at a time to keep from
making noise. The campfire crackled and popped. Sergeant Morris stirred but remained asleep. The guards
watching the perimeter of the camp moved out of sight.

Connor untied his feet and rose up. His knees cracked.
He froze, but nobody moved. The orange campfire
flickered, but the light was too dim to illuminate him.

He took a step toward the fire. His boot crunched on
the ground. Sergeant Morris stirred again, but did not
wake up. If he couldn't slip away before she sounded the
alarm, then the general would have Connor's balls on a
grappling hook for sure!

He took another step, focusing on the metal tire iron
lying in the ashes to stir the logs. He took a third step
toward it. Bending down, he wrapped his fingers around
the heavy metal rod.

When he lifted the iron up, the smoldering wood in
the fire shifted, sending sparks into the air. Connor
froze, but he had gotten this far. Maybe something
would go his way—for once!

He tiptoed toward the sleeping form of Sergeant
Morris, one step at a time, approaching her as cautiously
as he could. The tire iron felt warm in his hand with the
opposite end glowing a dull red. He stood over her and
smiled.

Connor raised the metal rod over his head. God, she
looked ugly with her fat lips, chubby face, and mussed
blond hair!

Her eyes flickered open—and she saw him.

Connor brought the hot tire iron down with all his
strength.

The iron smashed into her skull with a muffled thump;

the sound seemed incredibly loud in the night. The red-hot metal sizzled in her face.

A log in the campfire slumped over again. He heard a few people talking quietly in another part of the camp.

She bled into the ground. Her body twitched, but he had smashed down on her eye—dead center—and she wasn't going to be spying on anybody else. Stupid bitch!

If she had just left him alone—if Bayclock hadn't assigned her as his bodyguard—Connor could have just taken his own possessions and gone quietly on his way. But, no, they couldn't make it that simple. So Bayclock and the sergeant had to deal with the consequences of what they had done. Connor felt no remorse whatsoever. How could he feel anything but scorn for military robots following the orders of a butthead?

He crept over to the wagon. The horses had been unhitched, though they stood nearby. The satellites were still there, but Connor didn't think he could take the wagon and still escape with his skin. After all, he had just killed one of Bayclock's sergeants. If he didn't get away—and get away *quick*—he wouldn't live to see another morning.

He reached into the wagon bed and quietly rummaged around. He found Heather's aluminum-framed backpack with the stupid neon-pink fabric—real camouflage! Still, it was large enough to carry what supplies he needed. He stuffed the pack with food, a canteen, and one of Henrietta Soo's metal-reflective blankets that had worked so well keeping the blistering desert heat away.

Mounting the backpack on his shoulders, he ducked low and made his way out of the camp. He crept quietly around the sleeping forms and out into the desert.

He intended to be far away by morning.

Well past midnight, Lieutenant Bobby Carron awoke with a start to the gentle touch of a knife.

Tense, Bobby lay absolutely still as the blade moved down to the ropes binding his wrists, then started to saw through them.

From the deep darkness and the constellations overhead, Bobby could tell that it was probably only an hour or two before dawn. The moon had already set, and the bone-biting chill of the desert night had settled into his joints.

"I know you're awake," a man whispered behind him. "I've got to get you out of here. The general's crazy, and you're the only one with nothing to lose right now."

Bobby opened his eyes. *The general's crazy? Thanks for telling me something new!* He felt a burning curiosity to know who the stranger was, but couldn't see. The ropes at his wrist finally fell away, and he brought his arms around, flexing them to get the blood circulating again.

His rescuer began to work on the bonds at his ankles, and Bobby looked down, astonished to see the gangly form of Lance Nedermyer. Nedermyer looked up at him, his mouth set. His gaunt face seemed swelled with fear, and his eyeglasses glinted in the starlight.

"Take the wagon, get the satellites away from here. Bayclock is going to destroy them tomorrow to call Lockwood's bluff."

Satellites? Bobby thought. Could these be the ones that were coming from the Jet Propulsion Lab? How did they get into the general's camp? "What do you want me to do with them?" Bobby said in a low whisper.

"Hide them. Keep them safe. Even take them to Lockwood if you have to. But I'd rather have you steal them than let the general smash the only ones left."

Bobby rubbed his ankles, trying to massage the soreness out. "I tried to tell you about the general when you left White Sands. Now do you know why I chose to stay down here?"

"Yes," Nedermyer said in a harsh bitter voice. "But I suppose it isn't the first mistake I've made in my life." He helped Bobby get to his feet.

"I've secured the horses to the wagon. There's no way you can sneak past the perimeter. What you'll need to do is just drive the horses like a bat out of hell and keep going into the night. The guards will shoot at you. Bayclock will send out search parties, but you have to get away."

"You're telling me!" Bobby said.

When they reached the wagon, Bobby saw that the campfires had burned low. All three horses had been hitched to the wagon; they stood stamping and restless, as if they could feel the excitement.

"Your best bet is to charge south for about a mile, then veer due east. The terrain is flat and hard, and you won't really need to watch where you're going in the darkness. You just need to gain distance. When you veer east, you'll head into the mountains. You can hide there. It'll be daylight in another hour, and then it'll be up to you."

Bobby gripped the thin man's shoulder. "Thanks, Dr. Nedermyer. I've got to admit you surprised me."

Nedermyer took two steps backward, as if uncomfortable with the compliment. "I'm doing it to keep the satellites safe. Our civilization has fallen far enough. I can't let Bayclock intentionally destroy what hope we have left."

"I'll hide the satellites . . . or die trying."

"I hope you don't have to," Nedermyer said, then waved him off.

Bobby smacked the reins and shouted. The three horses burst into motion, lurching forward in a full gallop. Rearing against the harness, the three mounts gained speed rapidly; the wagon and its cargo rolled across the flat hardpan of the desert. Within moments they flew beyond the perimeter of the military encampment.

Behind him Bobby heard sudden shouting and alarms being raised. He heard other horses, but none of them came toward him.

Within minutes gunshots sounded in the night. He ducked low on the buckboard. Only once did he hear a bullet whiz past him; all the other shots went completely wild. He drove the horse team by cracking the reins again and again, and they ran in blind, hot panic through the flat darkness. Bobby prayed they wouldn't stumble across a sudden ravine or arroyo.

After about ten minutes of hard riding, Bobby pulled the reins to turn the horses eastward. Against the blotted backdrop of stars, he could see the craggy silhouettes of the mountains. The terrain would get more rugged, and he would have to slow down.

He knew the wagon wheels left a painfully clear trail across the gypsum sands, but Bayclock's trackers wouldn't be able to see them before the morning light. If Bobby could ride into the hills by then, he could perhaps find a place to hide.

Across the clear silence of the night, he still heard gunshots, the turmoil back at the encampment. He had gotten away for now, but remaining free would require all his wits.

By morning Bobby had driven the wagon into the foothills. He made slow progress at first, forced to get down from the wagon and lead the horses along the winding, hilly path. More than anything, he wanted to get back to Spencer's enclave by the solar-power farm, but he knew he couldn't get past Bayclock's seige. Certainly, he could not take the bulky wagon with three horses up to Spencer's command center. He would have to hide the satellites in a safe place, hoping to retrieve them when, or if, the scientists ever managed to defeat the general.

By the time full sunlight penetrated the hills, Bobby found a steep arroyo. Its jagged corners were clogged with piñon, scrub oak, and mesquite. The dense branches and sparse gray-green leaves provided good cover, and Bobby tied the horses while he tried to camouflage the wagon.

He covered it with branches, masking the wagon from sight unless someone stumbled directly on it. As he worked, he thought that this was something Rita Fellenstein would enjoy, playing some sort of mind game with the general. He smiled as he thought of her—

she certainly wasn't the prettiest woman he'd known, but she was the most interesting, and the only one he knew who wouldn't take any baloney from him.

As he finished, Bobby knew he had to get back in touch with Spencer. If he got killed before he reached the microwave farm, then no one would ever know where the satellites were—and Bayclock might as well have destroyed them. The smallsats might become a sought-after treasure like the Lost Dutchman Mine.

But Bobby would do his best to keep that from happening.

Bobby packed some supplies and ate a quick breakfast. He picked the strongest-looking horse and mounted up, turning the other two loose to run wild.

Bobby rode down out of the hills in hopes of finding a good route to the solar-power installation. He would try to make his way there after dark.

The time passed quickly as he tried not to follow the way he had come. The White Sands valley stretched out below him as his horse picked its way down. Who would have ever thought that only months before he had been a carefree naval aviator—

A gunshot rang out, a loud crack that echoed around the hills. The horse neighed, startled, and trotted ahead, rolling its head from side to side. Bobby looked around to try and find the source of the gunfire. Another shot rang out, closer this time, and he spotted four riders emerging from the hills, all of them wearing air force uniforms.

Bayclock's men. Another rider charged out in front of him.

Bobby shouted and urged the horse into a full gallop. He hurtled out of the hills, desperately seeking a place to hide, as the other riders launched into pursuit.

He hunched low over the horse's neck, the mane whipping in the wind, stinging his face. Hooves thundered as Bobby's horse leaped over a cluster of rocks and kept charging downhill.

Behind him, the riders split up to intercept him. They

shot again, and Bobby knew they had no interest in capturing him alive this time. At least he had fled far enough that the satellites were safe—but these riders must have tracked the wagon trail. How many men had Bayclock sent out after him?

The gunshots came in faster succession now. The riders tightened the distance. Another volley of shots—the loudest so far—rang out in a sudden echo like firecrackers.

The horse whinnied and reared as Bobby saw a sudden scarlet blotch appear on its ribcage four inches in front of his own thigh. The horse stumbled, falling over and throwing Bobby.

He tried to hold on, but then rolled free as the horse thrashed on the ground to get to its feet again. The horse was bleeding heavily from the large gunshot wound close to its heart. It stamped up and down, then staggered back, limping.

Bobby stood gingerly. His leg was sore, but nothing was broken, nothing sprained. He looked around for some rocks to hide in, anything for shelter.

Then the hoofbeats of other horses pounded down on him from all sides. Four riders came up, each with rifle drawn.

Bobby stood slowly with his back against a wall of sandstone, and raised his hands in surrender.

By late morning, Bobby Carron found himself Bayclock's prisoner once more. They tied him helplessly on the back of a horse, then rode off toward the foothills on the opposite side of the valley. The encampment had already moved, and from his rocking position on horseback, Bobby was dismayed to see that the general's army had succeeded in taking over the damaged railgun facility in only a few hours.

The troops had marched up to the control buildings at the bottom of the miles-long electromagnetic launcher. From what he could tell, the scientists had not put up much of a fight.

Bobby stumbled when his captors hauled him off the horse and dragged him to his feet. Smears of soot blackened the launcher control building. He tried to see other people he recognized. He hoped the scientists had gotten away.

General Bayclock strode out of the burned-out control building. His eyes were bloodshot and he looked at Bobby with disgust. "This time I'm taking no chances. Lead the prisoner to the telephone pole. Right now."

One of the guards shoved him down a path toward an old creosote-covered utility pole that had once carried electricity to the launcher facility. Spencer's people had already removed the wires from the pole—but Bayclock had another purpose in mind.

"I knew you were a traitor, Lieutenant, but I didn't believe you would team up with a slimeball like Connor Brooks to steal the satellites. We'll find him, soon. Which one of you murdered Sergeant Morris, or did you take turns bashing her head in?"

Bobby stared at him. *Sergeant Morris, dead?* He said numbly, "What are you talking about?"

"Don't insult me," said Bayclock. "I think we'll go the high road with you." The general looked up to the wooden crossbars on the electrical pole. "We'll hoist you up so we don't have to cut down Dr. Nedermyer."

Bobby wavered as the guards pushed him forward. He saw the blue-black clenched face of Lance Nedermyer. Bayclock's men had thrown a loop of rope around his neck like a garrote, inserted a short stick, and then twisted it to draw the rope tighter and tighter until it crushed Lance's larynx and severed his trachea. Bobby saw scuff marks in the sand and fresh gouges from the bottom of the utility pole where Lance had kicked and struggled. His body had already begun to bloat in the bright morning heat.

"I have no patience left for traitors," Bayclock said. "It's about time my people realized that."

SEVENTY-THREE

ALONE AGAIN

Standing on the south balcony of the White House, President Jeffrey Mayeaux watched his military troops patrol the Mall. The National Guard had forcibly removed angry crowds from the Ellipse. Even the cherry trees along the Tidal Basin had been cut down and stored as firewood for the winter.

He crumpled the handwritten communiqué in his hand and let it fall to the floor.

The commander of the San Diego naval base had been assassinated while trying to stop a rally against the military crackdowns. The crowds had gone wild, killing the admiral and at least fifty naval officers around the city. A self-appointed ruling council had seized control of the shipyards and the base facilities. According to the report, the other navy personnel on duty had surrendered willingly.

What the hell was he supposed to do about that?

"I want a meeting with my Joint Chiefs in five minutes!" he said without turning. He heard one of the

Secret Service men leave the room. He wished Franklin Weathersee would get back from his expedition.

Everybody blamed Mayeaux for their problems, and nobody listened when he issued orders to take care of anything. For God's sake, *he* hadn't caused the petroplague!

He hadn't heard a word from the old bitch Emma Branson at Oilstar for more than a month, and he was glad—she could fend for herself out in California. He had heard one report that mobs had burned down the Oilstar refinery, but he didn't know if he could believe it. Probably.

Around the country the citizens had begun to throw up their own defenses and forget the big picture. Mayeaux was in charge of what he had started to think of as the "Humpty Dumpty Squad"—no matter how many long hours he put in or nights he spent without sleep, he still could not put the pieces together again. But if the population thought their president was just going to pick his nose while the world went down the toilet, they were in for a hell of a surprise. He hated not knowing what to do, what would work, what would snap the mobs out of their pigs-fighting-over-a-corncob anarchy. People just didn't make sense.

Mayeaux had the chance to pull off the biggest change in history and set the tone of the country—hell, the world!—for the next century.

The U.S. could get back on its feet, according to the advances projected by NIST scientists—petroplague-resistant plastics, the change to a hydrogen-based energy economy . . . if people could resist turning into post-holocaust barbarians.

But they wouldn't listen to reason. *United we stand, divided we fall*—dammit, every kid in the country had that slogan hammered into him from grade school on.

Mayeaux followed the Secret Service men down to the Situation Room. Only the military officers stood for him when he entered, a sign of disrespect like a slap in the face. No one greeted him, no optimistic "Good morn-

ing, sir!" from the staffers. Where the hell was the rest of
his cabinet? He hadn't even seen the Vice President in a
month.

Two military officers sat at the table—General Wacon,
chairman of the Joint Chiefs, and the CNO, the Chief of
Naval Operations. Both men looked grim. Mayeaux
didn't recognize any of the White House staffers wearing
blue WHS pins as substitutes for laminated badges.

"Have you forgotten how to stand when your commander in chief enters the room, gentlemen?" he said.
This was worse than he had thought.

Grudgingly, the two remaining staffers struggled to
their feet. Mayeaux pulled up his chair and dispensed
with niceties. "I called a meeting in five minutes! Where
is everybody else?"

"They won't be joining us," General Wacon said.

"Why the hell not? This isn't a RSVP party invita-
tion."

The general ignored the question. "How can we help
you this morning, Mr. President?"

Mayeaux scowled and got right to the point. "I trust
you've been briefed about the San Diego incident?"

"Yes, Mr. President," the CNO said, clearing his
throat. "To make things worse, we've also just learned
that the San Diego ruling council has commandeered the
installation's radio network. They are broadcasting their
'victory' over the entire Atlantis Network, actively trying
to incite other similar uprisings."

"As if we didn't have enough trouble already! How
do you intend to deal with it, gentlemen?"

Wacon drummed his fingers on the table. He spoke
smoothly, using years of experience honed by testifying
before congressional committees. "We've made the decision that it is prudent not to antagonize the public, not
to take unnecessary risks. There may be some options
that the military can use, but our primary mission is to
defend our national security."

Mayeaux pressed his fingers together. "So, you made
that decision yourselves? Thank you very much, Gener-

al. It's nice to know I don't need to bother running the country anymore. You thought it 'prudent' just to let cities overthrow their military bases, assassinate commanders, and secede from the United States at will?"

The general stiffened. "There are certain degrees of response we may consider, Mr. President. The army still has access to point weapons—grenades, bullets, bazookas, all of which work effectively only if coordinated by the chain of command. Since our communication is sporadic, and the troops do not have the necessary logistical or transportation support, such weapons cannot be utilized effectively to suppress large mob-type disturbances. The military might prevail initially, but they would quickly be overrun, as in San Diego."

Mayeaux tapped on the table. The general had told no lies, but he had not told the whole story, either. "I find that hard to believe, General. Are you insisting that this plague has eliminated the military's ability to respond decisively if a city openly defies a direct presidential order?"

"I wouldn't say that, exactly, sir—"

Mayeaux broke in. "I've been informed that we still have ten Trident-class nuclear submarines on underwater quarantine and as yet unaffected by the plague. Wouldn't you say that sub-launched missiles are a bit more substantial than a few 'point weapons'?"

The Chiefs exchanged glances. The temperature in the Situation Room seemed to plunge.

A Secret Service man barged into the room. His arrival startled the other guards enough that one placed himself in front of the intruder.

"Mr. President!" the newcomer said. He panted, then stopped as he drew several deep breaths to calm himself. Mayeaux recognized him as one of the agents who had hauled him out of bed in his Ocean City condo to tell him of President Holback's death.

"Yes, what is it?" Mayeaux snapped.

The Secret Service man drew in another lungful. "Sir, it's Mr. Weathersee. Your . . . your chief of staff has been killed, sir. We were ambushed on our food-requisitioning run. A large group of civilians swarmed over our wagons. Someone threw a grenade at the convoy. I believe they simply intended to appropriate the food, but they killed everyone they captured."

A roar of pounding blood filled Mayeaux's head. Weathersee! "Are you certain it was him?"

"I was with him. Mr. Weathersee was assassinated, sir." He squirmed. "Uh, there is no doubt in my mind that he is dead."

Mayeaux gripped the table. Franklin Weathersee had been his legislative assistant since Mayeaux had taken his first political office, accompanying him for years as a silent companion as his career climbed. What was he going to do without the man's dispassionate competence, especially in such a terrible crisis?

"How?" Mayeaux said, sounding like a croaking toad. "How was he killed?"

"Uh, he was . . ." The Secret Service man swallowed and stood stiffly, staring at the far wall. "He was decapitated, sir."

Mayeaux's vision seemed to grow warm and black, fuzzed at the edges. What was he going to do without Weathersee? He took a long, shuddering breath and forced himself to focus on the people gathered in the Situation Room.

"You have my sympathy, Mr. President," General Wacon said.

"I don't give a damn about your sympathy," Mayeaux said. He took a long slow breath and spoke each word like a heavy footfall down a long staircase. "I believe you were about to answer my question about the availability of nuclear-tipped missiles on Trident submarines."

The chairman's face fell slack. "Mr. President, you can't consider launching a nuclear missile against *American* targets. Even at the height of the Cold War, using these against the Soviet Union was considered only a last resort for survival—"

"Just what the living hell do you think this is?"

Mayeaux shouted. He struck his palm on the table, scattering two pencils beside his coffee cup. "By your own admission, the military cannot function. The greatest nation on Earth is decaying into pockets of barbarism, even here in our capital city! *Just when do you draw the line and say that things have gone far enough!"*

Mayeaux breathed hard as he looked around the room. He was surprised to feel tears on the verge of spilling from his eyes. No one spoke. The Joint Chiefs returned his icy stare; two of his cabinet members looked down, shaking their heads.

Mayeaux took another deep breath, but his pulse kept pounding like a drumbeat in his head. "The United States must be willing to cauterize a wound to keep this nation from bleeding to death. We *cannot* tolerate this situation any longer. Look what's happening in our own neighborhood."

The general tried to calm him. "Mr. President, maybe you should reconsider the options, wait until you have calmed down from this shocking news. Within a few days we can prepare an extensive list ranging from a light to intermediate response against San Diego—"

Mayeaux's Louisiana drawl got worse as his anger rose and he lost control. "*Mais*—let me tell you somethin'! The people must be utterly convinced that the President is still in charge! Abraham Lincoln did it, and so can I. Lincoln suspended the writ of habeas corpus, jailed political leaders and newspaper editors in Baltimore to prevent Maryland from seceding from the union."

Wacon sat rigid, masking his emotions. Beside him, the CNO's eyes widened when Mayeaux turned his attention to him. "Admiral, I want you to give me a list of the surviving Trident II submarines within range of San Diego."

The admiral threw a glance at the chairman; General Wacon nodded stiffly. Mayeaux scowled. Who the hell was in charge here, anyway?

The admiral avoided Mayeaux's eyes by glancing at a

sheet of paper. He cleared his throat. "Of the subs still in contact, two are in position to strike targets on the west coast of the United States." He fiddled with his paper, as if it was very important for him to file it away at that moment. "However, Mr. President, I cannot assure you that the crews of either vessel will carry out war orders that require them to retarget missiles against their own country—"

"Thank you, Admiral," said Mayeaux icily. "I'm sure the captains of those vessels remember who their commander is, even if my Joint Chiefs do not."

He felt giddy, detached, as if he had just been swept up by a giant invisible hand. Within days of the first strike—one decisive strike—word would spread like wildfire over the available channels of communication. The rebellious cities would be shocked, then afraid, then repentant. Time for everyone to work together, not break apart. History would hail Jeffrey Mayeaux as a savior, the architect of the future United States.

Mayeaux leaned back in his seat and tapped his fingers together. "Very well, Admiral. I've made my decision. I want you to transmit the order that one nuclear missile be launched at the heart of downtown San Diego."

The chairman and admiral exchanged glances. General Wacon's face looked blotchy with submerged fury.

Mayeaux turned to the chairman. "General Wacon, work with the NSA to broadcast in the widest possible manner that unless the nationwide rioting stops and all of the new city-states rescind their claims of independence, one city after another will be obliterated in a similar fashion. The leaders advocating secession must resign their posts and surrender."

No one spoke. Mayeaux looked from person to person. Each member of his staff looked away, not meeting his glance.

He drew in a breath. "Well? What are you waiting for?"

The military officers sat erect, hands on the table.

Mayeaux felt his face grow warm. "Admiral, I gave you a direct order. The navy will fulfill its legal obligations under my authority as commander in chief. Do I have to repeat it? Is something not clear?"

The CNO spoke slowly. "No, Mr. President. I understand completely." Still, he made no move.

Mayeaux felt his heart rate quicken. A flush of adrenaline flooded his system, now that he had finally made his decision. "General Wacon—do I have to remind you, too? I am your commander in chief."

The general pushed back his chair with a sudden motion. His silver hair contrasted with the dark blue of his worn air force uniform; his eyes looked glazed as he glared straight at Mayeaux and spoke in a level tone. "My allegiance is to the Constitution of the United States of America, sir, and to obey the legal orders of those appointed over me. I'm sorry, but I respectfully refuse to obey your illegal order. You cannot use nuclear force against our own citizens."

Mayeaux leaped to his feet, his eyes wide, his breath coming in short gasps. "General Wacon—you are relieved!"

The chairman picked up his papers and walked away. Without a word, the admiral also stood up and followed him to the door. Mayeaux's voice sounded shrill in his own ears. "History will brand you a coward, General! Both of you!"

Wacon was halfway out the door when he turned and pointed an angry finger at Mayeaux. "Nuremberg set the stage, Mr. President—ask any American military officer since Lieutenant Calley. We're responsible for our actions, and we have to pay the price. And as far as I'm concerned, using nuclear missiles to make an example of American cities is bullshit." He hesitated, then added "Sir!" before whirling to leave. The admiral followed him.

Two other members of the president's staff got up and walked out the door. "Sorry, sir," one of them muttered.

Mayeaux shook; he felt his teeth grinding together as his jaw worked tightly. Where was Weathersee, dammit?

"Come back here!" he shouted. "I'm still the president!"

One by one, the President's staff exited the Situation Room, their heads down, muttering as they left, and not meeting his glare. They didn't have to impeach him. They had stripped him of power in a much simpler way.

"Weathersee! Where are you!"

In a moment, Jeffrey Mayeaux stood alone—the most powerful man in the world, in the most important room . . . with no one around to hear him rage.

SEVENTY-FOUR

THE STAND

A white flag of surrender dangled from a broomstick as Spencer Lockwood and Heather Dixon approached the burned-out control building for the electromagnetic launcher.

Early that morning, Bayclock's main forces had occupied the place, taking prisoner the few scientists and technicians who had remained after the railgun explosion, including a seriously injured Gilbert Hertoya. Holding the EM launcher and the scientists hostage, Bayclock had sent a courier demanding Spencer's immediate surrender of the entire antenna-farm facility.

Spencer felt he had no choice. If only he had succeeded in getting the increased satellite power directed at the general's troops! He had tried everything possible, but he could not get the orbiting Seven Dwarfs to respond, and the makeshift circuit board would not be worth anything for quite some time. Instead, the smallsats would pass overhead in just a short while, unaffected, beaming their increased solar power down onto the field of microwave antennas, oblivious to the conflict below.

Spencer idolized fictional scientists, geniuses like the professor on "Gilligan's Island" who could kludge together a solution to the wildest problem with the skimpiest resources—*and it would always work!* But despite Spencer's expertise and the help of his team, his desperate measures fizzled as often as not: the transformer at the water-pumping station, Gilbert's railgun defense system, and Spencer's attempt to reprogram the smallsats.

Bayclock held all the good cards right now. He had demanded surrender, and so Spencer had rigged up the white flag.

Back at the solar-power farm, Heather Dixon had astonished him by asking to accompany him on the journey.

"What for?" Spencer blurted.

"Because I want to." She fidgeted and then flashed him a smile. "Besides, the general is less likely to shoot at a man and a woman coming to meet him, than just a lone rider."

He stared at her; then she smiled at him. Actually, Spencer didn't think Bayclock would kill anyone coming in under a white flag, since the general seemed so anal retentive about law and order. Bayclock lived by a clearly defined code of honor—*and that might be his weakness,* Spencer thought, *because it lets us predict what he will and won't do.*

Now, as they rode toward the launcher facility, dangling the surrender flag in front of them, both he and Heather stared straight ahead. The long rails extended up the side of Oscura Peak, flanked by debris, rocks, and underbrush. Plenty of good places to hide.

Spencer seethed at seeing the troops occupying the ruined facility—how many prisoners had Bayclock taken? Given his code of honor, the general wouldn't abuse Hertoya or the other captives, but he seemed to have no compunction against destroying irreplaceable technical apparatus. A true barbarian.

In the rugged foothills by the base of the launcher, Bayclock's scouts saw the two of them approaching and rode out. Spencer swallowed. "You ready for this?"

Heather reached over and squeezed his arm. Together, they waved the white flag.

The scouts rode up on either side of them. Spencer halted his horse as the air force men looked them over, guns leveled. "Are you unarmed?" one of the scouts asked.

"Yes," Spencer said. The two men nodded. Somehow, he had known they wouldn't bother to check. Bayclock, with his sense of military honor, would automatically expect everyone else to play by the same rules. He would be bound to accept Spencer's surrender and offer terms.

But Spencer's mind didn't work the same way. He preferred the model of one of his other heroes, Captain James T. Kirk: promise the world, stall for time, and keep working to find a way to win. And that was exactly what he planned to do now. He just hoped this would work.

"Take me to your leader," he said to the guards.

His hands bound behind him, Lieutenant Bobby Carron stood facing Bayclock's wrath.

One of the airmen threw a rope over the crossbeam and dropped the rope down, letting the noose dangle at the height of Bobby's shoulders. They would slip the noose over his neck, tighten it, and yank him into the air. No quick snapping of the neck for Bobby—he would kick and twist as the rough rope squeezed his throat shut.

Arnie, the scientist who had accompanied Bobby and Caitlyn's first expedition, stood watching by the ruined aluminum building. His hands were loosely bound, another of Bayclock's prisoners of war; he looked as though he were reliving the nightmare of when his family had died under martial law.

Gilbert Hertoya sat with one broken leg crudely splinted and the other bandaged from several bloody gashes he had received in the explosion of the railgun. Unattended, Gilbert rested in the scant shade beside the wrecked capacitor banks and the long metal rails of the EM launcher. Both captive scientists looked angry, unable to believe what Bayclock was about to do.

The air force captain gripped the noose, opening it wide as he stepped toward Bobby. The captain kept his eyes down, avoiding Bobby's eyes. Bobby wished he could remember the officer's first name, but his mind blanked.

General Bayclock stood with his hands behind his back, scowling.

Bobby could think of nothing to say. His stomach knotted, and his vision seemed sharp, too focused, as if trying to absorb a lifetime's worth of details in just a few minutes: a cloudless sky, the dry dust, the sweet smell of sage, razor-sharp shadows.

Bayclock was not kidding. Not kidding at all.

A rider came up the path to the blockhouses. He had pushed his mount hard, crossing the foothills to the general's new base of operations. Breathless, he dismounted next to Bayclock, glanced at Bobby and the ready noose, then saluted the general.

"What is it?" Bayclock asked. "Report!"

"A white flag, sir!" the airman said. "The scientists have sent two representatives to surrender. I believe one of them is Dr. Lockwood himself, sir."

Bayclock suddenly looked relieved. "Very well. Bring them to me as soon as possible."

"They're on their way, sir."

Bobby wanted to collapse in dismay. He couldn't believe it! Why would Spencer give up after all they had accomplished? Bayclock's army had been severely wounded by the scientists' efforts, and their morale was shot. The general had occupied the launcher facility, but that was already ruined by the explosion. The cracks showed in Bayclock's forces; they were ready to crumble in another few days, and he was sure the general knew it.

Why couldn't Spencer have held out just a little longer? Bobby had no other choice, nothing to lose. He raised his voice. "You better hang me in a hurry, General. Now that they've come under the flag of surrender, can you justify executing prisoners of war?" The general ignored him.

Bobby spat hard at Bayclock. "Yeah, General, I'm talking to you! If you string me up right now, I'm sure you can convince every one of your soldiers to pretend you hung me *before* anybody saw the white flag. That would cover your ass. In fact, why not just threaten to shoot any soldier who says otherwise?"

Bayclock turned from the courier, and his face became livid, deeper than the sunburn on his broad face. The black bristles of his hair stood on end. Bobby thought of the old fighter-pilot adage: balls the size of grapefruits, and brains the size of peas. He wanted to continue provoking Bayclock, keep him torn between his conflicting wishes.

"What's the matter, General? Can't make a snap decision?" *Balls the size of grapefruits.* "Good thing you're not flying real aircraft anymore! You're still fighting the last war. You're better off flying a desk."

Bayclock took one step forward, shoving his face less than an inch away from Bobby's. Bobby didn't flinch. Bayclock backhanded him across the cheek. *Brains the size of a pea.*

His face stinging, Bobby spat at him again. "You're a coward, General, if you have to strike a man while he's got his hands behind his back and waiting for a noose around his neck."

Bayclock yanked the combat knife from his belt and sawed at the ropes around Bobby's wrists. Bobby couldn't believe how easily provoked the man was. The general tossed the cut rope and the knife over by the metal rails of the electromagnetic launcher. "All right then, traitor! Come at me!"

Bobby did not wait for the numbness to leave his hands. He charged at Bayclock, swinging with both hands as the other spectators stepped back.

Conner Brooks knew that even if the general's troops moved at top speed, they'd still be hours behind him. He had walked all night, and the only thing he could see to the far distance was scrub brush and frail yucca plants. Overhead, some kind of hawk wheeled around, a dark check mark in the clear sky.

Another few miles and he'd be at the solar-power facility. *Then* he could do some fast talking.

Earlier that morning, Connor had hidden as a group of people headed out from the metal trailers by the antenna farm, making their way north toward Bayclock. The idiots carried a white surrender flag—as if Bayclock would have mercy! The general would probably try to draft them too, or throw them in a dungeon somewhere.

He saw the snowy tops of gypsum sand dunes south of him, shimmering in the distance as heat rose from the desert. To the north, immense metal rails of the electromagnetic launcher rose up the side of Oscura Peak. If he could make it to the trailer at the microwave facility, he might find something he could use as a bargaining chip. Connor had always considered himself a resourceful person. After all, he had managed to walk away in the middle of the night, right under Bayclock's nose.

He twisted his face at the very thought of that butthead general. *Damned Napoleon.* There had to be something about command that turned people into assholes. First there was Captain Uma on the *Zoroaster,* and now General Bayclock.

Connor laughed at the thought of getting back at the general, just as he had with Uma. If the solar-power facility was so precious to the son of a bitch, maybe Connor could even sabotage the place. That would really piss Bayclock off! In fact, the troops might even rebel once they discovered that their forced march all the way from Albuquerque had been for nothing.

Connor Brooks pulled the aluminum frame of his pack higher on his back and arrowed straight for the trailers. The pounding sun was high in the sky, and he cast very little shadow. If he could get to the trailers by noon, he'd have plenty of time to wreck some of the equipment, or snatch something with which he could barter.

The sunlight seemed magnified by the glittering white sands. If he had only swiped a hat from one of the soldiers, anything to keep off the sun.

"I'd like to see Bayclock's troops march through this shit!" he muttered. He stopped and shrugged off his backpack. He pulled out the reflective thermal blanket and fixed it around him like an Arab *kaffiyeh*. "If the towelheads can do it, so can I," he said to himself. Connor donned the makeshift headgear and soon felt cooler. He picked up his metal-frame backpack and whistled.

As he hiked toward the trailers, he spotted glints of sunlight reflected from the harsh ground in front of him. He walked up a small rise, and the bright flashes grew stronger, like a mile-wide field of whiplike chrome wires covering the basin between himself and the trailers.

He could see the blockhouse trailers more clearly now, even with just one eye. The three aluminum-sided structures with corrugated tops sat at angles to each other, forming a triangle. If he cut straight across the basin of whip-wires to get to the trailers, he could trim at least a mile off his path.

He looked behind him. Still no sign of Bayclock's troops, but Connor didn't want to screw up by getting there too late. He knew the importance of timing—he remembered his good timing running up the stairs on the *Oilstar Zoroaster* after setting off the fire alarm; he remembered finding out just in time about that lunatic Uma back at the camp . . . and he remembered getting double-crossed by Bayclock, because of bad timing. No way was he going to let that military fuckhead get there before him!

Connor grinned and started for the trailers.

As he stepped into the field, he discovered that the glints came not from wires, but from thousands of slender metal poles low to the ground, like a giant pincushion in the desert.

He ducked through the strands of a barbed-wire fence that ran around the antenna complex. It felt weird, walking through the field of metal poles. He stepped on fine wires that ran from the bottoms of the poles, kicking a few loose.

Picking up the pace, he made his way to the trailers. It wouldn't be long now.

From his team's camouflaged position at the top of the EM launcher rails, Todd Severyn watched Bayclock's soldiers camped near the control building below. The troops had dug in, pitching their tents in the foothills, while the general set up his command post inside the burned shell of the building itself.

Todd saw Spencer's white flag approach the encampment, surrounded by escorts. Waiting within view on the other side of the long metal rails, Rita Fellenstein signaled Todd. She had seen Spencer's arrival as well.

Time to move in.

Todd jammed his cowboy hat on his head, then bent low over the horse's neck. Rita tightened the string on her bush hat, and waved for the ranch hands to follow. With Todd came seven other ranchers from Alamogordo, all on horseback and carrying crude grenades made from the potent-smelling citrus-based explosives.

Todd and Rita both led their horses, picking up speed as they galloped down the service trail on either side of the long electromagnetic launcher. They would attack in two prongs, striking from either side of the supply camp. He just hoped they could manage not to blow themselves up when they lobbed the homemade grenades into Bayclock's troops.

Unable to restrain themselves once they urged their

horses into a full gallop, Todd's attackers let out a loud war yell as they charged toward the camp.

Sitting in the shade near the blockhouses, Gilbert Hertoya watched the confrontation between General Bayclock and Bobby Carron. The two men crouched in a coiled stance, circling and glaring. The empty noose still dangled from the utility pole, and Spencer Lockwood was coming in under a white flag.

The short engineer felt his hope draining. He didn't want to give up, but their chances seemed to be fading away. It had been absurd in the first place to think they could drive off a fully armed invasion force.

The nerves in Gilbert's legs hurt with a throbbing, insistent pain, but he tried to ignore it. He had to focus his thoughts to formulate some way he could help Bobby, or stop Spencer from surrendering—or at the very least hurt Bayclock.

Bobby Carron lunged at the general, feinting with a left-handed blow to the stomach, which Bayclock blocked, then lashing out with a quick hammer-punch to the general's face. Bobby struck him squarely in the nose, once, twice, before snapping backward to avoid a counterpunch.

Though he himself wasn't much of a hand-to-hand fighter, Gilbert knew that the nose was a noncrippling but singularly effective place for a blow to land. Bobby's punch would have sent a bright explosion of pain into Bayclock's head, blinding him with a sudden flood of reflexive tears. A splash of scarlet blood dribbled out of his nostrils and splattered on the pale sands.

"Face it, you're too old, General," Bobby said.

Some of Bayclock's troops had drawn up as spectators, but they remained oddly subdued and silent, as if they refused to cheer for the general but were afraid to cheer for his opponent. They stepped back, giving the two men fighting room.

Bayclock launched himself forward, moving his legs like pistons and butting Bobby in the stomach. Bobby let out an "oof!" but managed to sidestep part of the attack. As Bayclock crashed into him, Bobby caught the general's foot with his own and tripped them both. They tumbled to the ground.

Bobby scrambled to get to his feet again, rolling away from Bayclock's grasping hands. "Can't fly, can't fight—what else can't you do, old man?" he gasped.

Bobby got to his knees, white dust covering his blue air force uniform. Bayclock's nose continued to bleed onto the sand.

Gilbert tore his concentration away from the fight and looked into the sky. He had no way of telling accurate time, but the sun stood at about noon, and the Seven Dwarfs would orbit overhead any moment now.

He lay by the wreckage of the railgun. In the explosion, the capacitors had ruptured and the banks of storage batteries had burned. During the day of waiting and recovery, Arnie had lovingly disconnected and removed the blackened shapes. Given time and resources, they could repair everything—but it did not look like the general would give them the opportunity.

Every day at noon, though, when the Seven Dwarfs passed over the White Sands antenna farm, the solar energy beamed down to the collectors was distributed through the repaired power grid, charging up caches of batteries to run various equipment. A direct power line ran up to the EM launcher to charge the batteries for the railgun, but now those batteries had been destroyed and the ruined capacitors taken off line.

The solar smallsats didn't know that, however. They would continue to beam their power, and the electrical lines would run the current up to the railgun facility. Disconnected from any source, the cable would become a live wire for the twenty minutes that the satellites passed overhead transmitting their energy.

A live wire. As everyone watched the fistfight, Gilbert Hertoya took the disconnected cable, praying as he touched it that the deadly current wasn't already flowing. No guard watched him closely, with both of his legs heavily bandaged.

Gilbert dragged himself to the metal superstructure of the railgun. He jammed the end of the wire into the steel base, then backed away—ignoring the sharp darts of pain jabbing his legs in a thousand places. He collapsed back on the dirt, trying to keep from passing out.

From the other side of the group of buildings, Arnie saw what Gilbert had done, and his eyes widened. Gilbert winked and crossed his fingers. In response, Arnie crossed his fingers, too.

Bayclock attacked Bobby again, and the fight went on.

Seven hundred kilometers overhead, seven satellites flew in a constellation of four planar orbits, inclined at forty-five degrees from the equator. Tiny solar-electric thrusters boiled plasma off their electrodes, keeping the satellites positioned in orbit, canceling perturbations caused by gravitational variations in the Earth's crust.

The satellites updated their position using the military's still-functioning Global Positioning Satellites, making necessary corrections. Each smallsat carried a tiny atomic clock, attuned to the energy of a certain fundamental transition frequency to know *when* they were. Isolated from the events taking place below, the satellites functioned as programmed.

One minute before noon, Mountain Standard Time, the lead satellite swung its gimballed antenna toward the horizon. Energy collected by the array of inflatable solar-cell panels was converted into electricity, which trickled into the transmitter.

The satellite silently began to irradiate the microwave-antenna farm at White Sands.

Connor Brooks was within two hundred yards of the edge of the antenna farm when he heard sparks jumping from the metal poles of his backpack. The sound scared him—it was if he had fallen into the middle of a huge popcorn popper.

At the same instant, his head began to grow hot. Very hot. The thermal blanket felt as if it had suddenly turned into napalm. The searing fabric pressed down upon his skull, across the back of his neck. Only seconds earlier, he had enjoyed the relative coolness of being shielded from the sun, but it now felt like molten lead.

Connor screamed and tore at the metal-backed cloth. But already the fabric smoldered. The metal snapped and popped in an inferno of blue sparks; the poles on his backpack burned hot-iron slices into his back. Acidic smoke billowed out; even the metal eyelets on his boots crackled with tiny arcs of flame.

The pain went on and on. Connor fell to his knees, clutching at the melting blanket that spread over his head, over his skin.

In a final effort, Connor tried to pry the covering from his scalp, but his fingers refused to respond, turning into burned, bloody stumps by the boiling metal. Sparks continued to crackle in a cocoon around him. He screamed, and hot arcs lanced from the fillings in his teeth.

The pain . . . wouldn't . . . stop. . . .

Seven hundred kilometers above the Earth, the second satellite locked on and started to beam its microwaves down to the target.

Five others waited patiently behind for their own turn.

Todd and Rita galloped in on either side of the base camp near the burned-out railgun facility, yelling their loudest battle cries. Todd set the spring-loaded timer on his crude grenade canister and lobbed the explosive toward a supply tent.

The air force men saw what he had thrown, and they scrambled in the opposite direction. Some ran for their rifles, but most ducked for cover.

Rita Fellenstein headed them off from the other direction, tossing another grenade in among the campfires. Following closely behind, the ranch hands fired their own rifles and shouted.

One colonel stood in the middle of it all, with a wounded arm in a sling, staring at Todd and the other riders. Very carefully, the colonel tossed his own rifle to the ground.

Bayclock's other troops, as if waiting to surrender, took this as a sign of permission. Other explosions erupted from the citrus-based explosives. Gunfire rattled around the hills, but nobody seemed to be shooting *at* anything.

Todd had intended only to ride in, cause damage, panic, and confusion, make the troops scatter, then hit the road as fast as possible to hide in an overgrown arroyo.

Rita pulled up beside him, and they stared as more and more of the soldiers either ran or tossed down their weapons.

"Now what do we do?" Todd asked.

"Beats the hell out of me." Rita shrugged. "We didn't plan on *winning!*"

Carrying their white flag like a shield, Spencer and Heather were escorted up to the main buildings of the railgun only moments before the first explosions and gunshots broke out in the camp below them.

Heather gripped his hand hard enough that her nails bit into his skin. Spencer felt himself trembling, knowing he was crazy even to be making this attempt. He tried to keep a straight face, although his guts had tangled into knots.

The first thing he noticed near the control building was the fistfight between Bobby Carron and the general. A small group of Bayclock's soldiers had formed a ring around the combatants, like gamblers watching a cockfight. But they did not cheer, simply watched the pummeling in silence.

Spencer's attention was yanked like a metal filing to a

magnet when he noticed the noose hanging from the utility pole—and the bloated body of a strangled Lance Nedermyer tied to the creosote-smeared wood.

"Oh, Lance!" Spencer said, and his breath went out of him. Even his cocky plans evaporated in his mind. If Bayclock could do this to one of his own supporters, then he would have no qualms about slaughtering Spencer or Rita or anyone else who dared to defy him.

Lance Nedermyer had been a real pain most of the time, but he had a good streak in him—a streak that Lance himself tried to extinguish. Maybe that good streak had been his downfall while trapped in Bayclock's hell.

Farther down the long rail launcher, he heard the first shouts of Todd's charge as they struck the base camp. Gunshots. Explosions. Several of the spectators ran off to see the attack, while others seemed afraid of leaving Bayclock's side.

Bobby Carron and Bayclock rolled around on the ground, pounding each other with fists. The general clawed the back of Bobby's head, attempting to grab his hair. Finally, he dug his fingers into Bobby's ear until it bled. Bobby cried out and smashed his forehead down on the general's skull, butting him viciously.

Blood poured out of Bayclock's nose and sprayed in red foam every time he took a heaving breath. Bobby hammered the general's side with his sharp elbow; Bayclock bit and grabbed, sinking his teeth into Bobby's shoulder.

With a scream, Bobby tore himself free and scrambled away. Bayclock climbed to his feet and charged, but Bobby met the attack with a double blow to the general's stomach, making him stumble back toward the railgun launcher. Bayclock's eyes were bloodshot and his skin looked like a cube steak. Bobby didn't look much better, but he remained on his feet as the general wobbled and fell to his knees in the dirt.

Todd and Rita rode into the area, with a tall solemn-looking colonel striding between them. The colonel cradled his wounded arm as he absorbed the situation; then he took another step toward the beaten Bayclock.

"General . . ." He hesitated, but Bayclock did not acknowledge him. Colonel David didn't seem to care.

"It's over, General." The colonel flashed a glance behind him to Spencer standing with his white flag. "I believe these gentlemen are in a position to discuss terms."

Rita leaped from her horse and ran to help Bobby up. Bobby swayed on his feet and flicked blood out of his eyes. Sweat ran in rivers down his exposed skin, and he shuddered like a shack in a hurricane. "That's it, Bayclock. Your troops have caused enough damage."

Bayclock collapsed, but Spencer saw that the man's eyes were open and calculating. In the shadows by the railgun supports, he fished around on the ground. After a moment, he snatched up a hunting knife that lay beside severed strands of rope.

"I don't surrender!" He lurched to his feet, brandishing the wicked-looking combat knife. Bobby stiffened; Rita tightened her grip on his arm. One of Bayclock's men grabbed a rifle, but didn't know what to shoot at.

The general turned, holding out the knife. As he backed up, his arm brushed against the metal supports of the electromagnetic launcher rails. The live wire, disconnected from the battery banks and capacitors, dumped its electricity into the bottomless ground of the miles-long rail, waiting for a load.

Bayclock completed the circuit.

He froze as if caught in amber; then in an instant he seemed to go out of focus, with a million nerves in his skin suddenly misfiring, every strand of muscle fiber in his body scrambling. Sparks flew from the point of contact, and his skin blackened.

His mouth cracked open in a long silent scream, and then his lips curled away from his teeth. When General Bayclock finally fell to the white sands, his entire form steamed from the moisture boiling inside his body.

No one spoke for a long moment.

Finally, Colonel David turned to them all. He looked strong, even with his wounded arm in a sling. The other troops kept staring.

"The general is dead, as is Colonel Nachimya. This leaves me in command of the expeditionary force."

He met Spencer's gaze, Todd's, Bobby's, and Rita's. "We have a lot of details to discuss, you and I."

SEVENTY-FIVE

LIVE, IN CONCERT

The breeze picked up in the late afternoon on Labor Day, rippling the golden grass along the Altamont Range. The wind turbines, like metal flowers lining the hilltops, whirled around and around, generating a silent river of power that flowed to the speedway stadium.

At last, the great concert got underway.

Next to Jackson and Daphne Harris, Iris sat alone on her blanket, elbows on her knees. She had worked too hard to make this event a reality, and she didn't want to miss a note. The fluttery feeling of anticipation in her stomach during the morning had disappeared, replaced by a spreading warmth of amazed relief. She looked around to see the same excitement in the eyes of the other spectators.

Jackson and Daphne Harris held each other close, as they stared at the band on the raised stage.

Iris and many others had forsaken the closer seats in the repaired bleachers to sit on the grass. She felt the lumpy ground beneath her, but it didn't matter. Sitting on the grass for a rock & roll concert seemed perfectly appropriate.

The first band got a laugh and a resounding cheer by opening with their rendition of Jackson Browne's "Running on Empty," which they followed with rock classics from the seventies, then a few folk songs that everyone knew. The murmur of the audience singing along as if in a trance sent shivers through Iris. The musicians used improvised musical instruments, and the songs didn't sound much like what Iris remembered—but the sheer delight of *music* again was enough. The notes vibrated through the speedway's metal loudspeakers, sounding tinny and muffled. Iris found it absolutely wonderful.

The crowd cheered, nearly loud enough to drown out the sound blasting from the improvised amplifiers the engineers had cobbled together. Iris couldn't wait to see if they had indeed managed to build a working electric guitar. She knew the energy drain was stupendous, and they'd be lucky to finish the concert. But the wind kept blowing, the windmills kept turning, and the music kept blasting through the air.

The bands were a mishmash of musical talent that had arrived after hearing word of the proposed concert. Many of the musicians had played in bar bands around the Bay Area, working day jobs and performing on weekends. The only "professional" they counted among their number was the lead singer from Visual Purple, a late-sixties alternative rock band, who had been stranded in San Jose during a rather unsuccessful attempt at a comeback tour. He had worked with the volunteer musicians, directing the others and getting upset when they spent more time tuning up than they did performing. But the singer's rough voice wrapped itself around the lyrics of all the old classics, even two country & western hits, but he really began to shine when he managed to work in the few chart-scratching songs Visual Purple had released.

The musicians kept playing for an hour. Iris expected

any moment for some fuse to blow, some component to fail, and the concert would be over. But the only pause occurred when the first band took a break to stand down while the second group came onstage.

The next lead singer had a softer, warbly voice—due in part to nervousness, Iris was sure. But the crowd received the music with full enthusiasm, almost growing too introspective with Crosby, Stills and Nash's post-apocalyptic "Wooden Ships."

Sitting on her blanket, Iris looked around at the crowd. Thousands and thousands had arrived, most from the local cities, but some had come all the way from the Monterey Peninsula to the south, others from Sacramento to the north. It seemed like a holy pilgrimage to them. They couldn't believe what they were hearing.

She wished Todd could have been there to share it. Maybe seeing how the music affected all these people would get through his thick head and make him see what he was missing. Iris felt very isolated as she sat by herself, trying not to notice Jackson and Daphne Harris snuggling next to her. . . .

As darkness fell, everyone grew silent, stunned, as the stadium lights came on, flooding the stage and the abandoned racetrack.

Powered by the windmills, the incandescent lights blazed with a warm white light that dazzled the viewers; the lights flickered, but they kept up. After a breathless pause, a spontaneous wave of people stood up and applauded, cheering. The lights and the music made them feel as if they had come home again.

Up in the tower, the kid Harley ran the lights, standing by the controls like the captain of a spaceship. He had begged Jackson Harris for the job, and Harris had given it to him. Iris had never seen Harley look so proud or so determined to do something right.

When the audience finally fell silent after seeing the electric lights, the lead singer from Visual Purple took the stage again, accompanied by two Livermore engineers who had each crafted an electric guitar. Hooked up to the amplifiers and the speedway loudspeakers, they began to play.

The first chords came out, gentle but with a biting memory that sent a liquid tingle down Iris's spine. People struggled to their feet again as the strains of "The Star-Spangled Banner" echoed over the speakers; the crowd sang along, but Iris felt a lump in her throat.

Many of the audience members sat back, sucking in a collective audible breath. As the darkness deepened, battered back and defeated by the brilliant stadium lights, the guitarists on stage played "Stairway to Heaven."

In the bleachers, the crowd swayed and sang along with the lyrics they all knew by heart. On the grass, people got up and held hands, adding their voices in a swell of song that rang across the hills. Behind her, on one of the blankets, Iris heard two men arguing about what the lyrics really meant, but she ignored it—she had been hearing *that* discussion since her high-school days.

To her left and down the slope, she noticed the teenaged couple from Oakland standing next to each other; the young father cradled the new baby in his arms, rocking it back and forth to the chorus. The young mother rubbed fingers across her boyfriend's shoulder blades.

As the music and a flood of other memories poured into her, Iris felt tears brimming in her dark eyes. She had seen other people in the audience crying during the concert, but never as many as now. Many of their voices broke as they tried to sing along.

With barely a pause, the singer slid into "The Long and Winding Road" by the Beatles, which kept people standing and stunned, wrapped up in their own thoughts. Finally, continuing with the Beatles, he lightened the mood with the now-absurd song "Drive My Car."

When the band finished, cheers pummeled them, and the singer turned to his two electric guitarists. "Are you ready to do what you came here for?"

Cranking up the volume, the trio, joined by the drummer and keyboardist, launched into the strangest mixture of music Iris could have imagined, Top 40, new rock, more folk songs, even a pair of Broadway show tunes. Everyone began moving, dancing, swaying, stomping. They seemed to care only that they were hearing music again, an icon of their lost civilization. Iris felt that the entire silent post-petroplague world must have been able to hear them.

The music continued late into the night. Iris was exhausted, but she never wanted it to stop. The people had shouted and chanted and sung until their voices were hoarse; they had clapped until their hands were sore. The magic in the air was intoxicating, and she felt in her heart that the dark ghosts from the previous violent concert at the Altamont must have been exorcised that day.

She saw Doog standing near the stage, his face tilted toward the stars in rapture, his round John Lennon glasses like shining coins in the stadium lights.

Iris looked around to see the hills glittering with a thousand yellow gems, tiny flames raised high. In another concert, the fans would be flicking their lighters, but this time they had brought candles, saving them until the very end in a gesture of their heartfelt appreciation.

"Nice touch, don't you think?" Daphne Harris said, giving Iris a look that made it apparent *she* had been behind it.

A thousand points of light, Iris thought.

Civilization might come to an end, but rock & roll would never die.

SEVENTY-SIX

EARTH ABIDES

In the aftermath of the desert battle, Bayclock's expedition force broke into a confusion of smaller groups with different agendas.

Many of the soldiers and camp followers gathered to make preparations for the long trip back north to Albuquerque, this time without the general's martial law. The consensus seemed to be that Mayor Reinski would be able to hold things together even without a reign of terror.

In the following days, others teamed up with some of the Alamogordo ranchers and dispersed, deciding to stay near the solar-power farm in the hope of eventually turning it into a bona fide settlement, an Atlantis out in the sparkling gypsum sands. Given the extra manpower, Spencer Lockwood told them they could lay new power lines and dig wells to the aquifer.

With Rita Fellenstein riding beside him, Bobby Carron fetched back the wagon and the ten precious solar-power satellites he had hidden in an arroyo. Spencer lightly touched the metal shells resting in the wagon bed, blinking back tears, as if he'd found the Holy Grail.

Already, Gilbert Hertoya limped among the remnants of Bayclock's army, talking to some of the enthusiastic air force troops about taking a military contingent back to the Jet Propulsion Laboratory for the rest of the satellites. Some of the soldiers, anxious to atone for their forced attack against the scientists, were willing to go without delay. Armed with functional rifles, the new military escort would provide a much safer expedition than Todd's crazy quest had been.

Ten more smallsats remained in Pasadena, and the parts for more were readily available. Someday, there might be enough to complete the orbital ring for uninterrupted electrical power from the antenna farm. Spencer was sure he could convince his old mentor, Dr. Seth Mansfield, to accompany the second mission back to White Sands.

Meanwhile, Todd Severyn felt at a loss, wandering among the blockhouse trailers and reluctantly relaxing. He felt the inner depression of having successfully completed a major goal and discovering that he had no idea what to do next.

Sitting in the noon shade, he watched Heather and Spencer chatting, walking to the aluminum water barrel. Spencer poured a cup for her; she drank most of it and, when he bent over to fill a cup for himself, she playfully trickled the rest down his back. Startled, Spencer dropped his cup and sputtered.

Just watching them together, Todd could see that Heather had fallen for Spencer, though he didn't know if they realized it themselves yet. He remembered when Heather had offered herself to him out by the stream in the hills. But Heather had made the offer out of desperation; and the memory of that one time was irrevocably stained with blood and violence. He and she could not look at each other without being haunted by the ghosts of Casey Jones and Henrietta Soo.

"Hey, Todd!" Gilbert Hertoya came around the corner of the blockhouse. "I want to talk to you about something."

By the water barrel Heather looked up, suddenly aware that Todd had been watching. She flushed, then turned away to follow Spencer, who knew nothing about what had happened between her and Todd.

He cocked back his cowboy hat and looked up at the short, peppery-haired scientist, who stood propped on a wooden crutch. "What do you want, Gilbert?"

Hertoya put one hand on his hip, covering a big leather belt that one of the ranchers had given him. "We're going to go back to California in a few months to pick up the rest of the satellites, and I wanted you to come along. This time we'll be armed, with plenty of help. What do you say?"

Todd looked west to the dim line of mountains. He had considered going along—it would be another major effort, an important quest, something to keep him busy. It would extinguish the restless indecision that had been bothering him.

But he slowly shook his head. "No, I don't think so. I've got to get going." He sighed, then tried to put his reasons into words that made sense to himself. "I'm going to try saving the world in little ways from now on, not by meeting it head-on."

Hertoya scratched his head. His grizzled face plainly showed his disappointment. "What does that mean?"

Todd tipped back his cowboy hat. "I think I'm going to go back to the Altamont, to stay this time. I made a promise. And it's the closest thing I have to home."

Grateful for his help, Spencer gave Todd his pick of the horses for his journey back. Todd pondered the choices from the Alamogordo ranchers and the air force troops; finally, somewhat uneasily, he selected Bayclock's black gelding.

He saddled up, took two of the working rifles and some ammunition, and as many supplies as he could cram into the saddlebags. The ride would be long and arduous, at least a month or so, but he didn't care how long it took him—just the fact that he was returning made it worthwhile.

Spencer and Heather, Gilbert Hertoya, Juan Romero, Bobby Carron, and Rita Fellenstein watched him as he departed. He waved back at them, saying nothing special to Heather, then turned and guided the gelding westward, once again riding off in the direction of the sunset. . . .

Over the following weeks, he rode across New Mexico and Arizona, stopping again at the ranch of the dead diabetic man. Todd took an extra few hours straightening up the house. He got a good night's sleep, replenished his supplies, then set off again.

He had nothing to do but think as he sat astride the horse throughout the heat of the day and into the cooling evening.

Part of him wished he had never left Iris, but he also knew that wouldn't have made him happy. If he had not gone to deliver the smallsats to White Sands, if he had not made some sort of tangible difference, Todd would never have been able to settle down for the rest of his life. Iris had reached a point where she wanted to put down roots, but Todd hadn't been ready for that; he'd spurned her offer to share her bed, sticking to his morals. He couldn't calmly accept the fate of the world without trying to make his mark. And he had succeeded.

But Todd didn't need to *keep* seeking bigger dragons to slay, wilder geese to chase. He'd had enough.

Would Iris have him back? He had left her without saying goodbye. She had no reason even to think he might return, despite the message he had transmitted from JPL. Had she waited for him? She was so intelligent, and so beautiful . . . someone else had probably claimed Iris the moment his bootprints faded from the dry grass in the Altamont hills.

Then Todd forced a bittersweet grin. Iris Shikozu did not allow herself to be *claimed!* She might have changed her mind, gone with somebody else because of her own decision—but she would not have been wooed away by a sweet talker. No way!

He passed into California and headed north, following abandoned highways and the line of the mountains. He came upon a former dude ranch in the Sierra Nevada where a tall man named Carlos Bettario had established thriving, comfortable quarters.

Bettario's group of workers had managed to keep themselves supplied with cut firewood, fresh fish and game, as well as meat from a herd of beef cattle. They powered their equipment and lights with electricity generated by water wheels turning in a hydroelectric plant on a nearby dam. One of Bettario's men, a grizzled old man named Dick Morgret, showed Todd the wild horses up in the mountains and how they had already begun to barter with people living not too far away.

Todd stayed there for a day, helping to repair a long fence to pay for his room and board, then set off again.

He pondered trying to find someplace where he could send a shortwave signal, to let Iris know he was coming. But he was afraid to. He didn't want to know if she was with somebody else.

Crossing the Sierra Nevada well before the first snows, Todd rode up the flat Central Valley, living off the generosity of farmers who shared their produce with him. In exchange, he told them all the news he knew, entertaining them with stories about the battle for the solar-power farm, Casey Jones and his train, and crumbling Los Angeles.

As he reached Tracy, moving westward to the grassy Altamont Range, he caught his first glimpse again of the white windmill towers lining the hill crests. He pulled Bayclock's black horse to a halt and stared up at them with a pang. Anxiety shuddered through him, and he seriously considered turning around and heading back to White Sands, or making the long journey off to his parents' ranch in Wyoming.

But he couldn't do that. Todd could never live with himself if he gave up now. He had braved armies and murderers and mobs—he could not let a five-foot-three-inch woman make him turn tail!

As he approached the Altamont commune, he saw that it had tripled in size in the months since he had been gone. Most of the windmills whirled in the breeze. Looking around the settlement, Todd didn't recognize most of the people, but they somehow looked less . . . weird.

Daphne Harris came out to meet him. Her skin was dark and glistening with perspiration as she worked in the garden; her colorful tie-dyed blouse looked as startling as a gunshot. She strode up to him with a grin. "Hey, look what the cat dragged in!"

Todd dismounted and tied up the gelding as other people came to see who had arrived. Jackson Harris appeared, his hands grimy from working on wind-turbine rotors, but he clapped Todd on the back. "We already heard what happened! Over the shortwave, Dr. Lockwood made sure we all knew what a hero you were down at the solar-power farm. Even Tibbett at Sandia got excited telling the story, if you can believe that."

"We were wondering when you would finally haul your butt back here," Daphne said.

Todd couldn't restrain himself any longer. "What about Iris? Is she still in the same old place?"

Daphne and Jackson flashed a knowing glance at each other that made Todd uneasy. "Go see her for yourself, Todd," Daphne said.

On weak knees—which he told himself was just from too many hours on horseback—Todd clumped up to their old trailer. His cowboy boots crunched on the dry grass. He spotted Ren and Stimpy off to the side, munching on dry grass.

The battered white aluminum siding of the trailer looked the same, with water spots and algae in the crevices; the rusty wheel rims still sat on concrete blocks.

The metal screen on the door had been fixed; Todd wondered if Iris had done it herself.

He stared for a moment, terrified; then he finally rapped on the doorframe.

Deep inside, Todd *knew* another man was going to answer. And what could he say to that? It was his own fault he had left. But darn it, he *had* to. He made up his mind just to shake hands and leave.

But Iris opened the door herself, blinking up at him in the bright late-morning sunlight. Her almond eyes widened. She flashed an instinctive, shocked grin, but then she recovered. She cocked her head and looked wryly up at him. "So you came back."

"I promised, didn't I?" He took off his hat, wringing the brim in his big hands. "I'm ready to take you up on that offer—if you still want me. But you'll have to marry me," he said doggedly.

She was silent for a long moment, then made a *tsk*ing sound. "And you still didn't remember to bring flowers."

Iris laughed; then she hugged him.